The runner reached the crest of the steep hill and paused, jogging gently on the spot. The sky above was a cool pale blue, hazed with thin veils of white cloud, that promised a warm bright day. Along the horizon puffballs of cloud were forming a warning of possible rain later. He raised his face to the warmth of the spring sun.

"Breathing slow and steady, heart rate slow and steady. Not bad for an old 'un," he murmured out loud and grinned. He felt glad to be alive, and that rare feeling surprised him. The tightness across his chest eased after a couple of minutes of relative stillness. He pressed his hand to the tee shirt over his heart, imagining the fading scars concealed by the thin cloth. He was glad the sharp pain that had speared through his hip and lower back at every step, when he started out, had faded to a dull constant ache. At least today he was able to run. The enforced inactivity of the previous two weeks had almost driven him crazy. He tried to remember the last time an injury had healed as slowly, but it was so long ago that he could not recall. He checked his watch, an annoyed frown furrowing his brow. The run was taking much more time than he had anticipated. He grimaced, realising he had overestimated how far his injuries had healed. He was going to be late for lunch. Unconsciously he shrugged. It made little actual difference; he had no place he needed to be. His housekeeper had said she would provide a cold meal. He smiled at the memory. She knew him better than he knew himself. His frustration was founded in how long it was taking to return to his usual fitness level.

A shudder shook his body when sudden, vivid, random images of those desperate three days attacked his mind. He closed his eyes and shook his head, trying to shatter those nightmare images. He would not surrender to fear. He grasped the earlier feeling of joy like a talisman for the future.

"Only one more week," he stated out loud. It was the bargain he had made with Thomas, his doctor. One more week of patient recovery, then he would take charge of a new team. As long as Thomas didn't find out about these daytime nightmares. Still, they were fading little by little, just like his scars. Soon the horror would be easier to control, he hoped. Taking up his new post would help, keeping his brain busy, focusing his mind on other things.

Beneath the beauty of the early morning bird song, he had been aware of a constant, low monotone drone. Until he had paused at the top of the hill, the sounds of footfall and breathing during his run, had masked the annoying hum. From the crest of the hill, he could see the blue-grey haze above Malford. The blurring polluted mist acted like an arrow, marking the nearest town, three miles to the north of the hill, at the end of the twisting ribbon of road. The Easter school holidays had begun, but still a caterpillar of queueing traffic undulated slowly around each bend. The silver, grey, black and white of expensive, powerful cars competed with the bullying bulk of four-wheel drives. The runner watched, fascinated by the slow undulation of the queue that blocked the road, despite the early hour. He chuckled at the image in his head: processional caterpillars, with black heads and monochrome camouflage creeping along the tarmac. The road was an infamous bottle-neck. The County Council had discussed a new plan that would destroy a lot more of the familiar countryside. Destruction justified by the need to ease the traffic flow, feeding left onto the motorway towards London, or heading straight on, to pour workers into the factories, offices and shops of the town. He had seen the changes happening at increasing speed, until today, the town and the motorway dominated the entire area. A heavy sigh longed for the good old days, then he laughed at himself. Had they really been that good? For him, perhaps, but a hard existence for most.

He turned to face west along the ridge, gazing across softer hedges, greening fields and narrow lanes, down the slope towards the village of Daneley. Once it had been all his village. Even there more change had happened. Around the village green stood the Norman church and the manor house. Further along, the war memorial, built on the central island, dominated the crossroads. It divided the village primary school, and the inn built on two opposite corners. There, was the ancient core of the village, with its attendant cottages. A harlequin mixture of Tudor, Stuart and Georgian, of thatch and slate roofs, the heart of the village still existed and thrived as it had in Domesday. Beyond them, newer housing had sprung up

IS WAITING

Patricia Simpson

TSL Publications

First published in Great Britain in 2023
By TSL Publications, Rickmansworth

Copyright © 2023 Patricia Simpson

ISBN: 978 1 915660-37-4

Cover courtesy of : Dave Slaney

For Alan & Holly

to satisfy those who wanted to work in the city, but have their own private piece of the countryside.

Had it been a mistake to live in the village all this time? He could see the midnight blue roof of the manor, partially obscured by the medieval bell tower of the village church. It was the only place he had ever felt at home. The London flat, where he had lived and worked for the last four years, never had the same feeling of peace and permanence. It had been the weekends spent at the manor which had enabled him to return, energy renewed, to the capital. No matter where he went, no matter what he did, he was always drawn back to Daneley.

Shaking his head, he started to turn south east, preparing to run the minor road through the valley. A light breeze rippled the tall grasses around him, teased his nose with a too familiar scent that fired his senses. He stopped, closed his eyes, lifted his face to the breeze, and took a deep breath. 'Aah! yes, a deep metallic note almost masked a touch of decay, still early.' His tongue licked his lips, tasted the air. His entire being altered, no longer relaxed and leisurely, but aware and tense. A hunter stalked the irresistible scent onward down the slope.

He ran slowly, carefully avoiding the potholes, wary of traffic, along the uneven narrow lane between the tall hedgerows. He turned right from the cracked and broken tarmac, avoided the open barrier, onto car-park compounded gravel, that crunched beneath his trainers, allowing him to increase his speed. He kept going, following the scent as if he could see it like a delicate trail of mist. Shining trunks of silver birch enclosed him. He moved from gravel to a hard earthen path weaving through the trees' pristine new whiteness. He leapt a broad dip in the path without breaking the rhythm of his running.

An overwhelming floral perfume, heady, dizzying, momentarily hid the scent trail. He slowed down, caught glimpses of the blue and green tapestry carpeting the woodland. The wild flowers flowed from one clearing into another until lost in the distance, a knee-high haze of bluebells between the silver birch trees. He hesitated where the path bridged a chuckling stream highlighted with ridges of white water. He crossed, then turned to follow the dry compacted bank upstream. The original scent, stronger now than the floral perfume, guided him along the stream. The scent became more concentrated, and he knew he would not need to run much further. Less than a hundred yards into the quiet woods, he stopped abruptly. He had found the source.

The body was sprawled face down and appeared to be sunk into the soft mud of the stream bank. It was slender and of medium height, most likely a young female victim. One arm trailed into the water as if reaching for something lost. The coat sleeve, soaked by the stream to black, and the blurred shape of a white hand could be seen just beneath the surface. The other hand grasped a handful of the reddish-brown earth beside the head. He knew there had been no rain for several days. The earthen path around the body was softened and soaked with blood. A long, tangled mass of dark brown hair obscured the head and face above the collar of the charcoal grey coat. The coat itself was dragged and bunched sideways, as if it had been used to manhandle the body. Beneath the twisted hem of the coat, he could see a floral-patterned skirt or dress.

He sighed, a mixture of regret and anger. No need to approach any closer. He could hear no heartbeat, no flow of blood through veins and arteries. The woman had died within the last few hours as far as he could judge. When the iron tang of her rare blood group began to overwhelm his senses, his whole body reacted. He realised he was already too close. He noticed he was growling low in his throat and forced himself to retreat back along the path. At a safer distance, he stood still for several moments, breathing slow and deep, until he regained some control and the terrible need eased. Eventually he stopped shaking and was able to focus on the scene. He returned to the stream bank, standing about two metres away from the body.

Off to his right he noticed two parallel lines of crushed flowers, slashing diagonally through the largest clearing towards the stream. The bluebell flowers had been bent so that the flower heads pointed in the direction of the stream. The direction of the crush indicated the body had been transported from the smaller car park on the other side of the woodland. The double track implied the body might have been carried through the clearing on some kind of trolley. Had she been dazed, unconscious, or already dying? He knew from the condition of the stream bank around her, despite several days of dry weather, that she had been alive when she was dumped. He couldn't see any signs of a struggle around the body, which suggested she had been attacked elsewhere and the killer or killers had left before the path turned to red stained mud. Why had she been dumped carelessly face down? The action suggested a callous disregard for the woman's fate. Left like fly-tipped rubbish.

He carefully glanced at the area around the body. There was no sign of a bag of any kind nearby. Had she had one? Perhaps it was beneath the torso. If so, it would have to wait for the forensic team. Strangely, she still had both shoes on her feet, dark green and either recently heeled or, a new purchase, from the lack of wear pattern. Unusual that they should have stayed on through all the activity, he would have expected one or both to have slipped off like Cinderella's glass slipper.

He pulled his phone from the pouch on his arm, but was not surprised when he couldn't get a signal. He decided not to follow the double marks across the clearing. Instead, he retreated out of the woods the way he had come, to disturb the crime scene as little as possible. Disregarding the reawakened severe pain from his hip, he forced himself to run back along the path until he reached the larger car park. At the entrance, his phone showed a strong signal Then he crossed over the road to the layby opposite, before he dialled 999. A hard cynical smile thinned his lips. He could appreciate the irony of Lady Fortune's nasty little jest.

The call was answered swiftly.

"Emergency Services. Which service do you require?"

He found it slightly awkward to be on this end of such a phone call while he reported the discovery of a body. He gave the location: "alongside the Halcut brook in Tolland wood".

"Yes, I will wait here. My name?" He paused, "Detective Chief Inspector Justin Mortmain, Major Crime Unit."

2

While he waited for the first responders to arrive, Justin called the Chief Constable, informed him of his discovery of a body and requested permission to take on the investigation rather than waiting another week. He was rather surprised how little persuasion was needed to get his senior's agreement. A third call ended abruptly when he heard the first faint sound of the sirens.

The smoothly organised process impressed Justin. It had been some years since he had been part of the initial team at a crime scene. The duty officer arrived with a team of uniforms who cordoned off the entire woodland. Surprisingly, for a rural death, a uniformed inspector was duty officer.

Justin understood he was an object of curiosity. The frequent cautious glances in his direction from the large number of people bustling around the car park was proof of that. However, nobody had approached him to give a statement, so Justin assumed they were waiting for the senior detective to arrive.

The ache of tension in his shoulders began to ease when a familiar Range Rover pulled up in the layby beside him. The driver got out, a mischievous smile sparkling in his eyes.

"Here's another fine mess you've gotten us into Stanley!" Dr Thomas Doubleday remarked with a grin, tossing his car keys to Justin. "Your phone call just beat the call out from the police. Jeans, et al., including shoes on the back seat as requested. You can change in the car and keep the keys for me." He scanned Justin's pale features. "Also, a quick snack in the cooler should you need it?"

Justin shook his head. "Thank you, Thomas, I am fine. With any luck, this lot will decide I cannot stand the sight of blood, not a bad reputation to have considering. Many thanks for this. Can I ask one more favour?"

Justin's best friend and closest neighbour paused, bag in hand.

"A lift back to my car when I can leave?"

Thomas grinned, "No problem. I'm off duty at the surgery today."

Justin knew that Thomas served as the police doctor, but was also one of the local practice GPs who served the area around Daneley. Thomas wanted people to believe it was just another way to make up for a misspent youth. Only Justin knew the truth, and possibly Thomas's husband Ryan.

"With all the police comings and goings, I take it running the distance at this time of day, or getting a police lift might be … umm … rather awkward?"

Thomas didn't wait for confirmation, but went over to the crime scene manager and registered his attendance at the scene. He changed into the regulation plastic overalls and overshoes he had collected from the boot of his Range Rover. The crime scene photographer arrived as he was pulling on the regulation gloves. Thomas waited for her to suit up and together they walked through the cordon of blue and white tape into the woods.

Justin unlocked the car and got in. His change of clothes was neatly folded on the back seat, along with his wallet and police credentials. He was glad of the privacy afforded by the car's tinted windows to get changed. Even he felt less vulnerable once he was more suitably dressed than in grubby shorts and sweaty tee shirt. He placed his running clothes and trainers into a plastic bag, in case the officers needed them, to eliminate any of his trace from the enquiry.

A varied assortment of transport had almost filled the long layby opposite the car park. The latest, a van marked Science Investigation Unit, disgorged its cargo. The white overalls, hoods, masks and overshoes made the forensic scientists look like macabre clones. Two were carrying the sad little tent which would cover and protect the victim's body until she could be moved to the local pathology lab, once the photographer and forensic team had done their part.

Justin leaned back and closed his eyes. The memory of another bluebell wood teased his senses. "What was her name? A tasty piece in all senses of the word on that long-ago, hot spring, day. … Ah! yes, Abigail. So very long ago."

A brusque knock on the window jolted him from sleep. He jerked upright and stared unseeing out of the car window. His mind, still replaying some extremely enjoyable memories, was slow to catch up with his physical reaction. He shook his head to clear it and focused completely on the woman outside the car. She was trying to peer in through the darkened glass, one hand shielding her eyes from the glare. Tall with short-cut mahogany brown hair, from the red gleam of sunlight seen through the darkened glass. Justin carefully opened the door and stepped out of the car. In response, the woman stepped back and raised her warrant card for him to see. The photograph did not do her justice. She was not beautiful in the modern fashion of beauty. Instead, she had the kind of face Justin had always envisaged for Helen of Troy: subtle and intelligent. Full of character that could keep friends and lovers fascinated for a lifetime.

"Acting Detective Inspector Anne Richards sir," she introduced herself, looking up into his face. "You are Detective Chief Inspector Mortmain?" She stumbled over his surname. Her voice was pleasant, with just a hint of a different accent than the local one on certain sounds.

Justin nodded and showed her his credentials. "DCI Justin Mortmain," he acknowledged, "Good to meet you in person DI Richards. I have already spoken to the Chief Constable, and he has agreed this will be our first case together. I did not see the point of waiting another week when this poor girl fell at my feet, so to speak."

Anne nodded, then looked over her shoulder as another person approached.

"I hope my taking over early will not cause any problems for you?" Justin asked out of politeness.

"No problem at all sir," she replied, her tone noncommittal. "This is DCI Luke Benson. He's the other Major Crime team's senior investigating officer, and in temporary charge of our team, at least he was until now." She managed to say before the stocky figure strode up to them. He had overheard their exchange, and disliked what had been heard, from the scowl on his face.

"Yeah, well, we'll see about that. I'm still the guy in charge at the moment," DCI Benson commented as he reached them. "Can't expect you to investigate yourself, can we? Still, who am I to disagree with the Chief Constable?"

Benson hawked and spat on the ground.

Justin stiffened at the insult, feeling an instant dislike of the man that clenched his fists at his side. Then he noticed Benson's sidelong glance, watching for a reaction and forced himself to relax, deciding he at least, would be civil. He would probably have to co-operate with Benson for some time to come. Justin needed to be patient and try to discover why Benson was going out of his way to provoke him. Or, possibly, Benson just had disgusting habits that he could not break.

"Have you heard from the Chief Constable? I spoke to him just after I found the body. He said he would inform you officially straight away that I would be taking this case." Justin paused, waiting for a response and appearing to consider Benson's last remark.

Benson nodded reluctantly and muttered, "Yeah he called me."

"It is true I cannot investigate myself, but then neither would I jump to the conclusion that the person who found the body was the killer. If you want witnesses to where I've been and what I've been doing over the last few days, I can supply them, including the Chief Constable, for most of yesterday, including quite a lot of the evening. Oh, and the Lord Lieutenant of the

County. I was at his place for dinner and stayed overnight. From what I can see, our victim died in the early hours of the morning, by which time I was deeply asleep twenty miles away."

"And have you got a witness to that as well?" Benson asked sarcastically.

"As a matter of fact, I have, if you really need to know." Justin realised acting Inspector Richards was just managing to hide a grin at Benson's resentful expression."

Benson grunted, "I take it you can get yourself to the station later? The acting Inspector here can take a statement from you, before you take over the lot." He said over his shoulder as he stalked off towards the crime scene.

"You may need these, particularly the trainers." Justin handed the plastic bag from the car to Inspector Richards. "There are likely to be traces near her feet on the stream bank, footprints at the least. You should be able to use these to verify which prints are mine. You don't need to worry about fingerprints since they are on file. I doubt there will be DNA contamination. I was not close enough, and the breeze was blowing from her towards me."

Anne Richards relaxed slightly when Benson left. She accepted the bag of clothes and put them down at her feet. "I could take your statement now?" she glanced up at his face, "Then we could have it ready for your signature at the station. If you are starting today?" She took out her notebook and a pen.

"Sounds good to me," he said and gave a clear concise account of how and when he discovered the body after deciding, on a whim, to run through the woods before turning for home.

"Here comes my ride," Justin said as Anne picked up the bag and turned towards the forensics van.

Justin headed to meet Thomas as he emerged from the trees. His normally cheerful face was unusually sombre, and he looked pale. They walked over to his car, where Thomas removed the white overalls and tossed them in the boot. He looked at Justin and grimaced. He didn't need to say anything.

Justin nodded in understanding. "Not a pleasant death, alone, growing weaker in the cold and dark. Poor girl!"

"She was young too. Just beginning her life." Thomas responded, stepping up into the driver's seat of the Range Rover. "The PM will tell you more, but from what I saw, it was a brutal attack driven by vindictive rage. Whether that rage was directed at our victim personally or at the fact she was female is for you to discover. She'd been dead about three, maybe four, hours. The body could've been dumped between two and four in the morning," Thomas's face twisted into a grimace. "She bled out onto the path."

"I agree. She was moved here, so we need to find the primary crime scene. Some kind of trolley or cart was used to move her, from the tracks crushing through that bluebell clearing. I did not follow them back in case I confused the forensics. Besides, it was far too late to catch the culprit. The way the broken flowers were withered and crushed down in the direction of the stream suggested the killer or killers had not used the larger car park I passed through. As I remember, there is another small car park on the other side of the wood which matches the track direction. A bit isolated, used by what we used to call 'courting couples' or, more likely, sex workers. She did not seem to me, to match either of those categories, but you never know. Probably a van of some type was used to transport the trolley and the victim. My bet would be whoever dumped her would have used that car park."

Thomas nodded. "Yes, I saw the forensics team heading through that way. OK, so where am I taking you?".

Justin looked guilty. "Sorry Thomas, I parked up at the Ashridge Estate. I had planned to circle back but got distracted at the top of the hill."

Thomas sighed. "Thirty miles from where you discovered the body. Justin, I hope you gave a convincing account or they don't ask you too many questions. For a start, scenting a body from half a mile away isn't all that believable in a human. Neither is going for a run and expecting to do sixty miles and then drive home for lunch while still recovering from injuries. How are you feeling, by the way?"

"I hope I have dealt with that. I said I was running through the woods on a sudden whim before heading home to Daneley. Strangely, I feel fine thank you for asking. Back to normal, in fact. I was getting bored after two weeks of convalescence."

Thomas glanced sideways at his passenger. "I'm not sure I actually believe you about back to normal. You going to run with this case?"

Justin nodded, a slight smile acknowledging the pun. "I already have a vested interest and official permission, so why not start the job early?"

"Good, the poor lass and her family have a chance of getting justice with you on the case."

"You do not like Benson?"

"I've never met a police officer like him before and I don't want to meet one in the future. During his most recent case, he held the person who found the body on suspicion. When the evidence came in, it showed the death was a suicide. The victim was fifteen and the person who found him was his mother. He was her only child." Thomas shrugged. "I knew the family. His team is more inclined to work with the evidence and usually manages to minimise the damage. This time, well, the only reason I can suggest why he's not on his way to some quiet backwater, or out of the force altogether, is the sudden loss of the other team leader. Now you are here, things might change. Watch your back where Benson's concerned Justin. He won't go willingly or without trying to cause some damage. He's a nasty piece of work who likes to have something to hold over everyone he comes into contact with.

"Trouble is Benson's been around long enough to demotivate your entire team. Anne Richards, well, she's an excellent detective, but she's requested a transfer, although that could be for personal reasons. She's gone through quite a nasty divorce and her ex-husband is also a police officer. That and the way Benson blocked her recent promotion." Thomas shrugged. "She might want a fresh start, but she'd be worth keeping. Detective Constables Paul Selsdon and Julie Rawlings follow orders, but again I would say with the right leadership and encouragement, they could step up. They both have the makings of real detectives. DC Ray Williams tends to emulate his senior officer, or so it seems to me, although occasionally I've suspected that's a bit of a tease because he's aware of what I think. He was once a Detective Sergeant but had an argument with a senior officer. That senior officer is now in prison, by the way and Ray may yet get his stripes back. Charles Ensbury is a fairly new, replacement DC who I've had little to do with so far."

"You fill me with confidence Thomas, you really do."

Thomas laughed, "You'll manage, you always have."

Another silence followed, giving Justin plenty of time to mull over what he had learned of his new team. He didn't doubt Thomas's appraisal since they had been friends, he and the "rock and roll" doc, from the time Thomas and the band had gained their first platinum disc. Now they were friends and neighbours and Thomas had returned to his original career choice as well as senior partner of the local practice.

Justin leaned back into the passenger seat, passing a hand across his eyes.

"Are you sure you're feeling fit enough for all of this?" Thomas asked, glancing sideways.

Justin turned to look at Thomas's profile. "Sorry Thomas! Either I have just been around too long or I am getting old. Not sure I want to waste valuable time building trust with another team. Perhaps it is time for a change of career for a while. Something to keep in mind during the investigation."

He heard Thomas choke back a disbelieving laugh. "I doubt that very much. What else would you want to do? Become a wealthy jet setter? How about dabbling in the stock market or becoming an entrepreneur? There's always farming you've got more than enough land?" Thomas was not impressed with his own suggestions. "You'd be bored in a heartbeat. What you need is a little more time to get back to normal, that's all. Welcome home Justin. I'm glad you're back."

"Thank you. Strangely, I am truly glad to be back. Daneley is the village I have lived in the longest in my life and the closest to a real home I have ever had. I think that is due to you and the village families."

"Happy to be of service. We are all very proud of our very own v … villain catcher," Thomas grinned.

"Careful Thomas, the villagers are as proud of their very own rock and roll superstar. I was at the manor when they turned a pretty penny from the tourists, showing them the gatehouse, and regaling the punters with the stories of the "wicked doings" going on in your home. You and the band were touring Australia at the time, I think. Amazing imaginings they came up with. So, take care Thomas! I might, just accidentally, tell the villagers a true story."

Thomas laughed out loud. "It would be too tame for their taste," he stated smugly. "I'd be dead if I'd attempted half the things that reached the newspapers."

Justin heard the wistful note in his voice. "You miss it still?"

"Yes, and no. All I have to do is remember what happened to Aimee, and then it's definitely not. It was fun, and we made it huge for quite a time, but, like you, I'm glad to be home doing something that is different but totally worthwhile. Especially now, sharing my life with Ryan."

The conversation faded into a companionable silence. Justin looked out of the window at the passing scenery of fields, trees and farms each side of the dual carriageway. The car journey of just over twenty miles was convenient but lacked the interest of the longer route through villages and along lanes that he had run that early morning. It was hard to believe he had set out from Daneley just an hour or so earlier. They turned off towards Hatcham onto the minor roads, until five miles and six roundabouts further on, they turned left and headed uphill, following a winding, narrow road. Just below the peak of the hill, Thomas turned left into the Ashridge estate parking area.

From the entrance to the estate, across the wide flat land they followed the track past several gaps in the wooded area that led to small car parking areas dotted between the trees. The wide area of grass was clear of trees so that arrivals could see the tall column, much like Nelson's Column in London, ahead of them. More than twice the height of the nearby woodland, and erected on the top of the hill, the Bridgewater Monument was intended to dominate the area. It celebrated the life and work of the third Duke of Bridgewater in the eighteenth century. He had understood the value of canals for transporting heavy loads and financed his own canal to carry coal from his mines in Worsley to the town of Manchester. He made a huge fortune from selling coal to the new factories and workers' houses as well as the fees for other industrialists to use his canal.

The various clearings where cars could park had begun to fill up, unloading dog walkers, serious hikers and locals out to enjoy the views. In the clearing closest to the café and shop, Thomas drew up behind Justin's car.

"Would you and Ryan care to join me for dinner tomorrow? Beth would be very happy to cook all your favourite dishes."

"You have a genuine treasure in your housekeeper Justin and a dream of a cook. Yes, to the invitation for me at least. Ryan has started writing up a piece on the people trafficking and prostitution racket he was researching. He needs to push on if he wants to meet the deadline." Thomas's forehead creased into a frown, quickly gone. "To hell with it, yes for both of us. It's about time Ryan got his head out of his arse, at least for a little while."

Justin stepped down from the passenger seat, amusement flashing across his face. "Beth is still your biggest fan Thomas. She always pulls out all the stops when she knows you will be visiting." He closed the car door and stepped back, waving goodbye as Thomas drove away.

3

When Justin arrived at the Shady Lane headquarters it was early afternoon. After a shower and change of clothes, he had hastily eaten a cold lunch and driven to the station. His neatly typed statement was waiting for him to review. The statement contained the basic facts as accurately as he had given them. He read it through carefully and signed it.

After handing it back to the waiting officer, he made his way to the second floor, where the Major Crime Unit had its offices. The open space gave the impression of waiting, making Justin feel very much on trial. The entire team was present in the main area. Five pairs of eyes focused on him. Anne Richards had probably given them a brief description of their new boss. Now they had their first chance to see for themselves. He felt like a catwalk model and wondered if he should turn around for them to get a full view. He knew what they were seeing. A man around average height with proportionally wide shoulders and a narrow waist, emphasised by the quality of the tailored suit he was wearing. Dark hair with no sign of grey, still slightly damp from his shower, swept across an intelligent forehead. Unusual midnight blue eyes returned their stares from beneath dark brows, a slightly aquiline nose and high cheekbones balanced by a strong jawline. The whole office seemed to be one frozen tableau and Justin felt a bubble of amusement rising within him that added a sparkling gleam to his eyes and a softening twitch of laughter to his mouth. However, he ignored all five of them for the moment. Justin walked across to the incident board, currently blank except for the date, a single photograph of the body, face down on the stream bank and a sketch map of the woodland. The photo was labelled unidentified female. The dump site was marked on the sketch map, as was the trail indicated by the crushed bluebells. As he had suspected, the trail had led back to the small, more secluded, car park, also marked on the sketch.

"Let me introduce you to the team. There are others but they are about other duties at the moment," Anne broke the silence then pointed to each of the other people in turn. "Chas Ensbury."

The tall, broad-shouldered figure, who had been standing next to the board when Justin arrived, waved a hand then added two pictures below the map. One showed the trail crossing the clearing, the other showed where the double track began at the smaller car park. Chas labelled them then stepped quickly back into the safety of the group.

"Ray Williams, Chas's partner and supervisor."

An older man acknowledged the introduction, "Sir."

"Julie Rawlings and Paul Selsdon"

The pair both looked up and nodded before returning their attention to the board.

Justin also continued to stare at the board for another couple of minutes, then turned to face his team.

"Welcome all of you to what HOLMES has officially designated 'Operation Stoker'. Right, what have we got so far?"

Anne began. She shook her head, saying, "Not so much. Doc's verbal report at the scene suggested she had been dead between three and four hours before you discovered the body at 7.15 a.m. We know this site was a body dump and not the original crime scene. If you look closely at the photo of the tracks across the clearing you can see blood drops at intervals along the trail."

Paul continued their report, his west country accent accentuated by nervousness. "Her clothes are blood stained and muddy from the stream bank, but despite her dress and coat being disarranged, she was fully clothed and there are no obvious signs of sexual assault. The post mortem results will verify if that is the case. Although initially it looks as if the coat was put back on the victim after the attack. That's according to the forensic officers at the scene and has not been verified in the lab yet. The search team didn't find a bag, purse or phone near the body, so," Selsdon grimaced, "no identification yet."

Julie added her information from behind the computer screen that almost hid the delicate looking blonde from view. "No matches from missing persons, but given when she died and how quickly she was found – all pretty close together – she may not have been reported missing yet. I've put together a description so we could still get a match." She raised her gaze from the screen. Doctor Doubleday suggested she's pretty young, somewhere between eighteen and twenty-three, he thought."

Justin nodded. "Anything from forensics yet?"

Anne shook her head. "Too soon! Preliminary report at the earliest tomorrow afternoon."

The information given, everyone stopped talking. Into the silence, the phone trilled, drawing everyone's attention. Ray answered, listened, then looked around at the team. His jaws still chewing on the nicotine gum Justin had seen him start as he had entered the office.

"Pathologist – post mortem set for 9 a.m. tomorrow."

"Inform the lab. I will be there. Anne, will you join me?"

Justin felt her hesitate for a fraction of a second before she seemed to sigh silently and nod her agreement.

Ray relayed the information and put down the phone. "Maybe the dental work will help with identification or she might have a unique tattoo. Let's hope so."

Justin turned back to the board. "Our initial priorities then: one: identify the victim; two: find her bag, purse or phone, preferably all three. Who has these items? Where has one or more of them been discarded possibly? Three: find the initial crime scene."

Justin looked at his new DI.

"Four: request a full search is organised through the woodland area in case something slipped away from the transport unnoticed in the dark. Concentrate on the bag/phone for identification, and also any potential weapons. Doctor Doubleday suggested a sharp single edged implement that caused the stab wounds. Anything!" he emphasised before turning to scan their faces. "We cannot identify the weapon any closer until the pathologist does the post mortem, so anything sharp enough to stab deep through flesh. Five: find the means of transporting the body used by the killer. Did the photographer take a picture at the car park end of our trail?"

Chas searched through the stack on his desk. Selected one and fastened it to the board.

"Good. Anne, can you organise a team of uniforms, perhaps traffic as well, for the next couple of days, day and night, to drop into the car park and question people parking up? Most of the regulars anyway, before word gets around and they avoid the area for a while. Someone may have information we can use." Justin stopped in front of the photo of the car park, where something caught his attention. "When did the county install CCTV in the woods?"

The team glanced at one another, a shake of the head here, a shrug there. Ray answered. "We didn't know they had."

Chas came to Justin's shoulder. "I can't see…"

"Get the owner of that bird-cam, or whatever it is, traced. It may have been recording last night and captured something we can use." Justin pointed at the tiny black dot of a lens in the crotch of a tree branch.

Chas nodded, "We'll get on to it now." He grabbed his jacket and headed for the door, followed by Ray.

Justin turned to Julie and Paul. "I know it is a bind, but I want you to go through traffic camera footage. Record the details of any van or 4x4 large enough to carry a body and some kind of trolley but small enough to get into that car park."

Alone in the main office, Justin made his way to the internal glass cube meant for the senior investigating officer. It was small but perfectly formed, Justin thought with a twisted smile, except a gold fish bowl would have more privacy. He shrugged, looking around. If the walls had been anything but glass, it would have been claustrophobic. What saved it from mediocrity were the extra-large windows onto the outside world, giving a wide panorama clear across to the old town. He also had a perfect view of the comings and goings of his new team because only the wall shared with the corridor was not glass. Justin immediately decided it would be perfect for his own floor to ceiling action board. The outer office would be empty for a while, so Justin got started moving things around. With no one watching his every move, he could be himself. In less than fifteen minutes, the two full filing cabinets had moved into the corner formed by the two walls to the outer office. He had rearranged the desk space to leave clear the blank wall and allow a fabulous view over the town for when he needed to think. The various cables, for computer, phone, printer, were just long enough. He shifted the "ergonomic" chair behind the desk, adjusted it for his height, logged on to the computer and pulled up a set of personnel files.

The information about his new team soon absorbed all his attention. What he read gave him a feeling of optimism, despite the recent issues, since Benson had become the temporary senior officer. For a start, Thomas had been right about Ray Williams taking the piss out of him. Ray was a highly decorated officer. His record as a detective showed he had worked successfully on several teams from domestic violence, through gang related and organised crime, to the murder squad. Ray had been partnered with Charles or Chas Ensbury, originally from Carlisle Bay, Antigua. Chas was on the fast stream training and had a first-class degree in criminology. It was a good choice, old experience and new eager detective. He was even more surprised by Julie Rawlings. She gave the impression of being a fragile gentle individual, which had probably been an advantage, doing undercover work that made Justin wince. She looked very young but had been part of a child protection group before joining the Major Crime Unit. That was a hard job for anyone to do. Paul Selsdon, like Julie and Justin himself, was a trained firearms officer but had transferred to serious crimes rather than risk burn out, having spent several years with the armed police units.

Potentially, it could be an excellent and successful team when not dragged down by poor leadership. Justin nodded to himself. Thomas had always been a good judge of character. The most surprising element was why Anne was not already a full, rather than acting, inspector. No wonder she wanted a transfer! From what he was gleaning from the records, she had been enduring some pretty strong harassment from Benson, although she had made no complaint. If, as Thomas had inferred, her private life was a mess, she was justified in making a transfer request. Now he understood why he would have a hard job convincing her to stay. The others, so it seemed, needed only a reminder of what success was. Justin hoped this case would be the necessary catalyst.

His mobile buzzed just as he finished reading the records. He glanced at the text, a smile curving his lips. Marta! He replied agreeing to dinner that evening but explaining he had taken on his first case and could not tell her when he would be leaving. Thirty seconds later, she replied. He laughed out loud on reading the text, although a certain heat reddened his cheekbones and added a gleam to his dark blue eyes. From the moment they had first met, she had understood and accepted that his job had first call on his time. She too had an important career, often travelling the world where her architectural work was beginning to bring fame and fortune. Most of all, it was her courage and intelligence that had attracted him more than her beauty. She had emerged from an abusive relationship with the strength of character to try again, and he felt privileged to be sharing that adventure with her. He replied, then tucked the phone away.

He was still thinking about Marta when he heard footsteps along the corridor before Anne walked into the outer office. He stepped into the open doorway and invited her to join him. She stood in front of the desk stiffly at attention, looking like a probationer hauled before a superior for some misdemeanour.

"No need to be so formal Detective Inspector." Justin commented quietly, then said, "please take a seat."

She sat down stiffly on the very edge of the chair.

Justin sighed. "I am hopeful that you and I will be able to work well together. In order to form a professional partnership, I think we need to clear the air. If you are willing to do so, that is?"

Justin watched her refocus on his face; her attention caught by the emphasis he laid on professional partnership.

"Look, I am aware of the rough time you've had for a while now, and I understand why you would want a transfer to make a fresh start. I want to ask you to put that idea on hold until we conclude this case. If, after that, you still want a transfer, I will support you. Yes, you have been held back. That is obvious from your record. You should have made inspector already. But your last two applications never got further than this office. I have already sent on your most recent application."

Anne stared at him hard, searching for something, but what, he could not tell.

"You seem to have been honest with me, so I will be the same. I don't know if I want a transfer at the moment, and that's down to you."

"Me?"

"Yeah, I checked you out through some people. There's a lot I couldn't find out, but enough to show you have a phenomenal success rate. I definitely could learn a lot from you, so they said. What no one can tell me is why you've decided to leave the Met and come to a little town like ours?"

Justin frowned. He needed to keep her confidence in his honesty but could not tell her everything, not now, perhaps never.

"I was working undercover at my last job. I cannot tell you why a DCI was undercover. Someone betrayed me to the international gang I and a colleague were infiltrating. What happened after that was not very pleasant and left me with certain injuries which have taken a while to heal. The officer I was working with was tortured and killed. Those in charge felt it would be better if I returned to work in a less harsh environment. I was born and live in Daneley, so in reality, I was returning home when I chose to take this opening. That is all I am allowed to tell you officially. The case has been designated 'top secret', so I cannot tell you anything more."

Anne was silent for a while. Justin allowed her time to consider, waited patiently, but certainly felt more nervous than he had for a long time. He could not understand why he felt that he needed Anne Richards to remain, only that it was important for the future of the team.

"OK," she said, her voice quiet and slightly doubtful. "I agree to a trial period until we solve this case. After that, well, the old phrase holds true, 'time will tell'."

Justin grinned. "Good, now let's get some decent coffee. You must know somewhere nearby that does a decent cup. I cannot stand the machine stuff from the canteen. Then you can fill me in on the rest of our merry little band. Oh, not the basic facts," he added, seeing her look towards the computer screen. "Their files have given me those, and they are impressive. Now, I want your insight into their strengths and weaknesses as someone who has been working with them. But first, save me from dehydration and caffeine withdrawal. Where can we get some decent coffee?"

"I think I know a reasonable place for decent coffee, although it's not that close," Anne stated.

She went back into the outer office and grabbed her jacket before leading the way out of the office and down the stairs. Justin made a mental note to get a machine set up in the outer office as soon as possible.

They left through the main door and walked along Shady Lane. The afternoon had gradually darkened and all the promise of the morning's sky was lost beneath a continuous, pale grey, cloud blanket. Even so, outside was still pleasantly warm, and the cloud was high enough to hope there would be no rain. They turned onto Clarendon Road lined with a variety of office buildings, from Victorian business premises housing legal firms close to the courts, to small nineties glass and steel buildings, rented out as company headquarters, nearer the main railway station. The road that joined the High Street to the station was the commercial heart of the town. They had to wait, as usual, for what seemed far too long, at the pedestrian crossing among a small group of shoppers and a trio of secondary school-age children. Justin guessed they were making the most of their freedom to meet up and have some fun around the town centre. His nose wrinkled at the smell of catalytic converters where car engines had not yet warmed up. He heard Anne cough, above the quiet murmur of voices around them, when the fuel fumes caught in her throat. Eventually they were able to cross the three lanes of the one-way system that divided commercial Clarendon from shopping Clarendon, the smaller section of the same road.

A homeless man sat on the pavement, his knees up under his chin to avoid blocking the path. "Spare some change?" the question asked so often was quietly muttered and barely heard.

It didn't look as if he had had any luck until one woman returned from the direction of the High Street, a takeaway cup and sandwich box in her hands. Justin watched her give them to the homeless man. Their eyes met as she started to turn away. She smiled and shrugged as if to say what else can we do? He understood, money could buy anything, but the gift of food and drink would keep hunger away. She passed them again, heading quickly back to the High Street, as they strolled along the Victorian façade of the town's theatre.

They followed the curved glass front of the Three Counties Building Society around the corner and left into the High Street. Here it was busy with pedestrians in a new traffic free zone. The road widened into a broader square, once the space used by the Medieval market. Now, it had become a paved performance area between two ornamental posts topped by the masks of comedy and tragedy. Behind and slightly to one side of the square was the town's large parish church.

They crossed over to the church side, hearing the melodious sound of Andean pipes from further down the High Street, where a group of buskers were playing and selling their CDs. The music cut off abruptly once they entered the Italian coffee shop Anne had selected, a part of a good country-wide chain.

Sitting together on a small two-person table in the window, Justin watched the comings and goings on the High Street while they waited for their order. He grimaced then muttered quietly, more to himself, "NIMBY!"

"Who's a NIMBY?" Anne asked, a hint of indignation in her tone.

"Me!" Justin answered quickly, then paused as the assistant arrived with their order. "I was feeling uncomfortable about the new 'fashionable' set that has invaded Malford and what this gentrification is doing to my town. It was a really pleasant place when we first came here."

"When was that?" Anne asked before taking a sip of her tea.

Justin grinned, "Pretty recently really. About 1070, I think, when the original Justin Mortmain was given the manor of Daneley as a reward by William of Normandy."

"Justin Mortmain? William the Conqueror?" She chuckled, "well, you can't say the place hasn't changed since then."

"Some changes do not have long-term benefits. That is the problem. What happens when the fashion changes and half these places shut down? The High Street would become deserted." He smiled and held up his hands in surrender. "Sorry, I have stepped down from my soap-box and we can now get down to business." He glanced around, but they were the only customers currently in the shop. "Anne, I need to ask you something before we start discussing the rest of the team."

She looked up at him. "Oh, what?"

"I know it is usual for the SIO to do the public appeals and be the face of the investigation. But I need you to do that job, if you will."

"Oh, why? Benson revels in doing the public appeals. He can't get enough of the TV companies or the press conferences. Why don't you want to do them?"

"I am not Benson," Justin snapped, then raised a hand in apology. "For the same reason, I could not tell you everything about my last case," he replied more quietly. "Will you do it, please? The television people have already discovered we have an unidentified body. They have given us a space on tonight's late news. Our press office has agreed a meeting at five this afternoon on the station steps to include the rest of the press. Then the appeal will also make tomorrow morning's papers. It will be a quick statement only, a two-minute appeal for information. You will not need to answer any questions."

Anne shrugged, "Fair enough. I suppose you don't want some hulking great bloke with a gun suddenly arriving in your village. Is that it, fear of reprisals?"

"Something like that,"

"Then yes, I'll take your place with the press."

Even though she had agreed, Justin sensed it was a reluctant agreement. He decided not to pry into her reasons until they had worked together a while longer.

"Thank you." Justin tasted some of the hot coffee, enjoyed the kick of caffeine, and decided it wasn't such a bad brew, then asked, "I've read the files and I know background and achievements for all the team. On paper every one of you would be my first choices to work with. It is also obvious something has gone badly wrong and they seem as disillusioned with the job as you are. Now I want to hear your honest opinion of our team's strengths and weaknesses."

Justin stretched to ease his aching back and shoulders, and decided to call it a day. His panorama had long since darkened to a nightscape highlighted by the street lamps and a sliver of bright moon where the clouds had slipped away. The last of the team had left after a good day's work. Although all they had done, yielded only a little more information so far.

His phone buzzed, and he glanced at the text then at his watch. Damnation, he was going to be late! He signed out of the system and headed to the car park, where he paused beside his car. After the rain had ended, the sky had cleared, and the night was mild. Justin decided to leave his car where it was parked. His destination was only a quick walk away. He turned out of the security gate and headed down the lane towards the High Street. It was a quiet time of evening; most people who worked and shopped in the town during the day, had already gone home. Those on late shift or heading out with friends were not yet on the streets. Just before he turned right onto a narrow side road that led to a square of Georgian town houses, a warning prickle shivered down his spine. A shoddy, clapped out, Nissan was driving slowly along the road behind him, going in the same direction. Justin stopped and looked back. The windscreen was filthy, but he saw enough, a single occupant driving the car. He relaxed, realising this was no revenge attack in connection with that last case, just a fool trying to gain an advantage. He continued along the road, relieved there was no immediate danger from the driver. Laughing silently, Justin turned onto the side road, too narrow for cars. He heard the engine rev angrily, and the Nissan accelerated past the turning.

Peace and quiet enfolded him within the elegant square away from the deep burr of the traffic. The walk was a pleasant way to begin an evening heightened by anticipation. Justin followed the pavement around to the opposite side of the enclosed garden at the centre of the square. He stopped at the base of two shallow steps leading up to a typical Georgian frontage. He paused there, waiting until he saw the headlights of a car turning into the square from the opposite end. There was no need for him to use the brass, lion-head, knocker. As he reached the top of the steps, the door swung wide. A woman's silhouette filled the doorway, highlighted from behind by the brightness of a crystal chandelier. Walking up the steps, Justin kissed the offered lips and smiled, angling his head to bring his mouth closer to her neck.

"I'm sorry to be late Marta. Will you forgive me?" He said quietly below her ear.

She nodded, smiling, "Just this once I suppose I can make allowance."

He felt her strong quickening heartbeat and sensed the flow of blood through her veins.

"Mm! You have the most wonderful perfume my darling Marta," he whispered into her ear.

Marta pushed him gently away and slapped him lightly.

"Behave, supper is almost ready and I am not the aperitif."

"You cannot send me such an interesting offer, then go back on your word," he replied softly, pulling her back into his arms.

"I never promise what I can't deliver." She laughed as she felt a butterfly light caress across her neck that made a shiver run down her back. "Not on the doorstep my darling Justin. Let me at least close the door." She gave a shocked gasp as he swung her up into his arms instead, in full view of anyone passing. Even pausing for a moment before pushing the front door shut with his foot.

"Anything you say," he agreed lightly, then saw her frown.

Before she could say anything, he ran lightly up the curved staircase and placed her gently into an armchair in the living room. Then, he went to the tall narrow window and looked out over the square. He beckoned her to join him, keeping close to the curtain. "See there, the orange-brown Nissan?"

Marta looked and nodded.

"Well, it was following me here. I simply thought the driver deserved to see something interesting, considering the trouble he has gone to." He caught the flash of fear in her eyes and hurried to reassure her. "No, you do not need to worry. The driver is not linked to what happened to me. Far from it, in fact. You don't mind, do you?"

"Not really, besides I know you will make it up to me for making use of me. I think supper first, yes, to make sure you have the strength."

Supper had been much appreciated. Marta was a wonderful cook, and he had not realised just how hungry he had been until the delicious aromas made his stomach groan. They settled for coffee and liqueurs in the living room. Marta closed the curtains slowly, ensuring it took long enough to look around the square.

"He is still there, this man who followed you. You are sure there is no connection?" Marta asked irritated by the intruder disrupting their precious time together.

"Yes, I am certain. Now come, sit and enjoy your brandy. Would you mind if we watched the news? My first case with this team will be mentioned tonight and my colleague is making an appeal."

"I would be interested myself. You were supposed to be on sick leave for at least another week. How did Thomas feel about you going back to work?" Marta warmed her brandy lightly between her hands.

"He made no objection."

Marta looked at him, her face showing disbelief. "Did you actually ask him?"

"Not exactly. It was more of an unspoken understanding between us. The victim was a young woman and that has affected quite a few of the team, including Thomas."

"So, tell me, before we watch, what happened exactly?"

He explained his run and finding the body, which had made him feel as if he had to take on the case. "I found her, so somehow, in my mind, she became my responsibility." He tried to explain his feelings of that morning.

Marta nodded, then pressed the button on the remote just in time for the news to begin. They watched in silence through terrorist reprisals in the Middle East; broken water pipes flooding railway lines; the usual delays and cancellations for commuters; another political resignation and then the newsreader began.

"Early this morning, the body of a woman was discovered in Tolland Woods. Our reporter, Mike Edwards, was at the press conference this afternoon." The picture changed, from the studio to outside the Shady Lane station and Anne standing in front of the main doors. Text at the bottom of the screen showed "Detective Inspector Richards of the Major Crime Unit".

Justin watched intently. "Excellent," he murmured after the news had given way to the weather forecast. It was a good interview. Anne came across as intelligent and experienced, both of which he knew she was. She pointed out immediately that the investigation was in its initial stage, then explained that if anyone had information regarding the identity of the victim, the investigation team would be pleased to hear from them.

The screen went dark as Marta switched off the television and turned to him, smiling while her eyes shone with mischievous intent.

"Well Justin Mortmain, are you prepared to keep your promise? I will be more than happy to keep mine."

Justin stood up and bowed. "My lady's wish is my command. I always keep my promises."

† † †

The early morning light illuminated the rectangle of window, shining directly on the back of the house. Justin blinked and squinted against the brightness to check the time. Marta groaned and tried to hide under the covers, then gave up and emerged, tousle-headed, from beneath the quilt. Sleep lidded, green eyes blinked at Justin and she groaned.

"Why do you always look so fresh and bright this early in the morning?" she complained, flopping back onto the pillow.

"Because, my dear girl, I do not need much sleep, unlike yourself. Now, what was it you were going to tell me when I interrupted you last night?"

Marta put a hand over her eyes. "I'm sorry Justin. I have to go to Switzerland for a consultation and discussions about the new office building my company is tendering for. It's a series of meetings that could keep me there for about a week. I cannot go to the restaurant's anniversary party with you."

He turned towards her, kissed her lightly on the nose. "That is not a problem Marta. Good luck with the negotiations, I hope you get the contract." Then he paused before asking, "Call me, when you arrive?" He pushed the quilt back, "I can pick you up from the airport if you let me know about your return flight. Now, what can I get you for breakfast?"

Justin got out of bed, giving her an interesting view of broad shoulders, narrow waist and naked bottom and wandered out of the room, returning five minutes later chuckling.

"The idiot in the Nissan is still there," he commented before heading for the shower.

An hour later, Justin carefully balanced a full plate on top of a mug of tea as he kissed Marta farewell. She watched, as he crossed the narrow road between the house and the green heart of the square, to where the dirty coloured Nissan was parked.

Even through the closed window, he could hear heavy snoring. Placing the plate and mug on the car roof, he rapped gently on the steamed-up window. The snoring grunted into silence; one bleary eye looked through the glass at Justin before the window rolled slowly down. Justin collected the plate and mug, passing them both through the opening.

"Ms Drogalova thought you might be hungry after an all-nighter," he remarked. "She would also like to offer you a chance to clean yourself up before heading for work." He glanced down at Benson. "She will not answer your questions, so do not bother asking. If you want to know about me, then ask me." His voice had lost its amused tone, grown harsh. "However, if I find you following me again like some private Dick," he emphasised the word, "you will not like what happens."

Benson shivered and looked away. The smell of the hot bacon sandwich and fresh, strong brewed tea made his mouth water.

"Have a nice day, as our American cousins would say." Justin left him tucking into a hearty breakfast and headed for the station to collect his car and Anne for their appointment with the victim.

† † †

They arrived slightly early for the post mortem and Anne introduced Justin to the pathologist, Doctor Amardeep Shah, and his assistant, Nev. Anne greeted the pathologist like a familiar and valued friend, asking after his wife and family.

Doctor Shah frowned at Justin, then asked, "Anne, shall I ask Nev to stay near you? I thought, after last time, they might spare you another post mortem. I'm not sending you home with a black eye again."

Anne's face went from pale to blazing rose in an instant when Justin turned to look at her questioningly.

"You haven't told him, have you?" Shah said and sighed with exasperation.

"No, but thankfully you have," Justin intervened. "There is no reason I should make you suffer. I can manage perfectly well. Take my car and head back to the office." He handed her the keys. "You can collate all the information from the team. I will make my own way back. Oh, and Inspector Richards next time there is a problem, tell me, please."

Embarrassed, all she could do was nod, grab the keys, and hurry out.

Doctor Shah put down his empty mug. "Right, let's get this over," he said.

Justin hated this part, had never grown used to looking at the empty, earthly, husk after life had been torn away. When eyes, that had been bright with laughter or shimmered with tears, were blank beneath closed lids. The animus, the spirit that made each one an individual, gone forever. He looked at the unidentified young woman, now washed and naked beneath her sheet. Her clothes and any external trace already collected. Doctor Shah glanced at Justin, then began.

"The body is that of a young woman, identity currently unknown, aged between 17 and 25 ..."

Justin was as pale as Anne had been, his expression bleak, having spent the walk back to Shady Lane reviewing the details of Doctor Shah's findings. He entered the building, keyed the code into the security door, and climbed the two flights of stairs to their team offices. Anne caught up with him in front of the information board, and the rest of the team gathered around the pair. He pinned the post mortem photograph of the victim, a head and shoulders shot, to the board beside the original picture.

"Our victim died of exsanguination from multiple stab wounds over the stomach and upper thighs." He began, his voice soft and quiet. "She had suffered several blows to the face and shoulders before being stabbed. Bruising had started to show."

Justin turned to face the team, a deep sadness reflected in his face. "She was pregnant, about three months, when she was killed. Blood alcohol level was high. Either she had been celebrating or drowning her sorrows."

He pinned a second photograph next to the first. "She has an unusual birthmark on her left shoulder, shaped like the silhouette of a phoenix rising from flames. It should help to identify her. A recent tattoo, a swallow, was on her right ankle. She had a rare blood, type AB negative. Only about one percent of donors have that specific blood group. She was approximately one point six five metres tall, weighed about sixty-four kilos, fit, and other than being dead, seemed in good health." He turned back to the team. "Ideas? Anything at all, any questions, any motives. No matter how wonderful or weird they seem."

"Was she sexually assaulted?" Ray asked.

"Not according to the PM, nor had she had consensual intercourse recently."

"Older married lover killed her to prevent his marriage going down the toilet?" Julie contributed.

"Boyfriend not prepared to settle down, and she was insisting he take responsibility?" Chas said.

"High alcohol content – random attacker? Vulnerable young woman out on her own?" Paul suggested.

"Yes, but was she alone? Could she have been with someone or a group? Maybe things got out of hand."

"Stalker issue? Gets a bit too intimate – she fights him off, tells him she's pregnant, if she knew – he becomes enraged, his perfect woman is not so perfect – kills her in anger. Those injuries sound pretty frantic?" Ray added another scenario.

"Why are we assuming it's a man?" Anne asked. "Why not the wife of the cheating husband?" She paused, shook her head. "Of course! Statistics suggest an attack like this is more likely by a male than a female attacker."

"What kind of blade are we looking for?" Chas asked. "Did Doctor Shah give us any ideas?"

"Yes," Justin nodded, "it is a single-edged blade with an asymmetrical point. The sharp edge being the shorter while the blunt longer edge curves down to meet it. The blade is around 10cm long, excluding the handle." He turned directly to Anne. "You are right. We should not rule out a female attacker on statistics alone, but the attacker pushed the blade in to the hilt multiple times. There was tell-tale bruising forming around the deeper wounds. Doctor Shah counted twelve deep wounds and around fourteen other slashes. That takes a lot of strength or fury, or both."

Anne smiled. "And we no longer talk about Cold War Russian 'female' shot-putters."

The atmosphere lightened a little. Justin also smiled. "True."

He returned to the information he had gained from the PM. "Her coat showed no damage despite all the bloodstains, but her dress had significant damage. The coat had been replaced after the attack before dumping the body. If so, why?" Justin answered his own question. "I suppose it could be a sign of remorse to hide what the attacker had done? Or simply to hide the injuries while he or she dumped the victim in the dark. How did all this happen with no one hearing anything? What stopped her from screaming?"

Julie had returned to her desk and was bent over the keyboard. Something had caught her attention. Her screen lit up.

"Sir, I think we have a hit on the missing persons – new tattoo and birthmark. A report has just been uploaded. The missing person is a local girl named Chelsey Harris. Her parents, Laura and Greg Harris, made the report when she didn't return home last night." She turned her screen so the team could see the photograph. The happy, smiling girl in the picture bore a very strong resemblance to their victim. The picture showed the same defined bone structure and a slightly pointed chin. It was a copy of a professional photograph possibly taken at a school prom. Despite being a few years younger, there was a good match with the post mortem head and shoulders shot.

"What's the address?"

"35 Stanhope Road," Julie read from the screen. "It's the family home. The girl still lives with her parents which is why they reported her. She usually lets them know if she is not expecting to get home."

Justin nodded he knew that district. "Stanhope Road used to be two-up two-down terraced houses a couple of streets from the railway line. Is it still the same?"

"Pretty much, although it is being gentrified, loft conversions and so on," she responded.

"You and Paul follow this up. Visit the house, see if you can get one of the family to provide identification, get something that we can use for scientific proof as well with their permission. Have someone from family liaison meet you at the mortuary. I think we have an identity for our victim, but we need formal confirmation. Let us know the result of the ID as soon as possible."

He looked over at Chas. "Any news on bird cam?"

Chas said, "Yeah, we found the owner, but he set the camera up to monitor the area but is now on holiday. Mr Tony Byett of 34 Laertes Close. One of the new builds on the Dalton Estate. It backs onto the woodland about a hundred yards south of the car park. Neighbours said he and his wife could be away some while. He owns a house in Spain so he isn't constrained to the usual one to two weeks like the rest of us. The camera records directly to his home computer, apparently." Ensbury frowned. "Tech boys said the camera angle would record the comings and goings in the car park. No nests anywhere in camera range."

"Can we find out where in Spain? Get on to the Spanish police. Perhaps they have a registry of property ownership and can track him down for us. Check with the neighbours if he has a cleaner or a friend keeping an eye on the house while he is away. See what else you can find out about him. Ordinary people do not usually place cameras to watch country car parks." Ensbury nodded, and Justin turned to Ray.

"Any forensic reports in yet?"

"Still waiting for most of the test results," Ray replied. "The scientists confirmed the route from the car park to the drop site. They followed the tracks which show a trolley with two wheels was used, possibly one of those old-fashioned trolleys you see used on stations during the steam train era. The techs also taped off where the vehicle had been parked, marked by blood pooling where the trolley was stationary, possibly while the killer locked the vehicle." He paused, then snarled "Poor Bloody Cow!"

Chas looked at his partner, eyes wide. Ray went red and wouldn't meet his gaze.

"I know, I know. Keep it impersonal, do your job, don't let it get to you. I've heard it all before, but sometimes it doesn't work, does it?" He looked at Justin. "Not every time. I look at that photo of our victim and I remember my sister on her prom night. What if it was her murder we were investigating? Sorry if that makes me unsuitable for the team, but there it is."

Chas said nothing, just placed his hand lightly and briefly on his partner's shoulder. It was all that was needed.

Justin felt some of his tension drain away. Perhaps this team could make it after all. "Fair enough. We all have at least one case which hits close to home."

Ray looked down at the desk.

"Mind you, it will cost at least one round at the pub for us to keep your secret."

"Sorry sir?" Ray looked up at him puzzled, meeting his gaze, embarrassment forgotten.

"Why, that you do have a heart despite pretending you do not." Justin grinned and moved on. "What about last night's car park trawl, anything, apart from scaring off the sex workers temporarily?"

"About twenty evening users were questioned by traffic officers, but none admitted being there the night before. Four were with familiar faces, sex for money. One cocaine dealer is now in the cells and two people were arrested on suspicion of sex with a minor. One was with a girl of fourteen and the other with a boy who looks about twelve but is, in fact, fifteen and well known to us," Ray grimaced. "It's a good haul, but we might have scared off people who have the information we need."

"Very well, suggest they leave it for a couple of nights. The incident board that was set up at the entrance might encourage people to come forward anonymously. Some car park users could have a regular visit pattern, including Tuesday evenings. If we get nothing in forty-eight hours, we can send the team in again. Those who are breaking the law can always be picked up later."

5

Stanhope Road was one of the smaller terraced roads that linked the railway lines and station to the High Street. Justin looked down its length, feeling it was a half-finished project. The part of the road, where they stood, was typically Victorian working class. The local pub took up the top corner of the road. Justin remembered many a Saturday night ending with blood on the Victorian floor tiles outside the main doors. The rusty stains decorating those same tiles suggested nothing had changed. Yet there was a disconnect between the early numbers on the road and the higher numbers. A change that began with the house they were approaching. The further you were from the pub, it appeared, the more upwardly mobile the households became.

At the front door, they looked at each other for reassurance. Both feeling sympathy for the individual who had told the living of the death of one of their treasured souls. It was one of the worst parts of the job that neither had become accustomed to.

The Family Liaison Officer, PC Romney, must have been looking out for them. They didn't need to ring the doorbell; the door opened as they approached it. Anne smiled at Romney and received a nod of recognition in return.

"How are they?" Justin enquired.

Romney shook her head. "Still very much in shock, Mrs Harris particularly is in denial. The younger daughter, Kate, seems extremely angry but also afraid of something. I don't know why. She won't talk to me yet." She looked through the archway from the lounge. "Mr and Mrs Harris are in the kitchen; Kate is upstairs, I think. SOCO hasn't yet arrived to search Chelsey's room."

"Any sign of the press?"

She shook her head. "No, but I doubt it will be long before they appear. Come on through, there's coffee ready or tea if you prefer."

Justin paused, one hand lightly touching Anne's coat sleeve. "I want you to lead, if you don't mind. I want to watch their reactions." Anne nodded her agreement before they walked through the archway into the back room.

An attractive woman, in her early fifties, sat at the dining table, beside her sat her husband holding her hand. Justin, watching the woman, felt she was unaware of her surroundings or of the comfort her husband was trying to offer, despite his own sorrow. She seemed isolated by the horrors she was imagining for her daughter. Mr Harris looked up and saw they had visitors. He was so tense he squeezed the hand he was holding, drawing his wife's attention back to the present. She looked directly at Justin, agony and hope at war in her eyes, before she shifted to Anne.

"I am so sorry Mrs Harris, Mr Harris," Anne began.

Justin heard nothing more. The mother's agony clawed at him. From a vast distance he sensed more than heard the despairing whisper of a broken heart: "Oh God, why?" Justin understood that cry. He too had asked that question long ago, "Oh Jupiter, why me?" He received no answer and doubted the current version of that deity would respond either.

After a lengthy pause, Anne introduced them and asked if they felt able to answer some questions. "Mr and Mrs Harris, we are sorry to have to intrude at such a time, but anything you can tell us, at the start of the investigation, about Chelsey's life could prove essential in finding the person responsible."

Mr Harris nodded, still holding on to his wife's hand. Romney poured them all mugs of coffee, then walked back to the living room. Justin and Anne sat down at the table opposite the bereaved parents.

"Did any of the family know where Chelsey had been going?"

They both shook their heads. "No," Mr Harris said. "She was an adult, and we respected her independence. She knew we'd come running if she needed us whatever time of day or night. But that night, we heard nothing from her."

"Was Chelsey in college or university?"

"No, she had the grades, but she decided she wanted to get a job and see where that might lead. She tried a couple of things that didn't really work out, then went to Donne & Partners on the High Street, that new fancy estate agent. She's been there about eighteen months and seems to be really enjoying it. Doing well she is ... was," his voice grew husky as he corrected himself.

"She had a fiancé, Sean Trent," Mrs Harris continued. "They got together in the sixth form and then broke up for a while. Recently they've taken up together again."

"I didn't know they were engaged," Mr Harris commented abruptly.

"You never did like him, did you?" Mrs Harris shook her head. "Going to be, I should have said. He came around while she was at work a couple of weeks ago. Asked for one of her rings to get the size right. He didn't actually say engagement ring, I admit, but it seemed right." Anne asked for his address and Mrs Harris told them.

"Mrs Harris, I wonder, is there any particular reason why you thought of an engagement? Did Chelsey believe in marriage?" Anne continued.

Mrs Harris shook her head, "No not really. She always said we were a good example of what she wanted if she ever got married." Her hand tightened around her husband's and she shook it gently. "Still, I wondered why she never even discussed going to live with Sean at his flat."

Anne glanced at Justin and took a deep breath. "Mrs Harris, Mr Harris, had Chelsey spoken to either or both of you about the fact she was pregnant?"

"What?" Mr Harris' shocked response mingled with the gasp of "Oh No!" from his wife. They had known nothing.

A strangled noise drew everyone's attention to the archway. A young teenager strode towards them, anger, resentment and fear driving her across the room. She sat on the other side of her mother and cuddled her arm for comfort, glaring at the two strangers who had just intensified the sorrow and pain her parents were enduring.

"I'm so sorry to tell you like this. It's possible she wasn't sure herself."

The silence stretched while the devastated parents sat, heads touching. They reminded Justin of a pair of swans he had watched that morning on the lake renewing their bond. This couple was strong, he had no doubt. They would carry on despite that permanent feeling of loss. Not least because of their other daughter. Justin contemplated Kate, their youngest. It was as if a young Chelsey had charged into the room. The strong family resemblance between the women of the house showed what Chelsey had been and what, in later years, she could have become. The waste of so much potential saddened him.

"You must be Kate?" Justin said, then explained who they were.

Kate didn't respond except for one quick, almost fearful glance.

"What about other friends she might have talked to?"

"Well, yes, there's Gina, she and Chelsey have been best friends since primary school. Gina Crane. She rents a place in Tangrave Close. There's quite a little group from secondary school as well who still go around together," Mr Harris continued. "Gina or Sean can probably supply their names and addresses, I should think. Darren might know some of them, but he's still on base. We expect him tomorrow."

"Darren?" Anne repeated.

"Yes, our son. He's a sergeant in the army. He's just got back from deployment overseas. We only contacted his commander when we knew ..." Mr Harris cleared his throat but couldn't continue.

"Would it be alright if we just had a look around Chelsey's room?" Justin asked gently. "I just want to get some impression of Chelsey's character. The scene of crime team will need to do a much more detailed search and may need to remove some items, such as her computer, for further analysis. I know this is another intrusion into your grief, but all of this is necessary if we are to understand what happened to Chelsey on that last day. For example, did she take a bag with her that morning?"

Mrs Harris looked up and gave a sad little smile.

"Yes," she replied. "It was a large shoulder bag, dark green leather with a garland of red poppies along the top flap. Chelsey used to make her own leather bags and belts and sometimes sold them at the local craft market. She had a genuine talent for design. Some of her friends said she should make them and sell them online. I know Chelsey was planning out how she might try that." The smile faded and tears traced a track down her face as she realised that would never happen now.

Both parents nodded permission slowly. Shock compounded the tragedy. Not just a daughter but a grandchild, their first, had been taken from them violently.

Justin and Anne crossed the dining area back into the living room and climbed the open plan stairs. Chelsey's room had originally been the master bedroom until the Harris family had extended outwards and upwards to make room for their family. To make sure they knew whose bedroom was whose, a pretty pottery tile, matching one on Katy's door, announced "Chelsey's Room".

Justin put on a pair of gloves taken from his pocket, then turned the doorknob and walked in. Anne had already made a note of their visit and they would log it on the record for the SOCOs reference.

Justin glanced slowly around. All of her belongings would now be handled by strangers, starting with himself and Anne. It was one necessary part of the hunt that he genuinely disliked, an invasion of the victim's privacy.

The first impression was of modern elegance and a space designed to meet specific needs. Photos of the family were grouped on one white wall above Chelsey's computer desk. Opposite was an expanse of built-in wardrobes equally well organised. To their right were the windows, letting in plenty of light. Below the windows, a shelf unit with some interesting antiques, including an antique writing slope. The tidiness of the space impressed Justin. Chelsey had appreciated and cared for her possessions.

Anne looked around, a rueful expression lighting her eyes. "I have an entire apartment that resembles the local recycling centre with all my stuff. Yet Chelsey kept her life tidy in one reasonably sized room. I am truly impressed."

Justin nodded, "Except for the bags on the bed."

There were three: one from a high street shoe shop and two from a high-end chain store that catered to younger professional women. Justin lifted one side of each bag in turn to peer at the contents. Silk and lace in one, black taffeta in the other. All the contents bundled and creased. Anne frowned at the sight – it was out of place and out of character in comparison with the rest of the room. The shoe shop bag held two shoes loose on top of the box.

"Why would someone who kept their personal space spotless leave these expensive items in this state?" Anne asked, speaking more to herself than to Justin.

Justin shook his head, most of his attention on the wastepaper basket.

"Someone, as tidy as Chelsey was, wouldn't just stuff things back into the bag to get crumpled, especially if she had changed her mind about them. Unless something had happened to upset her?" Anne continued to follow her train of thought. "Yes, something had upset her, but what?"

"I think Chelsey was going to wear them. She certainly tried them on, or so it seems." He commented, voice muffled by the basket. "The price tags and all the other security and size gubbins shops stick over their goods these days, are in here." He straightened up. "We will wait for forensics to do their magic. Perhaps she tried them at home and changed her mind, though that does not seem likely. She took the time to lay the receipts out here on her workspace next to the computer. They are dated the day before I found her body at the brook." Sadness for the loss of two young lives made his expression cold and severe. "There's a positive pregnancy test in the basket, half pushed back into its box."

Anne looked around the room and over the bed, headboard to footboard. "No sign of any kind of bag she might have been using and no mobile either. There's a little rest for it on the bedside table. She probably used it as her alarm clock." Anne opened the wardrobe and closed it again. Everything of good quality, easily mixed and matched for work in one section, and casual clothes neatly organised in the other, divided by sets of drawers used for underwear, mostly.

Justin paused before asking, "If you purchased something like these," he pointed at the newly bought items, "what would be the reason?"

Anne considered, eyes roving over the bags. "If I were Chelsey's age possibly for a date with someone my mother told me had borrowed a ring of mine. Especially if I wanted a closer relationship with my 'baby daddy', having just discovered I was pregnant. A nice way of breaking the news if he didn't know?"

Justin was nodding. "Yes, that was my thought too. Our visit to the boyfriend could prove very useful. Time to leave the place to forensics I think."

He opened the door and pulled off the gloves, tucking them into his pocket. On their way through the lounge, Justin had a quiet word with PC Romney asking that she keep a close eye on the youngest daughter. "She knows more than the rest of the family. See if you can get her to speak to you sooner rather than later."

Even with the double-glazing, Justin felt that the street outside was far noisier than when they had arrived. It was not yet time for school finishing or for the earliest of workers to be arriving home. He lifted one side of the blind, which blocked the window, and grunted with annoyance.

"The reporters are massing," he commented to Anne, nodding towards the kitchen. "We will take the back way out."

"They're damned quick. How did they find out?" Anne asked exasperated by this complication. She looked at Justin, who raised one eyebrow. She shook her head, "No! Despite everything Benson did to damage the team, none of them would jeopardise the enquiry."

"I did not really believe they would," Justin replied then shrugged. "Reporters always seem to have contacts in the most unexpected places. Phone for a guard at the door to stop them from harassing the family. We need the PR people to put a press conference together. You did a great job last night by the way. Could you do the next as well? The Chief Constable will probably join you this time."

Anne nodded agreement, but Justin felt it was a reluctant agreement just like before.

"Is there a problem?"

"No sir, I'm happy to deal with the press on behalf of the team." She shrugged and her mouth tightened for a moment. "It's just that my ex-husband's little coterie of friends is taking the piss on social media and I've let it get to me."

"I think we need to talk about what is going on with your life. I can certainly help with your being harassed like that. Thank you for helping me out, especially as you knew that would happen."

Justin went back into the kitchen and with the Harris's permission, slid open the glass doors into the small square of garden. At the end of the garden was a gate into a back alley. They turned left and followed it to the end, where it joined the top of the road near their parked car.

Justin phoned in a request for a check on Sean Trent and to set up a guard to protect the family while Anne drove away from the reporters. Luckily none of them took any notice of the unmarked car. Anne turned onto the one-way system known locally as the inner ring road.

"Tell me sir, you've lived around Malford for most of your life, you said."

"Yes, I was born in Daneley. What do you want to know?"

"Why is this road known as the inner ring road when, as far as I know, there never has been an outer ring road?"

Justin laughed and admitted he had no idea either.

It took them about fifteen minutes to arrive at Sean Trent's imposing block of flats bearing the name Richmond Mansions. Looking up at the block, Anne shook her head. "If the owners did some restoration and repairs to the building, they could triple the rents. This must be one of the last remnants of Art Deco left in town. Even without the restoration, it still has that faded elegance. You could imagine Poirot living in one of those apartments. Sean Trent is the tenant of number 30." She released her seatbelt. "It's on the second floor."

Justin was considering the building as Anne opened the car door. She was right about the maintenance. He glanced over the façade, mentally noting some very obvious defects as they walked together to the main entrance. The managing agents had let things seriously slide. While Justin had no interest in "tripling the rents", he felt a personal visit to the agents should be a serious priority.

The front door to the main lobby opened as they approached. They nodded politely to the couple leaving the block and slipped inside. The lifts didn't need a code or key card and the doors stood open.

"Chelsey's boyfriend, lives in a corner apartment with a large lounge diner and two double bedrooms. Wow! Wonder what the rent on this flat would be?" Anne remarked as they rode the lift to the second floor.

They reached the flat's front door, rang the bell, and waited. No response.

Anne pressed the bell again, a longer peal, until a disgruntled voice shouted from inside the flat. "Stop leaning on the bloody bell! What the hell do you want? If you're here to read the meters, I'll …"

The door jerked open, and the grumbling stopped abruptly. Bleary brown eyes peered at the two warrant cards displayed for his inspection. Despite the hung-over look, Justin had to admit the boy was attractive. His features were clean cut, the skin smooth and tanned. The slight designer stubble suited the barefoot, shirtless look. He was confident in his fitness and youth and obviously worked out regularly. Despite the apparent fatigue from a late night, Trent had that irrepressible twinkle in his eyes that could be interpreted as attraction and experience by the unwary. An expression that could also suggest he was looking for someone very special. Justin caught the guilty flicker of appreciation in Anne's glance before she looked away. Pity they weren't yet on sufficient terms to tease each other was the thought that brought a quick smile to his lips.

"Mr Sean Trent?"

The young man nodded.

"DCI Mortmain and DI Richards, Major Crime Unit. May we talk inside?"

Trent frowned, but stood aside for them to enter. There was no instant denial of crimes committed, just a sudden alert stillness in his expression.

"Go through to the lounge and make yourselves comfortable. I'll just finish getting dressed and join you."

Trent headed for the door at the end of the hall. Justin and Anne went through the door immediately in front of them, which led to a bright lounge dining area. The stylish furnishings impressed Anne. A large HD TV faced a corner suite with a recliner positioned at one end. Between the seating was a low coffee table, its top littered with empty beer cans, a half bottle of whisky and a game console controller. All the signs of a lads' night in. Another controller peeped out from the gap between the seat cushion and the arm of the recliner. The dining table and its matching chairs and sideboard also of good quality marred by the remains of a group night in, including open cartons of a takeaway meal. Four congealed plates hid in the debris. On the sideboard, Chelsey's face smiled out from a professionally taken picture, neatly framed. They turned back to the lounge area as Trent strolled in.

"Right. What's all this about then?" He pulled the controller out of the recliner, put it on the table and sat down, waving a hand for them to do the same. Justin felt Trent was too calm, not at all concerned by two police officers arriving on his doorstep. He was far too sure of himself to be real. Even people who had done nothing wrong were nervous when getting a visit from the police.

"Were you aware that Chelsey Harris's parents had reported her as missing?"

Trent's eyes widened, then he looked away and shook his head. "Nah, nobody told me."

"They became concerned when she had not returned home since leaving for work on Tuesday morning." Justin watched him closely. "Perhaps she came here, or you met up somewhere after she finished work? We are trying to get a clear timeline of her movements."

There it was a flash of alarm before Trent's expression closed down and he shook his head. "Sorry, no, we didn't meet up. We hadn't been together for about a week. We both had a lot on."

"Could you tell us where you were on Tuesday night?"

Trent stared into the distance for a moment. He was about to reply when the doorbell rang. With a muttered "'Scuse me," he left the room.

Justin caught Anne's attention and raised one eyebrow in question. In response, Anne grimaced showing she shared Justin's suspicions of Trent. They looked away from each other when he returned, followed by a young woman.

"This is Evie, Eve Jordan, a friend. She lives downstairs on the first floor."

Evie, in her baggy jumper and pocket decorated cargo pants, was all energy and bounce, like an overlarge puppy trying to please its adored master.

"So sorry Sean. Didn't know you had company. Just wanted to check if you could come around tonight to finish that shelving unit? Didn't mean to interrupt anything?" She looked from one to another, curiosity oozing from every pore. Justin and Anne stood up to be introduced.

"No worries, Evie These are police. Chelsey's parents have reported her as missing."

"Oh! Wow!" She turned to them eagerly. "How exciting! Did she decide to run away? Had they had an argument? Do you think you'll find her?" Evie seemed to find the idea amusing.

Neither of them appeared to have thought that something serious might have happened to Chelsey. Justin looked at them both, young, confident, and so extremely vulnerable. His expression was as neutral as his voice when he replied. "I am afraid we have found her. We have just confirmed the identity with her parents, Chelsey's body was discovered in Tolland Wood early yesterday morning. So, Mr Trent, when was the last time you and Chelsey met up?"

"No! Oh no!" Trent bent double; arms wrapped around his torso. Tears welled in his eyes. Shock suddenly transformed him from a cocky young man into a sorrow-struck boy. "You're sure it's her? It is Chelsey?"

Trent was shaking with the shock. Evie, standing wide-eyed by his side, reached out to steady him. She led him to the corner seat and sat down beside him, arms around his shoulders.

Trent looked up at Justin and Anne, horror reflected in his eyes and his voice when he asked suddenly. "Was it a suicide? Did she kill herself?"

"Why would you think that, Mr Trent?" Anne asked first. "Was there any reason you know for Chelsey to take her own life?"

Trent froze, then slowly shook his head. "No, not really. She was mentally strong, you know. Could cope with anything. Was it an accident? It can't have been, what do you call it, 'natural causes', not at our age."

"No sir. We are treating her death as suspicious. It's our job to find out what happened to her and who was involved," Anne replied.

Justin, satisfied that Anne could deal with the pair, left the lounge. He found the kitchen. The kettle was already hot, so he switched it back on while he hunted around for mugs, milk, sugar and tea bags. He couldn't find a teapot so shrugged and put a tea bag in each mug.

By the time he returned with the three steaming mugs on a tray, Trent appeared calmer. Evie was speaking quietly, murmuring into his ear. Anne was looking out of the window. Justin offered tea to Trent and Evie. Trent accepted the mug, enclosing it in both hands, appreciating its warmth. He refused both milk and sugar.

"Sorry, can't seem to stop shaking," he said, an echo of that tremor in his voice.

Evie shook her head. Justin put the tray on the dining table. He added milk to one of the remaining two and took it over to Anne. She looked surprised. "Milk, but no sugar," Justin said quietly, with a slight smile. "I notice little details about people." He turned back to Trent. "You are in shock, Mr Trent. Hearing this kind of news is always horrific even when you don't know the victim very well, and you did know Chelsey very well, so it is hitting you much harder. We can finish this at the station tomorrow if you prefer?"

Trent shook his head. "No, let's get on with it," he stated brusquely. Beside him, Evie looked doubtful and anxious.

"Are you sure, Sean? Maybe tomorrow would be better when you've had time to process what you've been told," the girl suggested.

Trent shook his head. "No, let's finish this. I'm fine." Even so, he grasped her hand.

"OK, Mr Trent. Let us go back to when you and Chelsey last met up. You said it was about a week ago?"

"Yes, we went for a meal together, then met up with some of our crowd at the Blue Boar. It was a good night. We left at the same time as the others and I walked Chels home. I got the bus back here about ten to midnight."

"You didn't see her again, say, the night before last?"

Trent shook his head but looked down at the floor, not making eye contact. His cheeks had a slight flush. Justin was uncertain why, but he knew this time Trent was lying. Before he could follow up, Evie spoke.

"Oh, that was when Sean was helping me. We had fish and chips at my place and spent a lot of hours trying to work out how to put my new shelf unit together." Evie smiled slightly. "At one point, the unit nearly had us beat, but we ended on an honourable draw. That's why I came around today to see if Sean was free to finish the job."

Trent seemed to grasp the alibi a little too eagerly in Justin's opinion.

"Yes, that's right, I remember. Sorry, the last few days have blurred together. Been on a bit of a bender without Chels around."

"Oh, do you have a job Mr Trent?"

"Oh yeah, I'm a financial advisor with the local bank. I took the last few days of my holiday before I lost them to the start of the new holiday year. They don't allow you to take time across unless there are exceptional circumstances."

"Mrs Harris said you secretly borrowed one of Chelsey's rings to get the size right. She wondered if you might be buying an engagement ring?"

Anne thought she saw a flash of surprise cross Evie's face but it was gone very quickly

Trent looked even more shocked, if that was possible. "Bloody Hell no! I wanted to get her one of those Claddagh rings. You know, a heart held between two hands."

Justin nodded. He had bought such a ring for his wife once upon a time.

A beep, beep, beep sounded loud but muffled. Evie grabbed at her thigh pocket and pulled out her phone. She looked at the screen and gave an annoyed hiss. "Sorry Sean," she said. "This is an appointment with a potential client. I have to go."

Sean was frowning, still hazy with shock, and nodded. "Yeah, OK."

Justin glanced at Anne to see if she had any further questions. She shook her head.

"Thank you, Mr Trent. We will leave it there for today, but I'm certain we will need to speak to you again just to follow up on a few things. You do not plan to be away from Malford for any length of time, do you?"

Trent shook his head. "No, I can't afford to go away this year. I'll probably stay right here." He saw Anne's surprised look and gave a brusque, harsh, bark of laughter. His face grew hard and his voice held a stark, nasty edge.

"The flat is courtesy of my mother's guilty conscience. She walked out on Dad and me when I was ten. Suddenly last year she reappeared out of nowhere and wanted to be mum again. Comes in useful when I need something expensive."

Evie patted his shoulder. "I'll come back later, see how you're doing, OK?" She waited for his acknowledgement, then all three headed for the door, leaving him alone with his troubled thoughts.

They watched Eve Jordan drive a new blue mini under the arch from the residents' car park and turn out of the driveway.

"What did you make of her?"

"Clingy," Anne said, "definitely clingy, but I couldn't tell if it was because she liked their friendship and doesn't want it to change or if she wanted something more than friendship with young Sean. What did you think?"

"I am not sure. She seemed to react as any good friend would when someone they care about was hurting. Although I agree with you about how deep that friendship might be. Her reaction to Chelsey's disappearance I found strange, but then there are people who get excited by finding themselves suddenly having an adventure and forget they are not in a TV drama. That people really do get killed."

† † †

"Phew!" Thomas said collapsing onto the sofa and patting his stomach gently. "I always eat too much when I come here."

Ryan laughed "That's because Beth is a temptress. She's fattening you up like Hansel, so she can roast you on the barbecue."

He sat down beside Thomas.

Justin stood behind them and handed each a generous measure of brandy. "Then here is a little something to help the digestion." He poured another for himself, then relaxed into the embrace of an armchair to one side of the marble fireplace. "Help yourselves to coffee." He waved his glass towards the tray Beth had left on the low table between them.

There was a comfortable pause in the conversation broken only by the chink of china and glass. Justin warmed the brandy balloon between his hands, allowing the amber liquid to swirl gently. A contented smile softened the usually tight set of his lips. In his own home, with this particular friend, he felt safe and content. Ryan was still somewhat of an unknown and he sensed from the frequent glances in his direction that Ryan had a great deal of curiosity about the relationship between his husband and Justin. Despite his being best man for Thomas at their wedding, Ryan knew very little about him. On occasion he had sensed suspicion bordering on jealousy from Ryan. Tonight, might be a good time to deal with those feelings for good. Justin gazed through the French windows and out beyond the terrace. It was a clear night alive with movement if you could see past the darkness of early April. He sipped his brandy enjoying the warm glow spreading through his body, listening idly to his guests' conversation. He leant his head against the chair back, eyes half closed.

"You can ask anything you want Ryan. I promise to answer as much as I can."

Ryan glanced at Thomas who chuckled. "Told you, you were being too obvious."

Ryan shrugged, "OK," then he stopped, unusually uncertain for a journalist.

Justin understood his dilemma. "I was a fairly new detective constable when Thomas and I first met. I was undercover as part of the band's security working the European tour. An organised crime group were using touring bands to transport concealed drug shipments across Europe and into Britain." Justin smiled across at Thomas. "After a while it became clear that neither Thomas nor the other band members had anything to do with the illegal shipments. It was two of the roadies who were raking in a lot of extra cash for hiding the shipments in the equipment lorries. Enough extra money to get violent when they were confronted. Thomas had been suspicious something was going on and believed I was part of it. He challenged me and having convinced him I was not part of the gang, we joined forces successfully. Thomas also saved my life when we arrested the suspects. After that we became good friends. Thomas needed somewhere to stay between tours, and the gatehouse was vacant. It seemed ideal."

Justin got up and filled his glass from the decanter. He offered them a top up too. Ryan accepted but Thomas shook his head, his hand covering the empty glass.

"Save some for me. I'm going to help Beth with the washing up."

He heaved himself out of the clutches of the sofa with a groan and wandered out of the door.

Justin laughed.

"Beth will have everything cleaned up and put away already. Thomas has timed his visit perfectly. He is after more of that delicious dessert to take home. He will succeed because to Beth he is still her particular superstar."

Ryan sipped his brandy before asking, "How did Thomas save your life?"

"When we reached Dover, my team were waiting to arrest the suspects. Unfortunately, they were warned and came out shooting. I was injured and bleeding in the struggle. Thomas found me and stopped the bleeding otherwise who knows what would have happened."

"I knew about the band after all they were pretty big for several years but he's never said a word about this adventure."

"No, well he could not do so for quite a while because I was still working undercover so I suppose it became a habit to say nothing." Justin hesitated for a moment then asked. "He has told you about Aimee, I think?"

Ryan raised his head from his contemplation of the glass in his hand. "Yes, she was special to him and she died of an overdose of bad drugs."

"Yes, that was the end as far as Thomas was concerned. She was an innocent almost child with an amazing singing voice. Her death was a changing point for Thomas. It was the push he needed to do what he had wanted for some time – leave the band and take up his medical career again. So, he retrained and became one of our local Gps, then he met you and his life has been a thousand times better ever since."

Justin watched, gently amused, as a blush of embarrassment heated Ryan's face. Ryan cleared his throat before he spoke again.

"You've done quite a bit of undercover work. What advice would you give to someone who might need to do the same?"

Justin tensed; his contentment smashed by the question. "Is that why Thomas chose to visit Beth?" he asked, his voice hard and cold. "Well, here is my advice. Forget it, if it is you contemplating such a crazy action. I was specially trained and have certain qualities which made me ideal for undercover work. You have to eat, sleep, fuck and live as your undercover personality. Sometimes you have to do things with a smile that turn your stomach in real life. One hesitation or mistake in front of the wrong person and you are finished. Ryan forget it, please. It is too easy to slip up or be recognised. This last time my partner and I were betrayed, he was tortured and killed and I was kept alive just for several days. I was fortunate that I was finally able to break free."

The door opened and Thomas came back, a neat package carried carefully in both hands. "I really love Beth," he said and smiled at Ryan, "If you ever leave me, I shall definitely murder Martin so I can marry her and keep her tied to my kitchen." He glanced at Ryan who shook his head and said with an effort.

"Or, you could just learn to cook her recipes Thomas, it would be much safer."

Nothing further was said about undercover work but Justin was left with an uneasy feeling when the couple left to stroll home through the grounds.

6

Everyone was in the main office for the morning briefing. Justin was leaning against the desk closest to the whiteboard. From his team's expressions this meeting was likely to be short if not sweet.

"Right let us get everything up-to-date. How did the search of the woodland go?" Justin took a drink from his bottle of water.

Anne responded, "A lot of stuff was bagged and tagged that might lead to something but nothing that definitely related to Chelsey Harris and nothing that could have been the murder weapon." She frowned, "Nothing that looked like the actual crime scene, no phone or purse and nothing close to the bag her mother described."

"The CCTV recordings have shown up nothing so far, we'll keep looking." Julie reported.

"Anne and I will take over checking the CCTV for this morning. I want you and Paul doing background checks on the immediate family and their neighbours," Justin said, and saw Anne frown. Before she could say a word, he held up a hand. "I know they were devastated but it has been known for a relative to fool the police before now. I agree with you their grief was genuine and deep but we still have to check." He turned back to Paul and Julie, "Check for anyone known to the family as friends, co-workers or whatever who might be on our records."

"We've asked the Family Liaison Officer, PC Romney, to pay particular attention to Kate Harris. She's very angry and sullen. She may know more about Chelsey's death that she's bottling up. It could be very useful if she can be persuaded to tell us what else she knows." Anne continued the briefing.

"Any responses yet to the appeal?" Justin asked. He turned to Anne and smiled. "I watched the news last night."

Ray shrugged and commented, "Several possibilities were phoned in that we've got teams following up."

"Good. Can you and Chas look into background on Sean Trent, Chelsey's boyfriend according to her mother." He glanced at Anne, "He was definitely in shock when we spoke to him but he did say they hadn't seen each other for about a week. What does he do? Who are his friends? You know the kind of thing I want."

Tasks had been allocated and the meeting ended. The rest of the team headed back to their desks and Anne and Justin went into his office. He had to switch on the lights because the backdrop to his view of the town had darkened with rain clouds, although the sun momentarily broke through and brought the stone and glass of the scene to sparkling golden life in stark contrast. They both sat down either side of his desk. He glanced across at Anne. She was looking out at the spectacular scene and seemed lost in thought as far as he could tell from her profile.

"Right! What do you think of our Mr Trent?" She suddenly asked turning to look at him fully.

"I was going to ask you the same thing. I am not wholly in touch with the youth of today." Justin inwardly laughed at that understatement. He had very little knowledge of the ways of the modern-day generation, although he would bet their actions and attitudes were no different to his own at that age or those of other young people he had known in the past. They just expressed those opinions differently.

"Well, I think he lied to us, but whether that was intentional or just his reaction to the shock of finding his girlfriend was dead, I couldn't say," Anne stated.

"I agree. He seemed to be hiding something, but I also found his attitude strange?" Justin thought for a moment, then nodded. "Yes. At the beginning, I am not sure he was telling us the whole truth. He said he and Chelsey were having a cooling-off period, but at the same time he had asked her mother for help in buying her a gift, a ring. Do people understand the significance of such a traditional ring?"

He pictured the ring he had given to his wife so many years ago, a golden heart cupped protectively between a pair of hands, and crowned by a coronet. She had been the ruler of his heart, his Antonia.

"Trent was deeply shocked when we told him that Chelsey was dead. But why in heaven did he ask if she had committed suicide?" Anne added.

"That question bothered me too. I wouldn't have thought suicide would have occurred to him unless he knew of some reason? Possibly shows he already knew about the baby. What do you think?"

Anne shook her head a slight frown on her forehead. "Timing doesn't seem right. That test was fairly recent perhaps done that morning. She could have phoned him I suppose. Then why the spending spree and the possible surprise?"

"I see what you mean. Well, we can keep him in mind and go back to speak to him again soon."

The phone rang and Justin answered. He put his hand over the mouthpiece and let Anne know who was calling.

"Chief Constable wanting an update." He murmured quietly, "Can you take over the CCTV trawl and I will join you as soon as I can."

Quietly, Anne stood up and headed out of the office as Justin started to reply to the Chief Constable. Twenty minutes later he joined her in the small, quiet room set aside for examining recordings. They worked side by side in silence until Justin felt his eyes beginning to ache with watching. He glanced at Anne when she paused the machine and rubbed at her eyes. He saw her surprise when she glanced at the clock on the wall. "I don't know about you, but I could do with a quiet time to think and something decent to eat," he commented.

Anne nodded, "Yeah, me too." Her stomach gurgled loudly. "See what I mean?" she laughed quietly.

"I know a nice place where we can get some space and peace to think, as well as a very good meal. My treat."

Anne thought about it for a moment, but another audible grumble from her stomach decided her. "Okay, your treat, but after today we go halves or pay for our own."

Justin smiled. "Fair enough." If she was setting boundaries on their relationship, she was considering the long term. At least he hoped so.

They left the rabbit hutch of a room and headed back into the main office. Justin's office phone was ringing so he went to answer it with an apologetic glance at Anne.

Anne kept an eye on the office and saw the call end. Justin shook his head as if to clear it, stood up and stretched. He waved so she grabbed her jacket and bag and they made their way down to the pool car they had been allocated. Anne got into the driver's seat with a challenging look at Justin.

"I am happy to be a passenger but not in the back," he said, sitting next to her in the front. "I have no doubt you have your advanced driver's course and probably several others too."

She started the engine and they made their way through the crowded car park to the exit. "Right. Where are we going?" she asked as they paused at the end of the driveway.

"Left into town, then I will direct you unless you know the restaurant. It is called Mama's Place."

The family-run restaurant had been a favourite of Justin's for a long while. It was owned by people from his village and had been doing business for fifteen years. They had struggled initially, but now it was known as one of the best places for Italian food in the entire county. Their lunch menu was a mixture of quality British and Italian food at reasonable prices for the local workers. In the evenings, Mama's Place transformed into a Michelin starred Italian restaurant. He smiled contentedly when Anne found a parking space two doors down.

The moment they walked through the door, the clatter of cutlery and a hum of conversation assailed their ears. Mouth-watering, stomach seducing aromas wafted from the kitchen, surrounding them like a hug. In response, Anne breathed in deeply, her eyes closing in appreciation. Justin couldn't prevent a chuckle at her expense, while looking over her head towards the waiter who grinned a welcome.

"That young man is Antonio, better known as Tony. He is the son of the owners," Justin said.

Tony indicated a vacant table tucked into a quiet alcove with a reserved sign on it. He threaded his way through the busy tables and had them settled with professional speed, menus in their hands.

"What would madame care to drink?" He enquired and then disappeared to get her order of still water. Anne flicked an enquiring glance towards Justin.

"Tony knows what I want. He does not need to ask. I eat here regularly when I am at home. Mama Rosa is at the till, Papa Pietro and sister Lucia are the magicians of the pots and pans in the kitchen. They come from Daneley, the same village as myself."

Anne looked at him with some scepticism. "Amazing that just coming from the same village gets you preferential treatment. A table that's reserved for you whenever you fancy turning up? You must either be here very regularly indeed or is there something you haven't mentioned? Do they do the same for all the villagers?"

"Not as far as I know." Justin hesitated when Tony returned bringing a pot of coffee and a bottle of still water. He waited for their food order. Anne opted for tagliatelle con funghi e Porcini and, Justin for a rare Bistecca with Porcini cream sauce and house salad.

"I helped them out when they had the original idea for the restaurant. It has been a very good investment for me so far. That's all."

"Oh!" Anne looked as if she suspected there was a great deal more to the story. When Justin smiled but refused to comment, she shook her head but said no more. In a short time, their food was being laid on the table. Justin enjoyed watching the pleasure on Anne's face as she tasted Papa's tagliatelle for the first time. He polished off his own food in quick time and drank his coffee. Tony returned for their plates and handed Anne a dessert menu then passed a folded note to Justin. He read the message then nodded.

"I'm just going to have a word with Rosa. Try the honey ice cream and poached pear. Thomas tells me it is to die for," he recommended before strolling over to the till.

Mama Rosa saw him and signalled to one of the serving staff to take her place. She slipped off her high chair and gripped Justin's hand in both of her own, drawing him through the double doors and into the office. There was a moment of silence, as if Rosa could not find the right words, though the grip on his hands was tight. Justin saw the glint of relieved tears in her eyes before she smiled at him.

"Thank you, my l…"

"Justin, Rosa, remember?" he interrupted her. "The title seems a little out of date these days. You need my help? Just tell me what is wrong."

She walked over to the desk and took some papers out of the drawer, placing them on the leather top. "About two months ago, we had a visitor, a young lad maybe sixteen years old. He walked in and handed this to one of our staff."

It was plain paper, strong and thick. The letters were glued on and had been cut from several different newspapers and magazines. The message suggested that £500 a week would buy the restaurant an insurance policy against damage or accident.

"Great Jupiter! Does this kind of thing still happen?"

Rosa nodded. "That's how we treated the whole thing, as some tired, ancient joke. We ignored the demand and when the boy came back, we told him there would be no money. He just shrugged and walked out. The next week the meat orders were cancelled. Our van wouldn't start, then someone smashed in our front door glass. We showed the police the letter but they too couldn't take it seriously, although after the police visit everything went back to normal for a while. Almost as if someone was on the lookout."

Rosa laid out photographs of the damage and copies of the cancelled orders, then picked up the second paper, same weight and quality, same style of glued on letters. "This came yesterday evening, hand delivered under the door, before we opened. As you can see, we are now expected to pay £800 a week."

Justin frowned. "Why did the wholesaler accept the cancellations?"

Rosa sighed, "Because one of our kitchen staff phoned them in. The good God knows why. She had been with us since we opened. We were going to ask her but the next day she never came to work and now we cannot contact her. Her flat mates say her mother was taken seriously ill. We telephoned her family, discreetly, you know, wages outstanding, where to send the cheque. Her family thinks she's backpacking around Europe with a group of friends."

"Will you pay?"

Rosa stood as tall as her tiny frame would allow, a look of contempt on her face. "Certainly not!"

Justin grinned and bent to kiss her gently on both cheeks. "Right! I will check to see what is being done and request a patrol pass by the restaurant regularly for a while. In the meantime, do you have a name or a picture of your little messenger?"

"Picture yes, we gave it to the police as well, a still from the security cameras, name …" she shook her head.

"Can you make me a copy and I will ask for a lookout to be kept for him? Rosa, you and the family will be careful until we can put a stop to this?"

She nodded. "There is one more thing. Tony has been chatting with some of the other businesses along the street. Others have had similar demands to ours, some have paid up. Only a few so far. It feels like someone is testing the waters for something bigger."

Justin hesitated, then said, "Rosa, I want to see if this can be sorted out legally, do you understand?"

She nodded and gently touched his hands. "Yes, I know what you mean."

"But, if any of you are put in danger because of these threats, I promise the would-be gangsters will be dealt with."

A gentle smile lightened the strain on her face.

"Yes, I understand, and I thank you."

"You have my number? Good, let me know if you get any more visits after the patrols start. I will keep you safe, and with your excellent food to tempt them I might be able to make this a regular lunch venue among my colleagues. DI Richards has certainly enjoyed her first visit here."

He caught the speculative look in Rosa's eyes and shook his head. "No Mama. Anne Richards is a colleague and a new colleague at that. As well as being a recent divorcee." He grinned at her obvious disappointment. "Believe me, I am content. Caring too much for one person only brings pain."

Rosa sighed, "True, but also great happiness each in their season."

"Enough Rosa." He gave her a hug. "I have to go."

Justin escorted her back to the cashier's counter and helped her back onto her chair. He paid their bill, then started to weave his way through the tables to their alcove.

Anne was already standing, her phone to one ear. She caught sight of him and advanced to meet him, shutting down her phone.

"We need to get back to the station," she said, leading the way outside. In the privacy of the car, she gave him more information. "Chelsey's bag, or at least one that might be Chelsey's, has been discovered by a passer-by, dumped in an industrial rubbish bin. The individual had seen the press conference and brought it into the station."

"Passer-by?" Justin questioned, securing his seatbelt.

Anne grinned. "Well, street person would be a more accurate description. Apparently, he took it to the reception desk at the station and admitted to stealing the bag in hopes of at least one night's bed and board. Until he realised, he could be charged with murder, then he said he found it. He gave the location, so Chas and Ray have been checking CCTV in the area. The location of the bin has been secured and SOCO is there now. Ray says they've found something or rather someone on the tapes."

7

Justin and Anne were eager spectators, leaning in over Chas's shoulders to view the black and white footage. A deserted back street, behind a Chinese restaurant, containing an industrial sized waste bin. The light was good and the image clear when their informant came into shot, heading for the bin. They watched his head and shoulders disappear under the lid, then emerge a few moments later. A take-away container was in one hand and the bag in the other. The bag which now lay in glorious technicolour inside an evidence bag beside them.

"Now we turn back time and …" Ray commented then chuckled.

Daylight reversed into early evening, full of shadows. One of those shadows slid slowly along the road, looking around for any potential witnesses, then looked up, directly into the camera. A clear likeness, easily identifiable.

Anne's voice held amused recognition. "Well, well, it's Lucky Larry!"

Justin looked a question. "Explain for the newbie please."

"Sorry sir," Anne responded. "You know, sir, when someone's given a nickname because they're so much the opposite? See, Lucky Larry is probably the unluckiest guy we've ever met. Lawrence Swale is his real name."

Justin nodded and touched Chas's shoulder. "Has this Larry been brought in?"

"Yes sir." The DC's amusement deepened, and he grinned. "He was trying to use Chelsey's bank card, complained to the teller that the machine had damaged it. Unfortunately, Larry chose an employee who had been to school with Chelsey. By the time we found him, he was already in custody. They delivered him to us just before you arrived." The grin disappeared. "The poor sod is a long-term heroin addict. He seems to be coming down from a high. That's probably why he was desperate for cash. We might need the doctor to check him over before interview. Not sure he's got much of a brain to think with these days."

"Any chance he killed Chelsey? Desperate for a fix, he tries to grab her bag and she resists. He gets violent and she ends up dead?"

The rest of the group paused, considered, and each shook his or her head. Anne answered for them all.

"Larry's never been violent. Never even shown anger when he's been pulled in. I would have said totally out of character."

Justin nodded. "Fair enough. Give Thomas a call. Anne and I will interview him. I would like you two to go to Chelsey's employers. See what you can find out about her last day. Check if she confided in anyone or if she had problems with anyone at work." He paused, then added, "Well done, both of you." Justin turned to Anne. "Is our homeless guy still here? I cannot keep calling him that. Do we have his name?"

She nodded. "Yes, he's still here. The only name he has given us is Anderson. He got his chance to sleep and have a hot meal."

"Thank you. I should like to talk to him informally so I will deal with his release. Give me ten minutes. After Thomas has given us the OK on Larry, we will tackle him together."

Julie and Paul came into the main office as Justin finished talking to Anne. A questioning look and a shake of the head. No new leads.

"I would like you to make enquiries at the flats where Sean Trent lives. I do not believe he is telling us all he knows. Find out what the neighbours might have seen or heard. Request any CCTV from their security cameras. If there is any difficulty with the managing agents, just let me know."

He turned back to Anne. "What was still in the bag when we got it?"

"Not much, a purse, empty of cash or cards; a comb; house keys. Nothing else."

"Still no phone!" Justin commented. "Ask the family liaison officer to get the number and the phone company. If Lucky Larry cannot say where it is, then we will have to check the call logs and see if it is still on so we can locate it. We might get something to move this enquiry forward."

He turned and left the office, heading downstairs to the custody suite. He introduced himself to Custody Sergeant Newton who was on duty and asked what he knew about Anderson.

"Well sir, we don't do much these days with the homeless unless we get a call from one or other of the shops in the High Street. Anderson hadn't been out on the streets for very long, I'd say. His clothes are shabby but decent and he seems clean enough." The sergeant thought for a moment. "Might be ex-army, from the way he stood in front of the desk here and the way he answered questions."

"Any indication of drug use?"

The sergeant shook his head "Not that I saw. Definitely hungry and probably tired, what with the weather and the street living. Doesn't like enclosed spaces though, freaked him out a bit when we shut the cell door. He was pacing about for quite a while before he slept. Do you want to interview him?"

"Not formally no. I would like to talk to him before he is released if there is an interview room free."

"Room five is free. I'll escort him if you want to wait in the room. Do you want anyone else with you?"

"No, I just want a chat before we let him go, there is no need for any witness." Justin replied then headed down to the interview room.

Five minutes later, Anderson was brought in. He stopped short in the doorway, eyeing Justin with suspicion for a moment or two.

"Please come in Mr Anderson. Take a seat."

Anderson hesitated then sat down cautiously opposite Justin.

"Thank you, sergeant." Justin said. "I will escort Mr Anderson back to the reception area."

Anderson turned and watched the sergeant leave the room. Justin could see the tension in his shoulders. He turned back to Justin and there was suspicion in the narrowed eyes. "What's going on?"

"I was curious about you, Mr Anderson."

"Nothin' to be curious about," he replied curtly.

"Oh? I think there is. Sergeant Newton got the impression you might have been an army man. Is he right?"

"So, what if I was? Don't make a difference out on the streets, does it?

Justin shrugged, "I suppose not. Where is the harm in telling me about yourself?"

He already knew far more than Anderson realised. Newton was right, Anderson was not a drug taker nor did he drink to excess. Anderson's blood was negative for those two traits. There was adrenalin pumping through his system, an automatic fear/flight response to the situation he was in. Beneath that was a deeper, subconscious fear which caused a dangerously high heart rate. The tension in Anderson's body suggested fight not flight, as did the uneasy glances that kept watch on the closed door. Justin went over and opened the door.

"You are free to leave whenever you choose, Mr Anderson. This is not an interrogation. Are you happy living on the streets?"

Anderson's heart rate began to slow as soon as the door was opened. He shook his head saying, "Would you like it? Filthy stone steps and underpass pavements to sleep on if the spaces aren't already taken. Drunken yobs disturbing your sleep because it's fun to torment the dossers sometimes to the point of a beating with fists and feet. Your life in danger there. Yeah, we all just love it. Food if you can beg for it or find enough coins to buy something." He shrugged carelessly but Justin heard the battered and broken pride beneath the "couldn't care less" attitude. "Yeah, I was an army man. On my last tour before my time was over, I got injured, buried by an explosion. Some of my men were killed. Those who survived got me out but it's left a legacy. Can't stand being shut up. I left the army and the wife left me. Don't blame her, couldn't cope with me wanting all the doors and windows open even in winter. So, now you know the whole sorry story – satisfied?"

Justin nodded, "Thank you. This is not idle curiosity, Mr Anderson. I am interested and, as it happens, in a position to offer you something else."

He took a card from his pocket and wrote a name and mobile number on the reverse. He held it out to Anderson.

"This has my name and number on it and this …" he turned it over, "is the name and number of my estate manager. There is a job outdoors and a cottage that goes with it. You can open as many doors and windows as you want there. It would be the first step on a new beginning if you want it."

Anderson hesitated, staring at the card, then at Justin.

"You don't even know me," he said curtly.

"Not true, I know enough and more than you realise. The offer is genuine. Martin will tell you about wages, hours, duties and so on. Now take the damn card, my hand is getting cramp."

Justin left the interview room with Anderson at the same instant Thomas returned to the front desk from examining Lucky Larry.

Anderson shook Justin's hand.

"Remember, the offer is open to you if you want it."

Anderson nodded and walked away, out of the station. Justin turned back towards the desk to stand next to his friend.

"Another lost lamb?" Thomas asked quietly.

Justin shrugged. "Perhaps just took a wrong turn. He's an ex-soldier who has seen and done too much."

"Aaah! now I get it – one soldier to another hmmm?"

"Something like that," Justin acknowledged with a slight smile, a gleam of amusement lighting his eyes.

Thomas nodded and changed the subject. "Your man is fit to interview at the moment, but I don't think it will be long before withdrawal starts tearing him apart. You need to get your questions in pretty soon. I'll wait around in case you need me."

Justin was grateful and said so. Thomas grinned.

"Good, then you won't mind if I steal a cup … or two of your decent coffee? I take it you have set up your own machine as usual?"

"Help yourself," Justin acknowledged. "By the way, come to dinner at my place tonight if you have nothing planned. I could do with the company. Marta is in London until late tonight."

Thomas sighed, "His deadline is still keeping Ryan tied to the computer so good company would be very welcome. I can always take him back a selection of Beth's cooking. Now let me at the coffee."

Thomas slid through the security door as Anne held it open. Justin wondered how long she had been standing there. How much of their conversation had she heard? He knew he would have to tell her and the team some of his story, but not until he was sure of their confidence in him. First, get the job done.

"Thomas says Lucky Larry is fit to interview if we are quick about it. Shall we?"

They walked down the corridor together. Anne had the file in her hand.

"Interview Room two, sir. The video is all set up and the duty solicitor is here. They've already spoken, and the solicitor has confirmed they are ready to be interviewed."

"Is there anything else I should know about our bag thief?"

Anne shook her head. "Not that isn't in the file sir."

"OK, let's get started."

Anne entered first. She set the video tape running and introduced herself and Justin. The duty solicitor's name was Lewis Jones and, with a little prompting, Lucky Larry introduced himself as Laurence Swale. Then there was a pause. Justin appeared to be studying Larry's file intently. After five minutes, he closed the cover.

"Mr Swale, can you explain why you were attempting to use a cash card belonging to someone else at the bank this afternoon? Mr Swale, did you hear the question?"

Larry was somewhere else in his head and found it hard to concentrate on the real world. Justin looked at the duty solicitor, one eyebrow raised. Prompted, Jones touched Larry's elbow and repeated the question for him. Another pause, then Larry spoke. "My girlfriend's innit."

"And what is your girlfriend's name?"

Larry shrugged, "Dunno!"

"How long has she been your girlfriend?"

Another shrug. "Can't remember."

"Perhaps because the woman we are talking about was Chelsey Harris, Larry and she was never your girlfriend."

"Chelsey, yeah, that's the name on the card."

"Mr Swale, Larry, concentrate please, and listen to me. Chelsey Harris was murdered. Didn't you see the press conference on television? Or read the newspapers' front pages? She was murdered, and you tried to use her cash card. Someone found her bag where you dumped it. CCTV showed you throwing her bag into the waste bin behind Hang Cheng's restaurant yesterday evening."

Lucky Larry began to shake his head vehemently, almost enough to strain his neck. "Not me, no, not me!"

Justin sighed, "Yes, Larry, you. You looked directly into the camera. We can positively identify the bag because it is unique, not from any High Street shop. Now what we want to know is, where did you get Chelsey's bag?"

They could all feel the vibration through the table where Larry's leg was shaking uncontrollably. Justin waited as Larry's attention wandered again.

After a minute, he said softly, "Mr Swale! Larry!"

Larry was looking around with short darting glances, fear in his eyes and pain.

"Where did you get the bag, Larry?" Anne repeated the question. "Come on now, focus! I know you wouldn't hurt anybody but my new boss here, DCI Mortmain, he doesn't know you. Tell him where you found the bag or he might decide to charge you with her murder."

Larry's eyes widened with absolute horror, his whole body visibly shaking at this point.

"No, no, no, no, no, no, never!" His eyes met Anne's. "You tell 'im Sarge. I found the bag, yeah. Old rec ground, posh 'ouses all round with gates onto the field. You know, where you arrested me that time?"

Anne nodded, "The Horsefield, you mean?"

Larry nodded "Yeah, the Horsefield, yeah."

"Well done, Larry! Now, was there anything else in the bag with the bank cards and the money purse?"

A moment's silence, then Larry bent and took off his right shoe, poking about in the toe area. He placed several pieces of thick paper on the table as he fished them out one by one. Justin pulled gloves from his pocket and an evidence bag. Carefully, he pieced the photograph back together inside the evidence bag and sealed it. Justin recognised Chelsey's face.

"Larry, did you tear this up, or was it already torn up inside the bag when you found it?"

"Already like that. Needed something to cover the 'ole in me shoe." He seemed annoyed at having to give up the pieces.

Justin remembered water seeping into his shoes one bitter winter, cold, dirty, and very messy. "We will find you something to replace that," he promised. "Now can you remember exactly where on the Horsefield you found the bag?"

Larry mumbled something, then looked up and said clearly, "Down by the school fence behind a couple of bushes where they grow thickest. Good place to do the business see. No prying eyes or wanting to steal your stuff."

Justin turned to the solicitor. "We have finished with Mr Swale for the moment. However, he will be charged with the attempt to obtain money fraudulently from the bank. You can use this interview room for your discussions after he is charged."

Anne terminated the recording, and they left the room, pausing in the corridor.

"I could see what uniforms are available and do an initial search of the Horsefield?"

Justin shook his head. "You know this Horsefield he was talking about?"

Anne nodded, a slight smile curving her lips. "I used to play there as a youngster right from the time my family moved here. All we had to contend with were teenage couples looking for some privacy, until we became those teenagers. Now, it's not so safe. Drug users and pushers hang out there. It's very secluded. It was a big house and grounds until a WWII bomb exploded, a direct hit apparently. No one claimed ownership, and it was expensive to rebuild, so the grounds became a field for horses. That didn't work out so well. Now, it's a recreation area surrounded by new, very expensive houses. They all have gates out to the fields from their back gardens. Oh, and a secondary school was built on about half the land in the sixties."

"Sounds interesting. You and I will have a look around. I do not want to waste forensics' time if there is nothing there."

They took the last parking space in the cul-de-sac, nose-to-nose with a gardener's van. Justin smiled at the name 'Gardeners of Eden (Malford) Ltd'.

Their car and the workers' van looked as if they should be hidden from view in such an upmarket neighbourhood. Like the tradesman's entrances of Edwardian times, around the back and out of sight. The air was pleasantly warm and heavy with floral scents, hinting at the summer to come. One house had a marquee in the garden just visible at the side of the exclusive, architect-designed house. Sounds of laughter, social chatter, and loud music clashed with the choral murmur of early bees and electric mowers.

They strolled down a wide lane alongside the garden's stone wall to the entrance of the Horsefield recreation ground. Justin noted that a small van could drive along the lane, although there was no space for two vehicles to pass. He looked ahead at the main entrance, a survivor from the Victorian Gothic estate which had once taken up the entire space. The ornate tall double gates could easily accommodate that same small van.

Justin paused between the open gates, remembering the beautiful grounds that had surrounded a large turreted house where the new detached houses now stood. He remembered a rich Victorian merchant had bought the land and built the house. The owner's daughter had had her eye on a young soldier about to go off to the Crimea. Justin grinned at the recollection. He had been very happy to facilitate their union to spite the father.

A few of the rare specimen trees still survived, living remnants of the once magnificent gardens standing out against the scrub areas of hawthorn, buddleia and brambles. The grounds were now divided between two football pitches, a skateboard park, and a couple of tennis courts. Dog walkers and cyclists had worn pathways through the grass surrounding the pitches. At the furthest end, a 1960s-built secondary school took up the footprint of the old mansion along with a third of the old grounds. Larry obviously knew the area very well. Despite all the houses having access to the recreation grounds, there were secluded spaces hidden within groups of overgrown shrubs and trees.

As they stood looking around, a couple of party guests slid through the closest gate onto the field, giggling together. A bottle of champagne and two glasses in hand, they were heading for one of those secret spaces. Further along the boundary, a mower box was emptied over the fence, grass cuttings like green rain falling onto the weed-choked neglected land.

"It's a busy place today," Anne commented. "Maybe it's quieter at night?"

All these houses must be double if not triple glazed, unlikely they would hear anything."

Justin wasn't convinced. If the murder had been committed here, why move the body? The recreation ground was almost as secluded as the dump site, despite its reputation for drug dealing.

"Let us take a look around, anyway. Larry suggested somewhere at the far end where the shrubs are thickest, and the gardens form a corner with the school grounds.

Justin could not accept this was the primary site. His senses were confirming that feeling as they walked across the ground. The freshest blood traces were animal in origin, the rabbit supper of a fox, the carrion left by a cat. There was old human blood here, yes, but nothing recent and nothing that might have originally matched Chelsey's rare blood group.

Over the very long time since the fateful day that had changed his life, Justin had become attuned to the many levels between the aroma of fresh and ancient blood. Fresh blood was like champagne, the rarer the blood group, the more like the best vintage champagne. As time moved on, the aroma developed like that of a mature vintage wine, then gradually decayed into the earthy tones of old blood that enriched the earth, until it was so old there was only the memory of blood, like the weakest homeopathy tincture. The freshest blood he had detected so far equated, in his mind, to a reasonable burgundy.

The weather had been mostly warm and dry for a few days, but Chelsey's leather bag had shown no sign of sun fading nor of damage by local wildlife such as rats or foxes. It was still fresh and relatively clean except for egg fried rice and the odd noodle. They walked on to the end of the field, past the tennis courts and around the other side of the football pitch, finishing back at the entrance. Anne looked disappointed but resigned when they stopped in front of the gates.

"It's more likely that after the killing, when Chelsey's body was wheeled across the wood, the bag was forgotten inside the vehicle that was used to transport her to the car park. Then later, the killer found it and disposed of it here. Do you agree?"

"Yes," Anne nodded, then smiled, "but there are an awful lot of security cameras on these houses. I think a house to house requesting copies of their recordings might give us something."

Justin conceded her point. "Fair enough. Organise a house to house when we get back to the office. There are cameras down by the school fields where they join the recreation ground. They may have recorded something. I suspect a lot of these houses have dummy cameras as a prevention measure, so do not be surprised if there is less security footage than you hope." He checked his watch. "We should get back; the others will be ready for the update meeting. I'll phone forensics while you drive, see what they think about the chances of capturing anything worthwhile from the ground."

They headed back to the car. By the time they got back to the office, the other members of the team were already gathered in front of the incident board. Justin grabbed a mug of coffee before beginning the meeting.

"Good afternoon, everyone. Anne and I checked out the Horsefield where Chelsey's bag was 'found'. It is not our primary crime scene." Justin felt the universal disappointment and nodded. "Only the bag was dumped there. I spoke to forensics about checking over the field, but they, and I, believe it would be a forensic nightmare. Footballers, skateboarders, dog walkers, and cyclists use the area daily and, at night it is the domain of drug dealers and their customers. We checked the place described by Larry, but there was no mobile. It had not slipped out of the bag when the bag was thrown away as far as we could see. Although it is possible someone else could have found it before Lucky Larry turned up. How soon can we get the information from her provider?"

"End of today at the latest they said." Ray remarked then add, "The phone is switched off, or the battery is dead so they can't ping for a location. Last known use shows the phone near Trent's place on Tuesday afternoon about four thirty."

Justin perched on the edge of a desk. "Near Trent's apartment?" He frowned, "He said he hadn't seen her this week." He turned to Paul and Julie. "Anything from enquiries around the neighbours?"

Julie nodded; notebook open. "Yes sir, Chelsey was well known at Richmond Mansions and well liked. One elderly resident, two doors down from Trent, told us Chelsey would run errands for him and always stopped to chat if he were out and about. Unfortunately, he'd been ill and stayed at his daughter's, to convalesce for the days covering the time frame we need to know about. Several other residents mentioned Chelsey's previous visits, but none of them remember seeing her on Tuesday. There were other close neighbours of Trent's who were out. We left a leaflet through the door asking them to call us."

Ray frowned. "In light of the phone evidence, Chas and I will follow that up if we don't hear from the absentees by tomorrow. With the press conference hitting the national news last night, everyone should be aware. Thought you did a great job there, Inspector," he added.

Justin agreed wholeheartedly. Anne had made quite an impact on the public and responses had increased after Anne's and the Chief Constable's appeal for help. "Well done. Now, how about Chelsey's work colleagues?"

Ray took the lead. "It was interesting," he pointed to where the timeline on the board had already been updated. "Chelsey had booked an afternoon off on Tuesday. She worked the morning as usual, then went to lunch with three of her co-workers. They had salads and *soup de jour* at The Lunch Counter in Lindon Place. The group left work around twelve forty-five and spent about forty minutes on lunch. They all walked back to the High Street together, then the other three headed back for work. They left Chelsey outside the shopping centre at one thirty and were back at work by one forty p.m. Chelsey had told them she wanted to shop for something special because she was planning to surprise Sean. That was the last time they saw Chelsey."

"Did she have any problems at work?"

Chas took up the reporting. "Everyone said no, but I got the impression they meant yes, but no more than any other female member of staff."

"Oh?"

"Sorry sir, this is more a feeling than clear-cut evidence. There was one guy. What did they call him?" Chas checked his notes. "Oh yeah, an associate partner, Adrian Dawson. Everywhere he went in the main office, all the female staff moved away. When he went off to show a property, a couple of the girls were having a tea break, so I asked them about him. According to Lisa and Chloe, he's a sleazy octopus! The type that stands just that bit too close, the odd touch that could be accidental, but you are never quite sure and it leaves you feeling uncomfortable. He's married to the daughter of the senior partner, Grayson Donne. Chloe said the rumour around the office was at least one female employee might have complained and another girl found a better-paying job before her trial period ended. She thought there had been some kind of payoff to the other potential complainant.

"There is no actual proof of this. It's all gossip." Ray reminded them, then continued, "Lisa reckoned Chelsey was his most recent target, but last week he suddenly started avoiding her. The suggestion was that his wife had found out and put her foot down. It's her father's company and her money that funds his lifestyle. Mrs Dawson is a barrister, Heather Donne QC."

Justin had encountered that particular barrister in court. A formidable defence for those accused who were rich enough to afford her. Given those rather painful experiences, he wondered how her husband dared even think of wandering off the rails. "Thank you. Anything useful come in on the hot line yet?"

Anne shook her head. "Not so far that definitely links to Chelsey. A couple of possible sightings. They are being followed up. It's still early days on that. What about our bird cam voyeur or naturalist? Have the Spanish police notified him?" she asked.

"Unfortunately, our flighty friend, Mr Tony Byett stopped at his villa long enough to unpack then went off on a cycling tour according to his caretaker over there. Only the caretaker doesn't know where or for how long." Justin shrugged. "We just have to wait for him to return to the nest I suppose." He grinned in sympathy at the audible groans from his team and stood up.

"Right, Anne has requested a door to door around the Horsefield for any security footage, so let us all start going through the footage we already have. We need more detail on the timeline of Chelsey's movements. She left her workmates at the High Street at one thirty. Her phone registered near Trent's apartment at four thirty. What did she do in between? Can we verify she went into Trent's building rather than passing by? When did she take her shopping home? Who did she meet along the way? Where did she go after her second visit home when she changed out of her new clothes? Come to that, why did she change again? How did she travel when she left the house a second time and how did her life end on a dark stream bank in Tolland Wood?"

Justin picked up the board pen and added the name of the associate partner. He glanced up at Anne. "I think a personal visit to this gentleman might be on the cards," he said before heading for his own office and shutting the door.

8

Justin groaned involuntarily, suddenly aware of a hollow pain spasm breaking through his body. "Oh, Hades, not now." He glanced at the silent concentration of his team in the outer office, then checked his watch. He saw the familiar red hue encroaching insidiously on the edges of his vision. Soon, he knew he would see everything through a red haze. "Damnation!" He closed his eyes, fumbling in his inside pocket for the tinted glasses he needed to disguise what was happening. He would have to get away soon, very soon, or they were all at risk. He slipped the darkened lenses on and opened his eyes. Fumbling for his phone with shaking hands, he pressed speed dial for Thomas's mobile. He could have howled when he heard "leave a message at the tone".

"Thomas, it is Justin. Sorry to bother you, but I am really hungry." He emphasised the last two words, knowing Thomas would understand the emergency. "I will try to make it to Marta's. Can you meet me there?" He rang off and speed dialled Marta's home, but again had to leave a message. Feeling frustrated and helpless, Justin sat back and began breathing slowly in and out, in and out, refusing to give in to the vicious desire that would soon tear his whole body with agonising pain. Gradually breath by breath, he gained a small measure of control just in time for a brisk knock on his door.

"Sir, you need to see this. We've found something on the High Street." Chas noticed the glasses and his face showed concern. "You alright sir?"

Justin gave a tight-lipped smile. "Yes, just a bit of eye strain with all this screen work. I'm surprised the rest of you are still so fresh." He stood up and indicated Chas should lead the way. Keeping a longer than usual distance between them, he followed.

"Here sir." Julie was smiling and waved him over. He went to stand behind her. On the screen was a scene from the afternoon showing Chelsey outside a lingerie store. Julie pressed play. A man appeared from across the road, standing blocking Chelsey's way. There was no sound, but Justin could tell from her stiff body language she was not happy with the encounter. Then he tried to touch Chelsey's arm, but she shrugged him off brusquely and side stepped. The man said something and Chelsey exploded with anger, drawing the attention of several other pedestrians. He finally took the hint, brushed past her and hurried away along the High Street.

Justin stepped back from leaning over Julie, suddenly very aware of the sound of her strong heartbeat and the fabulous aroma of her perfume, the same rare blood group as their victim. Its heady effect intensified the gnawing ache in his gut into stabbing pain.

"We can identify the man. It's Adrian Dawson." Ray's quiet voice confirmed, thankfully distracting Justin. "There's someone else you should see as well. Not someone we can identify yet, but he's definitely following Chelsey. He appears several times through the afternoon until we lose sight of Chelsey on the 325 bus back to her home. He queues at the bus stop but doesn't get on. Here he is."

A figure in jeans and a leather jacket, collar turned up, appeared on the screen beside a covered bus stop. Justin couldn't distinguish for certain if it was a man or a woman from the view. The figure avoided looking at the bus camera. Leather jacket watched the other passengers getting on the bus. From the width of the shoulders, the figure was most likely a man, and the clothing suggested a younger man.

"Well done, all of you." Justin glanced at his watch: 9 p.m. It was getting late in more ways than one. "We have completed the timeline to the point Chelsey heads home for the first time, and we have another possible suspect to add to the board. Let's call it a day and start fresh tomorrow. Anne and I will tackle Mr Adrian Dawson. The rest of you have two objectives: first, find out when and where Chelsey went after returning home and second, who is Leather Jacket. For tonight, you all have homes to go to, so get going. See you at eight a.m. sharp tomorrow." Justin went quickly back into his office, closing the door on all that glorious temptation.

He kept his head down, giving the impression of concentrating on what he was reading and not wanting to be disturbed. Justin stayed at his desk and avoided eye-contact until the last of his team left. He felt some of that dreadful fear fade when they were safely out of his space. He checked his watch and as soon as he thought there was a safe distance between their heading home and his leaving, he hurried from the building. Turning out of headquarters, he strode swiftly down the darkened street between the dull circles of light from the streetlights. Even through his desperation, he kept a watch for other people, slowing his speed to avoid their attention, and giving them a wide berth, always moving towards the safety of Marta's house.

Damn, he was starving, the familiar craving was barely held in check, increasing its demands every second it remained unsatisfied. Justin turned into the unlit passage between two of the shops, a shortcut into the Georgian square where he had parked his car in front of Marta's house that morning. He was hoping that Marta would be at home and would be able to offer temporary relief. He had not exhausted his supplies at her house as far as he could remember, but he was becoming dizzy with need and was no longer certain whether the remainder would be enough. She was not his possession, however, and led her own independent life. If she was away for the evening, then he would drive back to the manor. He just had to hope he didn't encounter anyone else before he could treat the problem. To distract himself from the increasing agony, he focused on thoughts of Marta. It was a genuine friendship which had blossomed first and friends with benefits suited them both for the time being. Did he hope for more? Justin was uncertain whether he could endure the pain and grief of losing another lover, and he knew Marta was not ready to commit long term to their relationship after her horrific experience of marriage. She had been in Europe the last time this mad hunger had engulfed him, and was unaware of the terrible effect it had, although he had warned her about his condition as soon as he felt he could trust her.

Despite the tantalising images of Marta that were partially distracting him from the increasing severe waves of agony, his instincts were sharply aware of a sudden soft rustling nearby. He paused, the rustling stopped, assuming it was a rat he carried on along the narrow dark alley, then turned into a wider unlit space leading behind the shops.

Thank the gods, Thomas had refilled his supplies at the manor yesterday. If neither Thomas nor Marta could answer his SOS and he had to drive home before he could feed, there would be enough to satisfy his hunger.

He caught the rustle of clothing to his left just a fraction too late. He cursed as a sharp slicing pain slid down his arm. His attacker had been ahead of him, then hidden in a shadowed doorway, a rat of a different kind. Giving a low snarl, Justin grabbed the slight figure by the throat, driving forward fast, until he forced his captive hard against the solid brick backyard wall. He could feel the warm thick flow of his own blood slowly soaking into his sleeve and sliding down his arm. A metallic tang invaded his mouth, setting his tastebuds on fire. The unique aroma of rich healthy blood seduced him almost to the point of losing control. The throbbing pain of the cut just prevented a complete loss of control. Justin tightened his grip and lifted until his attacker was up on tiptoe. Faster than the young man could blink, Justin grabbed his captive's wrist and twisted sharply. A grunt of pain and the knife was in his left hand. His night vision cleared just enough from dark, deep red to allow him to inspect his captive. Justin sighed. A teenager, maybe seventeen years old, male. Practically still a child. He loosened his hold to allow the captive to breathe. His own breathing was shallow and fast, his heartbeat drumming in his ears. He tried to ignore the increasingly heated temptation of his senses, then he caught the fast strong beat of the youngster's heart pumping a river of healthy blood around the body he was holding. Everything he could ever need was right there within his grasp. He managed to pull back for a few seconds but the enchantment was greater. He could feel his control being shredded.

"What the hell did you think you were doing?" he enquired, quite mildly considering that fierce internal battle. "You could kill somebody with this."

"Bastard piece of shit, let me go. Fucking prick! I will kill yuh. What the fuck are you doing to me?" The lad started to twist and lash out. "I told yuh let me go or I'll gut you."

Justin shook him lightly until he stopped struggling. "Why should I let you go? You attacked me, remember? If I called the police, you could be in deep trouble, actual bodily harm, perhaps armed robbery." He allowed the boy to get his feet on the floor, but kept a tight hold.

"Fuck yuh, call 'em if yuh dare. I'll tell'm yuh attacked me, wanted to rape me an' I defended meself. Better for yuh just to give me money and let me go."

He tried again to wriggle out of Justin's grip. Justin shook his head and hoisted the boy back onto tip toe. He lifted the knife so the boy could see it, the blade glimmering where his blood was not darkening the metal. Justin smiled, watching the boy's eyes widen as he leaned closer.

"You really should not have tried it lad," he said softly, "not with me, and definitely not tonight!"

Justin's attempt to maintain control of the uncontrollable weakened even more. His eyes glowed like bloody ice, reflecting what little moonlight was reaching the alley. He watched the boy's eyes widen with a terror that increased when Justin's lips parted, slender, needle-sharp fangs extending.

The alley was deserted and there was no sound from pedestrians at either end of its short length. There was nobody to hear the scream of terror cut-off at birth when Justin used a sleeper hold to knock his victim out. At last, Justin surrendered to the overwhelming need. Fangs pierced a large vein and the healthy heart beat faster, pumping rich, thick blood that flowed into Justin's body. He sighed happily, euphoria replacing the agony as the glorious tide reduced his hunger. He gave himself up to pure pleasure until he realised the boy's heart was slowing down, finding it difficult to pump the remaining blood around when the blood pressure was so low. Justin forced himself to pull away, watched as the twin punctures sealed up and faded.

Twenty minutes later, the dazed and terrified teenager struggled to his feet and staggered into the wall of the alley. He paused, shaking with the effort, then rushed overbalancing and fell into the opposite wall. Desperate to reach the light coming from the High Street, the boy stumbled on. Under the street lights he looked pale and his eyes were unblinking, dazed. He staggered, but instinctively headed to where his friends should have been waiting. Justin followed silently without being noticed until his victim crashed into his mates, leaning against the ornamental railings of the local museum. Once they seemed to be looking after him, Justin left them to it.

He decided to walk the longer route to Marta's house. He stretched his neck and eased his shoulders, enjoying being momentarily pain free. There was no longer any great rush, but he would need to feed again very soon. His phone vibrated, he looked at the caller ID.

"Hello Marta." Justin listened, smiling. "I am fine, no need to worry for the moment. I found a volunteer donor." He wiped a speck of moisture from his bottom lip as he listened. "Thank you. I shall be there in twenty minutes."

By the time he stepped into the light from the portico, he was exhausted and shaking with reaction where the effect of the relatively small amount of blood he had allowed himself was wearing off. The door opened and Marta took his arm, drawing him into the welcome warmth of the hallway. She continued to hold him as they walked through the door behind the staircase into the kitchen, where she pushed him gently into a chair at the table. Marta opened an ice packed cool box waiting on the kitchen counter, took out one of the bags of blood inside.

"Here you are. Thomas came around as soon as he heard your message. He told me what happens to you sometimes." Marta looked down at him, her face sad. "Is it bad?"

Justin nodded. "Yes, and unexpected. Usually, this hunger only occurs when an injury needs to heal. This last time was truly the worst and I guess it shows I am not yet fully recovered." A worried frown carved lines into his forehead. There was a note of fear in his voice as he continued. "I was with the team. I hate to think what they made of me tonight, but at least I managed some control. They are the ones most at risk if the Hunger becomes overwhelming, particularly DI Richards, as she is with me so much of the time. I had hoped, with another couple of weeks of healing, there would not be another incident."

Marta reached into the cool box and placed another bag of blood in front of him before resting her head against his, her arms around his shoulders while he fed. Justin felt her ease off his jacket and carefully roll up the once white shirt sleeve. "My poor love," she whispered before opening the first aid kit to dress the slash on his arm.

9

Justin tried not to move. The agony in his head stabbed worse than any hangover he had experienced in his youth. Marta muttered in her sleep and turned over. That small vibration intensified the pain exponentially. He slid out from under the covers, collected his clothes, and headed for the bathroom. Peering into the mirror, he winced at the bloodshot eyes and dark bruise shadows beneath. Cold water in the shower cold enough to make him gasp. Slowly, as the dawn brightened the sky between the clouds, the pain faded to just about bearable, like the weakening aftershocks following an earthquake. He turned off the shower, dried off, and dressed. Putting on the tinted glasses, Justin headed downstairs to the kitchen. He would make breakfast, a way to thank Marta for her kindness and understanding last night. He had it waiting, laid out on the kitchen table, when she glided in. She helped herself to a generous portion of eggs, bacon, and toast, then sat beside him, and, glancing at the cleared plate in front of him, nodded.

"At least you have an appetite for food this morning," Marta commented.

"Stop beating yourself up over what might have happened," she added severely, having no sympathy for the failed thief. "You had sufficient control not to kill that stupid child and you were safe here." He looked up, about to speak, but she stopped him with a finger to his lips. "With Thomas, and I, to help you, we should be able to manage the situation until you have completely recovered. Whatever happened on that undercover job must have been horrific if you are still healing three weeks later." She nibbled at the crispy bacon on her plate. "Mm! you can cook breakfast every time you stay from now on," she said, closing her eyes to enjoy the flavour.

Justin didn't respond, trying to bury the memories of those three days after his cover had been blown, and the gang had taken their revenge.

Marta gave him a critical inspection, her expression doubtful when she asked, "Are you in a fit state to work today?"

"I am in a better state than my poor victim," he answered. "The first forty-eight hours have already gone and we are no nearer a solution." He reached out, took her hand, and kissed her fingers. "I will manage. The worst is over for now."

Marta touched his cheek, "Very well stubborn one, I will drive you to the station. When all this is done, we will go to your place in France for a while, yes?"

Justin managed a smile, taking in her state of undress. "Dressed like that, you are going to cause a sensation at Shady Lane."

Marta laughed, stood up and let her silk dressing gown slide to the floor. Her chuckle of delight drifted back to him as she disappeared out of the door. Justin grinned despite his fears as he watched her. He promised himself a suitable revenge for taking advantage of his temporary infirmity.

Appropriately dressed for work, Marta pulled up outside the Shady Lane main entrance. Justin made his way carefully to the office and sat, blinds drawn over the outside windows. It was a relief for which he was thankful. The throbbing in his head had grown worse on the journey in, but in the shadowed office was fading slowly back to manageable.

The outer office was empty, although the team would start to arrive soon. Justin had time to take stock of their response to his taking over. Overall, he felt they were fitting together very well. They were all committed to finding the killer. He felt a justifiable ripple of pride in how much his team was willing to trust him despite their recent experience with senior officers. They might have reservations about him, he could understand that. It was early days, but there was hope for the future.

He took off his glasses and rubbed his eyes, then fired up the laptop to read through any new updates. He also checked for Donne and Partners, the estate agents. Justin decided a visit to the premises would be first on the list for the day. He checked the map and realised it would be easier and quicker to walk rather than drive halfway around the one-way system to the other side of the pedestrianised precinct.

Anne arrived a few moments later, only just ahead of Julie and Paul, then Ray and Chas. Justin gave them time to settle before the morning briefing, although that was truly brief, as there was little to tell, except that some of the help line leads had been followed up and proved negative. The others set about chasing down information from the various security cameras. Justin and Anne headed out to interview Adrian Dawson.

The day was fine when they joined the morning pedestrians on the street, but rain clouds were massing, threatening showers for the afternoon. Anne and Justin arrived at the office as the staff opened for business.

A smartly dressed woman smiled professionally, assuming they were potential house hunters. The smile wavered into a frown when they produced their warrant cards. "Sorry, but your detectives were here yesterday. What more can we tell you?"

Justin asked to see Adrian Dawson.

"Not here I'm afraid. Adrian has literally just rung in sick. I was allocating his prospective clients to other staff members." She glanced around then added, "perhaps I can help you?"

"Yes, I believe you could Ms …?"

"Langley, Thea Langley. Shall we go into Adrian's office? It will give us more privacy." She turned quickly as a member of staff came towards them. "Ahh, Joe, would you take Adrian's eight forty-five? I think that's them now." She nodded towards a couple coming through the door. Ms Langley told Joe the address for the viewing before leading the way into a smaller office. She waved them to seats around a low table placed in the corner of the office away from the desk. Justin could feel her uncertainty in the quickening of her heartbeat and the frequent darting glances at them and looking away.

"Ms Langley, you obviously want to share something that concerns you." He finally commented.

Ms Langley still hesitated, the confidence she had shown in dealing with business drained from her. "I'm not sure."

Justin nodded. "Anything, no matter how small, that you think might help us. The smallest thing could be the key to catching Chelsey's murderer."

The woman nodded, biting her lip then, "Chelsey was a good worker and had real potential," she said considering her words, then added suddenly, "she didn't deserve to be Adrian's victim. Oh, she was pretty enough, but too intelligent for his shenanigans and far too sensitive." Her voice held sadness and regret. "I know Adrian rather well actually." She saw Anne's expression and smiled. "No dear, not like that. I'm outside Adrian's age range. He likes them young. I found Chelsey outside in the courtyard one afternoon. She was so angry she was crying. We talked. Chelsey felt she was being forced out, and she didn't want to leave a job she enjoyed just because of some machismo stupidity." Ms Langley sighed. "I admired her determination and decided I would give her a little help. So, I told her something she could use to defend against his sleazy tricks. It seemed to work, you know, leave me in peace or I tell your wife about your mistress." Her brow furrowed and tears blurred her eyes. "I was certain Adrian was too weak a character and too fond of his current lifestyle to turn nasty. He is a typical unhappy bully, stand up to them and the bravado shatters. Sleazy bullies like him don't usually turn to violence. I thought he was trying to show how important he was because he felt intimidated, marrying the boss' daughter when she's a high-flying legal eagle." Ms Langley shrugged, then met Justin's gaze. "Was I wrong? Did my advice push him into killing Chelsey?"

"That is what we want to discover, Ms Langley. There is no evidence either way at the moment, but we do need to speak to Mr Dawson."

Ms Langley licked her dry lips. "Adrian has someone at the moment that I believe he is very serious about. At least, as serious as he can be, given the circumstances. I told Chelsey about them. I'd seen them by accident a few weeks ago. Adrian was so very different with her, gentle, protective. I was astonished. Before you ask no, it wasn't his sister or any relative, and I know his family rather well." She laughed. "Anyway, the speed Adrian changed from being Mr Grope to avoiding Chelsey was faster than his new Porsche can accelerate."

Justin and Anne thanked Ms Langley for her information, and Justin gave her his card in case she thought of anything else, before they left the estate agents. They headed back to Shady Lane under a typical April shower, sharp and heavy but ending quickly. They collected the car and set off to find Adrian Dawson.

"OK, where to?" Anne asked over the growl of the engine.

"Back to the Horsfield," Justin replied, checking the address on his phone. "We must have parked nearby yesterday."

"Oh, not the Marquee place?"

Justin shook his head. "No! The house is called 'The Briars'. It's the other corner plot to the boundary wall we walked along into the Horsfield itself."

This time, they turned into the driveway of 'The Briars' through the open electric gates and parked directly in front of the main entrance. Anne glanced around the bare drive.

"I wonder where the Porsche Ms Langley mentioned could be?" she commented, climbing the shallow steps to the door. They rang the bell and waited quite a while before the front door opened just a crack.

"Yes? If you're selling anything, I don't want it, so go away! I'm busy."

Justin saw Anne frown, staring hard at the figure half hidden by the door. Her expression showed puzzled recognition, as if the slurred voice was familiar, but the actual person wasn't.

"Not too busy for the police, surely, Mr Dawson?" She snapped, suddenly raising her identification for the door to see clearly.

There was a significant pause before the door opened wider. Justin noted Dawson's dishevelled state just before Anne marched through the door and into the hallway. Surprised and intrigued by his partner's unusually abrupt behaviour, Justin followed her in.

"Is there somewhere we can talk in private sir?" she asked.

Adrian Dawson glowered at his intruders through bloodshot eyes, then shrugged. "Through here. My wife's at work and the cleaner already finished for the day." He led them into a large lounge, sprawled in a deep armchair, and picked up his glass from the side table. He took a good sip of what looked and smelled like quality whisky. His other hand waved them to sit down.

"Right. What do the police want from me?" The tone was sullen, but Justin noticed Adrian Dawson was avoiding looking at Anne.

"An explanation of your actions concerning our murder victim, Chelsey

Harris, would be a good starting point, Mr Dawson." Anne snapped in response, her back ramrod straight, muscles tense.

Her hostile attitude added to Justin's surprise. He started wondering how this meeting would play out. Justin could feel a strange sort of recognition between Anne and Dawson, but nothing he could put a name to. It was just the feeling that they had met each other before and it had not been a successful encounter. He decided to let Anne have her head. He wasn't certain he could stop her anyway.

"I don't know what you are talking about," Dawson said slow and clear, with obvious effort. He emptied his glass and reached for the decanter for another refill.

"Mr Dawson, we have eyewitnesses to your intimidation of Chelsey. In fact, of sustained sexual harassment."

Dawson blew a raspberry. Anne's eyes narrowed, then she glanced at Justin.

"I didn't bully her, and I didn't harass her. It was only a bit of fun. When she told me to stop, I did as she asked."

"That's not strictly true, is it? Chelsey threatened to tell your wife about …"

Dawson interrupted, "What the Hell! I'm not answering any more of your bloody questions. Get the hell out of my house." Dawson slammed down the glass, spilling whisky across the polished table. He stood up, then made a bad mistake. He grabbed Anne's arm.

Reacting automatically, she turned into his body, grasped his arm with both hands, she bent forward fast and hooked his feet from under him. She looked up at Justin and shrugged. "Sorry, self-defence classes and a black belt in judo,".

Justin looked down at Dawson sprawled on the floor, face down, held still in a fierce arm lock.

"Mr Dawson, I am going to ask Detective Inspector Richards to let you stand up, but only if I have your word, you will behave yourself in a civilised manner. Do you agree?"

Dawson suddenly relaxed and nodded. "Yeah, get her off me."

Justin's lips twitched at the sight, but he nodded at Anne, who released her hold and stepped away. She still looked as if she would like to break a bone or two. Dawson got slowly to his feet, rubbing at his arm and slumped into the armchair.

Justin shook his head when Anne looked to continue the questioning. "Mr Dawson, I think it best that we continue this interview at the station. Bearing in mind you just attempted to assault my colleague, I think your best course of action is to agree. The evidence against you, though circumstantial as I'm sure your wife will tell you, does place you close to the top of the suspect list in our investigation of Chelsey Harris's murder."

After a long pause, Dawson nodded his agreement. He led the way into the hall, swaying from side to side, collected his jacket from the closet.

"You can contact your wife from the station. Is she in court today?"

Dawson nodded. "No need to bother her. I don't need legal representation."

He came quietly, subdued and definitely worried. He remained silent throughout the journey back to the station. When they showed him into an interview room, he asked for a cup of black coffee.

Anne headed upstairs to the office, but Justin stopped her, suggesting they should take a walk outside. They found a sheltered spot under an overhanging roof just before the rain started to mist the ground.

"You and Dawson know one another." Justin made it a statement of fact. "How?"

"Not know one another," she corrected, "more know of one another."

"Fair enough. I ask again how?"

Anne closed her eyes momentarily.

"I know of him because he was, probably still is, my ex-husband's whoring buddy," She finally said, fiery colour flooding up from her neck to the top of her head. "Apparently, they've been bosom buddies, no pun intended, since school days. The best friend who provides opportunities for weekends away, supposed conferences, the usual crap the other half doesn't get to know about for years then, crash, the whole cesspit explodes."

Justin was thoughtful. "So that's why he was avoiding looking at you after he had seen your warrant card?"

She nodded.

"But you've never met physically until today?"

Justin winced in sympathy, seeing the hurt in her eyes as she replied, "No, just a familiar voice on the phone. Ron's staying overnight with me because he's had a little too much to drink. Hi, I was wondering if Ron was available next weekend. You probably haven't caught up with the rumour mill yet. My darling other half is Inspector Ron Timpson of Traffic Division."

"And?"

Anne sighed. "I'm pretty sure he asked DCI Benson to persuade me to resign any way he could. I don't doubt the word has gone out that I'm fair game if his mates want to make my life uncomfortable, and Ron is a very popular man. He might even try the 'all boys together' act with you."

Justin laughed out loud. "Be certain he will not. It would do him no good if he did. I want you here! You are my link with the rest of the team, who respect you as much as I do. I believe we could, given a chance, develop a real partnership because you and I complement one another. I said to you when we began this investigation, only you have the power to decide whether you stay or transfer somewhere else. My only concern is the connection between you and our suspect. I think you should sit out of this interview, but I still want you watching in case we miss anything. I want to make use of that detailed knowledge of Dawson's ability to lie."

Anne nodded. "Fair enough sir. Who will you work the interview with?"

"Any suggestions? I was thinking a bit of brotherly bonding might loosen his tongue."

She smiled, "Ray Williams, Ray's your man. Just tell him what you want and he'll deliver."

"Good, let's see if he's in the office and get ourselves organised. I'm surprised Dawson does not want his wife contacted. We need to ask him again if he wants legal representation. I have encountered that lady in full flow and I am not prepared to put a conviction at risk if he happens to be the killer."

Ten minutes later, Anne and Justin watched as Ray entered the interview room where Chas was already with their suspect. Ray placed a cup of water in front of Adrian Dawson.

"Here you go sir, something to help clear your head before the boss gets going." Ray sat down and placed a file on the table, giving Dawson an obviously sympathetic look. "Between you and me, he's not too happy with you. Doesn't like what he's heard about you, womaniser, he said with that strait-laced look he gets."

Justin chuckled as he listened to Ray's assessment of his character.

"Bit of a hypocrite really, considering. Me I've seen Chelsey's photo, a real looker she was. Might have chanced my luck a few years back."

Dawson looked up, surprised, a suspicious frown on his face.

"You taking the mick?"

Ray shook his head and leaned closer, keeping his voice low and soft. "No, I guess as you know Inspector Richards' ex-husband, you also know our DCI Benson?" Ray gave a significant wink, his gum chewing going into overdrive. Justin wondered if he was overdoing it.

At Anne's name, Dawson scowled and muttered a curse. Ray smiled. "Yeah, our acting detective inspector makes a lot of men curse, and she was your mate's wife." Ray shook his head. "By the way, that's another black mark against you, as far as our boss is concerned. Might even charge you with assaulting a police officer if he doesn't get what he wants from you. If I were you, I'd rethink not having the family solicitor here with you."

Dawson held his head in his hands as if trying to stop the world from spinning. "I didn't intend anything by it. I grabbed her arm yes, but what I was going to do after that?" he shrugged. "I just wanted them to leave me in peace. I wasn't thinking straight." Dawson gave a short, bitter laugh. "Not sure I have a solicitor. My wife left me a letter this morning. She's left for good to live in Surrey with some high-flying legal eagle." He turned to Ray, looking for some understanding, responding to Ray's reference to his old school friend. "Dear God, I never touched Chelsey, not seriously. It was just a bit of a wind-up. I was sick of being told what to do by women all the time. She happened to be handy to relieve my feelings, I suppose." He looked between the two officers at the clock on the wall.

"Well, you tell your story to the boss, sir, not to me."

Justin grinned at Anne and headed out of the room next door, leaving her to continue watching. When he appeared in the interview room, he was grim faced. Chas stood up as Justin entered the room. Justin sat down beside Ray and placed his laptop on the table between them. Ray announced his arrival and Chas's departure for the record and the interview began. Ray explained the interview was also being watched by other officers then asked Dawson to give his account of what happened between Chelsey and himself.

It took very little prompting for the whole sorry story to spill out. From the moment Chelsey joined the firm through to the day she threatened to tell his wife and her father, his senior partner, what he was doing unless he left her alone.

"That was all she wanted, to be left alone to get on with her job, so I stopped." Dawson shook his head. "No, I more than stopped. I avoided her like the plague." He looked up at his interviewers, a sneer on his face. "Someone at the office must have told you about it. She'd found something out I definitely didn't want reaching the ears of my wife or her bloody father. I don't know how."

The complete confession tallied with what they had already discovered up to a point. However, Dawson stopped before the encounter with Chelsey shown by the CCTV footage.

"You've forgotten something Adrian. Think hard now, when was the last time you saw Chelsey?" Ray kept up the bonhomie with an effort.

Dawson looked puzzled. "I told you at the office …" His voice faltered into silence then, "No, you're right. I remember I saw her in the High Street."

Justin turned the laptop around so that Dawson could see the CCTV footage.

"Yes, there. I was going back to the office when she came out of that new lingerie shop. I went across to her to try explaining, maybe to apologise. It was an impulse. I don't know what I would have said because she shut me down and walked away."

"The CCTV shows you grabbed her arm, Adrian. Did you threaten her? You know, meet me later or I'll make things more difficult for you."

"No, I swear I didn't. I asked her to listen to me, asked her to let me explain. She said just leave her alone and she wouldn't say anything. I was relieved. I believed her. That was the last time I saw her." Dawson nodded at the footage as it showed Chelsey walking away.

Justin leaned forward his expression doubtful. "I am not sure I believe you, Mr Dawson. I think you went looking for her later. She had got the better of you after all, and you do not strike me as a man who appreciates being bested by a woman. Where were you between the hours of nine p.m. and five a.m. on Tuesday night?"

Dawson shook his head angrily. "I did not follow Chelsey. I went back to the office. If you don't believe me, ask that guy from the garden centre who was following Chelsey." He pointed at the screen where the unidentified figure they had noticed was visible. "Friend of her boyfriend's or his hanger-on, name of Gavin something or other."

Ray made a note as Dawson paused.

"As for where I was that night, all I'm saying is I was with a friend from eight p.m. to eight a.m. then I went to work." Dawson had the grace to look shamefaced. "My wife was away at a conference in London from Tuesday morning to Thursday evening."

Justin turned the recording back to the blurred figure. "How do you know this, Gavin?"

"He's brought deliveries from the garden centre to our contractor a few times while I've been working from home. I've also seen him outside the office with Chelsey's Sean when he's arrived to take her out after work." Dawson looked up from the screen. "What more do you want from me?" he said, his voice tired and monotone with resignation.

"Nothing further today, Mr Dawson. We appreciate your help today, but until we can corroborate your alibi, I must ask you not to go anywhere without informing us first."

Dawson was already nodding then snapped, "What the hell does it matter now my wife has walked out? Jody Pearce, that's who I was with. She means more to me than I ever expected, Jody and my child. No job, not much in the way of prospects, but she'll still stand by me. Can't ask more than that." He sighed. "So, are we done here?"

"Once you give us the address and telephone number of Ms Pearce so that we can contact her to verify your whereabouts, then yes. However, you will remain here until we get that confirmation."

Dawson nodded. "Yeah, just keep that awful coffee on tap for me, would you? If you also happen to have a couple of headache pills, that would be great."

Justin left the interview room with Ray. "Go visit that address and see what Jody Pearce has to say. Better still see if she will come into the station and make a statement."

10

The phone was ringing when Justin returned to his office. The irritating sound seemed to signify their current lack of progress.

"Mortmain," he snapped into the receiver.

A silence then. "Sorry to disturb you sir. One of Sean Trent's neighbours just phoned the dedicated line."

"I'm sorry Keval," Justin said, recognising the voice of the hotline supervisor. "A touch of investigation frustration creeping in. What did the neighbour want to report?"

"His name is Richard Waverley, and he was one of the absentees that the team leafleted. He'd been away on a business trip from late Tuesday afternoon until this morning. Mr Waverley saw our appeal repeated on the local news, then found the card in his post and phoned in. He saw your victim at Trent's flat as he was leaving for his business trip."

Justin's interest grew. Not only had Trent lied to them about seeing Chelsey that day, or so it now appeared, but they had a witness who recognised her and placed her in the building on the afternoon before her death.

"Thank you, Keval, and again my apologies for being so snappy." Justin put down the receiver and went in search of Anne. He found her with Julie and Paul, enjoying a quick sandwich lunch in the canteen. They all looked up expectantly as he reached their table. Justin signalled for them to stay seated.

"Finish your lunch. It is nothing that cannot wait. You all deserve a break. When you are done Anne, we need to go back to Richmond Mansions. The trawl through the neighbours has paid off. One of our absentee neighbours has rung in, who saw Chelsey that afternoon at Trent's place. I thought you might like to lead on questioning the witness? I will be in the office. Come get me when you are ready."

The roads were quiet for a change and they reached the apartment block in less than twenty minutes. As they approached the entrance, they slowed down, looking for a parking space on the road. Over the low hedge, they saw quite a crowd gathered in front of the building. Anne pulled into a gap just past the entrance. As soon as the car door opened, they could hear clearly, loud, excited comments from the crowd. They headed rapidly towards the action.

Justin elbowed a path for them to the front of the crowd near a terrified teenage girl he recognised as Kate, Chelsey's sister. Someone in the crowd shouted out that the police had been called. Flashing blue lights proved the point when two police cars came to a halt, blocking the exits from the building. Anne put an arm around Kate Harris's shoulders. "I didn't mean for this to happen," the girl said in a terrified frantic whisper. "I only wanted someone to show them to. I couldn't tell my parents they were in so much pain already." She turned and burrowed into Anne's side. "Please make them stop! Please, Darren will kill Sean and then I will lose my brother as well as my sister, and it's my fault."

Justin heard that appeal, even though he was already moving towards the combatants. He saw what he expected to see. Sean was getting the worst of the fight with a trained and experienced soldier. Justin had to give him his due, however, Sean was certainly brave enough or plain angry enough to come back swinging. He was getting up from the tarmac for the second time since they had arrived. One eye was swelling closed. There was blood flowing from his nose, and the corner of his mouth had split and was swelling. Justin saw he was slightly side on to his opponent, as if protecting his ribs from further damage. Chelsey's brother, on the other hand, looked ready to go on forever. His eyes glowed with a deadly hatred. Justin got between them as two other officers arrived at a run. Darren Harris glanced at Justin, one quick irritated glance.

Justin shook his head. "Stop now, Sergeant Harris."

Darren ignored the order, going for Sean again and found himself flat on the floor, not sure how he got there and unable to get back up. Justin gave another warning. "Stay down! It is over!"

"Not till I see him beg for mercy for what he did to Chelsey. Then you can have him," Harris snarled, trying to struggle against Justin's hold.

"No." Justin replied, putting more pressure on the elbow joint. Darren Harris grunted with pain. "I don't want to hurt you Darren, but I am not letting you go."

The pain finally pierced the haze of hatred, and Darren finally looked into Justin's determined face. Reaction set in and the murderous fury energising his actions disappeared. He shivered, and still grudging, nodded.

Sean was already being supported by the uniformed officers.

The police cautioned both combatants then both were handcuffed, and placed in separate cars. They would be waiting at the station for interview. Justin shrugged. They could wait. He wanted as much ammunition as the neighbour and Kate Harris could provide before tackling Sean again. He turned back to Kate and Anne.

"Kate, we will take you home. Do not worry about your brother. The doctor will treat both Darren and Sean at the station before we interview them. If it is necessary, we will escort them to A&E. You shall have your brother back at home by late tomorrow morning, I should think." He saw the apprehension on her face. "Yes, you are right. We want to ask you about what caused the fight, but not here and not now. It is time to get you home."

As they turned towards the entrance, Justin saw a man approaching. He was someone Justin had noticed standing apart from the eager crowd. Anne paused, but Justin signalled for her and Kate to go ahead to the car.

"Come on Kate, you're shivering. Let's go wait in the car where it's warmer."

Anne distracted the girl, leading her away.

The man tactfully waited until they were out of earshot. "I'm Richard Waverley. I phoned about seeing Chelsey."

Justin shook hands. "Pleased to meet you Mr Waverley, DCI Mortmain. We were on our way to take your statement when we were … distracted."

Waverley nodded. "Yes, a nasty business! Who was that young man? He seemed prepared to take on all comers."

Justin ignored Waverley's curiosity. "Regarding your statement, are you going to be at home this evening? I would like to hear what you saw, but our priority is to get that young girl back to her parents."

"I'm not going anywhere for a few days. Send someone when convenient. I'll be here."

Justin drove, leaving Anne free to sit with Kate in the back. It was a silent return journey. Kate was shaking in Anne's embrace, tears just held in check. They parked outside the Harris house, protecting Kate from a couple of lurking photographers as they headed inside.

Kate went straight to the kitchen, set the kettle on, then turned to face them.

"I'm sorry," she said, her words broken up by silent sobbing breaths. "I should have told you what I knew that first day."

"Tell us now." Justin kept his tone neutral.

Kate abandoned the kitchen and sat at the dining table.

"I hadn't felt very well that day, so at lunchtime I signed out and came home. It's a privilege the sixth form has. I was in my bedroom when Chels arrived. She was more upset than I had ever seen her. She just blurted everything out, as if all that pain and anger couldn't be held back, now she was home. Sean had given her a key to his flat a few days ago. Chels wanted to surprise him by making use of the key and organising a romantic evening for two. She'd bought new clothes, including some lacy underwear. When she came home, she was pulling and tugging at the material as if she wanted to tear everything to shreds and all the time the tears were flowing down her cheeks." Kate's voice broke on a sob, her own tears a mixture of sorrow and anger. "She was the one who got the surprise. She found Sean romping around the bedroom with another girl. They were enjoying themselves so much, they hadn't heard her come into the flat. She said she'd stood in the doorway watching them for what seemed like an hour before they noticed she was there." Kate looked up from the tabletop, her face reflecting a little of the same shock and hurt. "How could Sean do that?" She asked, frowning. "I tried to comfort her. We hugged, and she seemed to calm down, but then she told me to go back to my room and started changing. I left her to it but about fifteen minutes later I heard her go out again."

"Why did you tell your brother?" Justin asked Kate, "I assume that was the reason for the fight."

Kate nodded, "Yes. I need to get something from upstairs, may I?"

She wasn't away long and returned with a sheaf of papers, one of which was still half in an envelope. Kate gave that one to Anne. "It," she said, disgust showing in her tone, "arrived by post this morning after Mum and Dad went with officer Romney to begin arrangements for Chelsey's funeral. I opened it. I'd just finished reading it when Darren arrived home. He saw the glued-on letters and everything just spilled out. We found these others hidden in Chelsey's special place. They made me feel sick, so much hate and anger."

Justin pulled an evidence bag from his pocket, and Kate put the papers inside. Anne added the most recent letter.

"We will see what we can find. It is a long shot, but there might be some useful information from the content or the materials. Thank you, Kate."

Kate frowned, seemed puzzled by something, then blurted out. "She was there, you know, Gina, Chelsey's best friend, in that crowd. She looked excited about the whole ugly business. Strange really, why should Gina be anywhere near Sean's place? So was that yob Gavin who hangs around Sean all the time. He was hanging back rather than rushing to rescue Sean, and that surprised me."

Justin recalled the scene when they had arrived and felt no surprise at all. The trained soldier with hate in his eyes had been a formidable sight. Few civilians, no matter how tough they were, would have wanted to tackle a trained combat soldier like Darren Harris at that moment.

"Have you told us everything now Kate? No more holding back?" Anne asked quietly.

Kate nodded, tired out by the emotional upheaval. "There's nothing else I swear. If I find anything else or remember anything more, I promise to tell you first."

The whole ugly business had left Kate pale, so exhausted emotionally that she had nothing left to say. While they waited for her parents to return, they made a pot of tea, which brought a little colour back into Kate's face. After finishing the tea, she went up to her room to lie down. When Mr and Mrs Harris returned with PC Romney, Anne explained what had happened, then left the family in peace.

"Back to the station?" Anne asked, as Justin hesitated with the passenger door open. He leaned down, looking into the car.

"You go back and get one of the team to take Mr Waverley's statement. I need a walk to stretch my brain as much as my legs."

"What about our two gladiators?"

Justin grinned outright, then chuckled. Gladiators indeed! Neither man would have lasted the blink of an eye in the arena. "Leave them to worry about the consequences until I get back. Once we have Waverley's evidence added to what Kate just gave us, I think Sean will want to tell us everything. You could interview this best friend of Chelsey's again."

"Gina Crane," Anne added, "I'll take Julie with me."

"Find out if Chelsey confided in her supposed BFF about the hate mail or anything else. I am very tired of half-truths and evasions from people who should want Chelsey's murder solved. What the Hades are they all trying to hide?"

"See you back at the station then, and sir."

"Yes?"

"My money is on you to get to the truth in the end."

Surprised and gratified, Justin waved her off.

11

Justin walked steadily, automatically avoiding pedestrians going in the opposite direction. The occasional shopping bag brushed against him, but he barely noticed. The new eyewitness threw suspicion straight back on Sean Trent. Thanks to Kate, they now had a reason why Trent had lied, but there was still the possibility he had killed Chelsey later that night. Anne's interview with the "best friend forever" might also bring fresh leads for the team to follow. Now Dawson had added yet another puzzling ingredient to the mix. Why had Gavin, a loyal friend of Trent's, been following Chelsey that day? Where did he fit into this tangle of events? Had Trent sent him to follow Chelsey? Why would he do that? Justin's pace quickened as the questions piled up one after the other, with few answers.

Half an hour later, Justin glanced up at the police station that covered the area of Malford around Mama's Restaurant. On a whim, he crossed the road and walked through the main entrance. At the reception desk, he was just about to show his credentials when a uniformed inspector came through the security door.

Tall and distinguished with dark hair highlighted by grey at his temples, Inspector Holmes' lean face lit by the warmth of his smile. He walked up to Justin and said quietly, "Justin, good to see you again. How have you been?"

Holmes turned to the duty officer, "Don't keep him waiting, buzz him through. What brings you back here to Malford, and what do you need from me?" He grasped Justin's outstretched hand. "I've got some decent coffee on the go if you have time. Got into the habit, working with you in Cambridgeshire and now I'm as addicted as you."

Justin returned his clasp warmly, amused at the slightly stunned expression on the sergeant's face. "Sherlock" was as usual keeping his men on their toes with his 'my bark is bad but my bite is worse' routine. At least until this moment, when he'd proved himself a normal human being who actually had friends despite rumours to the contrary.

When they were both seated in his office, coffee mugs in hand, John Holmes exclaimed, "You've been away a long time Justin. It's good to see you again."

"Good to see you too. How is the family doing?"

Holmes was always happy to talk about his adored wife and twin daughters, who were also Justin's goddaughters. He always remembered to send birthday cards and gifts and kept in touch with the girls regularly, especially when they headed for university near where he had worked, until that last case.

"OK Justin, I've wittered on about Elsa and the girls for ten minutes and you probably know more about what the girls have been up to than I do. What's bothering you and how can I help?" Holmes paused. "Are you in charge of the Harris investigation? I wondered why Detective Inspector Richards was doing the press conference. She was a good choice, as well as being an excellent investigator."

Justin nodded. "Thank you, and you're right. I found the victim, so I requested the case and the Chief Constable approved. However, I am not here about that case. Do you remember Mama's Restaurant? We went there a few times for celebration meals. Your station has kindly been keeping an eye on the premises for me. I wondered if there had been any further incidents since your men had been calling in?"

Holmes shook his head, "Not so far, not at Mama's. Although since we've made our presence obvious, some of the other independent shop owners have also spoken out about being approached and threatened. Rumour is the 'protection racket' is fairly widespread through the town, but nobody can identify who is organising the whole thing. All we've got so far is a couple of young men well known to us loitering near Mama's place. There's no evidence to show they are involved, but they seemed to be keeping an eye on what my officers were doing. However, I've been given approval to investigate since we've shown it's more widespread than one small parade of shops. If we get anything, I promise I will let you know."

Holmes put down his own mug and pulled up a file on his laptop. "I don't know if this is useful to you regarding the Harris case. In line with your request to keep a watch for vehicles that could be used to transport the body, but be small enough to get into the Tolland Wood car park, something came in that rang a bell."

We had a report of a vehicle stolen from outside Richmond Mansions. A medium-sized van belonging to Gardeners of Eden (Malford) Ltd. The report was made by the owner of the company, Eve Jordan. She lives in the apartment block."

Justin blinked, surprised. "Yes, she's a friend of Sean Trent. He was in a relationship with our victim. In fact. Eve provided his alibi for Tuesday night when we interviewed him."

Holmes' eyes widened. "Well, well, that's interesting. What are you going to do?"

Justin grimaced. "I have Trent in custody for disturbing the peace and will be interviewing him again. It will be something else to add to the list." He drained his mug and placed it on the desk. "Thank you for all your help, John. Mama is a very determined lady, but even she cannot deal with a protection racket on her own. Trouble is, she will give it her best shot if I am not mistaken."

"We'll continue to keep a check on the restaurant. In fact, we have a volunteer competition since some of my men have tasted the food there. If you get any more information, you'll let us know? It's truly good to see you again, Justin. Elsa and the girls would love to see you in the flesh, so to speak. How about we arrange a social night while the girls are back from uni? How about next week?" Holmes eyed Justin up and down and shook his head. "You still don't look any older than when we joined the force. Me, I feel about ninety sometimes."

Justin chuckled. "Just a healthy lifestyle and a good conscience. As for feeling about ninety, that makes you a spring chicken in my book."

Holmes grinned, "True, I keep forgetting you're a few years older than me."

He escorted Justin back to the entrance, reminding him again about getting together. Justin walked out into the open air and turned back towards the Shady Lane station.

He arrived back at the office just as Dawson was leaving with a young woman holding a baby in her arms. It was obvious from Dawson's very protective attitude that they meant a great deal more to him than he had admitted in the interview. Justin stood aside at the bottom of the shallow steps for them to pass by. He knew that feeling, knew it and feared it, when a person becomes your entire world. Justin watched them walk away and hoped that Dawson never suffered that total loss, even though he despised Dawson's attitude towards Chelsey Harris.

The entire team was in residence and the outer office had the anticipatory atmosphere of a newsroom when a big story was just about to break. There was a buzz of chatter and quiet laughter that eased a deep tension that remained from the start of the investigation. The demoralised and cynical men and women he had inherited so short a time ago were now melding into a dynamic and exciting team. All the signs boded well for the future. Smiling and content for the moment, he joined the group and started the meeting.

Anne began with the interview of Gina Crane. "Gina Crane, supposedly Chelsey's BFF, knew nothing at all at first." Anne shook her head, a frown on her face. "Her answers appeared false to me. There was something in her attitude, secretive and excited. Yes, she was upset by Chelsey's death, but nowhere near as much as I would have expected from someone who had been a friend since childhood."

She looked across at Julie, who nodded in agreement. "She knew about Dawson but laughed that off as something all attractive women had to deal with." Anne shrugged. "She didn't seem to know about any other threats." Anne looked around at the team. "By the end of the conversation, I was beginning to wonder if we had the wrong Gina Crane."

Justin turned and added Gina's name to the incident board. "Let's add her to our list for the moment. Paul, you go next."

Paul had interviewed Richard Waverley. "Mr Waverley was leaving on a business trip Tuesday afternoon when he heard a loud commotion coming from Trent's apartment. He said Chelsey rushed out of the door, obviously upset. She almost bumped into him he said, because tears blinded her eyes. He knew Chelsey well from previous visits, and she had always been so cheerful and friendly. Mr Waverley put out a hand to steady her, but she brushed him off and hurried down the stairs. No one else left the flat while he was in the hall. However, he had overheard clearly some of the argument between Trent and another woman, after Chelsey ran down the stairs. It seemed Mr Trent was ... er ... entertaining another young lady when Chelsey arrived. 'There was hell to pay,' Mr Waverley's words. He had left at that moment to drive to Leeds because his first meeting was that evening. He called us as soon as he saw the televised press conference repeat on the local news early this morning and then found our card among his post. Mr Waverley has signed his witness statement."

Justin nodded. "Yes, Kate Harris was at the apartment block this afternoon. We took her home. She told us Chelsey had returned home after that incident. She was so upset she told Kate everything. Kate also gave us some seriously unpleasant anonymous letters Chelsey had received. They read as hate mail based on her relationship with Sean Trent. They are now with forensics. It was Kate telling her brother what she knew that set off the fight we had to break up."

Justin turned to Ray and Chas. "After this meeting, I want you two to question the brother, Darren Harris, about the fight. Get him home as soon as you can. I doubt Trent will press charges so we could let them both off with a caution. Anne and I will interview Trent again, if Thomas has given him a clean bill of health?"

"Yes sir, the doc said apart from a black eye and a bruised rib, he's in reasonable condition. No signs of concussion and no serious injuries. You managed to separate them in time."

"Good. Ray, you look as if you have more news for us."

"Yes sir, two pieces of information. First of all, Jodie Pearce verified Dawson's alibi. He had been at her place and the baby had been so ill, they had taken her to the hospital. The hospital security tapes supported his alibi, as did the time on the parking ticket from Dawson's car. You might have passed them as they left the station? They left together about ten minutes ago."

"Yes, I saw them leave. He was very protective of his girlfriend and the child. Not surprising if the child had been unwell enough to be taken to hospital."

"The other piece of information concerns our bird cam man. He's an inspector with the RSPCA and the camera is part of an ongoing investigation he's running. Tolland Wood has a large badger colony, and there's a gang of badger baiters, raiding the setts in the local area. The camera is recording arrivals and departures from the car park because Byett believes they will strike Tolland Wood soon. The RSPCA has a good idea who is involved in the baiting but needs solid proof. I called the branch he works at and they confirmed what was going on. Also, Inspector Byett has been with them for twenty years. He had a bout of ill health recently and went off to his family's villa to relax and get fit. If we can't get in contact beforehand, they say he should be back at work end of next week."

Paul took up the report. "While Ray was seeing Dawson released, we had a report from the pathology lab. Their test for Rohypnol came back positive. That's why no one heard Chelsey scream, because she was physically unable to do so."

There was a long silence. Each of them contemplated what it must have been like for their victim. Aware of what was happening but unable to do anything about it and then diving into unconsciousness that took away all but the vaguest memory.

"We've also heard from Chelsey's cell phone company. Her phone was switched back on and they contacted us straight away." Paul looked at Justin and Anne with a slight smile on his face. "You aren't going to believe this," He continued. "It was switched on at Trent's apartment block during the time the fight took place. Unfortunately, it was switched off again within five minutes. Where it is now, they can't say."

"Something we can ask Sean Trent about in the interview," Justin commented his tone grim. "Just as we need to discover who was with him when Chelsey arrived." He turned to the board and pointed at Trent's name. "The alibi we were given for Trent cannot be true if he was, as you put it, entertaining a young lady that afternoon. Unless, could it have been Eve, the girl we met at his apartment? Was Eve his playmate?" He looked across at Anne. "Did you get any impression of intimacy between them? I must admit, I thought Trent treated her like an irritating younger sister rather than a love interest."

"I thought so too. Nothing there that said we are lovers."

"So why did she provide him with an alibi for earlier that day? Mistaken the day and date or something else? Another thing we can ask Trent." Justin turned back to the group. "Just to compound the issue. Eve owns a gardening company, Gardeners of Eden (Malford) Ltd. On the morning I found Chelsey's body, Eve was reporting her gardener's van stolen from outside the apartment block."

Justin noticed one of the team had printed and put on the board the picture of the stranger following Chelsey. "Dawson reckoned Chelsey's shadow was a guy called Gavin, a best friend or follower of Sean Trent's. Why he was following Chelsey, we have no idea. We need to talk to Gavin as well as finding out from Trent whether he had asked his friend to follow Chelsey. Dawson reckoned Gavin worked at the garden centre used by several of the local gardening companies. Ray and Chas can pay him a visit once we have interviewed Trent and know more about this individual."

"Why, when we think we are making progress, do even more questions slither out of the woodwork? Do we see Gavin as another suspect? I think we have to until we know more about him. Right! We still need that phone, and to find out where Chelsey went that evening after she left the house for the second time. See what you can discover. Anne and I will tackle Sean Trent again. My office will be better for preparing for the interview. Have Trent taken to an interview room about an hour from now." He turned to Anne. "That should give us sufficient time to work out an interrogation strategy."

Julie nodded and picked up the phone while Anne collected her laptop and followed Justin into the inner office.

12

Justin stood just inside the interview room, looking down at Sean Trent slumped in a chair beside the duty solicitor. His face showed annoyance and irritation, but not one iota of sympathy for the pathetic sight. They had dealt with the formalities. Now there was silence in the room, broken only by Trent's rather heavy breathing. Trent glanced upward out of his one open eye, then looked away quickly. Justin sat in the chair next to Anne and completed the formalities.

"Why did you lie to us Sean?" Anne's mild question broke the quiet.

Sean glanced at her, mouth opening, but before his denial gained freedom, Anne raised one hand and shook her head. "Don't lie to us again Sean please. We have evidence Chelsey was at your apartment the afternoon of the day she was killed."

Trent's shoulders slumped. He put his hands over his face for a few seconds then: "Yes, Chels was there." He said at last, low voiced and reluctant. Dark red embarrassment crawled under his skin.

"So, why lie?"

"I think we already know why," Justin's icily precise words contrasted with

Anne's quiet calm. "What other reason is there than a guilty conscience? Look at him Inspector, what do you see?"

Anne nodded, then said, "Guilt sir, I agree. Why did you kill Chelsey Sean? Was it the baby? When she told you, did you get angry? You have a pretty good life now with Mum footing the bill. All that would have ended."

"You don't have to answer that." The solicitor told Sean then added, "And you are fishing Chief Inspector Mortmain."

Sean ignored the advice if he even heard it. "No! That's not true! No, I didn't kill Chelsey, I swear. I loved her," Sean burst out suddenly, his already damaged mouth cracking and bleeding.

"Then tell us what happened, Sean. Why did you lie about seeing Chelsey? The truth now!" Anne asked quickly before the solicitor could say any more.

Sean's breathing sped up through his open mouth, then he shouted, "Because I was screwing someone else and Chelsey caught us at it." He put his head on his arms and sobbed.

They waited for him to recover, all three knowing he had just provided another reason to be their main suspect.

"Tell us what happened Sean! Were you with Eve? She seems very protective of you. She even provided you with an alibi, which we now know was false. What other reason would she have to do that? Did she help you kill Chelsey and move the body?"

The solicitor started to say something but Sean was already shaking his head and interrupted him. "No, it's time I told them, for Chelsey's sake." He managed a chuckle, then winced at the sting from his split lips. "God no, not Evie! She's too much like a younger sister. I suppose I have to tell you now."

"Whoever she is, she is also your only witness at the moment. Give her up Sean." Justin told him. "Not much point in keeping it secret now that Chelsey is dead. Was that why her brother came after you?"

Sean sighed. "Yeah!" he looked at them resigned. "It was Gina, Chelsey's best friend Gina," he blurted out abruptly. "Sick, isn't it? Her and me, Chels' two closest people after her family. Chelsey was the one I wanted to be with, but I got scared. Commitment, settling down, betrayal, divorce. I could see it happening in my head. I didn't give us a chance. Gina turned up at the flat. Made it very clear she wanted to … You know the rest." He looked at them, his one open eye now clear and direct. "I think Gina did it deliberately. I don't know if she knew Chelsey wanted to surprise me that day, but I got the impression she was angling to get one over on her BFF if she could. It didn't seem to matter then, but now … I guess I have to hope she will be honest about what we did."

"When did Gina leave? Straight after Chelsey found you, or did she stay longer?"

Sean sighed. "Once Chelsey caught us, the way she looked …" Sean's face echoed Chelsey's pain. "It didn't seem to matter anymore. I knew I'd lost her. We got dressed and sat in the lounge, drinking. She left not long after and the boys came round, Gavin, Paul and Ashley. I wasn't in the mood but I had arranged a games night for us so I went through with it. Paul and Ashley went off on holiday Wednesday afternoon, and I haven't seen Gav recently. I don't know if you could find them, but they should back me up. All three left my place on Wednesday morning."

Anne allowed her curiosity loose. "Did Gina know how serious you two were getting?" she enquired. "It seems strange that Chelsey's BFF would screw her, what were you Sean, boyfriend, fiancé, baby papa?"

"Seemed strange to me afterwards when I was using my brain to think. I asked Gina the same question. She was slightly tipsy by then and laughed at me but then muttered something like 'because you were hers'."

"Why did Eve lie for you Sean," Justin asked.

"Not sure she did. I was round her place the night before, Monday that would've been, helping with those shelves. I think she just confused the days."

"Know anything about her van being stolen?"

"No! When did that happen? Poor Evie!"

"The same night that Chelsey was killed, Sean. Stolen from right outside your apartment block. A van, Sean, that could easily transport a dead or unconscious body. Can you see why I am interested in your alibi for those hours after Chelsey ran out of your apartment?"

Sean's shock was genuine. He had never seen himself as a definite suspect in Chelsey's murder until now. He hadn't made any connection between what had happened that afternoon with Chelsey's death. Also, he had not known about the theft of the van. Motive, means and opportunity were all his, yet Sean had not realised how it mounted up to him being their prime suspect. Except Justin felt a niggling discomfort that made him doubt it was true.

"You had better hope that Gina, Paul, Ashley and Gavin support your story when we speak to them. Give us their addresses Sean, and we will follow up. You say this Paul and Ashley were off on holiday?" Anne said.

"Yeah, but only for a brief break. They were heading down to Cornwall for a few days because of the surf. Back this coming Monday, they said."

She handed over a sheet of paper and a pen. "Just write down their names, addresses. Oh, and their mobiles if you have those numbers." She instructed then watched the paper fill with his neat writing. "By the way, do you have any idea where Chelsey's phone might be?" She added as he returned the pen and paper.

"Sorry no, not now. That afternoon, yes. I followed her down the stairs once I had some jeans on. By the time I got to the entrance, she was gone, but her phone was on the floor in the main doorway. I took it back upstairs and put it on the dining table. I had some crazy idea I could take it back to her and we could get over this." Sean shook his head, "Stupid, huh? Anyway, I noticed it had gone just before you guys turned up at my door."

"Could someone have moved Chelsey's phone out of the way when your mates turned up? Did you look for it after we left?"

Sean nodded, then hesitated before replying. "I wondered if Gina might have taken it. I dunno. It just seemed likely when I thought about what she said. Funny, I never thought of Gina as jealous of Chelsey or something. Maybe she saw it as some sort of trophy."

"OK, leave that for now. Tell us about your mate, Gavin, is it?"

Sean looked up, obviously surprised by the question. "What? Sorry, what has he got to do with all this?"

"That's what we're asking you Sean. You seem to be the only connection between Gavin and Chelsey. Tell us about Gavin." Anne followed through.

"OK! I told you my parents split up, well … I was a bit of a fool, no, a lot of a fool, and acted out. I ended up in Ockham young offenders for a short while. I met Gavin there, Gavin Lombard. He's a bit of a knucklehead sometimes. You know, hit first, talk second, if he gets angry about something. We looked out for one another inside and continued after we got out. He's a mate."

"Would this mate do anything you asked him to?"

Sean frowned, "What do you mean?"

"Well, would he take care of problems for you? Say you thought Chelsey was seeing someone else."

Sean grunted, "Not likely, not Chels."

Anne made a note. "Fair enough. However, if you asked, would Gavin follow Chelsey, to keep her safe or whatever?"

"I suppose," Sean answered slowly then, "Shit!" He looked directly at Anne; eyes narrowed. "Gav has made a try at a couple of my ex-girlfriends after we've split up." Sean shrugged. "Occasionally, he got lucky." Sean frowned, adding, "He would never have gone after Chelsey. He had a real soft spot for her. More likely, he was being protective of her. She was that kind of person you know, warm, generous, someone you want to be around." He shook his head. "Also, Gav knew Chelsey was special to me. Oh! Tuesday is Gav's day off from the garden centre because he works the weekend." He looked brighter, more cheerful when he asked, "Was he with Chelsey? Could he help with who killed her?"

Justin nodded, "Possibly. We have evidence that he was following Chelsey during the early part of the day when she was shopping and possibly when she went home. Did he say nothing to you about his following Chelsey when he came to the games' night?"

"No, I didn't ask Gavin to follow Chelsey. No, he said nothing at all to me about Chelsey that night. If we had been trying to protect her, or Gavin had on his own, we made a bloody awful job of it. I don't know why Gavin would have been following Chelsey that day."

"Fair enough," Justin remarked then, "we just wanted to know whether it was your idea, considering it was her relationship with you that was the motivation for the hate mail Chelsey had been receiving."

Sean sat frozen for quite a while, then he took a deep breath. "Oh God no," he whispered, "oh no!"

"I am afraid it was. She had deleted most of it from her computer, emails and so on, but our tech department retrieved the information." Justin grimaced. "Pretty awful stuff from their report. It made me feel sick. Every message was full of vicious hatred and there was a constant stream of them. Warnings to stay away from you and graphic descriptions of what would happen if she didn't. The technicians are trying to trace the origin. As well as that, Chelsey had been getting anonymous letters through the post. Same kind of thing but made up of glued on letters."

Justin's eyes narrowed as he watched for Sean's reaction. "She must have cared for you deeply to defy those vicious threats. You had no idea, did you? She never told you what was happening?"

Sean's reply was slow, his voice husky. "No, I didn't know. She never said." Unconsciously he emphasised she which caught Anne's attention.

"Chelsey might not have said anything to you, but someone else had?"

"Yes." a stronger response this time. "Not about Chelsey being threatened, but my previous girlfriend, the one before Chelsey and me got back together. She broke up with me over some nasty phone texts she'd received. She showed me one of them. It was pretty graphic, ugh!"

"Add her name and address to the list please Sean." Anne returned the pen and the list to him. "We need to speak to her. By the way, you haven't written down an address for Gavin, just his mobile number."

"Yeah sure. Oh, Gavin is sofa surfing at the moment. He got chucked out of his digs. He was staying at my place for a few days, then said he'd found something, but it wasn't quite legal. I thought he meant a squat, but he wouldn't say where."

"Thank you, Sean. We will be talking to Ms Crane, and," she glanced down at the list, "Ms Stacy Robson. For the moment, you can go home, but we may have more questions for you later."

Anne formally ended the recording of the interview and they escorted Sean to the front desk. Eve was waiting, had been waiting quite a while, it appeared. She turned at the end of her pacing when she heard Sean's voice. Striding to claim him as soon as the security door opened, glaring furiously at Anne and Justin. Sean shook off her concerned hug.

"I'm fine Evie. They don't rough you up in the back room anymore, you know." He took a deep breath and patted her shoulder. "Thank you for coming to collect me," he added more calmly, then turned to face his interrogators. "I guess I must be your prime suspect with everything you've learned. I know I didn't kill Chelsey, so find the person who did."

Evie grabbed his hand to lead him out of the building. "You look shattered. Come on, let's go home. You can stay at my place tonight. I can look after you."

Anne chuckled before commenting quietly for Justin's ears alone, "If our Mr Trent isn't careful, he'll be Adam to her Eve before he's aware of what's happening." She grinned, her dark eyes full of mischief, watching the possessive way Eve walked out of the station with her prize. Justin laughed, despite a slight frown when he thought Eve paused and her shoulders tensed for a fraction of a second. He shook off the feeling easily, distracted by what they had just learned. "We have motive for him, but means and opportunity are becoming more problematic. Take Julie and bring Ms Gina Crane in for an interview. Find that damn phone! I think Sean might be right and Gina does have it. Either she, Sean, or a resident of those flats switched it on this morning. Ray and Chas can assist with the CCTV trawl. It is even more important now, not only for Chelsey's movements that evening, but also Sean, Gina Crane and Gavin. Get Paul to speak to Sean's previous girlfriend about those threats, see whether she has any record of those texts, emails or ordinary mail."

"And you sir?"

Justin grimaced. "A chat with the Chief Constable and then a date with Mama. It is the fifteenth anniversary of the restaurant starting up." He caught her expression of envy and chuckled. "How would it suit you if I asked the restaurant to provide a buffet lunch for the team? I think it is time they sampled the family's magic touch with food."

"You've got a deal!" Anne confirmed enthusiastically and led the way back upstairs.

13

Justin caught Thomas's start of surprise reflected in the mirror where he was checking his appearance. He managed not to laugh out loud, but could not control the gleam of amusement in his eyes but it was tinged with sadness. He knew what Thomas was seeing. It wasn't Justin's attractive features or his broad-shouldered physique that had momentarily widened Thomas's eyes. They had known each other too long for that.

Thomas shook his head and grinned an apology. "I know, too much reading the wrong books as a boy," he commented. "I just can't equate you possessing a reflection with what you are."

"What am I really Thomas?" Justin turned to face him, suddenly serious. "You came up with the analogy for my condition. Perhaps we should think again if even you are afraid of the images the name conjures up."

"In all the years you have had this curse, no one has found a cure?"

Justin's voice was sharp edged with bitterness. "I doubt there is such a thing. Perhaps the cure will be when all the seven deadly sins disappear from humanity. Perhaps when there is no more greed, hatred, jealousy or desire that drives people to kill, rape or steal. After all these years, and there are many more than even you can conceive, I do not believe there is a cure, only a way of controlling the blood lust." His lips tightened and his face showed the heart-deep sadness he was feeling. "We had better get back to the festivities or Mama will come to find us."

Shame faced at the unintentional hurt he had caused his friend, Thomas nodded. "True, in which case I'd better hurry. No 'men only' sign will keep her out."

Justin strolled back into the main room of the restaurant and out to the marquee, erected for this special occasion, on the precious lawn in the garden. The evening was dark, sparkling with millions of stars. The soft cool glow of a full moon acting like a spotlight. A beautiful but cool night to celebrate fifteen years of Mama's restaurant's first opening on the High Street. The marquee was full of laughter and conversation, music and song. Justin looked around for Mama and her family. He spotted them on the far side of the marquee just as Thomas came to stand beside him. Beside Mama was a man in jeans and tee-shirt, about six feet tall. He was much bigger than Mama's diminutive five feet two inches. Tee-shirt guy loomed over her, standing far too close, in Justin's opinion. From the other side of the marquee Justin could see that Mama, as feisty as ever, was giving the man a piece of her mind in no uncertain terms. She emphasised what she was saying by waving her hands in the air under the stranger's nose. Justin hurried through the crowd to join them.

He arrived as Mama finished with, "Go back to your so-called boss and tell him to go to hell!"

The young man obviously had his instructions if the family refused his demands. He turned towards the nearest table, behind where Justin was standing. Justin glimpsed the pinpoint gleam of his pupils as he paused, gazing absently around the marquee. Tee-shirt guy resembled a robot programmed to follow orders without thought. He bent to upend the table. Before the contents crashed to the floor, drawing everyone's attention, Justin grabbed his arm and drove a knee into the back of his legs. Tee-shirt guy's knees gave way, unbalanced he bent down sharply over the table. Gasping, he stayed in that position to ease the pressure on his arm. Justin twisted just sufficiently to show his captive that he should not struggle, then spoke quickly into his ear. "Look around you fool. You should be able to recognise three-quarters of the people here. Have you any idea what will happen if you attempt to smash up the place?"

He knew he was not getting through the drug haze when the man began struggling despite the pain. Without hesitation, Justin knocked him unconscious and hurriedly hauled him out of the marquee through the entrance behind the family. Mama promptly closed off the exit with a pair of chairs. Only Thomas, saw what happened, everyone else being deeply involved in having a good time.

Outside the marquee, Justin held up the unconscious body with one arm. Tee-shirt guy's arms were trapped by the hold. To Justin's surprise, as he came back to consciousness, he didn't even try to call for help from the one distant passer-by Justin had noticed far down the road, heading in the opposite direction. They reached the car before anyone else appeared.

Justin paused, now in a dilemma. He had intended to hand his captive over to Inspector Holmes' men but, in his present state, he would tell them whatever they wanted to hear, then remember nothing when he came down from his drug of choice. Justin remembered Thomas's reaction to his reflection tonight, even though he had known Justin's secret for twenty years. Helped to overcome its difficulties, still he had shown fear. Even Thomas expected the mythical stereotype of Bram Stoker's *Dracula*. How would a stranger react to a horror movie scenario? He might gain more information from playing the role than doing the thing legally. Justin unlocked the Bentley and opened the boot.

"There you are, a nice cosy space to sleep. No one will bother you here," he said to his captive. Justin couldn't quite believe it when the young man simply climbed in and lay down. "What in Hades had he taken?" He shut and locked the boot. It would be a tight fit, but not for long. This particular addict was going to have the most nightmarish withdrawal symptoms Justin could devise. The thought made him smile tightly as he got into the driver's seat. He started the engine and drove smoothly away. In such a piece of precision engineering, it was a swift and easy trip back to the manor. With hardly any traffic, it took less than fifteen minutes.

Justin pulled up alongside a plain, insignificant wooden door that opened into the oldest part of the manor. He got out of the car, opened the boot, and hauled out his captive. Before there was any protest, Justin slung him over his shoulder, ducked through the door, and strode easily down a short flight of stone steps. The stairway spiralled down into what had been the under croft of the original medieval manor. Justin grinned in the utter darkness as he crossed the wide empty space. His foot knocked against something that gave a metallic ring as it slid across the cold stone. He reached down for the chain, allowing his burden to drop gently onto the floor. Tee-shirt guy tried to struggle to his feet and fight, but it did him no good. Locking the leg iron around his ankle, Justin stepped back.

"The chain from your ankle is secured into the stone wall, which is four feet thick under here." His quiet voice echoed around the vaulted chamber. "To your left is a bucket, should you need it."

Justin placed a large bottle of water next to his captive, then silently faded back into the darkness before he turned and walked back to the staircase. He listened to the rattle of the chain and his prisoner's grunts of effort, which made him smile. The youngster was certainly determined, there was no doubt of that. Justin headed back up the stairs.

Fortunately, the return journey was as easy, the road still clear of traffic. Justin parked the Bentley in the same space, arriving back at Mama's as the anniversary toast completed the congratulatory speeches. A reassuring nod and smile to Mama was all he could do in the crowded marquee. She blew him a two-handed kiss in response, although he knew she would want a full explanation as soon as he could manage it. Thomas joined him, handed him a glass of burgundy.

"I saw you leave. Anything I can do?"

Justin shook his head. "Thank you for the offer, but this is best left to me." He saw Thomas's look of concern and held up his right hand. "I solemnly swear there will be no lasting damage and no extra bodies." He grinned and pointed at the dance floor. "Go dance with your other half," he said noticing Ryan glancing their way. "The band is definitely playing your tune."

Justin watched the guests say their goodbyes to the family. There had been no further interruptions to the festivities, much to his relief, and now the celebrations were drawing to a successful close. The clear, slightly crisp, night offered Justin the opportunity to clear his thoughts. Knowing Thomas and Ryan had arrived by taxi, he offered them his car to get home. He gave the car keys to Thomas, anticipating the freedom that would be his on an early morning walk. They said their farewells to the family before Justin led his friends to where his car was parked. He waited until they drove away, then turned out of the back streets.

He walked steadily along the High Street, now almost deserted in the early morning darkness. The street lights having automatically switched off just after midnight. Here and there among the shops, the darker, larger shadows of people taking advantage of the shelter of the doorways to sleep for a while, shapes tucked into a sleeping bag or a nest of rumpled blankets. He walked silently past, careful not to disturb what rest they could get. Other creatures too were enjoying the absence of humanity: rats were investigating a pile of carelessly tied rubbish bags left out after the collection had gone through. Several cats, their eyes reflecting the small amount of light, crouched in the shadows, ready to pounce on any careless rodent. Justin turned off the High Street into the Lammas Fields, an area of green space dotted with ancient trees; criss-crossed with footpaths and bisected by a minor road. An ancient piece of common land so far overlooked by developers. Above his head, late feeding bats twittered as they fluttered haphazardly after the flying insects beneath the tree branches or headed for their roost beneath the railway arches supporting the main line into the capital.

His subconscious noted and dismissed the sounds of the night creatures while his thoughts concentrated on how to deal with his prisoner. He felt guilty about kidnapping the man, but knew this was an excellent opportunity to get useful information. He shrugged, guilty as charged, so there was no problem with doing far greater damage. Mischief sparkled in his eyes as a plan formed, then solidified from possibility to definite action. He could persuade his captive to tell what he knew without too much physical damage being done. He had not seemed to have a weak heart. Relying on autopilot, Justin suddenly stopped short, facing a brick wall. A silent chuckle acknowledged his mistake as he turned about face. After a century or more, there had indeed been some development in the fields. He had strayed into the grounds of a primary school, following his familiar route to the bridge across the river. He emerged back onto one of the pathways that lead into the centre of the open space. Justin realised that if he headed diagonally past the public playground, he could follow the street of houses down to the bridge. His night vision was as acute as that of any nocturnal hunter, which is why he noticed two darker shadows, one smaller than the other, beneath one of the ancient trees. From what he could make out, one was a bulky masculine shape with its back to the path. At first glance the other shorter figure looked vaguely familiar. Justin was thinking of tactfully veering away from the tree when the two shadows merged and two more figures hurried around the side of the massive trunk, one after another.

There was a shout of anger, then the sound of a blow, followed by a cry of pain. The smaller shadow staggered into the rough tree bark. The smallest of the attackers raised an arm for a blow, then suddenly doubled forward, landing on the ground. There was a vicious curse as he stood upright again, landing a hard blow that dropped their victim on the ground. A foot lashed out, connecting with the prone body now curled into a defensive ball against the confusion of fists and feet. Justin noticed the last arrival seemed to be forcing the original attackers away, standing protectively over their victim.

Justin realised who the body on the ground was. "Anne!" He shouted shocked and furious, then began running at full speed, towards the struggle. Two attackers hesitated, then another vicious kick landed before they took off at a run. The third attempted to lift Anne off the ground. Failing, he hesitated and was slower to escape. Justin grabbed at the last shadow, but his hand slipped on a jacket. A coughing groan from Anne lying on the root rutted ground stopped him from following. The running steps faded fast into the darkness, then he heard a motorbike roaring away into the distance. He had a picture in his mind of that last assailant. He was almost certain who it had been. Now, his first concern was Anne. She was trying to get up, but fell forward. Justin knelt beside her, talking to her so that she might recognise him, while he checked carefully for any obvious injuries. Anne pushed his hands away and tried to sit up.

"Will you keep still woman? You could have injuries I cannot see." He just avoided an unexpected fist, catching her hand in his. "Anne. It is Justin. You are safe now," he repeated quietly.

Her nose and mouth were bloody. One eye was already swelling shut. Her gaze was unfocused, suggesting concussion. Blood ran down from a cut on her forehead caused by the rutted tree bark. Justin was more concerned about internal injuries. She had taken two nasty kicks to the ribs and stomach area. He sat beside her, dialled the emergency services, and listened to her breathing ragged and shallow, hoping the paramedics would be quick to arrive.

He was relieved when the ambulance turned up within a few minutes. It must have been a quiet night. The blue flashing lights added a surreal blue tone to the scene. Two police cars followed, stopping nose-to-nose on the roadway and adding to the light show.

He stepped away, giving the ambulance team room to work. Anne was muttering broken phrases and words, increasing his concern. The first officer on the scene stood in front of him. Justin explained who the victim was and his own part in the incident. He pointed out the way the assailants had escaped. Even as he was answering the questions, Justin realised why he had recognised that last particular shape and frowned.

"Sir, is something wrong?"

Justin shook his head and then gave a brief description and a possible ID for who they might be looking for. "I think one of the three might be the same individual my team is looking for in relation to the Chelsey Harris murder. He was following her during the afternoon before her death. The boyfriend identified him as Gavin Lombard, currently of no fixed abode. Why he would attack DI Richards, I have no idea. I will go with the DI to the hospital. If you want to follow us, I can answer any further questions there, but I suspect you will have to wait until the morning to get any sense out of DI Richards."

He took a few steps away from the activity at the base of the tree and phoned Ray Williams. Ray answered quickly, despite the late hour. Justin explained what had happened.

"We have no address for this Gavin except for where he works, at Foxstones Garden Centre on Foxmoor Road. First thing tomorrow you and Chas get out there and wait for him, in case he goes to work as normal. Julie and Paul can organise search teams for the garden centre then join you. Ray, request permission from the manager for a search. I will wait in case we need a search warrant so call me if he agrees and will meet you there. I have to go, the ambulance crew are taking Anne to the hospital. I will stay with her and let you know the latest on her condition, as soon as a doctor checks her over."

The crew had got Anne into the ambulance by the time Justin finished his call. She continued to shift between almost lucid and semi-conscious incoherence through the brief trip to A&E. The ambulance slowed, then stopped. Anne, on a stretcher, was pushed through the automatic doors into the department, directly into a cubicle. The crew handed Anne over to the A&E staff and left. A duty doctor arrived, and Justin went back into the waiting area. He looked around and suddenly memories flooded back, as real as the room he stood in.

The urgent shocking phone call that had brought him speeding into the hospital. Bursting through the doors into a mass of pain and horror. Finding her at last in intensive care, broken and destroyed despite all their care, their expertise and the technology deployed to help her. The shattering of his dreams for the future as he heard through layers of cotton wool the consultant tearing his world apart. The long months of waiting, helpless, hoping, until his beloved wife followed their unborn child into that other place, leaving him empty.

Justin realised he was offering silent prayers to the long-lost gods of his youth on Anne's behalf. Why? He couldn't say. They had done nothing when he had to switch off Antonia's life support. However, Anne's case was not so serious and this time, perhaps, one of the Pantheon might just be listening.

The A&E doctor, having finished his examination of Anne's injuries, joined him and the police from the scene. He explained Anne would not be answering questions lucidly until the following day. She was suffering from a mild concussion. The officers completed their notes and sent their best wishes to Anne for her recovery before they left.

Justin was allowed to see her, but only for a few minutes, and given a warning that she would probably keep lapsing into unconsciousness. The staff were waiting for a porter to take her to X-ray.

Luckily, Anne was awake and more aware of her surroundings when Justin peered around the curtain. Her eye was closed, the bruising was developing into a purple rainbow very quickly. He knew the doctor was concerned about potential damage to the cheekbone and to her ribs, where the assailants had landed a couple of heavy kicks. Justin entered the cubicle and stood by the bed.

"Glad you are awake. The doctor is arranging to keep you in for tonight, possibly longer."

Anne frowned and attempted to shake her head, but thought better of it.

"Look, is there anyone who can get you some things from your apartment or do whatever you need?"

"No," Anne whispered, "Only me and Mr Claws, my cat. He'll need feeding." She smiled at the thought, then flinched when her cheekbone hurt.

"If you tell me where your keys are, I can feed the cat and pack some clothes for you. Is there a neighbour who would look after the cat or should I take Mr Claws home with me tonight?"

"Flat 3 really loves him too. Jane would be happy to look after him. She has a spare key to my flat. Just put a note through her door tonight. My keys are in my bag. The nurse put it under the bed."

Justin found her keys and reassured her he would feed the cat. He moved away from the bed as the porter and a nurse came to wheel her off to the X-ray department. He left the hospital and headed for her apartment. He would feed the cat and collect a case of clothes. After that, he had a different guest to take care of before dawn.

14

An agonised scream shattered the pitch-black silence, changing to a series of halting, gasping groans, fading into empty faint echoes. From oblivion to instant panic, the sleeper bolted upright. Crablike, he scuttled backwards until shoulders and head slammed painfully into the stone wall. Then kept pushing as if the solid bulk would give way.

Justin, leaning against the side of the stone pillar nearest his victim, watched with intense interest. He heard the terrified thudding heartbeat. The loud, fear fuelled panting masked Justin's own slight, involuntary cough after the effort put into the scream. He was relieved his prisoner's heart was healthy, and strong enough to take the shock. A dead man was of no use to him. Justin smiled slightly and shrugged. He had forgotten the depth of that primeval fear of the dark. It had been a millennium since he had experienced that feeling. He moved silently to where he had placed a brazier earlier and dropped a lighted match onto the prepared wood. The tall bright flames exploded upward; painfully dazzling eyes used to the windowless darkness of the under croft. The leg chain rattled as the youngster shuddered and shaded his eyes from the flames.

Justin waited until his prisoner could see fairly clearly, then stepped into the flickering light. Casually, he thrust an iron bar into the heat, then looked down and smiled. He knew the effect created by the flickering light, emphasising the white fangs; his eyes reflecting all the available light. Light and dark shadow combined created an unearthly face.

"What is your name?" he asked quietly. There was no answer except hurried gasps for breath. He wondered if he had overdone the horror film setting. "Your name!" he snapped coldly.

"Owen," was the whispered response. "Owen Thompson."

"Excellent Owen," Justin responded. "It is always wiser to tell the truth."

Justin already knew both his name and where he lived, having searched his pockets.

He grasped the poker, lifting the red-hot tip from the heat. Sparks scattered upward and faded. Owen's eyes fixed on the glowing metal.

"Well, Owen Thompson, why were you threatening Mama and her family tonight?"

"I didn't," he replied, then hesitated and frowned, "no, I wouldn't."

"You do not remember gate-crashing their anniversary party this evening?"

"No! I don't think I …" his voice slowed, paused, "but, but that wasn't real." He seemed genuinely puzzled and appalled by such behaviour.

"Perhaps your drug of choice gave you the idea. It seems a particularly potent medication."

For the first time, Owen showed defiance, even anger.

"I do not do drugs!" he stated emphatically, despite the visible trembling of his hands clasped tightly around his knees.

"But you did this evening."

Owen was shaking his head.

Justin attempted an evil chuckle, repeating, "But you did this evening. Why else would you be here, at this moment?"

Owen cringed, pulling his knees tighter to his chest, trying to become as small as possible. "Where am I? What is this place?"

Owen covered his face with his hands, trying to block out his captor, his surroundings, the image of the flames and the thick darkness beyond.

"Where do you think?"

There was silence. Justin waited. After all, he had many hours to play this game.

"I don't do drugs," Owen repeated. "Oh Fuck! Bloody Aston must have spiked my drink." He looked up at Justin's face, then looked away quickly. "Is this what tripping feels like? Why do people think this is fun?" he asked, then gasped as pain stabbed his stomach. Owen wrapped his arms around his legs, pulling his knees firmly into his stomach to ease the cramps. "This isn't real. It's just a nightmare. I told Aston I didn't want to watch a bloody horror film."

"Why would Aston harm you?"

Justin thrust the cooling metal back into the brazier. He leaned down close to Owen, face to face.

Owen shuddered, closed his eyes. "You're not real. I'm not really here," he said starting to rock back and forth. Owen was trying to convince himself rather than Justin. He continued. "Come on, get a grip. This isn't real. When I open my eyes, I will be back in the halls. I just need to concentrate. I will wake up in my own room. I will wake up in my own room." He repeated the last sentence, a protection mantra, then opened his eyes.

"I am still here, Owen. We are still in the hell of your imagining. You will not escape until you answer my questions."

He heard a sigh of defeat.

"Who is Aston and why would he dose you with drugs?"

"Aston was talking about busting up this anniversary party he knew about, as if it were some kind of joke. He said it would be a laugh. I told him I couldn't see the point. So, he poured us yet another beer and put on that weird film with an old lady who looked like my grandma. She was tough like my grandma too, even though there was carnage all around her, she stood her ground ..." Owen's voice slowed, "telling me off ... oh God!" Realisation hit him, a knockout blow. "It wasn't a film, was it? Did I really do that? Did I really scare that nice old lady?"

"Who is this Aston? More information if you value your health."

"Aston Buckland." He stopped abruptly, choking on his words as Justin grabbed his chin tightly, lifting his head sharply, painfully upward.

"Buckland?" he hissed the word, hatred throbbing in every syllable.

A gurgled gasp of pain from Owen made him ease his grip. The young man swallowed hard as soon as Justin released his stranglehold and rubbed the back of his neck to relieve the ache there. He flinched away from the menacing dark shadow on the wall when Justin took a step closer still. Owen quickly continued talking.

"Yes, Buckland. He's always bragged that his grandad was a real hard gangster in the seventies. Aston really looks up to him. He's always said he wants to follow in his granda's footsteps. I often wondered if he meant it." Owen sighed, "I guess he did."

"Did he tell you his grandfather's name?" Justin asked less forcefully.

"Yeah, really proud of him, Granda William, Aston calls him."

Owen began to slump down, still groggy from the after-effects of the drugs and the shock Justin had created.

Justin retreated into the darkness beyond the brazier's brightness. A kaleidoscope of images whirling like phantoms in his own head. William Buckland, a man he had thought long gone, dead in prison, after legal trial and sentencing. His expression grew hard, ruthless. Buckland still lived. Justin turned, took two steps towards the door, and stopped. He shook his head to clear the images, forcing himself to think. No! Vengeance could wait. There would be time to deal with that personal problem when he had dealt with the threat to the business owners and found Chelsey's killer.

"Hey! Hey! Come back! Don't leave me here," Owen called frantically.

Justin sighed and turned back. He could not leave his victim yet. He reached for an insulated mug he had left by the pillar before "waking" Owen. Owen was exhausted both emotionally by the betrayal of his supposed friend and physically from the terror Justin had put him through. The fear-flight reaction had turned to despair. Justin touched him lightly on the shoulder. Owen jerked away, but it was a weak protest.

"If this is my nightmare, why can't I make it stop?"

"Tell me where I can find Aston and it will stop. I promise, you will wake up safely in your own bed as you wished."

Owen didn't hesitate. He blurted out the address, adding, "Serves the bastard right after what he did to me."

"Thank you, Owen. Now drink this and all your nightmares will simply disappear. I promise!" He moved the mug so Owen could see it clearly. "You must be thirsty and hungry by now."

Owen looked up suspiciously, blinked rapidly, then grabbed the cup. He was so desperate to escape he didn't care if it was poison or acid or just plain hot home-made soup. He wrapped his hands around its warmth and sipped. Justin caught the look of surprise and pleasure on Owen's face and smiled out of sight of his victim. Beth's soup was delicious, he knew from experience.

He caught the empty cup before it hit the floor when Owen succumbed to the sleeping draught he had mixed into the liquid. Effective but otherwise harmless, the draught would even do him some good. The herbs would alleviate some symptoms of the hangover from the night's horrors. Justin unlocked the padded leg shackle, checking for any swelling or bruising, luckily there was none. He lifted the sleeping form onto his shoulder, carrying Owen with little effort up the stone stairs and out to the car. He would keep his promise to Owen and make certain he was in his own room before he awoke.

† † †

Justin pulled back the duvet on Owen's bed and lowered his burden gently onto the mattress, then covered him with the duvet. Owen muttered something and snuggled into the pillow. Justin grinned, waited for Owen's breathing to slow and deepen, then left the room.

Fate had been on his side: the party on the floor above, still booming energetically through the building, meant the hosts had left the front doors to the student flats on the latch. Not only that, but they had put up a sign outside to say so. Justin had simply walked in and carried Owen up to his third-floor flat. Luckily, all the other residents seemed to be at the party, or had made themselves scarce elsewhere. He had encountered nobody. The same was true when he left Owen in the arms of Morpheus, walked out of the block of flats, and headed back to his car. Justin checked his watch, surprised to see there were still several hours free before he could collect Anne from the hospital. He had the perfect way to use up the time.

With only the odd late night taxi driver to bother him, he drove to the address Owen had given him for Aston Buckland. It was in a rundown part of town. He pulled up at the corner of the road and walked to the house in the middle of the terrace. On one side, the front garden was being used as a car repair shop. From the thick layers of rust on the derelict engineless hulk, no repairs were happening. The other side had pretensions towards being the town rubbish dump from the number of split and decaying refuse bags spilling over the garden. Just to be different, Buckland's squat boasted an amazing crop of tall, energetic weeds. Justin waded through the dense mass towards the front door as the early signs of dawn lightened the sky. The door was in a surprisingly good sturdy condition with a shiny new lock. Justin took a small leather pouch from his pocket. Twenty seconds later, the door swung open into a dingy hallway. Justin replaced the picklocks with a lighted torch and entered cautiously over the slippery pile of advertising leaflets and circulars.

To his left a staircase lacking a banister rail and several treads led up to the bedrooms. He paused, listening, but could hear only a low vibrating hum. He opened the door to his right with some effort. The room was completely empty, no furniture, carpets, or curtains. The windows boarded up, allowing in very little light. A second room in the same state as the first, then the tiny derelict kitchen with signs of an old fire on its damp smoke-stained walls and ceiling.

Carefully testing each tread, he went up the stairs. A bathroom with a working toilet, from the way it was dripping, reasonably clean. A front bedroom deserted although there was a useable looking bed. An empty small bedroom, then Justin came to the third bedroom overlooking the back garden. The humming was louder upstairs. Justin listened at the door to the bedroom. This room was the source of the constant hum. He could feel the vibration through the wooden door. He opened the door to intense heat and bright light, illuminating many familiar potted plants, all of them shrivelled and dying.

He bit back a vicious curse and closed the door. Buckland, if he had been staying at the house, had left in a hurry. The condition of his marijuana stock was evidence of that. Those plants, if harvested, would have netted a good sum for the gardener. Justin had to decide how he could let his colleagues know about the drug farm without giving away exactly how he had found out. Owen was about to become an anonymous informant.

The sun was a little stronger and had burned off the pale pinks and blues of dawn into the bright blue of a warm spring day. He relocked the front door. Justin took out his phone and checked his watch. He still had a couple of hours before collecting Anne. Justin hoped she would not object to the Bentley when he drove her to his home, but guessed he was in for an argument. Tough! She would have to put up with it. He dialled Inspector Holmes' personal mobile.

"Holmes. Hi, Justin, what can I do?"

"Hello John. I had word from an informant late last night of a marijuana plant cache. I have always found his information accurate, so can I give you the address?"

Report made and sure John Holmes would take action, Justin wandered back down the road to his car, heading for the office for a couple of hours before collecting his acting inspector. He couldn't understand the reason for the attack on Anne. Was it some revenge attack from an old investigation? Had someone followed her from wherever she had been? They certainly knew where to find her, and the attack was serious. Whoever they were, they could not have known her personally. It had been obvious that her ability to fight back had been a surprise. Justin frowned, trying to recall the memory. There had been a few moments when he had not seen what happened except as a blur between other trees. At the beginning, his memories had distracted him. Then he had thought what he saw was nothing out of the ordinary until he had recognised Anne. He could have sworn there were three people involved, but he could not recognise them with any confidence. They had just been darker shadows against the night. Two of them had been wearing the typical youth uniform of hoodies and dark jeans. The one he had almost caught had been wearing a leather jacket. That was why his grasp had slipped and why he had suggested Gavin Lombard as a possible suspect. He switched on the engine and headed down the road.

Anne was looking a hell of a lot better, despite the very obvious bruising. Justin laid the case he had packed on the bed and went out into the corridor to wait. He was talking to the ward sister when Anne slowly emerged to join him, a small rueful smile on her lips.

"Now I know what a tortoise feels like. Completely frustrated because it can't keep up with everybody else."

A smile acknowledged her comment. Then when he produced a wheelchair for her use she protested strongly. Justin ignored her grumbling, took her case, and looked at her rather fiercely.

"It is hospital policy until you leave their care, so sit down or I will carry you out to the car and make a bigger spectacle of us in public!" he threatened, meaning every word. Then added more quietly, "I thought you might like to head for your place, see Mr Claws, who is fine by the way, and pack a few more clothes. You are staying at my place for several days while you recover, and where my housekeeper is happily waiting to pamper you."

She attempted to continue her protest, but he interrupted her.

"No! Stop being so damned independent! It was the only way the hospital would let you leave today. If you refuse my invitation then I leave you here and head back to the office, which you will not see for at least the next fortnight. Besides, I have kept my promise to you."

Anne frowned at him, a question in her eyes. "There is a buffet lunch from Mama's Place waiting at the house, and I want to get there before the rest of the team arrive and polish off the lot."

Anne managed to keep quiet until they got her into the car and were on the way to her flat.

"Thank you," she said brusque with embarrassment.

"You are welcome."

"But I can't stay with you. You're my boss! Besides, I have neighbours who can and will help me."

"Anne, you really can stay with me. You don't even need to see me except at the office. I have more room than I can use and a housekeeper who loves having the house full of people. Thomas Doubleday lives right next door if you take a turn for the worse, which I think is unlikely, but the hospital wanted to be sure you did not have a delayed concussion. Your neighbours seem to be lovely people and they are taking care of the cat and your flat, but they are working people and cannot be around all the time for you."

He pulled into a parking space at her place.

"Well?" He asked in such a way she knew she had no actual choice except between his place or the hospital for another couple of days. Justin had every intention of carrying out his threat to ensure she was on sick leave. He had recently lost a good friend and colleague. Anne was not going to be the second colleague he lost. He had hopes that in the future he could also call her a friend. Justin liked their developing working relationship. He heard her sigh heavily.

They had negotiated the stairs slowly and hobbled steadily to the flat because of Anne's bruises and now Justin sat in one of the cosy armchairs in the lounge while Anne, careful and slow, made her way around the flat. Mr Claws, a large long-haired silver tabby with amazing green eyes, had been fussed over and fed. He was now happily curled up, sharing the chair with Justin. Anne had phoned her friend and arranged for the cat to be looked after, although Justin had been quite happy to take the friendly furball to his place along with the owner.

"Look really, I will be fine here. You don't need to be so concerned about me."

So, she was feeling braver on home territory, was she? Not a chance!

"OK," he said to her surprise, then she frowned, suddenly suspicious. "But you stay here! No turning up at the office and no further participation in the investigation. You take official sick leave until you are a hundred percent better."

Justin chuckled at her expression. He knew she would hate being out of the loop. Anne was as hooked on finding the killer as he was. "Stay with me where I can keep you safe and you will recover more quickly. I will be happy to let you have office duty until you are not hobbling like a ninety-year-old. Well?"

"I'll get my case," she said rather subdued.

Justin halted the car as the imposing crest decorated gates opened automatically. He pointed out Thomas's house, which had originally been the gatehouse for the manor, and realised Anne was glaring at him, anger and shock on her face. He stayed silent as they drove smoothly along the tree lined carriageway and pulled up in front of the main house.

"Anne?"

Anne just turned and looked at him, silent.

He sighed, then said, "This is my home. I cannot help it if it is not a two up two down next to the railway line. I have lived here on and off for a very long time. We built the original fortified manor in 1070 and this house in 1750. Think of it as a fancy ruin or as a posh hotel if it helps."

He got out and walked around the car to open the door for her. Anne found it a struggle to get out of the Bentley and realised a smaller car would have meant the indignity of being pulled out of the seat, which would have been embarrassing and painful.

"I'm sorry, I'm just not used to being 'looked after'. Usually in my life it's been, deal with it yourself, and I've learned that lesson too well. Do it for yourself, Anne, because no other bugger will. I'm sorry and yes, I would love to spend time at this posh hotel. Tell me, does it have a pool, oh, and a spa?"

Justin grinned. "Actually, I do have a pool and a hot tub at the back of the house or there is the lake if you want a longer colder swim. As well as that, there is a couple in the village who are qualified beauty therapists and are happy to take new clients. I think we can accommodate Madam's wishes."

Beth the housekeeper, came through the front door, followed by her husband Martin, to welcome Anne. Justin introduced them to Anne. "Beth will show you to your room. Come down to the morning room when you are ready. Beth will show you where it is." He turned to glance down the drive and smiled. "I think by then reinforcements will have arrived."

15

Justin pulled to the side of the road. He switched off the engine and waited. If the garden centre where Gavin worked refused to co-operate, he was in place to get a search warrant should it be necessary. To pass the time, he went over his notes yet again, hoping something new would leap out at him. Unfortunately, anything new was still hibernating. His mobile filled the car with the theme from the Godfather.

"Mortmain! Hello Ray." He listened intently. "The manager is happy to co-operate? Excellent, I will not need to disturb the magistrate after all. Yes, Anne is sleeping and the X-rays showed no breaks, just heavy bruising. My housekeeper is happy to help her dress and ensure she eats something. Anne will not need to lift a finger to do anything for herself. She will probably hate it. What was that?" Justin grinned. "One tough cookie! Careful Ray or I will tell her you said that. I will collect her later and bring her into the office today." Justin listened again. "OK, I should be with you in ten minutes. I am on the right side of town to get to the garden centre. Are the others there? Good, wait for me."

He headed off down the tree-lined road. Some trees were showing pale pink blossom among darker red leaves while others were dressing in the fresh green of new leaves emerging into the sunshine. This was another of the more desirable parts of town. It backed onto the remains of an ancient estate given to the town by the last of a once aristocratic family. Woodland and parkland, by the acre, turned into public access with a trendy new coffee shop, a series of different water pools for children as well as several walks and rides for locals to enjoy in the summer months. Justin pulled down the shade against the glare of the early sun, low in a clear pale sky.

He managed the drive in the ten minutes, sliding into a space next to Paul and Julie's car. The team had gathered around Ray, who was talking to a man dressed in the green jacket and trousers of the garden centre uniform. Science Unit vans and police vans littered the car park. Beside them, uniformed officers and white overalled forensics officers waited. Ray introduced Justin to the garden centre manager.

"I can't believe Gav would do what your people said he did," the manager commented, shaking hands. "He's never been aggressive at all towards the female staff here. In fact, the opposite is true. He's always been very protective of them, keeping a watch on any stroppy customers they might have to deal with." He shook his head, then a guilty blush spread across his face. He looked down at the floor. "I was telling Detective Williams that I let Gav use one of our display sheds to sleep in for the last week. He'd used up his sofa surfing privileges with his mates. I know I shouldn't, but he also worked as an unofficial night watchman. It was an emergency and I've always found him a good kid, though rough around the edges." He glanced up at Justin, looking worried. "I can take you over there, but the staff will start arriving soon and we need to open not long after that."

"I am sorry, but this will take as long as it takes. We are investigating a murder and a severe assault on a police officer. Gavin is a suspect in both events at the moment. Unless we find something that indicates this was the original crime scene, we should be out of your way in a couple of hours. Could you put up a sign saying 'staff training'? As for the staff, could you ask them to come in a little later? We need to check any and all the areas Gavin would have accessed. As he was living here, did he have washing facilities, a locker where he might keep extra items? As an employee, I assume he had access to most staff and public areas?"

The manager nodded.

"Thank you. Now if you would show us where he was sleeping?"

It was a cathedral-like centre for a popular hobby, part of a smaller national chain. With two small but prosperous towns in its catchment area, The Malford branch made a considerable proportion of the chain's profits. They entered through a curving glass door that opened automatically into a display of suites of garden furniture. A display of various styles of garden lighting was hung along the walls and other 'got-to-have' paraphernalia. Beyond that were islands displaying bird food, ornate wooden boxes, gardening books, artisan cakes and biscuits on crowded shelves. To their right were shallow trayed tables of houseplants, succulents and exotics through which you had to weave your way to the checkout counters. Even here, no selling opportunity was missed and even more tempting goods were displayed.

Keeping the customer restaurant to their left, the group walked through a small corridor lined with gardening tools on both walls and out into the fenced off area between growbags, bags of soil improver and ornamental woodchip. They turned left through the displays of garden plants, shrubs and trees, all in their labelled sections from evergreens through perennials to tender annuals and herbs. Even Justin lost track among all the fresh growth, and the combined scents and perfumes were overwhelming. They went through an archway in the fence line to the garden structures area. Inside the enclosure, the buildings ranged from rustic pergolas, small sheds and summer houses to the latest designs in garden offices for working at home. One of the latter would have happily housed a family but was intended as an entertainment space.

The manager led the group to one of the smaller sheds with a row of tiny windows just below its roof on the two longest sides. He reached for the handle, but Ray stopped him with a word.

"Thank you, but we'll take it from here. Perhaps you could show my colleagues where the staff areas are and where Gavin mostly worked? Julie, could you take your team and search the lockers? Chas, Paul, and their teams can take the other outside areas. Direct our team here, please. Should you find anything, let us know."

Justin watched with amused appreciation when Ray realised what he was doing.

"Sorry sir," he said.

"Sounds good to me Ray. Let us see whether we can find anything here."

They both put on gloves and shoe covers before Justin lifted the latch and eased the door open. There were obvious but neat signs of occupation, although there was no one in residence.

"Our suspect seems to have done a runner," Ray commented.

"It certainly looks that way," Justin replied.

They stepped out of the shed, and Justin nodded for the forensics team to begin. It did not take long to search through the meagre belongings. A few blankets and a camp bed, the remains of a meal alongside a mug with the dregs of cold tea in it. A tattered paperback and a torch left on an upturned crate.

"Nothing useful," Ray said.

"No, only items that can be quickly shoved out of sight. I hope Julie has better luck."

One of the forensics people moved the pillow from the bed and eased it away from the wall.

"Then again …" Justin murmured as a rucksack was revealed between the wall and the end of the bed. On its side, it had been hidden by the pillow.

It contained clean clothes, neatly folded. One of the tee-shirts was wrapped around a passport. A wallet of cash and a credit card were discovered in the pocket of a pair of trousers.

Justin broke the silence by asking, "Would you do a runner without your passport and money?"

Ray shook his head, "Not unless I had an in with some of the illegal migrant gangs. Even then I would need more money than is in that wallet. Mind you, we have been given the impression that this Gavin is more of a wind-up toy than a thinker. Maybe he's just acting on survival instinct or he could know a guy who knows a guy."

"Yes, we have been given the impression that the density of his skull is slightly more than the density of a single brain cell by what Sean said and Gavin's own actions. We do not know that is absolutely true. Sometimes people judge on appearances too much."

"Well, the team is about done here. No weapon, in fact, nothing obvious." Ray looked at the damp and bare wooden walls. "It's a sad situation, so it is, for a young man to be in."

They left the team to bag and tag the shed's contents and wandered back through the myriad of outdoor plants for sale.

The noise of wheels on the tarmac path caught their attention. One older employee of the garden centre turned into the next aisle, going in the opposite direction. He had a large, Romanesque, garden pot balanced on an old-fashioned sack trolley.

Justin stopped abruptly, breathing in. He turned automatically towards the intense sweet aroma that teased his nose and mouth. Ray, two steps further on, stopped and turned.

"Hey you, stop!"

Mindful of Ray nearby, Justin called out before stepping quickly around the end of the shrub display into the next aisle. The man had stopped as requested, he showed no panic or upset. He simply waited calmly for them to catch up. Almost as if he thought they were desperate to buy the pot as just the right thing for their garden. He rested the base of the trolley carefully on the ground so the pot stood upright. To Justin, the dried blood glowed like warm red flames. To an ordinary human, they were almost invisible against the patina of the old wood.

"Show me your hands please."

The gardener shrugged and opened his hands palms up. His eyes widened when he saw the rusty stains caught in the creases of his palms.

"Well, I'm blowed! Damned trolley must have got damp. The blasted wood stain is leaching out."

"You came straight through to work. You did not see the manager at all?"

The man shook his head. "Just came through the gap in the fence at the back and started moving the stuff left from yesterday. I was a bit late y'see."

"If you would leave that trolley here," Justin asked, showing the man his credentials. "We need to check all the trolleys. Why not go take a break with your colleagues and clean off your hands. The work can wait until we have finished." He turned to Ray. "Get the team over here now. I think this is the trolley that transported Chelsey from the attack site to where she was found. See, two wheels about a shoulder width apart. I would swear that is dried blood, not wood stain." He did not add that he knew for certain it was Chelsey's rare blood group staining the woodwork.

The two scientists who had finished at the shed appeared. They tested the stain and confirmed the trolley stains as human blood. They logged and labelled the trolley. Then wrapped it in plastic and carried it away for further analysis.

"I hope they can type and match those stains to our victim," Ray commented softly.

Justin agreed absently, an uneasy feeling skittering down his spine.

"How come the trolley is here?" Ray continued, "Didn't the killer realise it was blood stained or didn't he care if we found it? Well, I guess that's pretty strong evidence that Gavin was involved somehow."

"Possibly, although it is still circumstantial. Just because the lad worked here does not mean he provided the trolley. Go talk to the manager about these trolleys. How many do they have and who uses them? Is it just staff or can the customers use them too? Meet me at the staff lockers. I want to see what Julie's team has found."

Ray went to find the manager and Justin headed into the main building, then through a door marked "staff only". The staff had a large reasonably comfortable room divided into a small kitchen area and a larger area. There were several sofas, a coffee table and several dining chairs. Along the length of the wall was a bank of staff lockers. Only one was open. It looked as if the locker was eating one of the science officers who was bending over, half in and half out of the long closet. Julie turned towards him.

"There's a bag of crumpled up clothes in here, possibly laundry. We're just going through the items."

There was a brief pause, then the scientist held up a black shirt by the shoulders. Across the front left was a medium patch of rust red-brown.

"It could be blood or it could be paint. My money's on blood from the lack of chemical smell," The scientist commented, voice muffled by the white mask covering her mouth. She placed the shirt in an evidence bag and it joined the other items destined for the lab.

Justin took a couple of steps back. There was altogether too much blood around this place for his comfort. The black tee-shirt had not soaked up Chelsey's blood. This blood group was much more common, O negative in fact. Justin's eyes widened with surprise. From the considerable time they had spent together since his arrival, he knew Anne was O negative with that slight suggestion of anaemia in her scent. Had his suspicion of Gavin Lombard's involvement in the attack on Anne been more correct than he had believed?

A short while later, the search teams headed for the vans. Paul and Chas came through from the stock areas to join Julie and Justin.

"Nothing obvious that links to our case. The people here, who knew Gavin were shocked we should suspect him, especially the women. They were unanimous that Gavin would never hurt a woman; that he was more likely to be protective. One thing, we had a chat with several garden contractors and a couple of delivery van drivers pulled up at the entrance to the stock area. Many of them use this room for a drink and a break when they deliver or collect. A couple said they had lunch with the staff here sometimes." Chas gave their report.

"So, it is not unusual to have relative strangers wandering around the private areas of the centre. Well done all of you."

Ray appeared through the staff door with the centre manager.

"Sorry sir, the centre sometimes loans out their trolleys to contractors and professional gardeners. They keep a log." Ray held up some photocopied sheets. "But it's not completely accurate." Ray glanced sideways at the manager, his expression resigned. "Also, the security system isn't all that good. The majority of the cameras are dummies. There is not a lot of footage, but I've got what there was." He sounded less than hopeful. "Something else that our friend here would like to tell you about Gavin."

The manager cleared his throat. "His staff record shows he came here from Colchester. He worked at a garden company there for quite a while before he got into trouble. I think he may have family there."

"Thank you for all your co-operation and please pass our thanks to your staff as well. My apologies for causing any inconvenience to your customers," Justin said as he shook hands with the manager.

The centre manager hurried away to open the rest of the garden centre. Only the shed area would be out of bounds until forensics gave the all clear. Justin thought the centre had been lucky. There had been no need to shut it down and keep it shut possibly for several weeks. He was sure the shed area would not remain closed for long, either.

"Right, I have to collect Anne on my way back to the office." He looked at each member of the team. "I'm reminding you now, just as I will remind Anne. She is confined to desk duty until I say otherwise. Don't let her persuade you into going against my instructions. She can collect and collate information on Gavin and chase up the possible Colchester link. Julie, you and Anne were going to interview Gina Crane again. Take Paul and go now. Your priority is Chelsey's mobile and the truth from Gina Crane. Bring them both into the station with you."

A tight-lipped satisfied smile from Julie, acknowledged his order. Julie and Paul glanced at one another. "She'll be there," Julie said, a determined note in her voice.

"Ray, I would like you and Chas back on Chelsey's timeline. We know she went home, changed and left again. According to Kate, she was extremely upset, feeling betrayed. Chances are, she was on autopilot when she left, so start from the bus stop near her work. Find where she went, who she met. Where can we trawl for witnesses?"

16

Justin collected Anne from the manor. She had been so eager she had been waiting in the doorway for him to show up. Justin helped her into the car, then drew in a deep breath and let it out slowly before joining her.

"Do not say a word until I give you permission DI Richards, that is an order," he said as he buckled his seatbelt.

Anne froze, mouth half open, then turned to glare at him.

"Yes, I am pretty sure you know what I am about to say, but I want to be very clear. You are on desk duty, no debate and no argument." A hint of anger lay behind his words, preventing her from interrupting. "The team all know and will not help you flout my orders. If you so much as set foot at any of our investigations sites before I give permission, I will insist on you taking two weeks' compulsory medical leave. Am I clear?"

Anne nodded, the facial bruising showing starkly beneath her still pale skin.

"Good, because Beth has already lectured me on taking care of you and I do not want to lose her good will." He started the engine and set off down the driveway.

Anne remained silent. Justin could feel his anxiety level increasing as the silence continued until they reached the office door.

"I was an idiot," Anne commented abruptly. "I went out to meet a supposed informant I knew nothing about, in the middle of the night, without being sure anyone had seen my messages. You have every right to be angry."

Justin realised he was rubbing his chest despite the scars having faded completely and forced himself to stop.

"Absolutely right. I am angry, but more with those who set the trap than with you, just about. You could have left a message on my mobile or called me. I was awake, I usually am. Jupiter Anne! Not so long ago, I was even more stupid than you and it cost me more than I can say. At least you had tried to inform somebody. You were lucky you came out with just bruises that will soon be gone. You will not wake in the night with remembered agony or attend a friend's funeral. We were careful and had full military support, even that is not always enough. You were out there on your own!"

"I can't even tell you why. I know better than that. Maybe I was trying to prove I could take care of myself. That I'm as good a detective and a better police officer than my ex? Hoping to get a breakthrough in the case? All the above." Anne shrugged.

"It does not matter why," Justin snapped back. "We have all done at least one stupid thing. Just do not do it again. You have nothing to prove to me or to the team. We know you are good at the job." He opened the office door and gestured for Anne to go ahead of him. He almost bumped into her when she stopped two steps into the room. It was then he realised the entire team had heard their loud conversation. He was aware of a silence and looked up to meet four pairs of very interested eyes. They were grouped around Anne's flower-filled desk. Julie and Paul both began to talk at the same moment, then stopped.

"Thank you, guys," Anne said quietly, her voice husky as she looked at the card. She sat down with a bit of a thump and winced. Her red face clashed with her bruises, while her unswollen eye was blurred with tears.

Justin heard her breathing catch and the sudden swift beating of her heart. Realising she was feeling emotionally fragile he stood behind her protectively. Then, to give her something to focus on, said. "Find out all you can on Gavin Lombard. You do not totally agree that he was one of your attackers. The women he worked with stated he is protective of women which supports your idea. Pull his records, his trial notes, anywhere else he has worked. You know." He left her to get organised and joined Julie and Paul.

"What were you two trying to tell me?"

They looked at one another and Julie nodded for Paul to report.

"We went after Gina Crane as soon as we left the garden centre. She's downstairs in interview two. She gave up the mobile immediately after we arrived, as if she had been waiting for us. It's with the tech boys now. Ms Crane seemed very subdued, perhaps realising how serious her situation actually is. She is now prepared to co-operate fully, so she says."

"Good! Then you two get organised and get down there. Get her statement about what happened that afternoon. Did she follow Chelsey or meet her later? What happened between Chelsey and her supposed BFF? Was Gina responsible for the anonymous letters? Get us some answers!"

They nodded and left the office. Justin walked into his own small space, closing the door to the outer office and shutting off the noise and activity. He paused, his mind distracted by nagging thoughts of William "Billy" Buckland — the name echoed down the years and he felt the tension and anxiety building. No! This time, if anyone got so much as a faint bruise, he would not wait for the law to take its course. He had checked and Billy Buckland, the man who had murdered Antonia, had been allowed out on licence. He was currently living in an expensively exclusive retirement home. Justin shook off what was rapidly becoming an obsession and sent off an email to Inspector Holmes asking for any update on the van and on the threats to Mama's Place.

He leaned back against the chair's headrest with an audibly heavy sigh, trying to concentrate on his own case. Chelsey deserved his full attention. He needed silence and time to make sense of the tangle of confusions. So much was still missing, so many suspects eliminated, then heading back to the top of their list. Justin searched for a pad and pen. He turned around to look at his own board of notes, pictures and chronology and began to work through every single activity one more time.

† † †

The email trilled a quick fanfare, breaking Justin's mental review of what he had been watching for the last forty-five minutes. As agreed with Julie and Paul, he had monitored their interview with Gina Crane. Even her solicitor had looked uneasy with the way she had answered the questions Julie and Paul had put to her. Chelsey's supposed best friend from primary school days had freely admitted a deliberate attempt to persuade Sean Trent into a sexual relationship with her. There was no remorse at betraying Chelsey, only a kind of spiteful triumph in her voice. Even the appropriation of Chelsey's mobile she viewed as a giggle, until Julie reminded Ms Crane that they could charge her with obstruction of justice. Gina Crane seemed not to understand the damage she had caused to her supposed best friend's relationship. Still, Trent did have free will. He could have refused her offer. Now that Chelsey's mobile was with the tech team for analysis, Justin was hopeful they would find something useful from the threatening texts if they were recoverable.

He watched the way his officers were working together and felt satisfied. Julie and Paul had formed a good partnership, which would only improve with time and experience. Already they were picking up on each other's body language and unconscious signals. That was possibly because of their budding relationship outside of work. Justin hoped it would not become a problem. Well, that development was his to watch with caution.

He glanced through the glass wall to where Anne sat, phone at her ear listening intently. The blue-purple bruising was starting to turn yellow around the edge of her eye. The swelling had reduced closer to normal. She was obviously a fast healer, although she was looking drained. He would have to persuade her back to the manor soon. His gaze moved to Ray and Chas face to face across their monitors, their concentration on the CCTV recordings collected from the various pubs, clubs, and eateries. The supposedly old-fashioned copper and the young fast-track graduate. They were learning from each other. Chas would fulfil his potential to be an excellent officer in the future under Ray's influence.

He turned his attention back to his screen, clicking on the email icon. He read the title and just managed not to cheer loudly. Time enough for that if things worked out the way he hoped. Although his Spanish was old-fashioned and stilted, closer to Latin than modern Spanish, he managed to whiz off a reply before closing the desktop and heading out to the main office.

"Listen up people!" he called out as he headed for the case information board.

Heads turned towards Justin, and his smile grew into a grin. "The Spanish police have contacted Mr Byett at last. I have just received an email from the local police inspector. Like a homing pigeon, Byett will be returning to his nest on the first flight landing at the local airport tomorrow morning. That is about six-thirty, according to the airline. I will meet him there and drive him to his house, where hopefully I can collect a download of the recording for the night of Chelsey's murder."

A mild cheer greeted his announcement, and a sense of cautious relief filled the room. "Ray, you and Chas must be square-eyed, considering the hours you have spent on CCTV watching. Anything worthwhile?"

Ray nodded. "We've found where Chelsey left the bus that evening. You were right, she was on automatic and it was her regular stop. She made her way to Nando's at the top of the town. She went in there but didn't stay all that long. Between road cameras and security CCTV, we've traced her to 'The Blue Boar' pub. Again, she didn't stay that much longer than having one drink. We'll be interviewing the early evening staff there today. After that she carried on up the High Street towards the club area. It might jog a few memories if we had some fliers we could hand out to the staff and the security crews at the venues." Ray's normal cheery tone shifted to quiet and thoughtful. He began tapping the end of his nose with a pen. "We can continue with the CCTV tomorrow." He looked up at Justin's face. "I think this might be the area she met up with her killer. Chas and I want to get up there and ask around. I know it might crash the budget, but we would also like to request a re-enactment of Chelsey's movements. You never know what we might get."

"That is worth doing. Just inform the Family Liaison Officer so she can forewarn the Harris family. It feels as if we have been trekking through a mire, up to our necks and not getting any closer to our goal. Now we have a few leads that will not, I hope, send us round in circles. Byett's recording might give us something or you two might find that perfect eye witness with total recall TV shows use regularly to break a case, but we never meet in reality."

Ray grinned. "In that case," he glanced across at Chas, "we better go find this mythical being."

Justin glanced at the office clock. "Phone me on my mobile if you find him or her. Otherwise, we meet back here tomorrow morning at eight for the update meeting."

Ray and Chas headed out of the door as Justin wandered over to Julie and Paul. "Anything stand out for either of you in Gina Crane's interview?"

Paul frowned. "Well, I think Gina Crane only ever saw Chelsey as some kind of rival. It seemed as if she couldn't wait to take away every little success Chelsey had that Gina didn't. She doesn't seem the type to have any deep feelings for anyone else, certainly not for Chelsey and I doubt for Sean either, except as some kind of trophy, maybe."

Julie nodded agreement when he looked at her. "Sir, I agree. She later tried to claim she was testing how genuine Sean's feelings for Chelsey were, but I doubt that. It gives us a motive though, jealousy of what Chelsey had achieved, good job, serious relationship, her own little business start-up. Gina's life, in comparison, has been chaotic since they all left school."

"So, you both think Gina should remain on our suspect list for now? What about opportunity? Could she have followed Chelsey or arranged a meeting later to 'patch things up'?" Justin considered, Gina alone, Gina and Sean together, or Sean alone. Every time they kept returning to these possibilities, none of which could be ruled out. He agreed with their thinking and said so. "Check her alibi for that evening. For the moment, they both remain on the board."

He turned back to Anne as she put the phone down at last. "Anything on Gavin Lombard?"

"Yes, something. I spoke to Colchester, and they are going to ask the arresting officer to call me. They are also emailing their file on Gavin Lombard. It wasn't a straightforward assault, was all they would say. The records will be here tomorrow and the officer will call when he gets back from court, but more likely also tomorrow. I gave them my mobile number just in case he is released earlier."

"Good. In that case, it is time I got you back to Beth's tender care. Until and unless the results of the CCTV follow up give us that breakthrough, or Gina Crane's alibi can be proved to be a lie, we have nothing that cannot wait until tomorrow. We can both be reached by mobile, if necessary," he added for Julie and Paul's benefit, then repeated to them the same as he had said to Ray and Chas, "Eight tomorrow morning, team meeting."

He waited for their wave of acknowledgement, then escorted Anne slowly and carefully from the office.

17

The dawn was still below the horizon, though the sky was a lighter blue-grey, hinting at a new day beginning, in the narrow spaces between the light grey clouds blown by the wind. There was a promise of warmth in the air, and the light cloud would soon burn away when the sun rose. Justin left his own vehicle at Shady Lane, choosing to take an official police car for the airport journey.

He drove through the mostly deserted streets around the one-way system and out towards the motorway junction. At this hour, the traffic on the motorway heading north was reasonably light. Justin saw the south bound carriageway was already slowing with cars queueing both for the Malford turn off and to join the motorway as the fastest route into London. He actually wondered whether it would be possible to drive the nineteen-mile route in the twenty-one minutes his sat nav calculated. If so, it would be the first time. He drove past the next two junctions and was into open farmland before the work traffic had built up sufficiently to warrant lower speed limits on the overhead signs. The sun was high enough to burn off the light cloud and deepen the blue of the sky. Beneath the warmth and light, the countryside shimmered in green, gold and blossom white. The trees and hedgerows had the freshness of new leaves and the first green shoots of planted crops were pushing through the dark brown plough soil. The grass shimmered like green silk where the ewes and their spring lambs grazed. Cattle were out on the pasture and horses cantered across tree sheltered fields. Everything shouted of new beginnings, a beginning that Chelsey Harris would never experience.

Justin couldn't shake off the sadness and anger that had rooted in his mind when he had found her. It had grown stronger with each piece of her story they had recorded. He remembered Ray's unexpected outburst that first morning. Some cases just got to you no matter how long you had been a police officer. Emotions he had thought long dormant were reawakening, strengthening his determination to find her killer.

The first sign for junction ten appeared and a short while later he pulled off the motorway and took a right turn at the first roundabout. Straight on at the next onto Airport Way. Two miles along the relatively new dual carriageway, Justin turned left into the main airport building precinct and parked in the passenger collection area as he had arranged with the airport authorities. Entering through the automatic doors, he glanced up at the arrivals' boards. Byett's plane was listed as delayed by thirty minutes with a new ETA of seven a.m.

Thankful to find a coffee shop open and Justin grabbed a takeaway, then settled on the plastic bench seats with a view of the arrivals' boards and the gates. His mobile buzzed, and he glanced at the screen. As he had anticipated, it was a text from Anne asking why he had left her stranded at the manor. He had done no such thing, in fact, had left her a note and got her a lift into town with Thomas, but she was not happy about being left behind. He sipped his drink and reflected carefully about how to respond. He had just finished a conciliatory text when the first arrivals were visible, coming along the corridor into the hall. A businessman, briefcase in hand and overnight bag on his shoulder, stepped out briskly towards a uniformed driver with a handwritten name sign. A pair of backpackers shortly followed the businessman. They paused, looking for signs to check directions to the coach stops and the railway station. A longer gap before the loudly announced arrival of an overtired brother and sister arguing. Harassed, fatigued parents shepherded the children along while pushing a luggage trolley between them. The nightmare journey with overtired children was one Justin could only sympathise with. He tossed his empty cup into a bin and stood up. The photo of Tony Byett in his RSPCA uniform was an unexpectedly good likeness. Brown hair speckled with grey, a suntanned face with a prominent nose and light hazel eyes, a mouth upturned at the corners that looked as if the owner was always enjoying a secret joke. The real-life man was just emerging from the luggage carousels via the green channel. Byett's tan had a new depth, though his face looked tired. Justin knew that Byett's journey must have started overnight, travelling to the Spanish airport from his villa. Then the long wait at the airport to book in and board the plane. A delayed flight so that the journey was longer than two-hours. Justin walked over and introduced himself, then led Byett away from where the main mass of passengers was now crowding into the arrivals' hall.

"Thank you for meeting me Chief Inspector," Byett's voice was quiet with an undertone of tiredness.

"My pleasure Mr Byett, to give you a lift home is the least I can do after you changed your plans to help us. I hope you were able to accomplish some of what you wanted in Spain?"

"More than I expected," Byett grinned. "I have some stunning pictures of mountain eagles and hopefully my recordings here will be of use to you. As soon as we get to my home, I can let you see what we might have caught." Byett nodded. "By the way, call me Tony."

Justin directed Byett through the exit doors and towards the car, thankfully clear of clamps and tickets. He unlocked the car for Byett to settle in while he placed the suitcase in the car boot. Byett relaxed into the passenger seat, continuing the conversation when Justin joined him.

"I'm sorry it took so long for the message to reach me. My partner and I were up in the mountains helping at a bird sanctuary project. I didn't expect to be needed here you see." He shook his head. "The camera was a means of getting some evidence against a badger baiting crew I know have been taking badgers from local woodland setts. Despite being illegal, badger baiting is on the increase. It's even rumoured that some minor landowners are allowing their lands to be used for what is a serious animal cruelty crime. Now you tell me I may have caught an even worse crime on camera."

Justin turned the car left at the exit and then around the next roundabout to head back past the airport towards the motorway.

"It is possible your camera caught something important to our investigation," he acknowledged. There was physical evidence of a vehicle parked where your camera was pointed. You may have recorded the point at which our victim's body was unloaded and taken into the woods." He slowed down as the traffic in front queued for the junction. "Was your investigation official?"

Byett nodded "Oh, yes! I had the landowner's permission and the support of your wildlife crimes unit. We have identified several people involved, but so far, they have avoided our attempts to catch them in the act." He glanced over at Justin. "I'm hoping there will still be some evidence of them being at the site which we can use?"

Justin nodded agreement. "I am hoping we can both benefit from your surveillance."

After that, Byett seemed disinclined to talk, content to relax into the passenger seat and doze through the stop-start return journey, which took more than twice as long as getting to the airport. The commuter traffic heading for the capital from the dormitory suburbs, had already built up. The density of traffic increased at each of the three further southbound junctions before Justin finally turned off the motorway and headed in the direction of the new housing estate where Byett lived. This part of the journey was less blocked with traffic. There was a natural pause between the work traffic already gone and the school run soon to start.

Byett stirred, yawned and stretched when Justin parked up in front of his house. It was a small, modern detached, indistinguishable from all the others except for the colour of the front door and the bright slightly shaggy front garden where one or two daring weeds were attacking the flower border.

Byett got out of the car and waved at the twitching curtains of the house across the road. "Ms James. Better than any CCTV she is." Byett grinned. "Probably keeps a detailed written record of everyone's comings and goings."

Justin opened the boot and Byett lifted out his case.

"Right! Let's get that recording for you and a decent cuppa for me."

He led the way down the narrow path, door key in hand. Through the front door, he placed his suitcase under the coat hooks to the left of the door, and scooped up a good handful of leaflets and post. These were tossed onto the telephone table beside the door to the lounge before Byett opened it.

"My computer's in here. I've only had it a few months, and it's got storage to spare even with the number of downloads from the woodland cam… Bloody Hell!"

Justin heard the shocked exclamation but could not see what had caused it until Byett stepped carefully back out of the entrance. He gestured for Justin to take his place.

"Sorry Chief Inspector, I don't think either of us is going to get anything useful now."

Justin silently looked around the living room and winced.

"I take it this is not your usual style?" he finally asked.

Byett shook his head forcefully. "No, I'm more of a neat freak." He was pale beneath his rich tan. He made a move to enter, but Justin's light touch on his arm prevented him. "Ah, of course, forensics and all that," he muttered, then added, "What do we do now?"

The devastation was horrific. Framed photographs on the floor, their glass smashed, books torn apart and scattered around the room from the bookshelves, a large mirror pulled from the wall and smashed over the desk that stood in front of the opposite wall. A desk which should have held a laptop and all its paraphernalia but was now adorned only with the shards of the mirror. The television was on its back, pushed off its stand, and the burglar had thrown a shelf full of DVDs to join the mess on the floor. A sound system had been partially removed but then left to dangle from the cables linking each part.

Justin twisted to look at the desk and grimaced. "I take it the desk was where you kept your computer?"

"Yes, locked in the drawer that's been smashed open. There's an awful lot of damage, but at first glance I can't see much that's missing. Shall I check upstairs?"

Justin shook his head. "No. Not at the moment. I think the best course of action would be to radio in from the car to report the burglary, then get you somewhere to stay temporarily."

Byett headed back out of the door. Still pale and obviously shaken by the destruction of his possessions, he managed to reply. "No problem. My brother lives not far away, in Swansmere. He's already looking after my dog. I'm sure he and his wife can find me a bed if necessary. How long do you think you will need my place?"

They reached the car before Justin replied. "Probably only for today. However, I want this place gone over in microscopic detail."

"Oh?"

Justin unlocked the car. "There are three possibilities here," he said. "You have been targeted by a random burglar, perhaps who discovered you were away from home, or your baiters have somehow discovered you are on their trail." He paused.

"And the third option?"

"Our murderer has somehow found out about your camera and realised what it might mean for them."

Justin reported the burglary and then phoned Anne to let the team know what had happened and that the morning meeting would be delayed.

They waited for the first police car to arrive and Tony provided an initial statement. Once the house was guarded and the forensics crew were on their way, Justin gave Tony a lift to his brother's home. It was a fairly short drive, although long enough for the urban scenery to blend into wooded countryside. They drove through the villages of Barham and Upper Barham climbing the long hill until they reached the traffic lights at the Common junction. They turned left and followed Common Road into Swansmere. Just the other side of the village Tony indicated they should turn right into a farm entrance. He got out and opened the gate for Justin to drive through. Justin pulled up to wait for Tony to close the gate. He was somewhat surprised at Tony's contented expression given the circumstances.

"You seem happier all of a sudden. Why is that?"

Tony chuckled, "My brother lives on what was the family small holding. It was always a happy place to grow up. I suppose that's why I always feel content when I visit here. When our mother died, we both inherited the properties here and in Spain. I was happy in my job and Dan's always been the farmer. We agreed that he would have the house and land and I would have the Spanish villa. Dan's bought more of the surrounding land over the years and now it's a proper farm."

As he finished speaking, they stopped in front of a pleasant detached house surrounded by a neat garden divided between vegetable patch and flower beds.

"Dan's wife, Judy does the gardening." He commented getting out of the car.

The front door opened and a large Alsatian bounded out of the house straight for them. The enthusiastically wagging tail and welcoming yelping were directed at Tony. There was no doubt he was Tony's dog. Just behind him, at a more sedate pace, a black and white, elderly collie added to the welcome. Dan and Judy Byett welcomed Tony with hugs and were introduced to Justin.

"Hope you've still got a bed for your brother at least for tonight?" Tony said with a rueful smile. "When we," he indicated Justin and himself, "got to the house it had been burgled."

Dan and Judy both showed their shock and concern. Dan called the dogs to order and suggested they all went into the house. Judy hugged Tony's arm.

"Of course, you will stay here. There's no question about that," she said.

Justin got Tony's case from the boot. Dan took it from him and carried it inside. Judy led the way into the living room.

"I'll put your case in the spare bedroom. We've just made a pot of tea and Judy was making biscuits this morning."

Justin sat down on one of the armchairs although he politely refused the tea on offer. Dan returned after a couple of moments as Judy bought in the tea things on a tray. Justin noticed Dan seemed worried about something. Over tea and biscuits Tony explained why he had returned early from Spain and what they had discovered at his home that morning. He was stroking the long dark fur of the Alsatian as it leaned against his leg. He took a drink from his mug.

"Bloody mess it is!" He shook his head angrily. "If whoever it was had got what they wanted, why do so much damage?" He looked across at Justin, "More important I suppose is, when did it happen?"

Justin agreed. "True. At the moment the burglary could have happened at any time from the day you left until last night. We will have to narrow down the time considerably."

Dan's worried look disappeared and his voice had quite a cheerful tone when he spoke.

"Well, I can help with that I'm certain." He glanced apologetically at his brother, "It could only have happened last night and after nine last night at that." Dan went rather red in the face. "See, we were there most of yesterday. Sorry Tone but Judy had a writer's group workshop at our place and I'd invited some mates to watch the England match. I borrowed your place. Your TV is better than ours anyway. After the match Judy came over, the guys left and we tidied up a bit. We didn't leave until gone nine I think."

"You are positive about the time?" Justin asked.

"Oh yeah, nine-fifteen at the latest when we left." Dan replied and Judy gave a confirmatory nod. "And we locked everything and checked all the doors and windows as we went."

"Thank you. Could you give me a list of your friends who were there with you? We will need to eliminate them from our enquiries as the saying goes."

"Oh, fingerprints and stuff, yes of course, although I met up with them again around nine-thirty at the Black Mare. It's our local in the village. We were all together until closing time." Dan went out of the room and returned with a hand written list of the invitees and their phone numbers and addresses. "Can I let them know the police will be calling, or should I not?" he asked as he came back into the room.

"I would ask you not to. The officers will explain what we need them for."

Justin took the list, folded it neatly and put it in his inside jacket pocket. Justin agreed to telephone Byett when they had finished at his home and said his goodbyes. Twenty minutes later, he was back at Tony Byett's house, but with little space to park, most of the parking space was now taken up with various police vehicles. There were people around the outside of the property, but none were inside until Justin supplied the keys he had borrowed. He then set a team of uniforms to go door to door and ask if anyone had seen anything out of the ordinary in the last few days. He glanced up at the house directly across the road, but there was no sign of twitching curtains and he suspected their potential prime witness was currently away from her house. Turning back to the crime scene, he noticed a familiar figure emerging from one of the cars.

"Good morning, Inspector Richards, and what are you doing here? I made it clear that you were on desk duty until I said otherwise."

"Sorry sir," she said without a trace of apology in her voice, "but I'm feeling a great deal better thanks to Beth's good care. I want to be back at work on the case proper. I promise not to tackle any suspects on my own …"

Justin could almost hear the silent addition of "for the moment". His coldly clinical gaze searched his partner from the top of her head to her sensibly shod feet. He had to admit Anne was looking much better despite the faded yellow and brown bruising around one eye. She was also moving more easily as they walked to the rear of his car to collect the required forensics' overalls. He sighed loudly enough for Anne to hear him and muttered something about insubordinate officers. He knew she would take that as permission and truth be told, he was pleased to have her with him.

As they headed for the house, Anne explained she had set the meeting back until the evening, Justin agreed that was sensible. They gave their names for the record and were directed to follow the path around the house to the rear garden. Being careful to step on the several protective plates already set onto the path, they eventually found Dr Elizabeth Caldwell, better known as Lizzie. She was the forensics team leader. She nodded a welcome to Anne and glanced questioningly at Justin, who introduced himself.

"Ahh yes, I had heard we have a new DCI," her voice was muffled by her mask but pleasant sounding. "This burglary linked to your murder then? We don't normally get such exalted company at a simple burglary."

"It is possible, which tells us there is an excellent chance that the recording had caught something vital to our investigation. Even so, there are other possibilities, one of which is an opportunist thief. We can take nothing for granted. This looks like an affluent area for the up and coming." Justin glanced through the open back door where the kitchen diner took up the back of the house. The large room appeared far less damaged than the lounge. He turned to glance back at the plates dotting the path. "Anything of interest?"

Lizzie glanced at the plates and pointed. "Possibly over there. We'll take photographs and moulds where we can." Her green eyes sparkled above the mask. "Take a look at this!" She moved aside the large leaves of a hydrangea to reveal a rubber cast, that was drying. "Your burglar left an impression pressed deep in the damp soil here. Your suspect stood here to cut the glass and get at the lock. In fact, you can see some dried earth patterns across the floor. Give me a few hours, then I should be able to tell you the shoe size, possibly the suspect's approximate height." She pointed at the gap between the plates, "From the stride pattern, also, if the imprint is good enough, the shoe database can tell us what type of shoe, more likely trainer, your burglar was wearing. Find me something to compare and I will tell you whether the wear patterns match or not."

She invited them to follow her in, avoiding other science officers in the kitchen area and some marked points of interest already indicated with yellow numbers in the first part of the hallway. "I have two of my team in here, but I suspect there is more destruction than evidence."

Anne looked around for the first time. "Why all this damage? It seems wanton somehow, as if the culprit was enjoying the destruction."

Lizzie nodded. "I agree, but whoever it was, they targeted the desk area the most. The TV and sound system seem like window dressing, but the desk has suffered some serious damage. We found the printer tossed behind the shed at the back of the garden. There are plenty of fingerprints around, but I would bet they mostly belong to the owners. I'm pretty certain our burglar was wearing gloves from the fibres on the broken pane where a hand reached for the lock."

"Either the evidence is gone because this burglar was linked to our murder or the RSPCA investigation was getting too close. None of this damage looks like you would expect from an opportunist burglary." Justin's forehead furrowed beneath the hood of the suit. "Six months in jail and a £5,000 fine would be serious enough to try for the evidence certainly, but how did they discover it was here? The same goes for our killer."

They left Lizzie and her team to their work and headed back to the car where they removed the sweaty hot overalls and stood to cool off before Justin unlocked the car for Anne. He stayed leaning against the car, deep in thought, before abruptly getting into the driver's seat.

"I hope the others have found something useful, perhaps a confession from the killer haunted by a guilty conscience, because at the moment we have hit a brick wall. Who knows what that recording might have shown? It could have provided us with a full view of exactly what happened and who did it."

Justin realised he was exaggerating and laughed shortly when Anne added, "On the other hand, it might have shown us absolutely nothing at all."

There was silence in the car. With both hands resting on the steering-wheel Justin leaned back into the headrest and closed his eyes.

"Three possibilities you said," Anne continued quietly, "opportunist possibly not, but the local boys can check that out. Forensics might get something as well. Secondly, the baiters Byett was investigating, what about them? Can't we check them out just in case they did get wind of Byett's investigation? Thirdly, our killer somehow found out about the camera, although I can't think how, and went after the recording. Is that likely?"

Justin opened his eyes and looked across at Anne, a slight smile softening his expression. "I like the way you think Anne Richards, I really do. There is a way we could help Byett with his case, and at least eliminate one of the three options at the same time. I need to talk to him again. I want his detailed information on the baiters."

18

Justin leaned back against the rough silver and black trunk of the birch tree, looking up through the shifting lace pattern of twigs and leaves shivering in the cool breeze. Across the blue-black sky, driven by the wind, dark grey clouds flowed over the face of the new moon.

His earpiece crackled, ending the nervous "what ifs" of waiting. What if the target stayed at home? What if the group chose a different site?

"Delta 27 to Delta 15," the crackle became words. "Target has left, travelling southwest towards your position."

Justin responded instantly, reacting to the adrenalin flowing through him. Good news! he confirmed receipt of the report. "Delta 15 to Delta 04, anything yet?"

The response was slow and whisper quiet in his ear.

"Delta 04 affirmative, two 4x4s in car park, six males I C one exiting the vehicles. Delta 04 moving down wind, four dogs with the suspects, now out and free. Looks like a digging out expedition. Two cages being unloaded, Delta 04 out."

Justin walked back to where his own team waited, along with other officers from the wildlife protection team. He moved silently, easily, over the rough ground between the trees. He heard an exasperated whisper "Ouch, shit!" in Ray's east London accent, followed by "Give me streets and pavements any day over this."

"Even with all the cracked slabs, rubbish and dog turds?" he muttered close to Ray's ear.

"Bloody hell sir," Ray responded, jumping at least a metre and a half in the air according to his delighted teammates. "You could've given me heart failure!" Ray turned to peer through the gloom at his boss. "How the hell do you manage so easily? It's pitch black out here when the moon is covered."

Justin chuckled softly. "I can see in the dark, of course. I did what my mother told me and always ate my carrots. She read about their goodness in a book about the Second World War. You should try some."

It had been agreed that each of his group would lead a team of three, and Justin would act as sheepdog herding the different individuals towards one or other of the teams. "Right! they have parked up on the other side of the wood. The badger sett is between us. You get to your groups, then wait. Do not move from your allocated site. I will not be expecting friends out there, so will act first and ask second, is that clear?" He waited for them to murmur agreement. "Good, now I will stir up the group and they should start to run."

"What about the dogs," Anne asked.

Justin grinned. "Nothing to worry about. I will deal with them." He turned to Paul, dressed similarly to Justin, with a camouflaged face. "You sure you can circle around between them and the cars?"

"No problem, just like an exercise with the territorials."

"Remind your teams that they get our suspects only after we have interviewed them." His earpiece buzzed and everyone froze until he nodded. "The leader has arrived, and they have moved out of the car park. They have a couple of spades and the leader is carrying a pickaxe, so be careful." He looked around. "Remember, they will come to you. Keep clear of the hollow, that is my area of operation." He pulled the night goggles over his eyes. "Go!"

As soon as the last person disappeared into the trees, Justin pushed the night goggles onto his forehead and the world sprang into life around him. A rustle in the undergrowth became someone's pet tabby out on the hunt. The trees took on their silver and black patterning rather than the shades of green of the goggles. Dark green floating dots became patterned woodland moths. Justin drew a deep breath redolent of fresh crushed herbs and grass, then set off at a run, aware of every tree root and shadowed dip along the rough path between the trees. He could hear men's voices and the excited whine of the dogs ahead. The rich loam smell of freshly dug soil, crushed leaves and badger informed him he was in the right area. He slowed, checking the direction of the light cool wind, and deliberately circled so the dogs could catch his scent. He stood waiting behind a large rhododendron bush, watching the men moving around the badger sett, two of them already digging down into the main chamber.

The moment the breeze blew harder, the dogs stopped nosing around and froze, before a cacophony of barks and growls erupted loud enough to wake the neighbouring estate. The body camera was recording all the events in the hollow until he switched it off. Then, free from any restraint, he strode forward, allowing the dogs to see him. They went frantic, drawing the attention of the men. One man shouted and signalled for his dog to attack. At first, the dog raced towards Justin, but then caught that strange disquieting scent again and slowed. Justin hissed, fangs gleaming, and the dog turned tail, racing back to the comfort of the group. The hunters had become the prey. The dog owner was Justin's first victim. He caught the man by the jacket, blocked a blow from the spade, and threw him into a dense clump of bushes. The man struggled to get out of the tangle just as the dogs were now straining to escape from the strange deadly predator. The other men were not so sensible. Justin watched what was happening. Three of them looked at one another, then advanced as a line of three, two burly men, more fat than muscle, and in the middle the leader, carrying his pickaxe, which he raised to his shoulder.

Justin chuckled, shifted his position, and grabbed the man on his right, shoving him with force into the axeman. They both hit the ground hard, while the left-hand man stopped, looked into the attacker's face. His eyes widened with horrified surprise then he turned and ran at full speed straight into a tree trunk. Justin watched him bounce and winced in sympathy. The final two, still near the badger sett, simply turned and hurried back towards the car park, accompanied by all the dogs. Paul's team would deal with them. The first man struggled out of the bush and also took off, but headed towards Julie's group. So far so good, Justin thought, watching the two on the ground untangle themselves. The one he had used as a club was moaning and trying weakly to get off the team leader. Justin waited until he struggled over onto his back, and his gaze focused clearly on Justin when the moon came out from behind the clouds.

"Run," was all he said.

The guy stopped pretending to be a stranded crab and made a good attempt at beating the four-minute mile following his colleagues. There were shouts coming from all around the hollow, his teams collecting the fugitives. The team leader still lay where he had fallen, axe cuddled to his chest. He looked up as Justin loomed over him.

"Are you going to try again with the pickaxe or are you going to put it on the ground and move away? Your choice! However, if you choose the axe, you will fail and I will stake you out, face to face, with that boar badger over there." Justin pointed to where the male badger had emerged from the sett and was watching them. "If you choose the other option, I will arrest you, but at least you will keep your face."

The axeman shoved the axe away and managed a decently speedy wriggle in the opposite direction. Justin gave a disappointed sigh, switched on his camera, and formally arrested the suspect. He helped him stand up and passed him to Anne's team, who appeared at the edge of the hollow with powerful torches switched on. A good enough excuse for not wearing the night goggles. He heard axeman babbling at his officers but didn't bother to listen, although he felt Anne look at him strangely she said nothing, turning away to supervise the prisoners. The back of his neck prickled uneasily as he wondered if he might have some explaining to do.

They separated the prisoners into individual cars for the trip to Shady Lane. Justin remained behind to supervise the dogs and the 4x4s. He knew, and hated the knowledge, that if the men were found guilty, or there was evidence that the dogs had been used for fighting, then the dogs would be put down by court order. He could only hope they would be spared, although that seemed a forlorn hope at best. Once the dogs were sent off to the pound and the cars were towed, Justin left the scene. It was getting on for four in the morning, which meant there was little traffic on the road and he arrived in time to see the last man being handed over to the custody sergeant. The sergeant also phoned Doctor Doubleday to come and treat some of their injuries. Justin was irritated. Now he would have to tell Thomas everything or Thomas would ensure he would never have a moment's peace until he confessed all. He headed upstairs to the Major Crime Unit offices where the rest of the team had gathered and were writing up their reports. He walked into the main room stood still.

"All of that can wait until tomorrow or rather later today. Go and get at least a couple of hours' rest. You did everything I asked of you and I appreciate your efforts. I need you fit and on form for the interviews. We are interested in whether they knew about the bird cam or any hint they may have been involved in the burglary." He paused and gave an acknowledging nod towards the Wild Life Protection officers. "After that, we can hand them over for charging to our colleagues here." He turned as if to leave, then added, "Oh, and there will be money behind the bar at the local tomorrow evening, which I hope will be sufficient for a pleasant and relaxed celebration."

† † †

"Sorry sir, absolutely bugger all from our suspect. Seemed to think we were having a laugh at his expense." Ray shrugged and grimaced. "I think the guy was genuine, and he had an alibi for the burglary. Took his family away that week to Wales." He paused and sighed. "We checked with the holiday park and he was there. Apparently his two boys were a nightmare and the owners remember them vividly."

"Nothing from our interview, either. Apparently, our man was working nights that week and had no idea about hidden cameras, either." Justin reported, then turned to Julie and Paul as they came through the door. "Anything?"

The pair both shook their heads. "Nothing, no knowledge of cameras in woods or of any burglary. He works as a night porter, would you believe, in one of the Park Lane hotels. Only goes out with his mates on his nights off. He was on duty during the time Mr Byett was away. The hotel confirmed he was working."

Justin sighed and leaned against the nearest desk. "Hand these three over to be charged, then we get to play the same game with our other four. Anne and I will take our leader with the axe and spade man. You four can toss a coin to see who gets which of the other two."

The axeman was the last to be interviewed. He had more than the others on his plate, having threatened to attack a police officer with the axe. Justin had no intention of bringing a charge that would be difficult to prove and possibly lead to some awkward questions for him to answer. He was glad to discover the man still seemed shocked, and that his memory of the night's events was blurred. From his pale face and worried frown, when Justin entered the interview room, sufficient memory remained to make him uneasy, but at least he had stopped gibbering about fangs and super strength. Justin wondered what the escorting officers had made of those comments but was not particularly worried. Who would believe such a story in this age of science?

Two hours later, Justin left the interview room with Anne close behind him. "An entire morning wasted!" he commented, turning to watch the last of the suspects being led away to be charged with the badger baiting offence.

"At least we can cross them off our list for the burglary," Anne said as they headed back up to the offices. "The local police don't have anyone in mind either. None of the usual offenders would leave such a mess. Apparently, it offends their professional pride. One of them was so totally disgusted by the suggestion he gave up the name of someone known for trashing the place when he broke in, but the offender has been in prison for the last six months with twelve more to go."

While Anne and Justin had taken the last interview with the axeman, the others had picked up their lines of investigation into Chelsey's death. The other four were all intent on screens and phones when the pair reached the office. A takeaway cup of coffee was waiting for Justin on the desk he usually leaned against, next to their crime board. He couldn't hide a grin of appreciation and gave a murmured "Thank you".

"You have probably realised already there was no joy from the leader, either. As Anne pointed out to me, we have eliminated them as suspects for the burglary. So, what have you got for us apart from coffee?" He paused then, "Julie and Paul, what about the ex-girlfriend?"

"We finally tracked her down living in Luton. She confirmed receiving obscene and threatening messages. She commented that Sean was a great guy but not worth what she had been threatened with." Paul frowned. "She did quote a couple of messages from memory. They were nasty, as bad as the ones Chelsey had received. She changed her phone and broke up with Sean before moving away." He looked over at Julie, who nodded for him to continue. "She also suggested a possible source for the threats. I quote, 'Is that little bitch still glued to Sean's side? When the threats began, I thought it might be her, always so possessive, always interrupting, always there!'" He turned the page of his notebook. "She then said, 'I'm talking about Eve Jordan. I never found any proof and Sean wouldn't believe Eve was capable of such a thing. I tackled her about it one evening. We'd all been drinking and I wasn't thinking straight, I suppose. She showed me her phone. She'd been getting the same abuse as I had. Well, then Sean got back together with Chelsey and I moved away. This is the first time I've thought about it since.'" Paul paused then said, "It's got to be someone who knows their phone numbers and emails." Paul shrugged. "It might not be a member of their group, though."

"Who else could it be?" Anne asked. "I suppose someone's phone could have been cloned. If the phone is cloned, does everything get copied? Another possibility is an unlocked mobile left on a table or a bar at a club where anyone can get at the contents or it could've ended up as lost property."

"Ray, what about your work on Chelsey's activities?"

"We've followed up on some of the serving staff, confirmed Nando's and the bar. The bar staff thought Chelsey met up with someone she knew, but they weren't certain. It was a very busy night for the beginning of the week. They couldn't say whether it was a man or a woman. They just saw someone standing near her table for a few minutes. None of them saw when Chelsey left or whether she left with someone, so we're back on the CCTV and uniforms are checking with the rest of the clubs and pubs at the top of the town. I think, if you can arrange it, we might do a reconstruction to jog people's memories and get it on the local news."

Justin added "met someone" to the timeline point and nodded. "Yes, I will speak to the PR office and get that arranged. Anything further on Gavin?"

Anne shook her head. "No sightings and no witness reports since you lot searched the garden centre. I received his record from Colchester. At first glance, it looks like a nasty unprovoked attack on his mother's partner that put him in young offenders."

"At first glance?" Ray questioned.

"Yeah! The officer who sent me the record also emailed me to say he had worked with the arresting officer, a Sergeant Don Taylor. Taylor had not been happy about the judgement. He left a message for me yesterday to say he will call me this afternoon to discuss what is not on the record."

"Not so straightforward then," Justin murmured, his thoughts elsewhere. "Right, I am going to visit Mr Byett and see who may have known he was filming the car park and when he would be away." He looked round the group. "Well done! I know it is slow work but something will break for us, eventually. Anne, stay here for your call. I will not need you at Byett's place. While you are waiting, check with forensics and the pathology report to see whether we can identify the weapon. It does have some unusual characteristics."

† † †

Tony Byett was clearing out the smashed and damaged items from the burglary into the back of his hatchback when Justin arrived. Byett closed the boot and waited beside the car when he recognised Justin.

"Good afternoon, Chief Inspector." Byett sounded remarkably cheerful considering what had happened. "Have you caught my burglar? Come inside and I'll put the kettle on."

Justin followed him inside and was directed to the lounge.

"Do sit down. I won't be a minute." Byett disappeared down the hall into the kitchen.

Justin wandered to the window, comparing the neat room with the mess it had been when they discovered the burglary. There were some gaps where the mirror had been and the damaged desk had left a large vacant space. In the bay window, a small table stood between two armchairs, all now upright. A litter of leaflets created a fan across its top: the latest pizza parlour offering delivery; get your clothes altered, a plastic bag with a request for old clothes to be donated; security alarm system installations; garden design and maintenance; a sale at a local department store and the opening of a new cinema in the local shopping centre.

The door swung open, pushed by the corner of a loaded tray.

"Here we are," Byett remarked, then placed the tray on top of the leaflets. Justin sat down in the nearest armchair, and Byett took the other.

"You have managed an amazing amount of tidying up. It must have taken some hard work."

Byett grinned. "Had to," he said, his expression rueful. "Nasmeen, my partner will be back tomorrow. She stayed on at the villa after we got back from the mountains. She claimed she deserved a couple of days' rest and recuperation after what I'd made her do." He grinned. "She's the one who suggested we went, so ignore the martyrdom plea." He poured tea into two china mugs. "The mirror can be replaced fairly easily; I've ordered a new one. But my lovely desk was an antique shop find." He drank from his mug. "Still, I've finally got rid of a lot of clutter that I'd always intended to throw out but never got around t0. I think I've earned a refuse disposal lifetime achievement badge." He looked across at Justin. "How good was our information?" he asked seriously.

"As good as it gets," Justin confirmed. "They turned up, and we arrested them. We have charged them but not with the burglary. None of the seven we caught were involved, I am sorry to say. They could all provide solid alibis."

Byett gave a whoop of triumph.

"Thank you," he said. "I'm sorry my recordings have been destroyed. I feel rather guilty that I cannot help you in the same way."

"At least we have eliminated your suspects from our inquiry," Justin smiled, "as my inspector reminded me. She seems to be a half full glass type. Unless there are more of the gang?"

Byett frowned then said, "No those seven are the organisers." He sighed. "If so, many others didn't gather to bet on the outcome or watch such barbaric entertainment, we could rid the modern world of an eighteenth-century blight."

Silently Justin agreed. It was one "sport" he had always avoided. "Who would have known that you and Nasmeen would be away?"

Byett absently drained and refilled his cup as he concentrated on a mental list.

"Well, my brother and his wife, they were looking after the dog; then my colleague, Tom." Byett grinned, "he's also a lifelong friend of ours, best man at our wedding. He was keeping an eye on the house along with my brother. He's away at a conference that started the day I got back from Spain. Apart from the milkman, that's the full list as far as I know. Oh, not quite. I think Ms James across the road knew as well. She and Nasmeen are good friends. When Nasmeen gets back, I can check with her if there are others apart from her work."

Justin stood up. "Thank you for your help. I will let you get back to the rubbish trips. If you think of anything else, please call me." He took a card from his pocket and placed it on the table next to the tray.

They shook hands, and Justin saw himself out. He paused at the boundary hedge, noticing the neighbour across the road was out in her front garden. She was leaning heavily on a walker and appeared to be waiting for him from the frequent glances in his direction. He waved and strolled across to her front gate.

"Ms James?" he remembered what Byett had said.

She nodded and smiled.

"Detective Chief Inspector Justin Mortmain," He introduced himself. "I know you will have spoken to our burglary team, but I was hoping you would not mind answering a few more questions?"

The look of concern on her face and the strain showing in her eyes eased slightly, and she gave a small smile. There was relief in her voice as well when she replied.

"Good afternoon Chief Inspector. I'm so glad you came over, won't you come in? I've had a terrible sleepless night going over in my mind what has happened. I rather think I am responsible for the burglary at the Byett's."

Justin followed the elderly lady's slow, unsteady steps up the garden path and through the house to the bright, open-plan kitchen. Ms James carefully sat down and invited Justin to take a seat.

"I just need to get my breath back, then I'll make us some tea."

"Ms James, allow me to make the tea," he replied, though his heart and stomach sank at the thought of more tea.

Ms James blushed, and her eyes sparkled. "Well, it would make a pleasant change to be waited on, and by a handsome young man," she said. "I must admit, my arthritis does sometimes make moving around slow and rather difficult."

Justin smiled. "Then you give the orders ma'am, and I will be your assistant." He threw up a salute.

The old lady laughed and began issuing her instructions. Ten minutes later, Justin set a tray down on the circular table before taking the seat across from his hostess. He moved a small heap of adverts to one side, noticing in passing they were the same bundle as Byett had received.

"When did these arrive," Justin asked, casually tapping a finger on the small stack.

"Oh, those things, I meant to throw them into the recycling." She considered, "I think they were put through the door Tuesday or Wednesday last week. Sometimes they have something good in among the rubbish."

Justin poured the tea into delicate china cups and set one on the table in front of Ms James. She added a little milk and carefully used both hands to raise the cup to her lips. By the time Justin felt she was ready to talk to him, the worried look had returned. She placed the cup carefully back onto its saucer before she spoke.

"The lad who delivered them is Olivia's boy. She's my cleaner cum helper. Apparently, he makes this kind of delivery to make ends meet while he looks for more permanent work. At least that's what his mother says." She paused and sighed, "Poor woman! He's been a bit of a problem these last few years. Boys will be boys and all that. We often have a cup of tea and a chat when she's finished sorting me out. She comes in three times a week." Ms James looked intently into his face. "The thing is, I can't help wondering if our little gossip sessions might have been how the burglar found out Mr and Mrs Byett were away."

"What makes you think that?" Justin asked gently. "Have you any suspicions about your helper?"

Before he could complete his question, Ms James was shaking her head emphatically. "Oh, good heavens, no, certainly not. Olivia is a very decent and honest woman. She's as much a friend as an employee, I assure you. It's just that these bits of gossip can get passed on, without any bad intention, to people who take advantage. As well as that, it was a lovely warm day, and we had tea in the garden." Ms James pointed at the garden beyond the folding doors with a sweep of her arm. "As you can see, the fencing is chain-link and there is a footpath running across the back of the gardens here. I don't always think about what I'm saying when I get a chance to talk to people you see. It's quite a rare opportunity, now I can't get about like I used to. I've been rather worried that I might be the reason Tony and Nasmeen were targeted. Then, of course, Olivia's lad, Ashley, Alan, something like that, arrived and joined us for a drink and a quick break on his leaflet round." She smiled, a very mischievous twinkle lighting her eyes. "He was doing a bit of courting too, had a young lady with him when he was putting the leaflets through the doors. I saw them together from the front bedroom window. She didn't come in with him, though, stopped at the corner before the back gate, then went back down the footpath while Olivia's boy came in."

Justin shook his head. "I doubt very much it was your chat that did any harm, Ms James. There are a good many reasons why the Byetts might have been targeted which I cannot discuss with you. But I do not think your little gossip, as you call it, did any harm."

Justin poured more tea and stayed chatting about things generally for another quarter of an hour before he carefully cleared the delicate crockery and bid his hostess farewell. He did his best to reassure her again before he closed her front door and made his way across to his car.

Once in the car, Justin sighed. He knew it was possible Ms James' little chats with her helper could have passed on the information about Byett's absence. It was only one of a dozen ways the knowledge could have escaped. He had reassured the elderly lady because none of the regulars were in the frame nor were the suspects linked to Byett's RSPCA work. The pool of possible culprits had narrowed down to a link with Chelsey's murder. He brushed one hand across his eyes, checked the clock on the dashboard, and reached for his mobile.

"Anne, I have a favour to ask. Would you give my apologies to the team and lead tonight's meeting for me?"

"Has something turned up?"

"No, nothing new. This is personal. I promised to meet Marta's flight this evening and I am running late."

"Not a problem. I'll email you the notes from the meeting. The PR people have organised the re-enactment of Chelsey's movements for tomorrow night and they've found a reasonable lookalike to play the part of Chelsey. The TV programme goes out the next day."

"Excellent! Are you happy to continue being the spokesperson for the investigation?"

He heard the frown in her voice when she replied.

"Of course. Why do you ask?"

"Two reasons, I suppose. The first was you did not seem happy with the situation at first. The second because I was wondering if that was the motive for the attack on you the other night."

"That's true, but I could name several others I've arrested who have threatened to get even. Let's carry on as we are and see what happens."

"Your decision," Justin confirmed. "Oh, one more thing, Byett's neighbourhood has had an advert drop in the last few days. Check the companies to see which one was responsible, who did the drop on their behalf and which adverts the delivery included. Belt and braces, really. It is possible that someone used the leafleting as a cover to check out Byett's place. Not necessarily our murderer but you know how people mention something unusual when they get into conversation."

"Will do. Have a good evening."

"You too."

19

In the four-poster bed, Justin lay awake. The window curtains were open, and he had been watching the crescent moon and the stars dancing their stately measure across the heavens until the building clouds had concealed the view. He enjoyed the warm feel of Marta's body against his own. He felt her shiver though still asleep, and unconsciously snuggle closer into his warmth. It felt good to listen to her breathing, catching the slight snuffle she occasionally made that always amused him. She gave a long, soft sigh as her body relaxed into a deeper sleep. Gently, he moved the duvet to cover her shoulder, then curled an arm around her before settling into a light doze.

He was instantly alert at the first vibration of his phone on the bedside table and grabbed it quickly, sliding carefully out of bed so as not to disturb Marta. She gave a sleepy snort of annoyance but thankfully did not wake up. He padded silently across the thick carpet into the dressing room before speaking.

"Martin," he acknowledged the caller, then glanced at his watch, four thirty in the morning. "What has happened?"

"We've just had a call. The Fire Brigade is dealing with a vehicle fire in Haydon's field. I'm heading down there now."

"I will come with you," Justin replied, hearing the rustle of clothes through the phone that showed his estate manager was getting dressed. "Meet you at the Land Rover."

Justin dressed hurriedly, then scribbled a note to Marta, placing it on the pillow, before closing the door softly and heading downstairs. He grabbed a waterproof and a pair of sturdy walking boots from the cloakroom where he heard the clatter of a powerful gust of wind throwing raindrops like gravel against the window. He headed out the side door, through the garden and round to the stables. The sudden squall was fading out, although the stormy clouds still darkened the sky, threatening more rain. Martin was already in the driving seat with the engine ticking over and the passenger door open.

Ten backbreaking bouncing minutes around the rutted field tracks, steaming up the windscreen each time Justin had to open and close the field gates, and they could finally see the place where a flickering, dancing glow just peeped over the edge of the hollow, topped by a pall of smoke darker than the fading storm clouds. The blue warning lights of the fire engine flashed and spun, the strobe effect sending blue lightning through the dark coiling smoke above the space where white-hot flames enveloped the burning vehicle. Martin pulled up at the top edge of the hollow where they would not interfere with the efforts of the firefighters. From that viewpoint, the two men watched in admiration the expertise of the firefighters as they steadily brought the flames under control, reducing the flaming wreck into a blackened damp mass. To Justin the final few moments were like a particularly brutal modern ballet, the climax of the piece, a great battle. The choreography was led by chaotic flashes and flares of flames challenged by individual firefighters until the last glimmer hissed into cold grey.

Justin led the way to where the crew was making certain the fire was completely out. Others were rolling up all but one hose and two of the firefighters were heading purposefully towards the back doors of what looked like the wreck of a small van. The Crew Manager came to meet them. Justin explained the dual reasons for his presence as landowner and police officer.

"What happened?"

The officer pointed to the lower road, little more than a lane leading to the next village. "It was a running call," he explained. "The two tenders were heading back from over Lownes Village way when we spotted the van in flames. It was a single engine call, so the other appliance continued back to base."

The three of them began walking towards the van.

"At the moment, it looks like a typical deliberate burn out. Probable use of an accelerant because the fire took hold pretty quickly, although I think the fire was set only moments before we got here."

Justin got his first close-up look at the blackened wreck. Windows were cracked into myriad straight lines by the heat and darkened by internal smoke staining. The tyres were gone, adding the stench of burned rubber to the smell of heated metal and melted plastic. Towards the rear of the van, the paintwork was charred, cracked and flaking. As they walked around the wreck at a distance, one of the team started to prise open the passenger door. The crazed glass shattered onto the ground as the door moved. The aroma of an overdone Sunday roast wafted over them and was gone. Justin and Martin froze, staring into the destroyed interior. They could not look away from the blackened corpse seated upright in the front passenger seat.

The Crew Manager turned to Justin.

"I think this has just become your problem Chief Inspector."

"I think you are probably right." Justin replied, hoping he spoke the truth, and Benson's team would not be allocated to the investigation. He took out his phone to begin the familiar process, calling in the incident while still staring at the blackened remains of another human being.

Justin sent Martin back to the manor and waited until the first responders arrived. After that, he felt able to return to the manor himself. He passed Martin returning with Beth and guessed they were going to set up a refreshment area for the people who would soon be swarming over every inch of the field. He waved but kept going at a jog. The rain had left the track damp but firm. Strangely, the feel of it brought memories of finding Chelsey's body. Justin grimaced, acknowledging his frustration at the whole situation. He increased his speed to a run, but he could not outrun his own feelings. Reaching the manor via the stables, he paused to hang up the waterproof and get out of the walking boots, then headed upstairs for a quick shower and change of clothes. He moved around quietly but realised the bed was empty. Marta was already up and about somewhere in the house.

The wonderful aroma of freshly brewed coffee and toasted bread reached him when he left the bedroom, suited and booted for the day. Justin followed the scent to the breakfast room where Marta was finishing her last piece of toast. She turned and smiled at him, pouring a large mug of coffee while he put together a breakfast plate from the hot buffet Beth had produced. He placed the plate on the table, then slipped his arms around Marta, kissing her cheek. She turned in his arms and lightly stroked a finger down his face. Justin thought she still looked a little tired.

"I am sorry I had to leave you. I hope I did not wake you up?"

Marta sipped her tea, then shook her head. "No, I slept well. I did wonder where you were, but Beth explained when she brought in the breakfast dishes. I offered to look after you so she could look after all the other people I assume are working on the site? She said someone had set light to a car in one of the fields."

Justin nodded and started to speak, but Marta stopped him.

"Eat first. You can tell me what happened while you drive me home."

Returning to the field after taking Marta home, Justin still had no word on which team would investigate the case, so expected to see Benson and his team at the site. There was certainly a lot of activity from the forensics unit. They were busy photographing and sampling across the damaged field when Justin pulled into the lower field between the lane and the crime scene. Several cars and vans were parked already, including a tow truck and an ominously discreet black windowless van to transport the body. There was no sign of Benson or any of his people.

Martin and Beth had set up along the hedge across the gate from the parking area and well away from the crime scene. Standing beside them, steaming cups in hand, were Doctor Shah, the pathologist and Doctor Lizzie Caldwell, who Justin had met at the Byett burglary scene. Despite the business going on around, it seemed as if everyone was waiting for something. Justin walked over to the group.

"Good morning." He shook hands with both the doctors. "Any progress?"

Before they could reply, Doctor Shah's mobile rang. He stepped away from the others to take the call. Lizzie smiled at Justin over the rim of her cup.

"Benefits of working with you?" She raised the cup in a toast. "Thanks for this."

Justin nodded towards Beth and Martin. "They are the ones to thank."

"You in charge of this one as well?"

He shrugged to emphasise his words. "This is my land, which is why I am here. I do not know yet which team will investigate."

"You do now," Doctor Shah commented, having finished the call. "Benson has gone on sick leave apparently and the Detective Inspector currently in charge of that team has his hands full with what they already have."

"So be it. Care to fill in some details?"

Justin glanced between the two, who finished their drinks, while he climbed into the required coverall and footwear the others were already wearing. Then they all headed back to the burned-out vehicle. The blackened corpse was still in place.

"Right! My initial report. The victim is most likely male and was dead before the fire started, in my opinion. I'm pretty certain we won't find smoke or soot in the lungs. The signs suggest his throat had been cut. We can check his teeth against dental records for identification as they are least damaged by the fire and also extract DNA to help us. Obviously, the DNA will take some time but we might get lucky with the dentistry. There is severe burning pretty much all over the body. I'll do the post mortem this afternoon." Shah looked at Lizzie. "If forensics has finished with the body in situ, we will take him to the mortuary."

Lizzie nodded her agreement and Doctor Shah signalled to his patiently waiting assistants.

"Thank you. I will see if DCs Williams and Ensbury are free to attend. Could you let them know the time?"

"Yes, of course," Shah replied, then turned and headed for his car.

Justin turned back to Lizzie. "What have you got for me?"

"Support for Doctor Shah's theory. The glass was shattered by heat and showed no signs of your victim struggling to get out. The striations are straight lines. If he had hit the glass hard enough to shatter it, the debris would all be cube-shaped. An accelerant was definitely used. In this case, it's probably petrol. I asked a couple of PCs to request any CCTV at the two nearest petrol stations." She took a few steps towards the back of the van where the doors had been opened and pointed. "The container was thrown in behind the seat after splashing the stuff about the interior. We can do more once the van is in our garage."

She walked away to the front of the van, then several yards further to where a cast was drying under a protective sheet.

"Motorbike tyre tracks, only two wheels, not four. Possibly two people on board from the depth of the impression." She looked over her shoulder at Justin, "Do you use motorbikes on the farm at all?"

"No, not in these fields. We have a couple of quad bikes up at the house. You are welcome to take elimination samples. Just let Martin know and he will show you where they are."

Lizzie nodded, then continued around the van to the driver's side. Again, she stopped several feet from the burned area. "This one's a footprint and not from the firefighters' boots. We've taken a cast and will compare it to the database and so on when we finish here." She paused and took a deep breath. "This is a gut feeling only, OK? Not a certainty until we check everything scientifically."

"I understand what you mean. Now, what is bothering you?"

"The footprint seemed familiar when I was preserving it, particularly the wear pattern. I think it's a possible match for that burglary the other day. Like I said, don't take that as gospel until we've checked."

Justin nodded to show his understanding, then asked, "What about the van itself?" He sounded doubtful even to himself, having seen the state of the vehicle. To his surprise, Lizzie smiled and shook her gloved finger at him like an old-fashioned school ma'am.

"Don't be such a pessimist. Once we get into the lab, we might find all sorts of goodies for you. We should be able to get the chassis number to start the owner identification process. We might even find some unburned areas which could help. after all it's likely the van was a commercial vehicle. Shall I ask for the petrol station CCTV to be sent to your team?"

"Yes, if you are right about the footprint, then this is linked to at least one of our current cases." His eyes narrowed on the van. "I too have a gut feeling, Lizzie. Mine is suggesting a further link to our original murder. I just hope you can find evidence to prove both of us right."

He checked his watch, surprised to find how little of the day had actually passed. He left Lizzie to her work and headed back to the car. There, he discarded the protective suit and then phoned Ray about attending the post mortem. His next call was to Anne to explain the expansion of their caseload.

"I am on my way to the office. I should be there in about half an hour. I will give you what details I have when I get there."

"Doctor Shah called. He's set the post mortem for four this afternoon." Ray said when Justin wandered into the main office. He turned in his seat to look at his SIO.

Justin raised a hand in acknowledgement. "I heard. Doc really did mean he would rush it. You and Chas are free to attend?"

Both men agreed they would.

"Sorry to add to your workload, but Benson's team cannot take anything else on at the moment," Justin paused, rubbed the back of his neck and looked around at his team, most of whom were looking amused. "This morning, the Fire Brigade discovered a burning van containing a body on my land. That is the post mortem I have asked Ray and Chas to attend. The initial suggestion from Doc Shah was the victim had been killed before the fire was started. Besides, I feel this is linked to our murder in some way. Lizzie is double checking to be certain, but experience told her the footprints in the mud at the fire scene may be a match for those at the Byett burglary. Her team of scientists also recovered a motorbike tyre track. The post mortem report and the forensic reports will confirm or reject a link with our current cases." He paused and shrugged, "for the moment we will assume a connection. We also have a stolen van we need to find. How are we doing with that?"

Julie frowned, met her boss's gaze and replied, "Not so good. We've tried to speak to Eve Jordan several times already and have asked uniform to follow up. None of us have managed to meet up with her, not at her flat, her office or any of the projects her company is working on."

"Right, Anne and I will see whether we can track her down. From what we have seen, she could just as easily be at Sean's flat."

Julie shook her head. "No, we tried there a couple of times. Sean was out at work the first time and the second, well, the second time we called, he was with Gina Crane." She saw Ray's raised eyebrow and shook her head. "No, not like that! I think they've been drawn together by guilt rather than sex. Both feel as guilty as each other, so they can be honest and comfort each other."

"What news on Gavin from your contact, Anne?" Justin caught the flash of triumph in her eyes before she spoke and sighed heavily, raising his free hand in mock surrender. "Let me guess, you were right, he is a knight in shining armour."

Anne grinned "Yeah!" The grin disappeared. "I feel for the kid, I really do. Yes, he attacked his mother's boyfriend, but at the time the boyfriend had punched her to the ground and was about to kick her for a second time, according to the arresting officer." Anne looked at her screen. "When she was released from hospital, she refused to press charges and refused to be a witness for her own son."

"Why?" Julie asked in disbelief.

Anne shrugged as she said, "Two possible reasons, you can choose which you think is correct. One, she was deeply afraid of the boyfriend and what he would do to her. Two, she didn't want to lose him. By the way, he was a dealer and well known to the local police."

"Lose him, bloody hell," Julie frowned heavily. "I'd love to ask her why."

"Afraid you can't. Three months into Gavin's sentence, the boyfriend beat her to death. He's serving life for her murder."

Just for a moment, the room went silent before Ray said quietly, "There are some people you just can't help."

Anne nodded in agreement. "Yes, but I'm damn certain, especially with a background like his, Gavin was trying to help me when I was attacked and that's how he got my blood on his shirt. The women at the garden centre also believed he was a good guy, and they were right."

"Which still means we need to find him and ask why he was following Chelsey that day. What did he know?" Justin was walking up and down between the desks. He stopped beside Ray. "Are we ready for the reconstruction? Extra staff to answer the phones, for example?"

Ray pointed to the door, "We're opening up the other area across the corridor. The technicians are setting up now: desks, chairs, phones and answer phones. Extra staff have been approved and will start as soon as the programme has aired. One of our police constables resembles Chelsey and we have a matching outfit for her."

Justin nodded approval. There was a noisy interruption from two civilian staff wheeling in another large whiteboard. It was placed next to the half-full original. Justin waited until the door closed behind them.

"So, my apologies for adding, at least temporarily, to your workload. Julie and Paul, I want you to focus on the burned van for now. Anne and I will pick up on Eve, starting with a full background check. I do not like the fact she did not mention the theft to us, considering it was the same night Chelsey disappeared."

Anne turned back to her computer.

"Ray and Chas will do the post mortem, then focus on tomorrow evening's reconstruction preparation. I understand the TV company will go with it the next night, so Anne will also need to be available from tomorrow afternoon." He turned to Anne and added, "Tomorrow morning, we will try to track down our elusive Eve."

20

"Where could the girl have got to?" Anne asked when Justin parked in front of her block. "She seems to have vanished off the face of the planet."

Justin shared her frustration, but could not restrain a chuckle at Anne's comment. "Do you have a crystal ball among your possessions? Or we could ask the local medium for assistance." He shrugged and got out of the car. Over the car roof, he continued, "We have checked her apartment, her business office and three of her major projects, just as Julie and Paul had done before us. Even the gardeners working on those projects today have not seen Eve Jordan in person for days. The team leaders all told us she had sent their instructions by text or phone call."

He followed Anne into the entrance. "We can try the last two projects tomorrow if we get no reply to our messages. However, she is not a suspect nor a witness in our case."

Anne nodded and stepped into the lift. "True, but don't you think it's strange that she's left Sean alone this long? At the start of our investigation, she seemed super glued to his side every time we visited him, yet now we want to talk to her, she's more elusive than a cat burglar." She pressed the numbered button for the floor hard, and they rode the lift in silence. Justin agreed with what Anne had said, but the questions they had for Eve were not likely to break the case, just anomalies that needed clarification. He glanced across the lift where Anne stood, facing the doors, her frown formidable.

"Are you prepared for this evening?" he glanced at his watch. "Is there anything you want to go over before we join the film crew?"

She shook her head. "No, this interview will end the segment on Chelsey's murder, its fine." She looked up and smiled. "Sorry, I don't know why I'm so bothered about Eve's disappearance. I didn't like her from day one and I'm allowing that to affect my judgement."

They stepped out of the lift, headed along the corridor, and Anne unlocked her door. Mr Claws, strolled out of the bedroom to greet them. While Anne was changing in preparation for the interview, Justin settled comfortably onto the couch where Mr Claws joined him. Justin tickled his chin, and he settled down, purring loudly, his head stretched out, eyes closed in pure enjoyment. Justin enjoyed the feel of his fur beneath his fingers and continued a gentle massage while looking out of the French windows across the balcony. The sun was shimmering behind the tall trees at the end of the landscaped gardens. He relaxed back into the seat feeling the tension in his shoulders ease. The movement of the leaves in the sunlight was hypnotic.

Anne stood watching them for a moment or two. "There's a lot to be said for coming back in the next life as a cat."

Anne's remark startled Justin from his daydream. "Mr Claws seems to like you. He's very particular who he keeps company with."

Justin glanced down at the warm area along his thigh where the cat was stretched out across the couch. He stood up slowly so as not to disturb the cat and turned to look at Anne.

"I like him too."

Anne gave a twirl and asked, "Will I do?"

Justin's glance went from the top of her head to the heels of her shoes. "Definitely. A perfect combination of elegance and professionalism. Shall we go?"

They arrived at the meeting point in good time and were introduced to the crew, including the young woman who would be acting as Chelsey Harris for the filming. The sun had set and the evening sky was clear, with a bright half moon. Although the evening was cool, the lack of cloud meant it was unlikely rain would disrupt their filming. There were some people already out and the clubs and pubs in the district had opened up. The dance rhythms seemed to tremble across the pavements while the music mingled with laughter and voices. Once the irritation of youngsters, and some not so young trying to get their antics on camera had been dealt with, Justin watched in fascination as the timeline they had put together painstakingly came to life for the cameras.

From the bus stop near her work up the High Street as far as the fast-food restaurant where she had eaten. Then, onto the bar where she was known and the unidentified friend or acquaintance who had stopped by her table. The scene faded into darkness and returned focused on the reporter who introduced "Detective Inspector Anne Richards".

"Inspector Richards is the spokesperson for the investigation into the murder of Chelsey Harris. Inspector, how can our viewers help you solve this awful case?"

"Good evening, Greg." Anne turned to face the camera. "We are asking anyone who was in this area on that Tuesday evening to ask themselves, did they see what happened to Chelsey Harris from the point where this unknown person stopped to talk to her in the bar? Did you notice Chelsey sitting alone? Did you recognise or could you describe the person who stopped at her table? If you are that person, please phone the number which will appear on the screen and let us know what happened. Did anyone see Chelsey leave? Were you and your friends outside on the street and notice Chelsey come out of the bar? Was she alone or with someone? We need to find out what happened between this point and the time her body was discovered in the woodland. If you have any information, no matter how insignificant you think it is, call the helpline. Thank you. Chelsey Harris was a young woman with most of her life ahead of her. She had a successful career and was in a steady relationship. Someone either alone or with another person brutally destroyed that future and devastated Chelsey's family."

The reporter took over reading out the helpline number, which would appear on the bottom of the screen when the programme aired. He also reminded people of the day, date, and time before signing off.

The crowd that had gathered to watch the filming began to disperse. Several figures slipped away from the groups in various directions. Justin watched idly until one couple started to move away. Both were wearing hoodies, but he thought at least one of them was familiar. With a frown, he ducked beneath the barrier and followed. The pair turned into an alleyway between the dessert shop and the night club already several metres ahead of him. He quickened his pace but, by the time he turned into the alleyway, they had gone. He walked to the other end, where the alley branched in three directions. With no sound of movement or moving shadows, he had nothing to follow. He went back to collect Anne but could not dismiss a niggling feeling that the recognition was important.

Anne was waiting outside the large TV control van.

"I am sorry to keep you waiting. Well done on the appeal, it looked good from where I was standing. I hope at least a few of the calls will have real value."

"Yes, it's always surprising how many people truly want to help, but the false sightings often outweigh the genuine by what? Ten to one, a hundred to one, would you say? Then there are the real time wasters on top of that." She shrugged, "we've a good team of operatives and the powers-that-be have authorised more officers to follow anything plausible." They turned together towards the car. "It feels as if we might actually get somewhere with this case."

Justin smiled. "You, Detective Inspector, are far too optimistic these days. We have followed up every lead and reached dead ends on each one. I am more of a realist than you, so I will wait and see what comes in."

He drove them back to Shady Lane, where Anne would have headed for the offices if Justin had allowed. Instead, she found herself escorted to her car and firmly ordered home to get some sleep and return clear headed for the next day.

Justin smiled as he watched her get into her car. "Just in case your optimism is justified," he said seriously, though his eyes held a hint of amusement. He waved her off, then made his way to the larger office where the phones were already on the overture and warming up for the major performance. He found a vacant desk, sat down, and waited for his phone to join the chorus.

† † †

Justin turned the shower across to cold and forced his body under the spray. He gasped as the icy droplets massaged and pounded his skin. His eyes closed as he leaned his forehead against the tiles. Having left the office at four in the morning when the flow of calls had eased, he had managed a couple of hours' sleep. Now he needed the tingle of the freezing water to wake up. Justin lifted his face to the spray and waited for it to complete the task.

The sun was still close to the horizon when he turned into the car park. He noticed Anne had arrived already and was pleased to see the local baker's delivery van just leaving. The team needed a sugar boost after last night's marathon and to set up the next shift for the new day. The expanded team had certainly made inroads into the mounds of croissants and Danish pastries when he wandered into the "call centre", as the new area had been labelled in his absence. Briefings would now include the supervisor, Keval, who would gather the reports and collate the evidence for them. Justin headed back to his own office, waving at Anne as he passed through the outer area. She waved back, then followed him.

"Morning! The local news wants an interview this morning. Apparently, the response so far to the appeal has been surprisingly good and they want to keep the momentum going."

Justin nodded his approval. "It was a good local response last night. Quite a few of the callers knew Chelsey or her family. Play up the popular local girl as much as you can this morning, loss to the whole community. You know the sort of thing." He was standing by the window and glanced down as several cars pulled up outside the gates. "I think you need to be ready. It looks like the wolves are gathering right now." He pointed down at the gates when Anne joined him at the window. "That looks like more than just local reporters down there. We have what, two or three local town or county newspapers? There are six or seven photographers alone. Where are you doing the interview?"

Anne glanced at the clear sky. "Outside the main entrance."

"Good luck to you. Did we get a copy of last night's filming, do you know?"

Anne shook her head. "I don't know. I have a souvenir recording of the programme at home if that would help?"

"Thank you, no. I asked for the raw footage."

"Any specific reason?"

"Yes, I thought I recognised someone in the crowd of onlookers. Not completely just a feeling, really. I tried to follow them to see if I could get a clearer look at them, but I lost the couple in the back area around the nightclub. Probably not important, but I want to see if the cameras picked up anyone who matches."

"Any names to go with the feeling?"

"No, not yet." Justin glanced at his watch. "There is a breakfast buffet across the corridor. I would grab something before the interview if I were you." He turned back to his desk and switched on his computer as Anne left. A check of his email showed he had his copy. He made a mug of coffee and settled down to watch the footage in the hope he would get a clearer, recognisable image.

Two further mugs of coffee had been drained before Justin stretched, then rolled his shoulders to ease the stiffness in his neck and back from sitting staring at the computer screen. Despite several re-runs of the recording, he had not found a clear image of the couple who had sparked his interest. He had been vaguely aware of Anne's return from the morning press briefing around halfway through the second viewing. He grabbed his mug and headed into the outer office, glancing at Anne's screen on his way through. Ahh, background check on Eve Jordan was her focus. He poured a fresh brew and turned back for his office just as Keval came through from the call centre, waving a sheaf of papers.

"We might have something here already," he said as he advanced into the room.

They all met at Anne's desk, and Keval spread his papers for them to see.

"We've had the usual set of long-distance claims from across the country. One from York." He shook his head. "They seem to think we are tracking Wonder Woman! At least five callers so far fit the time frame and the club land area of town. I sent uniform to get statements from all of them. One was anonymous, except I recognised the voice." Keval grinned, "A local door security employee at Carlo's Club, a hundred metres further up the High Street just before it's crossed by the one-way system." He swapped a couple of statements around.

"Here's more of your victim's timeline and the statements overlap slightly."

Justin and Anne leaned over to read the witness statements. Keval was right, they had struck lucky. Witness one had been in the bar and remembered seeing Chelsey talking to someone who had then left before Chelsey. The witness had left the bar at the same time as Chelsey and seen the same hooded person waiting outside, and Chelsey had joined them. They had both walked further up the High Street towards Carlo's. The next witness was the club doorman who had admitted the pair. Importantly, he had requested the removal of the hood before admitting them. He was one person who might be able to give a description. He had not seen Chelsey leave the club. Witness three had been at the club and thought they recognised Chelsey, who had seemed unsteady on her feet, but had not seen who she was with. Another caller had seen Chelsey leaving the club and had thought her to be very drunk, needing the help of her friend to stay upright. Again, the hood was in place, but this witness also might give a description having seen the pair under the streetlights. The caller had said the companion had glared hard at him before looking away and urging Chelsey to move on. The final witness had been walking home from a shift at the local hospice and had noticed when a van had stopped on double yellow lines right next to him. The driver had got out and waited for a couple of girls she thought, although one was hooded. The driver and the hoodie bundled the other person into the van. They then both got in and drove off along the one-way system.

Justin stopped reading and looked up at Anne. They exchanged a glance, and both nodded. Justin sent a text to the rest of the team, requesting a return to the office. Anne smiled and handed Kev a whiteboard marker.

"I think you should do the honours Keval. Thank you."

Justin watched the additions going up on the board in silence. The same person was mentioned, mostly wearing a hoodie that prevented recognition. The door man had seen the face as had one other witness. They needed to be put into contact with a police artist as soon as possible. Carlo's had good security, he remembered, and wondered why the club had not responded to the previous broadcast for information. The van was important and now they had a chance to track the van through the traffic cameras and CCTV to see if they could get some information on the driver.

"Two people! Two people, both of whom were keeping their identities hidden. Had they killed Chelsey, or was there more to discover?" He had spoken out loud, attracting Anne's attention. "We need to see what the club security might have picked up. Get a warrant for the recordings, as the club did not volunteer the information. Also, get one of the team on the CCTV and traffic cameras on the one-way system to track where the van goes from there. Do we have a police artist, or do we need to find one?"

"We have one and she's very good. I'll get that arranged as quickly as I can."

Justin turned to the supervisor. "Thank you, Keval."

Keval turned to leave, but Justin was responding to an uneasy feeling that usually meant trouble. "Keval, sorry, but could you send the York sighting to the local CID?"

Keval smiled and said, "No worries, already done. I might treat it as a joke here, but the callers were an elderly couple who insisted we were looking for their neighbour, a woman called Abigail Hutton. They haven't seen her since that same night. Ours won't be the only suspicious death that needs investigating. The local boys promised they'd visit the old couple." He went back to the ringing phones.

"How are you doing with the background on Eve Jordan? I noticed you'd started a search."

Anne shrugged and frowned. "Nothing regarding a criminal record."

Justin chuckled. "You sound disappointed."

Anne sighed heavily. "I don't know. There's something about that girl I just don't like. She seems so intense about everything and her attitude when we mentioned Chelsey's missing person report was rather bizarre. Anyway, she left school after A-levels and joined her father's company, Gardeners of Eden (Malford) which, at that time, was a one man, one van outfit and not doing very well. Our Eve, however, is quite a driving force, so much so that Dad's taken a back seat and it's now a very successful business." She turned and pointed at her screen. "There was a spread in the local press a few months ago, on successful locals, she featured as the most successful of all. They now have several lucrative contracts and employ twelve other permanent staff. Eve is also known for clever garden design and quality maintenance."

The story of Eve's career impressed Justin. Eve was managing a successful business and was still able to spend a large amount of time either comforting Sean after Chelsey's sudden death or collecting him from the station after his interviews. Added to the DIY action that had been Sean's supposed alibi ...

"She spends more time with Sean than his girlfriend could." He commented with a half-smile. "How does she manage all the rest, too?"

"The article did the usual about any successful woman, you know, love life, family or business and so on. Eve, according to the reporter, hinted at a very special relationship despite working all hours to get the business on a sound footing. She absolutely refused to name her partner, but I guess he or she must be someone very special." Anne drank from her cup and grimaced, "Euch! So much excitement and it's gone cold. Anyway, I'll keep digging into Eve, although so far everything looks legit."

Justin headed back to his office and opened up the long list of new emails. He felt a little disappointed that neither Doctor Shah nor Lizzie had yet sent in a report on the body in the van. He told himself to be patient and settled into the rest of the messages, awaiting his attention. Anything was better than dealing with the overtime and budget reviews, which sat deep in his conscience, niggling mildly but ignorable, every so often. He had just sufficient time for a yawn or two before the rest of the team arrived. He went out to join them as Anne stood at the board and explained the new timeline information. She paused, so he signalled her to continue and perched on the side of her desk.

"So, fair's fair guys. What have you got?"

Chas just beat Julie to it. "We went to the post mortem yesterday. Doctor Shah wouldn't be drawn on much."

"He never will," muttered Paul, raising a chuckle from the others.

"What he would say was the dead man was definitely killed before the van was burned, but not very long before. His throat was cut with a very sharp blade, slashed through to the backbone, Doc said." Chas' expression showed his shock. "That was some anger, or hatred, to provide the adrenalin to do that. "Doctor Shah did some X-rays of bones and dentistry. He also tried for DNA and will email any results and possible identification as they come through." He glanced enquiringly at Justin, who shook his head.

"Nothing so far, perhaps this afternoon or tomorrow morning."

"That's it so far."

"Thank you, Chas. Paul, Julie?"

Julie referred to her notes. "The burned-out van is with forensics. It was definitely deliberately torched. The accelerant was petrol, so we need to check the CCTV from the closest petrol stations. We'll …"

Justin's phone buzzed impatiently. He glanced at the caller ID. "Inspector Holmes," he explained. "I will have to take this."

21

Inspector Holmes' voice was almost lost in the background noise. Noise that occasionally crashed out an intelligible word or phrase in a stranger's voice. "Clear the way ... shattered glass ... Blood stains but not from the victim." Then the sound of a door shutting out the noise.

"Justin, I'm at Mama's restaurant. There was an attack this morning. One of my men has been injured. The ambulance crew has just taken him to the hospital. Mama and the family are shaken up but not hurt."

"I will be there in five minutes." Justin replied and looked up to find the whole team watching him. "Keep searching the CCTV and anything else you can think of. Find that van. Anne and I have to go now!"

Anne grabbed her jacket and hurried after him, arriving breathless at the car. Justin already had the engine running, the blue concealed lights flashing. He barely gave her time to belt in before the siren started and they were heading out. The barrier only just cleared the top of the car as they sped out of the car park. Justin heard a gasp from Anne as he overtook an elderly couple sticking to the speed limit, and another as he slipped between a BMW and an oncoming lorry. He accelerated along the one-way system, then slowed quickly to turn, against the lights, into the High Street proper. Justin pulled up hard just behind a marked police car.

The area around the restaurant had been cordoned off and was guarded by uniformed officers. There was an ambulance-sized gap in the street between the parked cars. Onlookers were gathering, which wasn't surprising, when it seemed every squad car in the county was parked nose to tail, crowded the High Street. Some were starting to head back to their duties, not being needed at the scene. The first emergency was now over and had settled into an investigation that none of the officers wanted messed up by destroyed evidence.

Justin got out of the car and looked across the roof at Anne's pale face. "Sorry," he said curtly but sincerely, then walked over to the officer with a clipboard. He gave his name and showed his ID. Holmes was waiting for him when he slipped under the tape. "John! What happened? Any word on your officer?"

"Serious head injury treated by the ambulance crew, then they rushed him to the local A&E. He was in the kitchen." Holmes pointed through the open front door to where the swing doors accessed the kitchen. "Mama and the family were in the restaurant area. They had just unlocked the door for the early lunch crowd when about half a dozen men barged in and started smashing up the place. My officer came out of the kitchen. One member of the gang was behind him when he came into the main room, who hit him hard. Papa thought the attacker used a wooden club. The gang then panicked and took off through the kitchen and down the back alley. Mama called an ambulance and us." Holmes' expression hardened. "I want these bastards hung out to dry! Steve, Constable Steve Godwin, he's a new father. His wife gave birth to their first child two days ago, for God's sake! At least they'll all be in the same hospital." He paused, turned away to get control of his feelings, then continued, "We're using the front entrance for forensics, but the rest of us are waiting for the all clear. The place is full of potential evidence. It seems sharp glass and crockery shards are just as damaging to those shits smashing up the place as they are to normal human beings. Mama and the family are with the greengrocer's two doors down.

Justin put a hand on Holmes' shoulder. "Between us, we will find them. Let me know as soon as you hear anything from the hospital about Steve."

Justin ducked back under the tape as Holmes turned to watch his officers questioning the growing crowd for witnesses. He signalled to Anne and pointed towards the greengrocer's shop.

In the back room of the shop, the greengrocer's partner had made the family comfortable and provided each of them with a mug of hot sweet tea "for the shock". He offered to make drinks for Justin and Anne but when they declined, tactfully left them to talk. Their conversation reassured Justin, especially when he saw for himself that all four of the family were unharmed, though very shocked by the experience. Mama immediately asked after the young police officer.

"I do not know any more than you, sorry Mama. Inspector Holmes will let us know when there is more to tell, I am sure." Justin bent over Mama and gently kissed her cheek.

"I will deal with this fool and his gang, if necessary, I swear to you Mama," he whispered in Italian. "For now, give the police a chance to investigate, yes?"

Mama patted his cheek and smiled. "Yes, but one way or another, they must pay for what they did." Her face showed the anger she felt. Justin understood her fury was for the injury to the young man who had been their guest and not because of the damage to the restaurant.

"Call the house when you want to go home. One of the staff can drive you. Also, let Martin know what help you will need once the forensics' officers have done their work. He will see to cleaning and repairs. Mama, if you need a loan for any replacements before the insurance comes through, just tell Martin and you shall have the funds immediately. Promise me!"

Once assured the family was safe and recovering, Justin was ready to return to the offices. He even gave a smile when Anne pretended to be afraid to get back into the car. He solemnly promised to stick close to the speed limit. One hand resting over his heart.

"Good," Anne replied emphatically despite the laughter twinkling in her eyes. "I've had more than enough excitement for one day and it's barely two o'clock."

"Excitement?" Justin laughed. "I thought you were a police officer?"

"I am, but I joined because the uniform is so flattering. It was that or an airline steward. Then I found I don't like heights."

The return was sedate and without incident.

"Next time you can drive, I promise," Justin said, following her up the shallow steps into the building. They both stopped short when they recognised Tony Byett at the front desk with another man. Byett turned and saw them. A huge grin lit up his face, and he waved something at them, tiny in his hand.

"I've got it! It wasn't lost when the laptop was stolen. This is Tom, by the way." He waved a hand vaguely towards his friend, then walked over to them.

"There you go." He placed a USB stick in Justin's hand, then lowered his voice. "Tom downloaded the recording when he checked the house last time. He wasn't sure if he would have time to get back again before the conference, you see. He came to see me this morning with the recording because he got back from the conference last night." Byett was so pleased that information was pouring out of him like a waterfall after the snow has melted. Tom stood by, looking bemused but pleased that his friend was happy.

Justin's hand curled protectively around the stick.

"Tony, thank you for this, and Tom thank you for downloading the recording. It may be extremely important to our investigation."

They said goodbye to the two men and hurried up to the office. Ray waved at them eagerly, his enthusiasm at odds with his habitual laid-back attitude. Pausing to plug the USB into Anne's computer, they went and joined the rest of the team.

"We've got something," Ray announced.

"So have we I think," Anne shot back, a touch of indignation in her voice.

Justin laughed even though he understood and shared their feelings. The frustrated tension of the last few days shattered by these potentially valuable new sources. "Wait a minute, both of you. Who has what information? Ray?"

"We've tracked the van."

Justin nodded, then waved towards Anne's computer.

"Byett's friend downloaded the camera recording before the burglary. We do not know exactly what the camera captured because we have not yet looked. Anne, you have the choice, Ray first, or us?"

"Ray first, it will fit the timeline better." She nodded at Ray to begin, and he blew her a thankful kiss before sitting at his screen. Justin and Anne stood on each side of his chair.

"We got the warrant, so the search started outside the club. The door guy gave us more information too."

Along the bottom of his screen were a series of minimised tabs. Ray opened the first. "The door guy was uncomfortable about the way Chelsey was being handled. Yes, he liked the fact that her companion was looking after her, but he felt he/she was being too rough with the girl. He watched the pair up to the road until he was called in to help with a few rowdies inside the club. What he did see was the van pulling up but didn't see the pair of them reach the van. Then we have this from the security camera."

They watched in silence; the security man had been right to feel something was wrong. Justin frowned when Chelsey tripped and was dragged upright with considerable force, then shoved forward to the van. The driver opened the door and helped haul Chelsey into the front seat, followed in by the other person. The door closed. Ray closed the tab and opened the next.

"We got this from near the Town Hall."

A still picture showed clearly, three passengers in the van and a front number plate, illuminated by the headlights of an oncoming car.

"Any luck with the number plate?"

Ray shook his head. "The result came back just before you came in. The plate belongs to a VW camper van, which our van is definitely not."

He changed the tab again, and the team watched as traffic cameras and CCTV followed the van around the one-way system, then south towards the motorway. The last recording showed the van leaving the motorway at the next junction south, heading towards the murder site.

Ray sat back. "And that's all folks!" he said. "The lanes aren't so well endowed with cameras or eye witnesses but by one thirty that Tuesday night the van was heading towards Tolland Wood and carried three people, one of whom was our victim."

There was a pause, then the whole team moved to Anne's desk. She sat down and took a deep breath.

"Right, let's see what we've got."

She double clicked to open the file.

They couldn't look away. No one so much as sniffed to break the silence. They were watching the worst horror movie imaginable, knowing what would happen, knowing it was very real. The recording was amazingly, dreadfully clear and detailed. Byett had obviously bought the best he could.

The van parked up, the rear registration visible and already familiar to them. Two figures left the van by both front doors, then hauled out a third. Chelsey, already deep under the influence of the drug, slumped between them. Their hoodies masked both their faces, but one was taller and broader, the other shorter and stockier than their victim. The driver opened the back doors, then together, they lifted Chelsey off her feet and almost threw her into the back. For whatever reason, the taller person who had driven the van then backed away, turned and walked off. The shorter one climbed in the back and appeared to straddle Chelsey's prone body. They saw the right arm raised, again and again, as if it would never stop slamming down into the flesh beneath. Even on the film they could see the strength and fury behind each blow. From experience Justin understood the impact, hoped her drugged state had prevented Chelsey from feeling the full unmitigated agony of the attack. He glanced at the intent faces of his team, pale, fixed, and knew they too were imagining the pain and fear.

Mentally stepping back from the view, he searched his memory of the last few minutes. The van had arrived in an empty car park and no other cars had entered during the attack. The pair had unexpectedly chosen a good night where none of the car park regulars were in attendance. He returned to the screen.

The single attacker tossed something further into the van, then slid out backwards, closing the van doors, before heading off in the direction the driver had taken. They were gone so long the recording stopped. The fascination of evil that had held them frozen lost its grip. Anne closed that file.

"There's a twenty-minute gap between the two files." She said, then opened the next file.

The two hooded figures came back together. They opened the back doors again. The driver pulled out a sack trolley and stood it in front of the open back door. Next there appeared to be an argument between the two from the angry jabbing pointing at Chelsey's body and gesturing at the trolley until the driver took off his belt and handed it over.

Paul shook his head, muttering, "They planned her kidnap, had a trolley available, and forgot about securing her to it?"

Justin nodded, eyes not leaving the screen. "So, it would seem."

The two attackers pulled Chelsey out of the van, ignoring what minimal resistance she could still make. Both belts were used to secure her to the trolley. The driver closed the back doors and returned to the driving seat. The other, shorter figure got the trolley moving and was soon out of camera view.

A third and final recording starting thirty minutes later showed the return of the trolley, then the van driving out of the car park.

"That's all of it," Anne confirmed, closing down the last recording.

"It confirms that she had her handbag with her until getting into the van. We didn't see it when she was tied to the trolley. So, the bag was dumped on the Horsefield by her attackers later. We also know now that there were two people involved in her abduction and murder, rather than just one." Justin paused, thinking. "Get the technical people to go through all the recordings frame by frame. We need to find clear views of either or preferably both faces. I think the shorter one's face may have been visible for a second or two when they drove into the car park and got out."

He turned to Anne. "You remember I thought I had seen someone familiar at the reconstruction, among the onlookers?"

Anne nodded.

"Well, I think we may have met the shorter of those two. There is something very familiar about it and I think both of them were in the crowd. They were wearing similar cargo trousers and hoodies as they were when they attacked and killed Chelsey Harris. They were definitely together. Add the unedited recording from that for the tech boys as well." He looked around at the others. "Ray, Chas, are there any views inside the van from the traffic cams other than the one that shows the registration as well?"

Ray shook his head. "Nah! We looked for those in particular. Once they left the woods, we lost them. They must've kept to the back lanes 'cos we looked for the van through to six the next morning and found nothing." He unexpectedly grinned, "Except for you pausing on the hill then jogging off down to the wood."

Justin joined in the laughter, relieved they had only seen the last part of his run where he was going fairly slowly, following that delicious scent.

"Thank you both." He turned to Julie and Paul. "You two had something to tell us when Inspector Holmes rang. My apologies for cutting you off the way I did. Something on the burned van, I think?"

"Yes, forensics reported on the van while you were out. They found the VIN and matched it. The van belonged to Eve Jordan. It was the one she reported stolen that night. They've also found blood samples that were protected from the fire. Lizzie was excited. Apparently, the plastic dashboard had melted over the samples and protected them. Her team is working on the samples as a priority."

Julie turned from her computer. "Sir, you need to see this as well. I think we can confirm the same couple torched the van. The petrol station on Loates Lane, probably closest to the field. We asked for the CCTV and they obliged. See here the couple on a motorbike. They fill a small jerrycan as well as the bike's tank. Having just seen the other recording, I think the taller rider is the van driver and his bike passenger is much shorter." Julie looked up into Justin's face a little nervously. "Sir, I think the passenger is a woman. Look here! Watch the way she walks across the forecourt and into the building, to the cash desk. She takes her helmet off just before entering and there!" Julie paused the recording. "There's a reflection in the glass door. I know it's a long shot, but …"

"Yes, I see it! I think you are right our passenger is a woman. Send it with the rest to the technical people. Though I would say that you and I are in the same boat here. While we think we recognise them, we need confirmation. A couple on a motorbike could just as easily be an ordinary couple that look like our pair but are just going about their legitimate business." Justin glanced at the time code. "The timing certainly fits and I know that petrol station. It's about ten minutes along the road from the field. I use it myself."

He turned to look at the two whiteboards. "Right, we need to find both Eve Jordan and Gavin Lombard as quickly as possible. They both have a few questions to answer."

22

"Did he give you any reason why he needed to see us?" Justin asked.

Anne looked at the text again. "No, just that he had something important for both cases."

She stopped, frowning over the wording, "Doctor Shah's almost as precise in his speech as you, so he does mean cases plural."

"It had better be good," Justin muttered quietly, walking into the pathology department office.

Doctor Shah swung around in his chair. "Oh, it is, I promise you," he replied. "Come and take a look at these."

They joined him at the light box on which the doctor had placed two sets of dental X-rays. Justin and Anne stared at them, even to a non-medical person, they seemed similar. Doctor Shah used a pointer to highlight the exact matches in the two pictures.

"A match, do you agree?"

"Looks like it," Anne said. "Who do they belong to?"

"This one we took from your fire damaged body and this one is from Ockham Young Offenders. Your burned body with the cut throat is that of one of your suspects in the Chelsey Harris case. Gavin Lombard was held at Ockham for ABH. Oh, and the blade used to cut his throat was similar to the one used on Chelsey Harris. The same shape and style." He frowned. "One of my assistants is an enthusiastic gardener. He thought the shape was familiar and suggested a larger version of his pruning knife at home. Possibly a one-off original made specifically for an individual. I think he could be right."

They looked at one another, and Justin frowned. At the garden centre, he had walked past an entire display of blades that had a curved top and a straighter, sharpened blade. No wonder they had seemed familiar.

He saw Doctor Shah grin, pleased with their reaction to his findings. Then the pathologist switched off the light box, stood up and stretched.

"More evidence for your theory, Anne." Justin acknowledged. "He may well have been protecting Chelsey, and that was the reason he had to die. If the killer thought Gavin knew something, it would be a motive for his death."

Anne smiled at his words but said, "It could be, but it could be a case of thieves falling out. There could have been an argument. We know Gavin was fit, and capable of defending himself, yet someone got behind him and slit his throat to the backbone. Either someone he trusted completely or someone he was confident he could handle." She sighed, "I don't know. We need more."

"I suggest another visit to Sean Trent. He knows Gavin better than anyone else and if anyone would have heard from Eve Jordan or know where she might be, he is our man."

"I emailed a full report of my findings to you just before you arrived. Now, I'm heading home on time for once. It's our anniversary and the boys have set up a 'surprise' party for us. My wife will kill me if I'm late and you guys have more than enough to deal with at the moment."

Justin smiled, "Thank you Doctor Shah and Happy Anniversary. Can we give you a lift home?"

The pathologist shook his head, "Thank you no, I have my car." He waved and wandered off into the changing rooms to get out of his scrubs and have a shower.

Justin and Anne headed back to their car. "Sean should have finished work and be heading home by now. We will head for his apartment building. We can check if Eve Jordan has returned at the same time."

The homeward bound traffic slowed down everything to a gentle crawl that doubled the time to reach their destination. The slow journey had Justin muttering about walking would have been quicker. He pulled into the parking area in front of the main entrance. They made their way up to Trent's apartment and knocked.

Sean had literally just got in and was inside his hallway when their knock sounded. He was still wearing a business suit and tie, although the tie had been pulled loose. The crisp white shirt showed off his tan to perfection. The suit was from a tailor Justin himself used, and the made-to-measure suits were not cheap. He was impressed, as was Anne, from the way she looked Sean over.

"Oh, hi," he said, recognising his visitors, "come in." He led the way into the lounge. "Take a seat. Can I get you a drink? It's been a pig of a day and I'm having one." He pulled his tie from around his collar and dropped it onto the back of the chair, undoing the top shirt button. He breathed deeply. "These damn things choke me," he commented, opening a decent single malt and pouring a generous measure.

"Thank you, no. It is a cliché I know, but we are on duty."

Sean sat down in the armchair while Anne and Justin occupied the couch.

"You haven't come to arrest me this time, that's clear. So, what do you want?"

There was a pause while Justin tried to find the words to explain. The wait for an answer alerted Sean to something serious. He sat up from lounging in the chair.

"What?"

"I am sorry Sean. We would like to talk to you about Gavin Lombard. I am afraid we found a body early yesterday morning, which has been identified positively as Gavin Lombard."

Sean went very pale beneath his tan and downed the remaining whisky in one.

"Bloody Hell!"

He looked at Anne and Justin with a narrow-eyed stare. "Are you sure? What the fuck is happening to us?" There was silence while Sean went over and refilled his glass. "It's too much of a coincidence surely," he continued quietly, "Gavin and Chelsey both dead. Do you think Gav killed her?" he was already shaking his head. "No, he would never do that. I don't believe that would happen."

"I'm sorry Sean, Gavin's death is being treated as suspicious. We wondered if you knew of anyone Gavin had argued with, or received threats from. Someone who would be violent if he'd upset them," Anne explained.

"No," he said, certain, "Gav looked like a typical tough guy but, in here," Sean tapped over his heart with his fist, "well, he was gentle, kind, caring. But all those feelings he kept hidden away, you know, where no one could see unless he let them. He had very few good friends, but a lot more people liked him. I don't know of anyone who was so much an enemy they would kill him. I suppose that's what you mean by suspicious, possibly another murder?"

"Had you been in contact with him recently, since Chelsey's death?"

"Come to think of it, only once, and he was quieter than usual. Seemed to have something on his mind, really troubling him, but he wasn't ready to share then." He shrugged, "I guess I could have pushed, but he is … was … a very private person. He could turn stubborn if you pushed too hard."

"Would he have confided in anyone else?"

Sean sighed and rubbed the back of his neck while he thought. "Not that I know. His family had all gone, if you know what I mean. Nobody left that he was close to. Most of the people he knew in Malford are my friends too."

"How about Eve Jordan?" Anne suddenly asked. "Did she and Gavin get on well?"

"No," was the decisive and immediate reply. "If anything, they just about tolerated one another, but no real friendship. In fact, I always felt Gavin was nervous around Eve, but I could never figure out why. Why do you ask?"

"We've been looking for Eve, but she seems to be missing as well. Have you seen her recently?"

"Oh, Eve decided to go away for a while, that's all." Sean frowned. "She went away not long after she drove me back from your police station actually. She does just take off occasionally, but never for very long."

"Any idea where? We really do need to speak to her urgently. We have some news about her stolen van, and given what has happened to two of your group, we would be happier if we knew where she was, and that she was safe."

He shook his head, "No, strange that. I never realised before, but she never does say where she's going. I know she has one particular cousin she's close to but who that is," Sean shrugged, "she never told me a name. She keeps in touch with her business wherever she goes off to, and I get a call or a text most evenings when she's away."

"Has she called you today?"

"Not yet, she might not. We had a long chat last night." Sean hesitated, and he looked agitated. "Strange that," he said, following his own thoughts.

"What was?" Justin asked quietly.

"Normally her name shows on my screen when she calls, but last night it didn't. Maybe her phone died, and she borrowed one."

"If she calls again, could you try to find out where she is, or ask her to contact us at the station? Tell her we have news about her van, would you?"

Sean agreed to their request, and they left him sitting in a chair, nursing the remains of his drink. His eyes focused on the wall, though he was obviously thinking about something else, probably trying to come to terms with what had happened.

"He looks lost," Anne commented, shutting the door to Sean's apartment.

"He does," Justin agreed. "How old is he, twenty-four, twenty-five?"

Anne nodded.

"And he has just lost two people of a similar age and as close to him as one person can get to another. He is in shock. Death has always been remote, insignificant, in Sean's world, like most young people. Now, two deaths have shattered that illusion of being indestructible."

"Did you ever feel indestructible, as if life would go on forever? I'm not sure I did."

Justin's laugh had a strange, hard edge. "Oh yes, once upon a time, in my youth. I remember that feeling very well indeed. However, death is waiting for us all. I suppose I have been lucky in some respects and the Grim Reaper has had to wait a lot longer for me than he intended."

"So, what happened that changed your mind?"

"I am not sure I ever did." Justin changed the subject. "How about we call it a day and start fresh tomorrow? I will even let you drive us back."

Justin found himself copying Sean's actions when he got home. Tie off, generous drink poured, Justin stood at the French windows watching the light gradually fade, enjoying the mellow warmth of the whisky spreading through him, helping to loosen stiff muscles and ease away some of the tension. Here, in his own home, he did not need to maintain a constant guard over his thoughts and actions. He could be himself among people he could trust and let his mind wander, to work on the nagging irritating unknowns that could hold the key to both murders.

Beth came in to switch on the lights and pull the curtains. She quietly left without doing either when she saw the dark familiar shadow at the window. Justin felt her presence, but it did not disturb him.

The glass was long empty before he turned away from the view. He checked the mantle clock and smiled, just enough time to freshen up and change before Thomas joined him for a quiet, casual dinner. He turned away from the darkened view and walked across the room. For an instant, the brightness of the chandelier in the hall dazzled his eyes and made him realise how dark the drawing room had become. Beth was in the doorway to the kitchen and came forward to take the glass from his hand.

"I am perfectly capable of washing up a single glass, Beth," he said and saw her smile. "You can make all cosy in the drawing room now, ready for Thomas." The delicious aromas of Beth's cooking tempted his taste buds, making his mouth water. He recognised the aroma of coq au vin and smiled.

"A favourite of Thomas's, you are spoiling us again Beth. He will want to stay here forever if you keep cooking all his favourites. I am not complaining, you understand, because I get to enjoy that extra special something you put into already wonderful cooking, and have good company to share it. What are you providing for dessert?"

"You'll find out when it's ready," she laughed. "Your guest will be here in ten minutes."

Justin kissed her cheek and headed up the stairs.

In the short time it took him to shower and change, Thomas had arrived and settled into a comfortable chair with a glass that he was happily emptying when Justin entered the room. Thomas greeted him lazily with a slight wave of the glass before taking another appreciative sip. Justin poured himself a drink and refilled Thomas's glass.

"You look very content," he commented.

"Who wouldn't be?" Thomas grinned, looking at the log fire burning bright in the Georgian fireplace. "Warmth, comfort, booze and a trip to soak up the aroma of Beth's cooking in the kitchen. I am a very happy man."

"You are certainly a privileged man if you entered Beth's domain while she was cooking and didn't end up with a butcher's cleaver in your head. But then you are her favourite. I always feel I need to ask permission to enter, or I sneak through the kitchen when I am sure she is absent."

Justin settled onto the couch nearest Thomas's chair. "How is Ryan doing with his piece on people smuggling? I have not seen him for quite a while."

Thomas sighed. "I don't know. He finished that piece and it's published. The editor seemed really pleased with it. But Ryan suddenly said he needed to go off on a research trip a couple of days ago and wouldn't tell me where he was going." Thomas leaned forward. "I'm not worried yet, but there is a nagging concern at the back of my mind. Normally, he leaves an address where I can contact him, but not this time. He hasn't even taken his mobile. He had been talking about doing a follow-up or even a series of articles on the same theme. Apparently, he heard rumours of a specific group about whom nothing factual is known." Thomas shrugged. "I'm sure he'll tell me everything when he gets back. He said it was just preliminary research and you know how many of these leads really turn out to be good."

"Mm, about as many as turn out well for us, or do you think Ryan has a slight advantage over us there?"

A faint, mellow chime was heard through the oak door.

"Aha, Beth's gentle call, food is ready. I hope you are hungry enough to do justice to Beth's superb cooking?"

"Lead on, I could eat a horse," Thomas commanded.

Justin laughed. "No, you could not. The meat is far too tough, I know." He led the way into the breakfast room. For some time, only the clink of cutlery could be heard.

"So, what's worrying you?" Thomas asked after a suitable time to appreciate the meal.

"Worried?"

Thomas nodded. "That or concerned might describe your mood better. You listen and sympathise with me often enough. How about this time I act as your sounding board?"

Justin sat back, pleasantly replete, his fingers tracing the engraving on the crystal wineglass. He watched Thomas refill his plate and took a swallow of wine before replying.

"Fair enough, as much as I can share. I am feeling … frustrated, I suppose. I had two people to find, both of whom could have had information useful to our investigation, and at least one of them was possibly in danger."

Thomas frowned. "How in danger?"

Beth came in, pushing a trolley, to clear the plates and place the dessert on the table. Tarte Tatin, with fresh cream from the home farm. Thomas sighed happily and took the opportunity to thank Beth, which brought a blush of pleasure to her face. She served the sweet hot flan, providing Thomas a generous slice. Then rattled the trolley quietly out of the door.

"You silver-tongued devil!" Justin laughed, watching Thomas shovel down his dessert, a look of total enjoyment on his face. "I can almost see your waistline expanding."

Thomas swallowed. "Yeah, rotund country doctor stereotype. That's me! Now you were saying?"

Justin shook his head, chuckling, "No distracting you, is there? One possible motive for Chelsey Harris's death, is her relationship with Sean Trent. We have found abusive communications, by post, text and email, to Chelsey. They are extreme. We then find out Sean's temporary girlfriend when he and Chelsey split up, also received abusive and threatening messages. Well, there is one woman who has probably had the longest ongoing relationship with Sean and she has now disappeared."

"What kind of relationship?"

Justin saw Thomas had emptied his plate.

"Shall we return to the drawing room? We can talk uninterrupted and let Beth clear in here and have the rest of the evening for herself."

He collected the bottle and his glass, then laughed aloud at Thomas's pretence of struggling out of his chair. "Beware Thomas, one day that problem may come true."

They settled contentedly in front of the fire, and Justin refilled both glasses.

"Sean's girlfriends, lovers, whatever you want to call them, seem to come and go quickly except for Chelsey." Justin paused, recalling his first sight of Sean Trent. "Trent is a handsome, fit young man with that twinkle in his eye that attracts the young women. Other than that, there is something about him that probably only a woman could explain. Chelsey was different in that he returned to her for a second time and seemed to make a serious effort at a long-term relationship. However, there is one person, Eve Jordan, who has been in his life through all his other relationships as far as I can tell, since they were at secondary school. Now, when we need to talk to her, she is nowhere to be found."

"So, you are worried about her safety?"

Justin shrugged. "I do not know really. We need to talk to her about a few things, not least the theft of her gardener's van on the night Chelsey was killed. We found the van with the dead body of our second missing person inside it. Gavin Lombard, Sean's friend and follower. Yes, I am concerned, and I feel some responsibility for Lombard's death. We wrote him off as a stalker, possibly even her killer. Now it seems he was trying to protect Chelsey, but from what, or rather, who? Did he know or think he knew who our killer was? Was that the reason they killed him?"

"Any suspects?" Thomas drained his glass.

"Sean Trent has an alibi; he was screwing Chelsey's best friend."

Thomas choked on his wine and gave a spluttering cough. Justin looked at him in alarm. Thomas waved a hand to show he was alright despite a red face, burning throat and gasping for air. Justin took his glass from him, got up, and poured him some water and a coffee from the tray on the sideboard.

"Why?" Thomas gasped and coughed again, then took a sip of the offered water. "Why is it when you use slang it always sounds really, really crude?"

Justin's confusion showed. Thomas shook his head.

"Never mind." Thomas smiled, "if the Trent guy has an alibi that solid, why do you sound doubtful?"

"Firstly, Chelsey had caught Sean and Gina Crane together the afternoon before she was killed. Secondly, the gardening van was stolen from the same apartment building. It could have been burned out to try to eliminate any forensic evidence that would link it to Chelsey's death, although obviously I have no proof of that yet. By chance, the Fire Brigade found the burning van with Lombard's body inside and we have evidence he had been following Chelsey at least part of that day, then …"

"You're sure it wasn't him?"

Justin nodded. "Yes. You see, there were motorbike tracks around the van and signs of two people at the site. The CCTV at the local petrol station shows two people filling the bike's tank and a small jerrycan. One is tall and probably male, while the other is much shorter and could be male or female. They might be innocent bystanders, but if not, then they could be Sean and Gina, the BFF. Lizzie's forensics may clear up a few things, but personally, I believe Sean may be a fool about women, but I cannot see him as a double murderer."

Thomas finished his coffee, looking at the chiming mantle clock.

"I'm on early surgery duty tomorrow. I think I will have to love and leave you unless I want my patients claiming I look worse than they feel."

"I will walk down to the lodge with you, then take a walk around the estate.

I need some cold air and exercise to clear my head. A few miles might help me see something we have, so far, missed."

23

Justin paused at the top of the three steps in front of the main door when his mobile buzzed for attention. It was a text that surprised him because of who had sent it. It read:

"Have something important. Can you wait for me to get there before you start the morning briefing? Lizzie"

"Of course! Where did you get my number?" he replied. When the head of forensics asked you to wait for something important, he wasn't going to argue. He did not expect a reply, but the phone buzzed again.

"I have my sources," this text stated, ending with a smiley face. Justin realised he was smiling in response.

Lizzie arrived like a miniature hurricane, having delayed the briefing by under ten minutes. The potential offered by her something important message had already generated a large amount of excited anticipation in the team.

"Hi people," she said. "Sorry to keep you waiting. I had to verify something with Inspector Holmes before coming here."

"So, what do you have for us?" Justin began the briefing.

"I'm going to start with the attack at Mama's Place, so please bear with me." She handed a written report to Justin. "It's all in there. At Mama's, we found identifiable fingerprints for several suspects already known to the police. We sent that information to Inspector Holmes. Alongside the prints, there was one particular footprint we picked up from walking through the victim's blood." She looked around, adding, "He regained consciousness late yesterday, you'll be pleased to hear, and seems to have stabilised. The footprint revealed a particularly unique wear pattern. I matched the pattern to casts taken, along with motorbike tracks, where your second victim was found and also with a cast from the Byett burglary. It links all three cases."

"You told Inspector Holmes when?"

"Yesterday afternoon. Since then, he's had teams out and arrested four people out of the six sets of fingerprints. My people checked their collections of footwear, particularly the trainers, and none showed the same specific pattern. That leaves two suspects, confirmed by fingerprint evidence as John Francis and Aston Buckland. Francis was front lookout and never went into the restaurant, from what the interviewees stated. Therefore, Francis could not have left the footprint in the blood."

"Ergo, Buckland is involved in burglary, arson, assault on a police officer and murder, as well as the protection racket." Justin's pleasure at the results vibrated in his voice.

Lizzie nodded, and her grin grew wider.

Ray picked up the hint. "OK, give with the rest!" his voice suggested a hint of boredom and resignation, as if he really didn't care about what she still had to tell, but his grin was almost as wide as Lizzie's own.

"I can link the burned-out van to Chelsey Harris as well."

"By what miracle can you do that," Julie asked.

Lizzie's infectious chuckle agreed with Julie's comment. "It was a minor miracle. The plastics of the dashboard melted over and protected a section of blood spatter. There were two blood groups represented, one was Gavin Lombard's, but the other, more rare blood group, was the same as Chelsey Harris."

"I would like to kiss you, Lizzie. Just to show my appreciation of your work, and if it was permitted," Justin stated. "Instead, how about you join the rest of us for a meal when the investigation is over."

Lizzie looked him over from head to toe, then laughed. "For you, I might give permission, once I know you better that is." She checked her watch. "Oops! Got to go. Yes, to the meal and good luck." She waved and shot out the door quicker than she had arrived.

Justin ceremonially wrote up Aston Buckland's name onto the board and boxed it in. He turned to face his team. "I have a confession to make," he said, and the buzz of conversation stopped immediately. "I have already been trying to track down Buckland. There was an incident at the restaurant on the same evening Anne was attacked. It was not reported because it came to nothing in the end. Buckland had set someone up to do damage on his behalf. He is no longer at the squat on Belper Road, the address an informant gave me. Inspector Holmes and the Drugs Squad raided the squat because there was a marijuana farm there." He looked around their intent faces. "Get to work and find me more information on Aston Buckland and any possible current locations."

He headed to his own office to call his friend about taking over the assault case. Now there was evidence to connect them with both his team's current investigations, he doubted there would be any problem in combining resources.

Three-quarters of an hour later, Justin felt a shadow cross his desk and looked up. Paul was standing in the doorway. Justin looked up and waited for him to speak.

"Sorry to disturb you sir, but there's an update on Buckland, including a possible location." He turned and headed back into the main office; Justin followed after him.

Chas was spokesperson. "Aston's father, Peter Buckland, is currently serving time for a failed jewel robbery. Crime seems to run in the family. The grandfather, Billy Buckland, had a reputation as a hard man in the seventies when he was involved in organised crime. The police then finally put him away for twenty years, for killing a pedestrian. He was driving the getaway car for a bank raid. It was supposed to be a life sentence, but he was released on licence. Grandfather Buckland now lives in a private care home, Longacres.

Aston's mother is Olivia Hardy. Several years ago, she divorced Peter Buckland and went back to using her maiden name. She has a house in Purbeck Street where Aston also lives according to the electoral register. She does care work for the elderly via a local care company."

"Ms James, Byett's neighbour, has a care package, and she called her helper Olivia. Chas, find her phone number and give her a call. Check what her helper's surname is. Anne, organise a search warrant for Olivia Hardy's house urgently. Well done, all of you. I will check with Inspector Holmes if he would like to be involved in the search."

Chas confirmed Olivia Hardy as Ms James' carer, slightly quicker than Anne obtained the warrant. The team headed out together in three cars, linking up with a police van on the way.

Purbeck Street was in the maze of small streets that formed the west part of Malford. It was a street of terraced houses built to house the railway workers constructing the main line through to London and the Midlands between 1860 and 1890. Much later, into the heart of the area, had been dropped the local football stadium, right next door to the hospital that was now being considerably extended. They followed the road, passing the local grammar school, then curved left before turning left at the lights into the main road along the front of the stadium. Between the stadium and the hospital, they turned right, away from the main road through a small thicket of "for sale" signs into the densely packed maze of smaller streets, following the closer turns right and left until they reached Purbeck Street. When they arrived, there was no one out in the street, except for a lone figure carrying shopping bags, who turned into the street at the same time as the cars stopped. The three cars and the van took up all the parking spaces around Ms Hardy's house. It was neat and well cared for, with a tiny front paved garden with pockets of soil spaced between the slabs where herbs and scented plants were growing. Justin opened the gate and walked two strides up the path to the front door. Anne followed through the gate while the rest of the teams waited in the vehicles. Justin rang the bell, and they waited; he was just about to ring again when a voice asked politely, "Can I help you?"

The question came from behind them and they both turned to see a neatly dressed, slender woman between two heavy bags of shopping. Her dark eyes were cool and her face guarded, but Justin could see the beauty of fine bone structure and flawless skin.

"Ms Hardy?" he asked.

"Yes, I'm Olivia Hardy," She replied, picking up the bags.

To have a son of Aston's age, she would have to be in her late thirties but looked much younger. She glanced resignedly at the line of cars.

"Let me guess, police? If Peter has escaped, this is the very last place he would come. You're wasting your time."

"We wanted to talk to your son, Aston."

Her mouth pulled tight, and she gave a resigned sigh.

"In that case, let's get inside before my ice cream melts and I'll put the kettle on."

She slid past them, door key in hand, and opened the door. Turning back, she inspected the mini cavalcade again.

"I've got enough mugs for all of you, I think. But someone will need to buy another pint of milk. The mini mart is just round the corner to the right."

She walked through the living room and on into the kitchen, expecting them to follow. The first thing she did was to put away the precious ice cream in the freezer, the second was to fill and switch on the kettle.

"Right! You can ask me anything you want as long as you don't mind me putting stuff away while we talk. I'm due at work in an hour and a half." She glanced around at them and noticed the piece of paper Justin was holding. She raised an irritated eyebrow.

"Search Warrant, I suppose?" she said and held out her hand.

Justin gave her the warrant. She read it thoroughly, then handed it back. "Aston is my son and I love him, but I'm not stupid and I know what he is like. Comes of being known as the infamous gangster family Buckland, I suppose. A bit like the Mafia, but not quite the same size of organisation."

She was making fun of their reputation, but there was a trace of hurt in her tone which hinted how much she hated that family reputation. She turned back and started putting tins in the cupboard.

"OK, you might as well bring in the troops. My bedroom is the one on the left of the landing, looking out onto the road. Aston's is on the right with a view of the back garden." She half smiled, "and yes, he has shinned down the drainpipe on occasion, when we have had visitors like you. Mind you, not all of them were as polite or careful as you lot. Just make sure you don't break anything precious to me, and try to put things back tidy."

She waved Justin and Anne to high stools at the breakfast bar and began taking down an extensive mug collection from the next cupboard to the tinned goods.

"To answer your questions, no, I haven't seen Aston for the last two weeks, except for a quick ten minutes to borrow some money from me on payday. Oh yes, and a chat and a cup of tea with Ms James when he was doing a leaflet drop in her area."

"What company does Aston normally work for, delivering those leaflets?"

Ms Hardy thought for a moment, "Mostly Halliwell's of Hope Street. At least that's what they call themselves. It's casual work, nothing regular and pretty poorly paid."

Justin and Anne shared a glance. The check on leaflet drops had revealed that no delivery had been scheduled for the estate where Byett lived, and the leaflets posted through the doors had mostly been old ones from a couple of months previously.

She poured water into a coffee percolator and set a full kettle to boil. Justin heard her mutter, "tea bags, sugar, mugs, teapot," then she turned back to them.

"I hope one of your lot did go to the corner shop, otherwise it's black tea and coffee all round, whether you like it or not."

A uniformed officer appeared at the door from the back room and walked into the kitchen. Before he could duck back out, Ms Hardy saw him and smiled. The milk had arrived. "Right, young man, kitchen here and you can deal with the drinks while you're searching. Utility room through there, including dirty washing. I won't ask you to load the machine for me." She pointed at the room beyond the kitchen arch that framed a view of the neat garden through glass double doors. For a moment, she looked suddenly lost, then her back straightened and her head went up. She beckoned Justin and Anne to follow her into the front room. "Not that he'll find anything. Aston hasn't brought his dirty laundry round for washing yet. As I said, it's been a while since I saw him. Please sit down. I know how long these searches can take."

"Ms Hardy, could you tell us who Aston hangs out with?" Anne asked. "Anyone who might do a job with him or help him if he was in trouble?"

She was shaking her head before Anne had finished asking the question.

"Not really. He doesn't tell me much these days, not since his dad went to prison. He used to hang out with a group of likely lads." She named the four they already had in custody. "There's no one I can think of who could hide him from your lot. He's very close to Grandad Buckland, but I don't think the care home would let him stay and Billy's very frail these days. There's his cousin, of course, but I don't think Aston would want to involve her in his shenanigans." She stopped and then asked quietly, "How serious is this? I know I've been treating this search as a joke, but it was a way of life for me when Pete was around. Aston has never been more than a two-bit yob, never a real criminal. How serious is it?"

Justin felt some sympathy for her pain. "I am sorry, Ms Hardy, but there are several potential charges that we need to clear up with Aston and yes, they are serious."

She let out a choked sob and turned her back to them. She fought the tears and won back control quickly. Justin admired her strength of spirit, knowing she must have dealt with the same situation many times during her marriage.

Now, her son was following the same path. She turned back to face them. Tears still showed in her eyes, blurring the look of determination on her face.

"Have you tried his dad's house? Aston has a key and uses it sometimes."

Justin mentioned the address of the squat he had visited unofficially, but Ms Hardy shook her head.

"No, Pete was shacked up in Durban Close with a girl a third of his age. When he went to prison, she trotted off happily to pastures new, about eighteen months into his sentence. Aston's been looking after the place for him since."

They finished their search and found exactly what Ms Hardy had said, nothing. Aston Buckland had cleared out most of his things and there were no signs of where he might be other than her suggestion.

The team polished off the tea and coffee in record time and headed outside to the cars. Justin and Anne were the last to leave. They were just about to walk out of the living room when a photograph on the wall unit caught Justin's attention. It stood proudly in a silver frame. A picture of most, perhaps all, of the Buckland family surrounding a wheelchair bound William Buckland. Even though the face had aged, it was one Justin would always recognise, but he hardly glanced at the image, then fixed on another figure standing next to Aston Buckland who was standing proudly beside the old man, one hand on his grandfather's shoulder.

"Is this all the family?" He asked their hostess.

She moved next to him and glanced at the picture. "Oh lord, yes. One of the staff took it, on Billy's 75th birthday, in the care home gardens."

"I can see yourself and is this Aston?" he pointed at the person to the right of the old man.

A smile curved Ms Hardy's lips, and her voice softened. "Yes, it was a lovely day. Aston and Pete hadn't been in trouble for a while and it seemed everything would be alright." She shook her head sadly, then named all the people in the photograph.

"And that is Eve standing next to Aston. She's his favourite cousin. She's Billy's daughter Yvonne's only child. Tragic that Yvonne died very young, a brain aneurism, and Lance had to bring up Eve on his own. She's done well for herself, she has." Ms Hardy laughed lightly. "Aston would do anything for her, soppy lad!"

Justin passed the photograph to Anne. She stared at the picture with interest but said nothing. Anne then returned the frame to the shelf on the wall unit.

"Thank you, Ms Hardy, and my apologies for the disruption." He signalled Julie and Paul, who walked back to join them. "To make up for us delaying you, please allow my colleagues to give you a lift to your first appointment."

"I have my bike, so I shouldn't be too late," she replied, but agreed when Justin insisted it would be no trouble. She headed upstairs to change.

Justin saw her mobile on top of her work bag on the sofa. "Keep her from trying to contact Aston if you can. Stay close until she goes into the home of her first clients. I will text you the location to meet us from there."

"I don't think she will try to call him." Anne said. "She seems to have had enough of trying to keep him out of prison. You saw her face when you said the charges were serious."

They went out to the car, and Justin gave Anne the keys. He got on the radio for the full address of Peter Buckland's house.

"You know where Durban Close is?"

Anne nodded.

"Peter Buckland owns number four. We need to get there quickly, but without rousing too much interest." Justin continued.

"It's the other side of town from here across the traffic and it's market day," Anne replied.

Luckily, crossing the main flow of traffic was easier than joining the queue that a snail could have overtaken. Durban Close was a private road of five widely spaced detached houses. The houses were just a level below the expensive modern mansions around the Horsefield. Though they were not so sizeable, they were impressive, a good enough reason for Anne's appreciative whistle.

"Oh boy! I'm in the wrong job," she commented. "People say crime doesn't pay. We should show them this."

"That is the one we need." Justin pointed at a house just as imposing as the others but looking slightly neglected when compared to their pristine exteriors.

Theirs was the only car to enter the close with the rest of the team parked on the neighbouring roads, to cover any escape routes at the back or sides of the houses.

Anne nodded "Yes. I think there's someone moving around in there. I saw movement across the windows."

Justin had also seen the shadow outlined by the sunlight filtering through from the back of the house.

"Yes, Zulu One to all units, standby," he said into his radio then he turned to Anne. "Shall we?"

She grinned, "Oh, yes!"

They walked to the front door and knocked. No answer. Justin used the knocker again for longer, still no answer and no sound or sight of movement inside.

"Stay here and keep watch. I am going to look around the back," Justin said.

Justin had checked the outside walls of the house and found no sign of security cameras. He also saw that the garage would hide his actions from Anne because the high wooden gate, his target, was set back a few feet and to one side of the garage. He jumped the two-metre-high fence, landing lightly on the other side, then paused, listening intently. When Anne knocked again and called Aston's name, he hurried down the side of the house where there were no doors or windows. Justin peered around the corner at the back of the house. There was a door leading out from the kitchen about ten feet from a set of bifold glass doors.

Something moved in the garden but it was only the local fox, put out to find a human blocking his usual route to his den. A noise came from inside the house. Totally disrupted, the fox turned and trotted back the way it had come. Justin froze into a crouch. The bifold doors opened with hardly any noise and cautiously Aston Buckland slid through the narrow gap. His back was to Justin. He half turned, heading for the back fence beyond the shrubs, when Justin spoke.

"Is this any way to treat visitors, even uninvited ones?"

Half a second of stillness, then Buckland took off. Justin reckoned he would have won gold at the last Olympics for the one hundred metres. He caught Buckland halfway across the expansive back lawn. A rugby tackle brought him down, but he kicked out, catching Justin on the shoulder. Breaking free, Buckland scrambled upright. Justin was already on his feet and grabbed his shoulder. Buckland lashed out and Justin leaned backwards, the wind of the blow grazing his face.

"Buckland, stop!" Justin avoided a second blow. "You are just making things worse."

He saw the desperation and terror on the young man's face, eyes glazed with panic, hearing blocked by the drumming beat of his own fear. Buckland would not, probably could not, stop. He broke free again, then grabbed a garden fork from the weedy flower bed. He turned and stabbed at Justin. Justin avoided the sharp tines, turning sideways on, like a farmer avoiding a bull's charge. He grabbed hold just above the metal tines and swung hard. Buckland, holding fast to his weapon, was hauled off his feet and catapulted head first into a large bush. He shouted in pain at the slashes from the spiky branches. Dazed, he still struggled weakly, entangling himself even more. Justin stood still, watching him battle with the bush. He was relieved Buckland was able to move. Buckland's defiance had irritated him, and he had not held back as much as he should have. He bent and hauled his captive out of the shrub. When he still tried to struggle, Justin shook him lightly, then clipped the handcuffs into place on his wrists, using the required legal wording to arrest him on suspicion of murder and mentioned other possible charges. Finally, Buckland slumped, defeated.

"Sir, Justin, are you alright?" Unable to see what was happening, but hearing the noise of the struggle, Anne hammered hard on the wood of the back gate.

"All is well," he called back.

He pulled Buckland back to the gate and opened it.

"Inspector Richards meet Aston Buckland."

He handed over the prisoner then called the other units to stand down, prisoner was secure. Anne's silence surprised him. Justin glanced at her and she avoided his gaze, her face very pale. She took Buckland's arm and led him quickly to the car.

Justin frowned, concerned that the rushing around had aggravated her injuries, although he could not see why, considering what she had done against his wishes over the last couple of days. He turned to pull the door shut and blinked in surprise. The heavy wooden gate hung from one fractured hinge. The top and bottom bolts had sheared, and the lock was bent and twisted.

Damnation. He had forgotten the door had been locked and bolted, which was why he had jumped the fence in the first place.

24

"I've asked Ray and Chas to take Buckland back to the station. Julie and Paul are supervising the house search. You and I need to talk!"

It was not a request. Anne's serious expression and stiff stance were flags of danger.

"Shall we?" she waved a hand towards the quiet sun patio at the top of the garden. Out of the way of the search teams but allowing them to see anyone who was heading in their direction.

"Very well." Justin led the way, then turned to face his Nemesis. Except Fate seemed to have lost her voice. Silence stretched until the third time Anne opened her mouth to speak, then stopped.

Justin lost patience. "Just spit it out woman, whatever you want to say I am certain I have heard it before," he snapped.

"Right, what the hell are you? An escapee from the MC universe, the missing son of the Incredible Hulk? Since the night we arrested the badger baiters, I've kept quiet. I saw you throw the heavy guy practically one handed into the bushes. How were you even able to see when the night glasses were on the top of your head? Then there's this bloody gate! You almost ripped it right out of its frame, hinges, lock and bolt."

Justin could have laughed. How the hell could he explain what he was able to do? He wondered if Anne realised quite how fantastical what she was saying could seem to any other human being? He thought not. She was too wound up to realise.

"Then there's the weirdness at the office, migraine my arse. You were perfectly fine when you went into your office, then you come out in dark glasses, avoiding us all as if we had the plague except you were drooling around Julie like a dog with a bitch in heat."

Ouch, was she keeping a diary of his actions? Before he could reply, Anne grabbed his arm.

"I'm not trying to cause you problems sir, I just want to help. Are you using steroids or something like them?"

"Gods no! I thank you for wanting to help, but there is no help, not yet. As for what is going on with me, that story would take a long time to tell and a suspension of disbelief that you may not be able to cope with. On my honour, I will tell you everything once we close this case. I will ask Thomas to join us. He can be my witness. Will that suffice for now? In the meantime, Julie is waving at us."

He waved back, acknowledging they had seen her. "Well?"

"OK, but no more superman tricks, clear?"

"I will try not to," he assured her solemnly and heard a "tsk" of annoyance before she marched ahead of him to where Julie was waiting just outside the house.

"We've found something," Julie said, leading them into the utility room where the washing machine door was open, its contents spilling out onto the floor. A white-suited science officer knelt beside the colourful cascade like an acolyte at an altar, but it was a bloody god being worshipped. In both gloved hands, he held a heavily stained hooded top and a pair of cargo pants similarly dyed. The smell of dried blood, and that it was Chelsey's blood, obscured all the other scents in the room from air freshener to soap powder except for the one wafting from within the machine. Another fainter, unique blood tang. He heard the officer say that the stains could be blood, as he placed the items into evidence bags, but the lab would confirm that. Justin didn't need to wait for the lab. His senses had already made the confirmation.

"Can you check the rest of the clothes inside the washing machine? I think there may be more evidence in there."

Why was such damning evidence still available? Justin frowned, his mind worrying at the puzzle. OK, these were not forensically aware criminals, but to leave bloody clothes for six days was sheer stupidity. Something must have happened in the meantime to prevent the washing from being done. It wasn't just the laziness of youth, surely?

Justin thanked the science officer, then wandered carefully through the house to get away from the smell. Upstairs, others were collecting and bagging all the footwear for comparison. With the evidence of his own sense of smell, Justin was reasonably certain one of the collected pairs of trainers would match.

"Well, well, what have we got here?"

Justin overheard the comment from another officer. She then pulled out a plastic bag taped beneath a drawer in the wardrobe. Inside were a multitude of smaller packets containing various types of pills. The officer held it up for Justin to see clearly.

"Nice little haul here. If they are what I think, then worth a pretty penny out on the streets."

Justin nodded agreement, and headed back downstairs, where he bumped into a distracted Anne in the hall.

"Sorry," he said, then noticed her expression. "What is wrong?"

"Would you say Buckland was a tall strapping lad?" she ignored his question to ask instead.

Justin remembered the wind of Buckland's attempted blows. "Yes, to both."

"I agree," then headed upstairs two at a time, leaving Justin waiting in the hall. Less than five minutes later, she was back, a thoughtful frown creasing her forehead.

"Those clothes from the machine, I don't think they are Buckland's. I got a look at the cargo pants' label. The size is too small compared to the clothes upstairs. He was doing someone else's laundry. The smaller attacker on the recording?"

"If that is the case, then Lizzie's team might get DNA or other trace from the clothes to prove who it was." Justin grinned. "Your optimism is proving right after all."

Paul came through the front door, his steps suddenly seeming quicker, more enthusiastic. He joined them at the foot of the stairs.

"There's a motorbike in the garage. I've arranged for it to be taken to the lab. They can check the tyres against the casts taken at the car fire. Also, the soil samples in the tread."

Julie came through from the kitchen area.

"Sorry sir. You were right, there's a second set of stained clothes in among the washing." She looked at Anne. "They're the same size as the first set. So not Buckland's?"

Anne nodded, "Not Buckland's."

"Right, let us head back to the station. We can leave the house to the search team. Paul, you and Julie bring Chas and Ray up to speed back at base. Julie, can you also chase up the tech department about the enhanced image from the petrol station door? Anne and I have a suspect to interview."

On the way back to the station, Anne and Justin discussed strategy for the forthcoming interview of Aston Buckland. There were so many possible charges it was difficult to know where to start their questioning. Certainly, it was going to be a very long and tiring evening!

Ray was waiting for them when they got back to the offices. Thomas was also there, his normally cheerful face serious, his eyes lined with strain.

"A welcoming committee. How nice," Justin remarked. "Which of you is doing the welcome speech?"

"I guess that's me." Ray said. "Buckland is in a cell and we've sent the trainers he was wearing to be checked with the rest. He had quite a deep cut in his hand, so we took photographs and called the doctor. It wasn't a fresh injury and there was glass inside the wound."

Thomas confirmed what Ray had said. "Slivers of what looked like wineglass, thin, sharp and curved. I've cleaned and dressed the injury. He's well enough to interview. Now I'm heading back to the surgery."

"I will walk you to your car." Justin was concerned about the tense strain Thomas was showing. No jokes, no puns, just straightforward business was not like him.

They walked as far as Thomas's car, where they were out of earshot of anyone else.

"Thomas? Something is wrong?"

"No, not really," Thomas shrugged. "I think I'm being paranoid, to be honest. Ryan got back last night. He said the lead was a dead end. I thought that would be the end of it." He shook his head. "Not finished at all. There's something very wrong. Ryan's restless, but won't talk to me. He seems afraid of something and doesn't want me involved. He's also hired a private detective and not your usual divorce and missing persons' type. This firm provides security for its clients. I overheard him on the phone this morning."

"At least he is taking precautions, Thomas. Ryan is no foolhardy beginner at this. He's aware of the dangers."

"I know, and I agree with you. It's not as if he's a war correspondent, but this particular investigation, it's drawn him in, become an obsession. I've not seen him this deeply involved before. Aah, well, he's a grown man and able to look after himself."

"If you, or Ryan, need my help, just ask." He was not certain Ryan would accept his offer. The guy had always been a little jealous of his relationship with Thomas.

"Thanks Justin. I'll see you later, maybe? Good luck with the suspect."

Justin watched him drive away. The Range Rover crossing with another car that was entering through the security gates. Justin groaned out loud when he recognised the new arrival. The Buckland family spared no expense when it came to their defence it seemed. They had a particular firm of solicitors on speed dial, expensive but successful in keeping their clients out of jail. The driver was relatively new to the firm, but had been to the station a couple of times since Justin had arrived. The cafeteria rumours were definitely unrepeatable regarding these particular legal eagles. No matter, he hoped this time, with so much evidence linking Buckland to their various cases, all they needed from him was his partner's identity. Justin waited a while longer, hoping to avoid the solicitor at the front desk. With a little luck, he would be in an interview room with his client. His luck was in, and the front desk was clear. In fact, he made it all the way to the office, where he checked with Julie about the image enhancement.

She shook her head. "No news yet sir. Lizzie is cursing us for sending over so much for analysis, but has also promised to fast track the lot." Julie finished her report.

Justin blinked as he thought about the costs, then mentally shut and locked the door on the budget concerns. They were too close now to quibble about additional expenses.

He joined Anne at her desk. "Can you pull up the father's criminal record please?"

Anne did so, and it made interesting reading. A career in petty crime begun as a teenager that continued into middle age. Burglary and car theft, nothing really substantial and the last event that could have moved him up a step on the career criminal ladder, was an attempted jewel robbery for which he was now serving time.

"Unlike the grandfather who was into some pretty serious stuff in his time, the latest generation of Bucklands don't seem to be in the top rank as criminals." Anne said, reading the report along with Justin.

"Yes true, notice anything else in the record?"

Anne shook her head. "Not really. The only attempt at anything like Billy Buckland's record is the failed jewel robbery."

"Show me the evidence log if it is up-to-date."

They were lucky in their case manager and everything from the house was now logged on the computer. They scanned through the listing, and Justin gave a half-smile. "What about now?"

Anne looked up at him and smiled back. "Of course, the father has no record of dealing in drugs. If the pills are illegal, then they are Aston's or whoever was staying with him since his father went to prison."

Justin turned to check with Ray. "Have we informed the solicitor of further charges?"

Ray grinned, "Yeah, as soon as he got here. Explained all the possibilities: about assault on a police officer and possible involvement in two murders as well as demanding money with menaces and the drug dealing. He truly looked shocked. First time I've seen anyone from that firm show emotion. Jonathan Anderson, the guy's name. I don't think he was expecting such a battery of serious charges at all."

"Did Buckland call him?"

"Yeah, we gave him his phone call. He called the solicitor."

"Thanks Ray." He turned to Anne. "Shall we go and talk to our Mr Buckland?"

It was quiet in the interview room, the only slight noise the ticking of a clock on the wall. The two men, already seated, were not talking to each other. Buckland looked up as they entered and sprawled further down in his seat. He was giving the impression of arrogant relaxation. However, the solicitor sat stiffly upright. Justin could feel considerable tension between the solicitor and his client. The reason for their silence might have been the uniformed police officer who had entered the room when their consultation ended. But it felt as if Anderson was unconsciously distancing himself from his client. He was half turned away from the younger man.

They sat down and began with the formalities. Buckland gave warning of how he intended to treat the interview when he refused to state his name for the recording.

"Aston, may I call you Aston?" Justin asked politely.

Buckland shrugged carelessly.

"Tell me, Aston, how did you cut your hand?"

Aston shrugged again and gave a sneer. "No comment."

Justin thought he was acting like an angry three-year-old rather than the adult he was supposed to be. He glanced at Anne. From her expression, he could see she was thinking the same thing. Buckland's attitude set the tone for the entire interview. To each question regarding Mama's Place and the assault on the police officer, the response was 'no comment'. However, when Justin asked him to account for his movements during the afternoon and evening of Chelsey Harris's murder, Aston paused and frowned, then forced out the usual 'no comment', although they got the impression he wanted to say more.

"Very well Aston. I do not think you have any idea just how serious these charges could be. We have enough already to charge you with the protection racket you were running among the shopkeepers and for the assault on our officer. Physical evidence such as fingerprints, bloodstains and witness accounts. In fact, would you be willing to take part in an identity parade tomorrow?"

"I will leave you to discuss that with your solicitor." Justin turned to the solicitor.

"I suggest, Mr Anderson, that you seriously discuss the idea of co-operation with your client. We will continue this interview tomorrow morning. I am sure you will be able to get here for say, ten o'clock. Please knock when you and your client have finished your discussion and an officer will escort Aston to the cells." Justin ended the recording of the interview, and he and Anne left the other two together.

"Stupid sod!" Anne exclaimed. "Is this the macho gangster attitude, or does he really think he's immune to our charges if he just says nothing?"

"Admiration of his grandfather, perhaps combined with inherited stupidity, I suppose. He must realise from his father's experiences that it is a dangerous game. His grandfather's long sojourn in prison should have warned him, even if he ignored his father's failures. Who really knows? I am not sure Aston himself does. I am hoping we will get the evidence we need for at least the arson and the murder of Gavin Lombard before the next interview. It would also be great if the tech boys can come back with a clear, recognisable image."

"Let's keep hoping," Anne said, turning as she reached the office door. "In the meantime, I'm going to try to narrow down where Eve Jordan might be. She might have information we can use as she's Aston's cousin or she could herself be in danger from the killer. After all, she is now the woman who's known Sean the longest."

They went into the office and gave the team a progress report on their stubborn suspect.

Sunset had come and gone, the sky had darkened into a star set velvet night clear of cloud and cold. Justin had ordered in sandwiches and pizza when none of the team wanted to head home for the night. They were all waiting, hoping for something from forensics or technical that would break the case at last. None of them wanted to be sleeping while their colleagues closed the case. It meant too much to all of them.

Sometime well after ten o'clock, Justin's phone buzzed. He was seated at his desk, looking at the town's silhouette against the clear night. His mind considered and discarded various theories and options while he watched the scene change, going over the evidence again and again. As soon as he saw who the caller was, he asked them to hold and went into the main office. He didn't need to ask for silence, everyone was already fully focused on him.

"You are on speaker, Lizzie. We are all listening."

"Hi everyone," the distorted sound of Lizzie's voice called out. "Ain't you got no homes to go to either?" They heard her chuckle. "Right, I can verify that the footprints at the burglary and at the car fire match Aston Buckland's trainers. The wear pattern is exact and the same wear pattern shows on several other shoes of the same size that were collected from the house. Also, on the trainers, there was blood present in microscopic dried droplets on the eyelets where the laces go through. There was enough to test, and it matches Chelsey Harris."

There was a concerted breath that released a massive amount of tension within the group, listening.

"The dark stains on the clothes in his machine were blood and one set was matched to Chelsey's blood group and the other to the same blood type as Gavin Lombard. However, Anne was right, the clothes were too small for Buckland himself. We found biological material inside both sets which we're analysing now. I'll rush the results to you as soon as possible."

"We are interviewing Aston Buckland again tomorrow morning just after ten a.m." Justin informed her.

"Right, well, we'll do our best to get the results to you by then. Good luck guys."

"Thank you, Lizzie, speak tomorrow."

He looked around and smiled. "We have a link to Chelsey Harris and to

Gavin Lombard. Another link to the burglary at Byett's where we know the killer or killers went to destroy the visual recording of the killing. Go home everyone. I have a feeling that tomorrow we will need every ounce of energy. I doubt anything else will happen tonight."

† † †

By three in the morning, Justin gave up trying to sleep. He put his hands behind his head and lay looking up at the canopied ceiling. It felt as if solving one problem would only release another more personal problem. So be it if it meant giving closure to Chelsey's family and peace to Gavin Lombard's soul. His mind settled on thoughts of Anne. How would she come to terms with the truth about his life? Sometimes it seemed fantastical to him, and he was the one living with the result. Also, he was more aware than she could be, that if Anne said anything publicly, she wouldn't be believed in this scientific age. But he had only just returned home and was not prepared to leave again so soon. Neither did he want to make Anne a laughing stock. There was no actual choice. She would have to be told the truth and the cards would fall as they wished. He wanted to work with her. That they suited one another and complemented each other had become more obvious as the investigation continued. She would have to accept him as he was if they were to work together with the team. He knew beyond doubt there would be other occasions when he did something weird in her eyes.

Thomas and Ryan crossed his mind, but he knew Ryan would not appreciate his interference. He had watched them walking together in the manor grounds when he returned home, late as it was. He had been relieved that Ryan was remaining close to the manor.

Justin stretched and got up. If sleep was avoiding him, then a good run with very few people around to slow him down would start his day early. Even after the run, a shower and breakfast, it was still very early when he reached the office. Yet, within ten minutes of his arrival, all the team had gathered. There was a sense of controlled anticipation filling the atmosphere. Justin believed their expectations were more likely to be fulfilled than not. So many pieces of the puzzle had now set in place that the picture was practically complete. The first visitor was Lizzie, who grabbed a cup of coffee as soon as she arrived, complaining it was the least they could offer her when she'd been up all night on their behalf.

Justin laughed, then said, "If your work gives us our murderer, then I will take you to dinner at the best restaurant in London that you can choose. As well as the invitation to the team celebrations."

She stopped, put down the mug, and gave him a considering look.

"Might hold you to that." Then she became all business. "Right, your results are done. The blood-stained clothes, both sets, were worn by a female. That female has a familial connection to your suspect, Buckland." She held up a hand when they started to comment. "The link is not close enough for a sister or mother, more likely a cousin on the paternal side. The same DNA was on the sheets of one of the guest bedrooms, but it was clear of any belongings. There were traces in the carpet, however, and these tested as potting compost." She drained the coffee cup and handed it to Justin. "Now I have to get back." She turned towards the door, then turned back, snapping her fingers and shaking her head. "Duh, almost forgot, must be the lack of sleep. The motorbike you sent to us; well, its tyre tread matches the cast we made in your field. It confirms Buckland's presence. Written report all official by …" She looked at her watch, "this afternoon after I catch forty winks."

"Are we looking at Eve Jordan for the murders?" Chas' tone was questioning, unsure. "But why? What motive could she have?"

"I would say definitely," Julie answered him. "Come and look at this."

They all crowded around her desk.

"The tech boys have done their magic and provided an enhanced picture of the glass reflection in the petrol station door. Who would you say it is?"

None of them who had met her doubted it was Eve Jordan staring back at them.

"Chas and I wouldn't know her from Eve," Ray grinned, "But we will take your word for it."

Justin nodded and Anne said, "Now we know where she's been staying while we tried to find her."

"More than that, I think she is the key to get Aston talking. Remember his mother saying he and she were very close and that he adored her?"

"But why did she hide? It drew attention to her rather than avoiding it?"

"We will ask her when we arrest her."

They were in the same interview room with the same ticking clock, only now it was much brighter where the morning sun snaked its beams through the small windows set high in three of the walls. Every so often, a gust of wind would rattle the panes. Anderson had arrived promptly and everything was now ready.

"Aston, tell me about Eve."

"Nn. ... What?" The change of topic had caught him completely by surprise.

"Tell me about Eve Jordan! She is your cousin, is she not?"

Buckland was confused, suspicious. He looked hard at Justin; his eyes narrowed with angry resentment.

"Yeah, Eve's my cousin, so what?"

No "no comment" answers now. Buckland was worried about these questions regarding Eve.

"Your mother, Olivia, said you two are very close, that you would do anything for your cousin Eve. Her words, not mine. What would you do for her, Aston?"

"What you talking to me about Eve for? She has nothing to do with the restaurant or that stupid sod who tried to interfere."

"Would you lie for her Aston? Or give her a place to stay if she needed it?"

"She's my cousin and my friend, 'course I would. Now you leave her out of this. She ain't done nothing wrong."

Justin shook his head, his expression mournful. "If you two are so tight, how can we believe you? Where were you on the afternoon and evening that Chelsey Harris was murdered, Aston?"

Anderson interrupted the staring contest between Justin and Aston. "Is this a relevant line of questioning, Chief Inspector?"

"Very much so, Mr Anderson. We have physical evidence placing Aston in the van where Chelsey Harris was killed and a recording that shows her murder by a smaller slighter individual. Evidence found at the place Aston was living links to his cousin, Eve Jordan." He turned to Aston. "Where is Eve?"

Aston's whole body was shaking with anger and fear.

"No, Eve didn't kill nobody. It was me, you bastard, me. I took out that bitch Chelsey Harris."

"I don't believe you, Aston. What about Gavin Lombard, Aston? Why did he have to die?"

Aston shrugged, looking away from them. His hands were trembling, so he hid them from view in his pockets. "Don't know what you're talking about."

"Surely you can tell us now? You just confessed to killing Chelsey and Gavin was killed in the same van. The same van, in fact, that you and Eve burned to hide the evidence. Why?"

Aston appeared defeated, no longer showing contempt, but Justin sensed he was still trying to fight them.

"Stupid bastard tried to stop, uh … me. Said I should go to the police and confess what I'd done or he would tell you." Aston's lip curled with contempt. "So busy telling me what to do and threatening he didn't notice …" his voice trailed off.

"Didn't notice what, Aston? That Eve was behind him with a pruning knife?"

"No comment."

"We know you did not kill either of our victims Aston. Oh, you drove the van and you helped to tie Chelsey to the trolley. You also helped with the murder of Gavin Lombard then, on top of everything else, you helped Eve torch the van. We can prove you were involved with all of that. We have all the evidence we need to charge you, as well as Eve. What I would like to know, however, is why the protection racket. You half killed a police officer and terrified a lot of people. For what?"

"The fucking businesses wouldn't pay thanks to that old Italian bitch. I was angry, and I hit the guy harder than I thought. I didn't mean it."

"What about the demand for money? You must have been making a few thousand with the drugs and the marijuana you were growing at the derelict squat."

"Me Granda needed it," Aston muttered.

"Sorry, could you speak up for the recording, please?" Anne said.

"Me Granda needed it," Aston spoke loudly. "He's run out of money and that posh home will kick him out if he can't pay the bill soon." He looked up, totally frustrated, "Dad bought that bloody house for him 'n' his bitch using Granda's stash. Now, Granda's got nothing. I was trying to get the money together to pay Granda back." He looked sullen. "He's still got some nasty friends that owe him. Dad was beaten up in prison and I got called by the prison governor to go and see him while he was on the medical wing. He said it was a message from Granda about what would happen if I couldn't get the money sorted out. Then Evie was angry that I'd left that damned washing for so long. I forgot about it what with going to the prison to see Dad. Then trying to sort out that shitting restaurant, I didn't get around to it until yesterday. Bloody hell she gave me. I was just about to get it done when you came noseying around the back of the house."

Justin terminated the interview but warned them they would be interviewing Aston again regarding the murders of Chelsey Harris and Gavin Lombard, then he turned to Anne. "Inspector Richards, will you see to the formal charges for Aston and ensure Mr Anderson gets copies of the recordings?"

25

The drumroll of knocking on the office door startled him. Before Justin could react, Ray was in the office as the last tap was fading.

"Sir sorry, but we've just had a call from Sean Trent. He's worried about Gina Crane. Apparently, she's been getting the same abusive threats that Chelsey had been receiving. They started recently, and she showed them to him the last time they were together. Now she's not answering her phone. He's left a message on the land line but there's no response at all from her mobile. It's been two days since she showed him the threatening texts, so he went round there this morning before work. There's no sign of her at home and the neighbours haven't seen her for a couple of days either. He said one neighbour thought she might be at her parents' place."

"Call him back, tell him we will look for Gina and see that she is safe. We will let him know when we find her."

Ray went back into the main office, already using his mobile to call Sean Trent.

Justin looked up the address for Gina Crane's parents, then collected Anne to go hunting for another missing young woman. They started at Tangrave Close, where Gina rented a property, but the house had been locked up. The curtains had been drawn as well, so no one could see in. While Anne checked with the next-door neighbour at the attached semi, Justin went around the back. He found a cracked but intact glass pane just above the lock of the back door. Whoever had tried to break in had failed. Either they had been disturbed or the toughened glazed door had proved too hard. Justin turned round hearing a deep growl from the garden on the opposite side. Above the trellis work fence, an old man was staring at him with the same suspicion and fixed stare as the elderly dog glaring through one of the lower diamond-shaped gaps. He had been so absorbed in his inspection of the door that he had not heard or sensed the man's presence until the dog growled a warning. Justin walked across to the fence and introduced himself to the old man, showing him his police credentials. The elderly neighbour stared intently at Justin's warrant card and his shoulders relaxed slightly.

"Can you tell me what happened here?"

The man nodded, resting his elbows on the top of the fence. "Yeah, somebody tried to break in last evening. I sleep light anyway and heard a bang. Old Sam, my dog, was growling. I opened the bedroom window and shouted, 'Show yourself or I let the dogs loose, trying to suggest there was more than Sam." He sighed and shook his head. "It was too dark to see much more than a black shape against the house. By the time I struggled downstairs, the sod had scarpered."

"Ms Crane was not home last night?"

The neighbour considered whether he should answer, then shook his head. "No, went away the day before yesterday. Don't know where, maybe her parents' place. She usually tells Cilla next door that side," the old man pointed across the garden, "where she's going and for how long, but the two of them fell out recently."

"Thank you, Mr?"

"Ryde, Tony Ryde."

"Thank you, Mr Ryde. You said a shape, there was only one person attempting to break in? Did you inform the police?"

"Yeah, that's right, one moving shadow was what I saw. Been waiting for the police to turn up this morning. They said they'd send somebody to take a statement. There was a young feller here, earlier but he was too young to be police and not in uniform. Then thought it might be you at first what with your partner knocking on Cilla's door."

"Will you be at home today?"

"Yeah, except for a quick trip to the park for the poor old fella." He glanced down where his dog was sitting watching him then looked back at Justin.

"Thank you. If Ms Crane returns home, could you give her my card and ask her to call me as soon as possible?"

Justin handed the card up to him and heard the dog's warning growl again. Mr Ryde chuckled. "Be still you daft dog. Pay him no mind, he's got no teeth anyway. He and me have that in common, we both still think we're fitter than we actually are." Justin left them with a final thank you and headed back to the front of the house. Anne was already there.

"Any luck with the neighbour?"

"No, the woman was just leaving for work and wasn't prepared to stop and talk about Gina. 'When that cow finally pays me what she owes, then I'll waste time talking about her'. That's what she said. Seems she owns both properties and Gina hasn't paid her rent for the last two months. Anyway, just before she walked off, she muttered something about try her parents' place, that's where she usually runs to when she needs help."

"Fair enough. Let us try the parents' place."

Anne drove across the town. It was another market day, but the delivery lorries had finished loading up the stalls and the shopping crowd had not filled the streets yet. They reached the series of tree-lined avenues where nineteen-thirties houses dozed contentedly in the sunlight. Gina Crane's parents lived in a very pleasant area on the outskirts of the town, backing onto a small reservoir and allotments that led into fields and woodland.

"Very des.res," Anne remarked.

"Yes. They never seem to have for sale signs up around here. There's a waiting list of people wanting to move in. Just beyond that curve in the road, you can get through an alleyway leading to the allotments and public footpaths through the fields for miles."

There were no cars parked in front of the small garden, or in the shared driveway next to the unusually large bay window. The family seemed to be out. They walked through the front garden up to the front door and saw movement inside the front room. Anne, nearest the door, peered through the side window of the bay, but the room was now deserted.

"Let's try round the back." She suggested, already heading across to the shared driveway separating the two houses.

A waist high fence and gate separated the garden from the drive, fixed from the corner of the house to the separate garage wall. The sunny open garden was obviously somebody's pride and joy. The lawn was neat and the borders, loaded with flowering spring bulbs, were weed-free. A long washing line was in use, and a young woman was pegging out more of the washing closer to the higher back fence.

Anne was about to call out, but stopped when they saw a figure clamber over the top six-foot fence and jump down into the garden, where the trespasser was hidden from their sight by the bulk of the garage. The enormous bed sheet she was pegging out hid the intruder from the woman's view.

"Hell, that's Eve," Anne snapped and burst through the gate. To keep up with her Justin jumped the small fence.

Eve was facing Gina Crane, with just the cloth of the sheet between them. Eve drew back her arm but the wind suddenly strengthened, billowing and rippling the sheet across the garden. With the sheet slapping at her like an angry housewife, Eve was forced to back away from Gina. Justin saw the glint of the curved knife in her hand as it slashed down through the sheet. He tried to get past Anne, but she sped towards their target and arrived first, catching Eve by surprise, so fixated on Gina that she had disregarded their presence. Anne grabbed her shoulder as Justin called a warning.

"Knife!"

The pull caught Eve off balance turning her towards Anne and further away from Gina. The sheet, freed from Gina's clasp, stretched and writhed in another gust of wind, enveloping Eve completely. Another flapping fold caught at Anne, wrapping around her. Clawing hands pulled the sheet off the line. Something fell to the floor when the sheet broke free of the clothes line. Free of the blindfold effect, Anne moved towards the spot where Eve struggled to free herself from the tangled material. The crumpled sheet caught at Anne's ankles. Off balance she fell sideways against Justin. They heard Gina cry out and a dull thud. By the time they untangled themselves Eve was gone over the tall fence and off across the reservoir lands. Gina, dazed and shocked, got to her feet, rubbing her shoulder and swaying. She looked with disbelief at the once pristine sheet.

"Are you hurt? Did she cut you?" Anne held Gina upright.

Gina shook her head. "No, I'm fine. She just shoved me over and jumped the fence. Wow, that was pretty amazing. I never realised how fit she was. Must be all that gardening." Gina seemed to realise the strangeness of the situation at last. "What the hell was Eve doing here, anyway?"

Justin picked up the dirty, trampled cloth. As he held it up to the light, they all saw the cuts striping its length. There was silence from Gina as he started to fold the sheet that had saved her life. She was looking down at what the sheet had hidden. Lying on the grass was a vicious looking, home-made, pruning knife that resembled a small machete. Gina bent to pick it up.

Justin said, "Do not touch it."

She quickly pulled back from the weapon. "It's only Dad's ..." Gina's voice trailed off and her brow wrinkled. "Shit, that's not Dad's pruner, it's way too big. What is going on?"

"It belongs to Eve, Gina. We think she came here to kill you." Anne said, then turned to Justin. "Will you call it in? I will stay with Gina." She guided the girl towards the garden chairs set out on the patio. Justin folded the sheet and placed it on the ornate metal table then headed onto the drive before calling the team.

They arrived quickly along with one of the science unit's vans and a patrol car. One of the patrol officers and the detectives began a house-to-house search. Justin and Anne left Gina, still shocked that anyone would want to kill her, with the other patrol officer on the patio, waiting for her parents to return. That left them free to talk. They stood in the driveway outside the small gate, now propped into the gateway. Justin smiled and turned to Anne, pointing at the gate.

"So, if I'm the son of the Hulk, what does that make you?"

Anne smiled and shrugged, "Practising?" she replied.

The pruning knife, bagged and tagged as evidence, was carried ceremonially past them to the van, as was the poor trampled sheet that had saved Gina from Eve's attack. Justin's phone buzzed.

"Mortmain! Thank you. No, we will do the follow up, thanks."

Justin ended the call and put the phone back in his pocket while he spoke to Anne. "The team has searched Eve's flat, her company offices and her father's place. They also checked where Aston and she had been staying. There's no sign of her. They are going to call in on the various gardening projects, but I do not think she will go to her employees for help."

"Where then? Has she got access to money, her passport?"

"No, the first pair at her flat found her credit and debit cards and her passport laid out on a table near the front door. The company's office staff accounted for all their vans. They are all out on various projects or in for repair at the local garage. There is no car at her father's house for her to borrow. He lost his licence last year and sold it. The description and registration of her Mini have been circulated."

Justin stopped, frowning, his lips pulled tight.

"OK, what else?" Anne wanted to know.

"What they did find at Eve's flat was a series of photographs in her bedroom. She had photoshopped Sean and herself into them. They were wedding photos. Around the room were other altered photos that showed her and Sean as a serious couple. When they checked her wardrobes, there were a dozen more albums, all containing similar. They went back years." Justin glanced at his watch, then headed out into the street. Luckily, Ray was just coming out of a nearby house. Justin waved, and Ray joined him.

"Ray, did you let Sean know we had found Gina, and she was safe with us?"

"Yeah, as soon as you called it in."

"Did you tell him who attacked Gina?"

"No, didn't think it was appropriate. Is that a problem?" Ray shouted the last sentence at Justin's back as he hurried to the car, calling to Anne.

"Sean telephoned earlier before heading for work. Did anyone try his flat?" He touched Anne's arm. "The banks are closed so Sean should be heading for home. He knows Gina is safe, but he was not told who attacked her. What better place for Eve to hide out than Sean's apartment?" His eyes glinted as he remarked. "How quickly can you get us there?"

With the aid of the lights and siren, combined with the lighter traffic, Anne managed to pull into the apartment block forecourt in just under six minutes. They entered the lobby and Justin made for the stairs while Anne headed up in the lift, that blocked both exits if Eve was in the building. With nobody watching, Justin hadn't needed to limit his speed and arrived easily before Anne. When the lift doors opened, he raised a finger to his lips in warning and pointed towards Sean's apartment.

The front door stood wide open. Justin could hear voices from inside the apartment, though the words were indistinct. The thick pile carpet helped deaden the sound of their footsteps as they moved closer to the door. A quick glance showed there was nobody in the hallway of the flat. The voices were coming from the main lounge. That door was also open, and they flattened themselves on either side of it. Justin took a quick look before ducking back. Eve was in the room with Sean. She had her back to the door, standing close to Sean, who was facing the door. He was looking down at her, his expression a mixture of surprise and puzzlement.

"Evie, what are you talking about? What's going on? I don't understand what you're saying. Why are you here, in my flat?"

"It's alright Sean, I've packed you a case and found your passport. You need to go back to the bank and get us some euros. Use my account. There's about ten thousand in there. We have to leave or they'll come for me. I won't lose you Sean, not now, not ever."

"What? Evie, are you crazy? What are you on? I'm not going anywhere until you sit down and tell me what the hell is happening. Why are you frowning at me like that?"

"Sean there's no time, not now. I'll tell you everything once we get moving. Now go transfer that money into euros. I've got some cash with me that we can change on the way, but not enough to live on for long."

"The bank's well shut Evie, I can't just go back and grab money from the vault. Can't you get what you want online? You can use my computer. I can't go anywhere with you because I've used up all my holiday allowance and I have to work. It's generous of you to offer, but it's impossible."

"Bloody hell Sean, stop acting stupid, don't you understand? If you hadn't taken up with that whore Gina after Chelsey was dead, I wouldn't need to run. Just when I need you to hurry, you can't see why we need to go? I thought you understood. I thought you knew we were meant to be together. I've waited so bloody long for you to realise. All those whores sniffing around you. Well, now it's my turn and we will be together for life, Sean."

Justin heard Sean gasp and risked another look. Evie and Sean had turned as Sean had tried to get to the door. Justin could see the large carving knife Evie was waving gently like a wand.

"No, no, not for you, my darling, not for you." She held the knife still, gleaming in the daylight and smiled. "This is for anyone who gets in our way, tries to stop us. Now, I saw the police sniffing around my place earlier. With them gone, I can get at my passport and clothes. We can have time in Marseilles. Dad's got a summer home there. That will give us time to decide where we're going. I like the idea of New Zealand. What do you think?"

There was a silence. Eve's revelations had left Sean frozen, speechless with shock. Justin heard voices from the main corridor. He saw Eve twitch, glancing towards the door and beyond to the main door, realising Sean had left all the doors open.

"Who's there? Show yourself!"

The voices were coming closer, two male voices in conversation.

Sean replied soothingly. "It's alright Evie. It's only Paul and Ashley, you remember them. We were going to have a boys' night out and catch up with what we've been doing since they went surfing in Cornwall. You remember. I'll tell them to piss off, they won't mind. You don't need to worry about them."

He started for the front door and, for a fraction of a second, Justin thought he was going to make it.

"No! You stay here with me. I can't let you out of my sight. We have to stay together." Her words came short and fast, reflecting the speed of her panting breath.

"But Evie …"

"No," she turned, waving the carving knife towards a chair. "You sit. They can come in." Her smile was catlike. "No need for you to worry about them," she said, echoing his words to her. She turned towards the door and her eyes widened, the smile wiped from her lips.

"Hello Eve, we have been looking for you. We thought you might need our help."

Justin stood in the doorway, blocking Eve's view of the hall. With a slight movement of his head, he tried to tell Sean to sit down out of the way. Luckily, he was bright enough to understand and sat where Eve had pointed. Behind him, Justin could hear Anne in the corridor, stopping Sean's friends from entering the flat and then using her mobile to call for back-up. Sean's next-door neighbour had come out to see what was going on and quickly pulled Paul and Ashley into the safety of their flat. Justin had heard what was going on, but his attention was fixed on Eve. She was pointing the carving knife in his direction.

"You're blocking my way." She said quite calmly. "You shouldn't try to stop me. I don't like that." She glanced quickly down at Sean and then back to Justin. "Sean, you really shouldn't try to leave me again. I'm your soul mate and you are mine."

"Congratulations on the wedding, by the way," Justin commented.

"Wedding?" Sean's voice rose in surprise.

"Oh yes, you were not there. Come to think of it, neither was Eve, but there are some lovely wedding photographs in an album, in her flat. When was that special day, Eve?"

"Shut your mouth. Those are private. Ideas and plans."

"Really, and the other ten albums of pictures, beginning at secondary school, were those ideas and plans as well."

"Shut the fuck up about them." Eve was red with a mixture of fury and embarrassment.

"Evie …"

"Don't you say anything Sean. I had to keep my dreams alive. You were so busy with all those whoring bitches." She smiled at him, "but I knew they weren't serious. No, any of them that hung on too long were easy to deal with."

"All those anonymous threats. Was that your way of getting rid of them, Eve?" Justin asked, trying to keep her attention on him.

"Yeah, not ready to die or get cut up if they stayed with Sean." Eve laughed, her voice harsh, her face contorted. "Then Chelsey came along. She was serious, wasn't she Sean? But just as always, you couldn't keep it in your pants. See, I know you so well. When you two broke up, I was glad, but then you got back together again. I won't be so tolerant after this though Sean. Not now you know we belong together."

Sean's face closed up. He suddenly looked older, more mature. His voice quiet and cold, he asked, "Did you kill Chelsey?"

"Sean," Justin spoke softly, a warning. Eve was getting more unpredictable by the second.

"Sean, get up, we're going. If he tries to stop us, I'm going to gut him."

"No."

"Fucking get up Sean, we're leaving."

Calmly, Sean looked at Eve and said, "No. I'll never go anywhere with you. Chelsey was my soul mate. Not you, never you."

Eve gave a great desolate scream, knife raised, and hurled herself at Sean.

Justin moved at full speed, got between them, but missed catching her wrist. The knife came down into his shoulder. He gasped with the sudden pain. He caught her by the throat and pushed her back away from Sean. He tried to control the waves of red fury pulsing in time with the pain. Even so, the force of his push sent her backwards over the couch. He pulled the knife out of his shoulder and dropped it on the floor, rounding the couch where Eve struggled to get up. She was on her feet when his arms forcibly held her arms against her body and he lifted her off her feet. She lashed out kicking and twisting to get free. Justin winced as she hacked at his shins with her booted heels. Eve continued to struggle until Justin squeezed just a little harder, then she went limp.

"Anne, if you would not mind, could you handcuff our friend here and arrest her?"

"Put your hands out in front of you, please Eve," Anne requested.

Eve obeyed quietly. Justin released his grip and handed her over to Anne. His shoulder felt as if it were on fire, but he knew within a few moments the wound would begin to heal.

"Will you be alright?" Anne asked, eyeing the blood on his jacket.

"Yes, it's a minor cut, that's all. I will see to it when we get back to the station." He turned to Sean, still sat in the chair, his face white with shock. "Your friends are safe next door. We will need you to come into the station with us and make a statement."

Anne nodded. "Yes, your neighbour has given them a place to wait. They saw nothing of what happened. Don't worry about them, we will explain the situation." She took hold of Eve and escorted her out of the room.

Justin looked at Sean. "Foolhardy telling her you would never be hers."

Sean wiped a hand down his face and looked up, meeting Justin's eyes. His voice was halting and husky when he replied. "I meant every word. No one will take Chelsey's place in my heart. I was so damn stupid I deserved to lose her, but she didn't deserve to die. She was special to a lot of people."

A group of people had gathered outside, and Justin heard Ray's voice in the corridor.

"Come on now. Show's over! Give us some room here."

He came into the flat and looked over at Justin.

"I've sent Chas with Anne to take the Jordan woman back to the station. We brought more men with us. They can cordon off the flat and secure things here. I'll drive you back." Ray also nodded at Sean. "Guess you'll be needing a lift too, sir."

It was a quiet journey back. Sean sat still, looking out of the window. Ray concentrated on his driving and Justin struggled to keep the pain from his face as the wound stopped bleeding and began to close up.

"How's the shoulder?" Ray finally asked.

"Minor injury, no problem, just bled a lot," Justin replied. "Thanks for asking."

"You gonna be OK to interview the suspect?"

Justin frowned. "Oh yes, Anne and I will interview Eve. You and the others can watch the video link. You all deserve that much."

He headed up to his office while Ray took Sean to one of the interview rooms where an officer waited to take his statement. Justin took a holdall out of the bottom drawer of the desk then headed for the toilets. He grimaced, teeth gritted, despite the careful way he pulled the spare shirt from the bag and gently shook out the creases. Carefully he hung it on a hook and began to strip off the blood stained, damaged shirt. Anne pushed open the door with her back, her hands full of cloth, antiseptic and sterile dressings. She placed them carefully on the wash basin then turned on the cold tap to fill the basin before taking the shirt from him and dumping it into the cold water.

"That should help to get rid of some of the stains though this shirt is probably fit for the dustbin." She said finally looking up at him then glancing at his shoulder. She dampened the clean cloth and handed it to him. "You need to wipe off the dried blood so I can see how deep the wound is. Try not to make it bleed again."

He moved to the next basin and followed her instructions. He caught a glimpse of her face in the mirror as the wound was revealed. She stared, eyes wide, then frowned ferociously. Her hand half reached out to touch then drew back.

"Guess I didn't need to do the Florence Nightingale act after all." Anne glanced at the bloody shirt in the basin, staining the water red, her frown deepened. When she looked back at Justin's shoulder there was only a barely discernible pink line where the knife had seemed to stab deep.

"If you bleed so much from a tiny cut, I think you should see a doctor and soon. There may be something seriously wrong." She said brusquely then slammed out of the door. Justin stood where she left him, deep in thought, a sense of failure gripping him. He needed to decide whether he wanted her to stay so much that he was prepared to tell her about his past. Whether she would believe him was yet another problem. Finally, he shrugged, buttoned the new shirt and rolled up the cuffs. He pulled the plug and emptied the basin, then wrung out the shirt and put it into a plastic bag then into the holdall. Feeling a little defenceless without his jacket and tie, Justin headed back to the office to prepare for this, hopefully, final interview.

The team crowded into the viewing room in eager silence. Justin explained for Eve's benefit that the interview would be recorded and that other officers would be overseeing the interview. Eve shrugged, her eyes were calm, her body language as relaxed as if she were with a couple of friends in a bar enjoying a chat.

"Are you sure you don't want a solicitor, Eve?" Anne asked.

Very aware of the Buckland family's legal eagle still sitting by the front desk, Justin asked, "For the record Eve, I need to ask you whether you are certain you do not want your solicitor, or the duty solicitor, to be present at this interview?"

Eve shrugged, "What would I need one of them for?" She seemed genuinely puzzled by the question then amusement curved her lips. "Yeah. Why not? I want a solicitor. Ask our Mr Anderson to be here."

Anne and Justin stopped the recording and left the room when Anderson was escorted to his client. They both knew there would now be a delay and headed for the offices to wait.

26

"Euch!" Justin exclaimed, mouth twisting in distaste as he forced himself to swallow the mouthful of cold coffee.

Anne looked up, a mischievous sparkle lighting her eyes. "If you will spend your time trying to wear a track into the floor, your coffee will go cold."

"How long does that damn solicitor need to consult with his client?"

Anne glanced at the wall clock. "About an hour so far. I'll bet he's trying for a no comment interview. Wonder if our Evie will agree?" She wandered out of the office while Justin got himself another hotter coffee. This time he leaned against Anne's desk and drank it slowly, listening for the tick of the clock marking the time second by second. Anne came back into the office about six hundred seconds later and nodded. "Consult over, they are ready for interview." She informed the team, collected her laptop and headed back with Justin close behind her. The others went back into the viewing room.

When he walked into the interview room, Justin felt a warning prickle down the back of his neck. He stood still, careful not to meet Eve's stare. She was utterly calm, heartbeat slow and regular, no hint of perspiration on her face. Her expression was almost serene except for the restless movement of her eyes from one to another of the people with her, then around the nondescript room, then back to the people. Each time she glanced at Anne a frown marred her calm expression. Justin sat down, still feeling uneasy and waited while Anne completed the formalities.

In contrast to his client, Anderson was red-faced, his heartbeat was almost at heart attack level. His movements were restless. He was frowning and tight lipped. In fact, he looked as if a double measure of a single malt would be very welcome. A clicking noise drew Justin's attention. The solicitor's hands were resting on his notepad. His thumb was continuously pressing the button on his pen: click, click. He didn't seem to hear the sound or even know he was being damned distracting. From the way Eve turned and glared at him, she agreed with Justin. The clicking stopped abruptly.

"Eve, you have had time to speak with your solicitor. We would like to begin the interview," Justin said, a question in his voice.

Eve nodded regally, "Yes, I would like you to know what happened."

Anderson's frown grew fierce. "Ms Jordan please accept and follow my advice …"

Eve's hand hit the table hard. She shook out the pain as she snarled, "You've done what Granda wanted, you've advised me to say nothing." She pointed at Justin. "How can he know I've done nothing wrong if I don't talk to him, tell him my side."

"Thank you, Eve, I would like to know what happened. Can you tell us what you were doing in the afternoon and evening of the day Chelsey Harris was killed?"

"Sure, I was with my cousin Aston for the afternoon, making plans. Then in the evening I went looking for Chelsey. You know the rest."

"Could you just fill in the details, please Eve?"

"Aston and me were at my place when Chelsey found Sean and Gina together." Eve shrugged and a slight smile twisted her lips. "Silly cow, I could have told her Gina was no friend of hers." Eve's smile widened. "Gina's always been more jealous of Chelsey than friendly, see? The whole thing was perfect." Eve went quiet, appeared lost in thought. The loudest noise was the clock ticking off the passing seconds. Then she shook her head and looked up at Justin. "I found her at the pub. She couldn't even get drunk and drown her sorrows." Eve giggled. "I suggested we go to the club together. I pretended to be on her side and called Sean a few names." She frowned. "Strange really, Chelsey didn't seem to like that. Anyway, I dropped some stuff Aston had given me into her drink and she went all woozy. I called Aston from the club and he brought the van to get us." Eve smiled, totally at ease. "She deserved what she got you know. She was in the way of our relationship, me and Sean."

"Had you warned her to stay away, Eve, like you did the others?" Justin asked softly.

Anderson stuttered a half-hearted protest that Eve ignored completely.

"Mr Anderson, we have technical evidence which shows Ms Jordan was using text messages to threaten any woman she deemed a threat to her imagined relationship with Mr Trent," Anne informed him. "I'm sure the CPS will disclose the information at the appropriate time."

Anderson leaned back in his chair then made an addition to his notes.

Eve simply continued as if there had been no interruption. "Yeah, but she ignored me. I tried everything, but she just hung on. She was a pain in the arse and I got rid of her that night, in the back of the van." Eve looked up straight at Anne and snapped, "What do you mean imagined relationship? Sean has always been mine," she chuckled. "It was girls like Chelsey and Gina who imagined a relationship."

A shaft of sunlight shone into Eve's eyes. She blinked rapidly then turned away. The brightness played across the yellow of a fading bruise drawing Justin's attention.

"Tell me Eve, why did you and Aston attack Inspector Richards?" he asked keeping his voice level and quiet, pushing down hard on his growing anger.

"You should teach your bitch to keep her mouth shut about things she doesn't understand." Eve's face twisted in fury. "She laughed at me, made nasty comments about me and Sean. Couldn't let that go, could I?" She glared at Anne, "I would've had you too except bloody Gavin came to the rescue. Then you!" Eve looked at Justin, "How did you get across the park so fast? One minute I was being shoved out the way by Gavin, the next you were there and we had to run for it. You were nowhere in sight when I grabbed her."

"Is that why Gavin had to die? Because he stopped you from hurting Inspector Richards?"

Eve shook her head. "Bastard shit warned me away from Chelsey when she and Sean got back together. He knew I hated her." She shifted in her chair, leaned forward towards Justin. "Then he helped her." Eve nodded towards Anne. "After that he worked out it was me that had killed Chelsey. Gavin wanted to meet, don't know why, he never got to tell me." Eve gave a small smile of satisfaction. "I agreed and suggested Aston would pick him up and bring him to me. He didn't realise I was hiding in the back of the van until I slit his throat." She looked down at the table, muttering, "He should have stayed out of my business." She started tapping with one finger on the table. "Can I go home now? I've told you what you wanted to know. I was only defending my property, after all. I haven't done anything wrong."

"Whose idea was it to burn the van with Gavin's body inside it?"

"Bloody Aston, thought he was being clever. I could kill him for that." She looked back at Justin and smiled, a smile that didn't reach her eyes. She turned to her solicitor, "Can I go home now?" Eve repeated adding, "I've got an awful lot of work to catch up on after taking these few days off."

Anderson looked down at his notes, unsure of how to deal with his client.

Justin answered her instead. "I am sorry Eve, but no, you cannot go home. We need you to stay with us for the moment. You have been very co-operative but we may need to clear up a few more things. Would you mind talking to someone else, Eve?"

"Oh, who?" She was interested rather than upset at the idea.

"Someone who could help us understand you better, who could clear up any confusion so we do not make any mistakes. We can arrange everything with Mr Anderson on your behalf." Justin glanced at Anderson who met his eyes gravely and nodded agreement.

"Of course. I would like a copy of any report sent to my offices as well. On that basis I would advise my client to agree to such a meeting."

Eve sat still, apparently considering his request, a small smile played around her mouth. Anne was restless, shifting her weight in the hard seat of the chair, running her fingers lightly around the laptop's keyboard. Justin just wanted to get out of the room, take a breath of clean air. He felt Anne shared that wish. The click click of Anderson's pen started up again. Justin's click count reached thirty before Eve spoke.

"OK, I'll see your psychiatrist." She said and laughed loudly. "Can't see that one more will make any difference. The one Dad took me to see when I was a kid was useless. Mind you it will have to be today. I've wasted too much time already and Sean and me have plans to make. Yes, today or not at all. I can come back for that. I don't want to stay here."

"Eve, I am sorry but you will have to stay here."

Eve's eyes narrowed and her mouth tightened. All emotion disappeared from her face. "Are you telling me what to do?" She stood up. "Are you telling me I can't leave?"

Justin tensed, "I am sorry, Eve but you have been arrested and we cannot let you go until a court tells us we can. Please sit down."

Eve began to shake her head, her hands twitching and fisting. She turned and grabbed her chair heaving it above her head. Screaming hoarsely, incoherently, she threw the chair straight at Justin. He went over backwards, the legs breezing past his face, then bounded upright in time to clear the desk and grab Eve, where she was raining blows down on Anderson as he crouched defensively on the floor.

"Eve, stop now." He growled in her ear pulling her round to face him. Her face was contorted with fury, spittle spraying from the corners of her mouth along with every swear word she could think of. He turned her back around and held her wrists behind her and bent her over the desk. Even then she kicked out at him. Anne had hit the panic alarm and other officers were coming into the room. One of them helped Justin to keep Eve still while another handcuffed her. Against two men she could not win and eventually that realisation hit home. She stopped struggling. The other officer escorted Eve out of the room, followed by a shaken solicitor.

Anderson glanced at Justin and shrugged. "I am her legal representative still." He said before he left.

"Interview ended seventeen fifty hours." Anne ended the recording with relief, and together with Justin left the trashed room. Out in the corridor Justin leaned back against the wall and slid both hands through his hair, eyes closed. Anne waited for him to speak.

"Can you arrange an urgent psychiatric evaluation? You know who to try?" There are definite underlying issues there." He opened his eyes.

"You mean she's a total psychopath. She has no remorse over killing two people who were supposedly her friends. Bloody Hell, she doesn't even realise what she did was wrong."

"If she continues to plead guilty, or admit what she did, then it should be over fairly quickly. That would be the best outcome for the family. I hope that being asked to speak to a psychiatrist will not alter her attitude. She is highly intelligent in some ways, just no emotional intelligence at all." He straightened away from the wall and rolled the tension out of his shoulders. "Come on, the others will be waiting for us in the office. It is time to celebrate completing our first case as a team."

Anne half smiled. "Yes, I suppose so, then we need to put everything into place for the CPS. Wonder what they will do with it?"

Justin shrugged, "Who knows. That is for tomorrow. Let us get today over."

The rest of the team were already in the main office. Ray was on the phone and the others were gathered around Julie's desk. Not long after Anne and Justin joined them, Ray finished his conversation. His face was noticeably paler than usual and he stared at the phone with unfocused eyes. Eventually he noticed their genuine concern and he grimaced. "That was Eve Jordan's father. He's pissed out of his head; seems to be how he spends most of his time these days. He's also a maudlin drunk."

Ray paused to drain the remains of a bottle of water as if he needed something clean. "He was crying down the phone. I could just about understand what he was saying." He half-smiled, "The advantages of a misspent youth, understanding drunk speak."

He tore a piece of paper from his notebook and handed it to Justin. "That's the name and address of the private psychiatrist he took Eve to see. She was ten years old when she killed the family's old dog by stamping on its head because, I quote, 'Yorkie didn't do what I told him to, Daddy'. Anyway," Ray massaged the back of his neck trying to get rid of the tension in his muscles, "this psychiatrist suggested a stay in hospital where they could have a series of meetings to work through Eve's issues. They never went back and, according to Dad, didn't tell anyone, not even the family, about the incident."

Ray stood up and stretched. "Damn, I could do with a pint. Let's go and celebrate. What do you guys say?"

They all looked towards Justin expectantly like a group of school kids at the end of term. He smiled and nodded, "OK, you deserve it. I have some paperwork to complete." He reached for his wallet and took out some notes. "Here put this behind the bar." He handed the cash to Ray. "I will meet you there once the psych assessment and the CPS paperwork are organised."

"We use The Falcon, it's the closest pub with decent beer and food. Oh yeah, you any good at that Karaoke? For some reason known only to them, Chas, Julie and Paul, all love it. Seem to think they're Pavarotti and Justin Timberlake rolled into one." Justin couldn't hide a wince at that information. Ray laughed, "Yeah, me too. Rather have a game of darts myself. The Falcon caters for all of us."

The team would most likely have given up on him Justin thought, pushing through the main door of The Falcon. He was nearly pushed back out by the noise and heat coming from the crowd around the bar. A laughing cheer from the far end of the room greeted his entrance. Ray was standing up and raised a pint in one hand, pointing first at the drink then at Justin. He understood the mime and waved acknowledgement before threading a way through the groups standing chatting nearer the door.

An empty chair miraculously appeared at their table and the pint was ceremonially placed in front of it. Justin sat down, lifted the drink and toasted the group, "Cheers everyone." Then downed the lot in short order. "I needed that," he said over their laughter.

"Right, now we've got you," Ray remarked laughter in his voice. He enjoyed Justin's puzzled look for a moment. "Bribery to remain quiet." Justin remembered Ray's anger at the way Chelsey had been killed. "So, now we get to name the punishment." Ray took hold of both lapels in the manner of an old-fashioned judge. "Justin Mortmain, you are hereby sentenced to remain as leader of our team for the foreseeable future." He stated solemnly to the murmurs of agreement from the others.

"Thank you. I accept the sentence as fair and just." Justin replied solemnly adding, "I think another round is in order." He glanced at Anne next to him. She was joining in with the laughter but he could see she was lukewarm in her agreement. He leaned towards her, using the laughter at Paul's terrible joke to distract the others. "I suspect you would like to stay with the team Anne. Would I be right?" She nodded silently and started to say something but he stopped her. "I want you to stay with the team, you and I complement each other." She sipped her apple juice and waited. Justin sighed then continued. "This discussion is going to need to be in private. I do not want you to feel threatened so I asked Thomas to be present. You and I are both off duty this weekend, so how about Sunday afternoon at the Gatehouse around four o'clock?"

For a couple of moments, she remained silent, long enough for Justin to be diverted by the announcement of a karaoke session just as Ray had predicted.

"Yes, I want to stay but I can't simply forget some of the things I have seen you do." Anne said quietly then paused and took a deep breath, "So, I will meet you and Thomas." She looked directly into his eyes, her own dark and unreadable. "After that it is up to you. That is all I will promise until I hear what you have to say."

Justin felt the tension release and nodded. "Thank you," he said before they both joined in the general chatter and laughter, battling against the varied abilities of the soloists and duos taking to the tiny stage. Justin waited a while longer then left them to enjoy their celebration at the same moment Paul and Julie stepped into the limelight.

27

His thoughts ran through his mind in rhythm with the soft sounds of his footfall across the fields and woods of Danely. The sky was paling to delicate blue streaked with the light pink clouds of early dawn.

Gods he was tired, less than two hours' sleep dulled his brain, but it was the bone deep, energy sapping exhaustion of deciding whether to let another person share his secret. Why did this time feel so much more important? How would Anne react to hearing his explanation? Justin reached the lake edge and dived into its coldly welcoming embrace. Rising to the surface he swam its full length, startling a few barely awake ducks. Wading out of its coolness, he paused looking towards the manor. Memories flooded through him of those he had confided in through the years. So very few really, some descendants of the original village families still kept his secret, still paid that special rent as if it were their privilege rather than a duty. His Antonia had known and loved what he was. He shut off that thought, that way lay pain he didn't want to feel again. Of course, there were Thomas and Marta, the two people closest to him, and now there was Anne. Why was telling her so important? The thought wheel turned again. Justin frowned and shook off some of the water. More slowly than usual, he jogged across the park towards home. Weary in body and wearied by the total lack of answers, he stumbled up the stone steps onto the terrace. Grateful to find a chair with a small table beside it. On the table was a glass and a decanter. He smiled slightly, bless Beth, then poured a brandy and slumped into the chair, sipping the honey-coloured liquid while the sun climbed over the horizon.

Justin's thoughts returned to his meeting with the Crown Prosecution Service and the long, detailed discussion of evidence including Eve's confession. Then followed on to Eve Jordan's court appearance, on the previous day, where she had been remanded in custody until her trial date, for murder, in a higher court. Now it was Sunday and it was his turn to be on trial. A few more hours needed to pass before he would discover his fate. He put the empty glass back on the table, leaned his head back against the chair. His eyes closed, surrendering to sleep.

Ryan had headed into London for the day to enable Anne, Thomas and Justin to talk freely. Justin was aware of how lucky Thomas was to have someone like Ryan in his life. Ryan had seemed to understand that the special bond between Thomas and Justin was different to the love that he and Thomas shared. Justin arrived at the Gatehouse early to help Thomas shift the table and chairs out into the walled garden. It was a fine warm day without a cloud in the sky, perfect for a traditional English afternoon tea. The stones of the walls around the garden were already warm from the sun and would keep out any cool spring breezes.

"You have known Anne longer than I have Thomas. What do you think of my chances?" Justin asked placing the last garden chair beneath the sun shade and looking round at his friend.

Thomas shook his head, his expression anxious. "I don't really know. I can only suggest from how I felt when you first told me. I didn't truly believe you until that night we were attacked and I saw you in action. Now, Anne has already been through a lot where men are concerned. I mean her ex-husband of course. I suspect fireworks and you may get badly burned."

Justin nodded. "I can see why. But Anne has one advantage over you. She has glimpsed me 'in action' as you call it. When we caught the badger baiters and when we arrested Aston. Perhaps I should agree with her that it is a drugs problem?" he sighed, "But, then I would have to waste time at rehabilitation and meetings and the whole rigmarole." His eyes grew cold, his expression ruthless. "No, the truth and if she cannot accept it …" His voice trailed into silence but Thomas understood.

"Come on, let's get everything sorted out. She'll be here in ten minutes." Thomas led the way back into the kitchen.

Anne arrived promptly, parking her car in the gravelled area at the side of the house. Justin heard her steps crunching across the gravel towards the front door. He headed out to the garden while Thomas answered the tinny summons from the Victorian pull-handle doorbell. He heard them walking down the tiled hall and then her chuckle at something Thomas said. A slight quiver in her voice suggested she might be nervous too. Nervous! Gods! He certainly was. He wiped the perspiration from his forehead and hoped she would think it was the afternoon warmth that caused it. Thomas came down the walk between the flower and vegetable beds towards the heart of the garden. Justin automatically stood when Anne reached the table. She looked at the traditional afternoon tea set out under the table umbrella and smiled almost naturally. The whole spread was worthy of a five-star hotel, neat little sandwiches and savoury tarts, fancy cakes with extravagant cream and icing. All displayed on two porcelain cake stands at the centre of dainty, matching, plates, cups and saucers.

She looked at Justin standing across from her and said, "From my experience at your house, I reckon it was Beth put all this together. It looks fabulous."

Justin smiled, "Yes, she worked hard on this. She likes you Anne, very much. Please sit down, and let us enjoy the fruits of her labours."

Thomas played host and kept the conversation light and flowing while they consumed the feast Beth had provided. There was tea and coffee on offer. Anne seemed more relaxed than when she arrived, influenced perhaps by the quaint normality of the tranquil garden and Thomas's conversation. Justin managed to force down the nervous dread and managed a semblance of normality. However, the conversation eventually faded into silence. Only the sound of early bees and a robin's song was heard for several minutes after the last cup was emptied and appetites were replete.

Justin put down the empty cup he had been holding in front of him, like a talisman. He looked at Thomas, who nodded encouragement, half rising from his chair. "If you would prefer to hear Justin's story in private and then come and talk with me, I have work I could do for a while," he said to Anne, gently touching her forearm.

She shook her head, "No, stay here. I trust you, Thomas."

Thomas sat back down. Justin looked out over the flower beds and focused on the mellow grey stone of the wall. Anne waited, her attitude tense. He turned suddenly looking directly at her, then down at the table. "Anne, what I am about to tell you will seem fantastical. Many years ago, I told Thomas what I am about to tell you." He smiled at his friend. "Since then, he has seen proof of my story which he can tell you. Marta knows my background, and Beth and Martin. They too will answer any questions you have. But only you can decide whether to believe me or not."

Anne seemed intent on inspecting a lavender bush in the border and didn't answer straight away. Justin was about to speak when she raised a hand to stop him.

"Fair enough, I want to know just what I'm getting into," she said. "I will listen."

Justin took a deep breath. "Thank you. I was born in what you know as AD 220, in Rome. My family were patricians and when I became an adult, I followed the family tradition and joined the army as an officer."

Justin had seen Anne's face change, her eyes narrowed and her mouth tensed.

"Why are you taking the bloody piss?" she snarled at them, looking from Justin to Thomas and back again. Her expression grew contemptuous. "Is that all I am to you both a fricking joke?" She stood up and so did Justin.

"No. I swear to you I am not trying to make a fool of you. I can understand why you would think so but hear me out. Please!"

"I felt that way too when he first told me," Thomas added quietly, "but I've seen and helped with things since that only confirm his story. Think about what you have already seen him do? Why did you think he was on steroids for example?"

"He told you?"

Thomas nodded, "Yes, when he decided to explain his situation to you. He told me what you believed." Thomas's expression was not that of someone enjoying her discomfort. "I hate to say this but you have seen only the smallest hint of what he can do."

Anne stood very still and Justin waited for her decision. She laughed short and hard. "What the hell, go on then. You said it was a fantasy. So far, I'm not sure if you two or I should be in the local secure facility." She sat down.

"I found I had a talent for leading my men and we were successful without the losses that most units had. The men recognised it and followed me. They gave me a sobriquet, a nickname in modern terms. It was Mortifer, it would translate as 'Death Bringer'. The name stuck. My unit was sent to Dacia, in AD 245 when the area was suffering a period of violent unrest. One day we were ordered to destroy a particular village, allegedly harbouring fighters who had attacked a supply column." Justin paused, "I make no excuses now for what happened then." He shrugged, "The information was wrong, fed to our informants by a rival group. My senior officers were eager for glory and were happy to believe it."

Thomas got up and headed for the house. He was back quickly a jug of water and three glasses on a tray. He poured a glass and handed it to Justin who took a drink then put the glass back on the table.

"The majority of the warriors were absent with their leader. It was the old, the sick and the young who were still in the village. When I realised, I tried to call my men off but the lust for battle had entrapped them." He had one hand over his eyes where he was leaning on the table as if to block out the memories. "I went into one of the huts. On the floor, there was a woman, a priestess dying from a vicious stomach wound." His voice had grown quieter as he told his story. Anne was intent on the tale, her anger gone. "She could not tell who I was, she was too near death but she knew what I was." His gaze locked with Anne's and she couldn't look away. "She cursed me with her last dying breath. 'Bloodthirsty you are and bloodthirsty you will remain forever.'" Justin's eyes were dull and his voice a monotone. He looked beaten, exhausted by reliving the nightmare "At first, I did not notice any change in me. I gathered the men and we returned to the fort. The commander praised us for our work even though I had reported the fact that our information was wrong." His laughter had a hard edge.

"That night we were off duty and three of us went out to the settlement that served the fort. Our little group was attacked in the darkness by a gang of thieves. They were carrying knives and clubs. One of them grabbed me from behind, but I got free and fought back. Then there was the smell of his blood, choking me, overwhelming me. I practically tore him to pieces in my need for that blood. Luckily my friends were also distracted by the attack and noticed nothing, not then." Justin looked up at Anne, frozen in her seat. "I will not bore you with the rest of my existence until now," he continued. "Just be assured I have gained greater control over the desire for blood and learned to know the warning signs."

Anne leaned back in her seat and reached for the water jug. She poured and drank down a full glass. Justin realised she was still not totally convinced. "Look at me Anne, please."

She looked up reluctantly, the spark of anger had returned to her eyes. Justin opened his mouth and his eye teeth extended into two, needle sharp, white, fangs. Anne's eyes widened with amazement and horror as they shrank back to normality. "The ancient area of Dacia included Romania, particularly Transylvania and the Carpathians. Given that geography and the fangs. Thomas named my condition after Bram Stoker's anti-hero." Justin shrugged, "I do not know if that truly explains my situation. The only time it becomes extremely dangerous to people around me, is if I need to heal. You noticed part of the problem with Julie." He smiled slightly, "not a dog with a bitch in heat, just a blood sucker finding the rarest blood group in the room in a time of desperation. I made a mistake starting back too early. Thomas had warned me. We were lucky that nobody was badly hurt." He leaned forward, "So, Anne, knowing what you do now, will you stay and work side by side with a blood sucking vampire?"

ACKNOWLEDGEMENTS

My grateful thanks to everyone at Watford Writers for their support and encouragement. Particular mention to David Elliott, Jo Morgan, Sumi Watters, Mike Lansdown and Ian Welland for specific help based on their particular areas of expertise.

Another thank-you to my good friend, Chris Holpin for her honest and valuable critique of the story.

To Andrew Wilson and Fiona Egglestone of the Professional Writers Academy and Faber and Faber my gratitude for their help especially to Andrew for his patience and positivity as my mentor.